THE
THIRD
MAGIC

THE
THIRD
MAGIC

MOLLY COCHRAN

A TOM DOHERTY ASSOCIATES BOOK   NEW YORK

THE THIRD MAGIC

Copyright © 2003 Molly Cochran

This book is printed on acid-free paper.

A Forge Book
Published by Tom Doherty Associates, LLC
175 Fifth Avenue
New York, NY 10010

www.tor.com

Forge® is a registered trademark of Tom Doherty Associates, LLC.

Library of Congress Cataloging-in-Publication Data

Cochran, Molly.
    The third magic / Molly Cochran.—1st hardcover ed.
      p.   cm.
    "A Forge book."
    ISBN 0-312-86440-X
    1. Arthur, King—Fiction.   2. Cheyenne Mountain (Colo.)—Fiction.   3. Terrorism—Prevention—Fiction.   4. Nuclear terrorism—Fiction.   I. Title
PS3553.O26T48   2003
813'.54—dc21

                    2003004001

First Edition: September 2003

Printed in the United States of America

0 9 8 7 6 5 4 3 2 1

For Devin, who still hears the song

THE
THIRD
MAGIC

PROLOGUE

Miracles often have odd beginnings.

On a January day in the mid-1990s, one particular miracle came into being when two crack addicts robbed the safety deposit boxes of the Riverside National Bank in a suburb of Chicago.

Although the thieves left the bank with nearly ten million dollars' worth of cash and jewelry, they were apprehended a few blocks from the scene of the crime less than an hour later. The loot, which had been stuffed into green plastic garbage bags, spilled out of the getaway car onto the street when the police made the arrest.

All but one item was recovered. This was a vaguely spheroid piece of greenish metal which resembled, more than anything else, a greatly overused croquet ball. Perhaps it was because of its unprepossessing appearance that no one noticed it as it rolled beneath the squad car and into the gutter, where it gained momentum on its downhill run, floated for half a block in a rivulet of melting snow, then came to rest in a heap of cigarette butts over a drainage grate.

It was here that a ten-year-old boy named Arthur Blessing found it. He wiped off the mud with his mittens and discovered that the ball was actually more like a cup, with a scooped-out cavity and an open end. It reminded the boy of the tiny handleless cups in his aunt Emily's Japanese tea set.

It was warm. Even though he could see his breath in the cold air, Arthur felt its warmth through his soggy mittens. He held it to his cheek and experienced something he could not have explained, something like the feeling he got when he hit the home run that won the game at summer camp. He felt like shouting, like laughing, like jumping into the air and never coming down.

He felt like a king. A king who would live forever.

CHAPTER ONE

THE BLUE MOMENT

JONES COUNTY, SOUTH DAKOTA

At the end of every day there is a fleeting time, easy to miss, when the sky is so deeply, purely blue that it casts its color on everything around it. The grass is blue. The hills are blue. The rock fingers jutting out of the earth, the crooked creek, the pines that shield the full moon like lacy curtains, all stunning, eerily blue.

And then, in an instant, everything becomes black. The trees cease to look real, transforming instead into silhouette cutouts, crisp, intentional, bearing leaves etched starkly and perfectly against the sky.

Arthur Blessing had been watching the mountain, and the man dancing upon its summit, since the blue moment. The figure looked like a Kokopelli drawing, made up entirely of knees and elbows, his long hair standing wildly out from his head. An old man; that had been obvious even from a distance. A blanket was sometimes clasped over his bony shoulders, sometimes cast away as the figure, stiff and knobby with age, danced steadily, ecstatically, into the darkening night.

He might have been a Lakota shaman, Arthur mused, admiring the dancer. The Lakota were populous in this part of South Dakota, and the mountain, known to locals as "The Puma" because its shape vaguely resembled a sitting cat, was sacred to them. At certain times of the year, only Native Americans were permitted to climb the Puma's rounded flanks. Most of the Lakota ceremonies were held then.

But this was not one of those times, and the old man was not a shaman. He was something much more.

After a time, the dancing man crouched on the ground. When he stood up again, a bright rag of fire blazed behind him. Arthur smiled and leaned comfortably against a low-hanging tree branch as the moon rose full.

This was a gift, Arthur knew. It was his eighteenth birthday, and this performance was the old man's gift to him.

Now the dance began again, this time against a background of brilliant flames. Sparks shot up out of the blaze like fireworks so that, from Arthur's perspective a half mile away and a thousand feet below, it looked as if a fountain of light were streaming out of the moon-dancer's body and spilling over the Puma's haunches. As the spark shower reached its peak, the old man stopped stock still in front of the fire, his legs wide apart, his arms spread out to his sides, so that he was surrounded by a nimbus of moving light.

Then, gone as quickly as the blue moment, the spectacle vanished utterly: the sparks, the fire, the old man . . . all of it was gone, plunged into darkness.

In the awesome silence that followed, in which even the insects grew still, the full moon floated out from behind a cloud and shone again, huge and silver beyond the crouching shape of the Puma. An owl called; the stars reappeared. A hundred thousand cicadas recommenced their hypnotic drone. The meadow pulsed with the soft light of fireflies. But the mountain was bare now, still, empty.

Arthur licked his dry lips. "Thank you," he whispered.

"You're welcome," a voice answered back. A moment later a tree limb crashed behind him.

Arthur whirled around, startled. The old man stood behind him, scowling, picking twigs out of his white hair.

"Taliesin!" Arthur grinned.

"Hello, Arthur." In the moonlight, his snow white beard, which curled softly down to the middle of his chest, almost seemed to glow.

Somewhere between his dance on the mountain and his appearance in the woods, he had acquired clothes. Arthur plucked a sizeable branch bushy with leaves out of his collar. "Where have you been?" he asked. "And how did you get here? You look like you fell out of a tree."

"Nonsense. One just got in my way. As to where I've been . . ." He looked about him, as if he were trying to get his bearings. "Oh, I don't know. Here and there, I suppose. Why, has it been a while?"

"Four years."

The old man stepped back a pace. "Good heavens, that long! Are you certain?"

Arthur laughed. "I'm sure. I've looked for you at every full moon."

"Hmm. Well, you do look considerably bigger. How old are you now, Arthur?" He squinted at the boy. "Oh, of course. It's your birthday. I knew that."

Arthur gestured with his head toward Puma mountain, awash with moonlight. "I enjoyed the show," he said.

"I didn't come out of it very well, I'm afraid." Taliesin plucked more twigs and leaves off his clothing. "Would you care to accompany me the next time?"

"To the mountain?" Arthur cocked his head. "Any special reason?"

"Most special," the old man said. "The Lakota called the sort of foray I have in mind a vision quest. I'm sure you've heard the term."

"Yes," Arthur said, feeling his heart beat faster. He had not been out of Jones County for four years. "I've heard of vision quests. They're rites of passage, I think. You go to some solitary place—"

"I'll be with you," Taliesin said. "I'll have to direct the vision, you see."

"Oh. Yeah, that'd be fine." Arthur could hardly believe it. What sort of vision would a being of Taliesin's power conjure? And why? There could only be one reason. "Is . . ." He groped for the right words. "Is it time, then?"

"Time?" Taliesin arched an eyebrow. "Time for what?"

"Time for me to leave," Arthur said with quiet insistence.

"Leave?" The old man shook his head so vigorously that his hair nearly stood on end. "Oh, no, no, no, no, no. I can't just release you like a trout in a stream, boy."

"I'm eighteen now. I can get along by myself, get a job—"

"Don't be ridiculous. A job!" His beard trembled with agitation. "Have you spoken with Hal and the . . . er, the . . ."

"Uncles," Arthur finished for him, trying not to sound disappointed. He had lived by the old man's rules for nearly half his life. "We call them uncles now."

"Ah," Taliesin said. "And what do they think of your plan to run off and find work, like some itinerant laborer?"

"There's no point in even talking to them." Arthur felt hot with frustration. "They'd never let me leave without them."

"Good. Although you're alone now," the old man added suspiciously. "Where are they?"

Arthur took a deep breath. Everyone treated him as if he were some kind of trained monkey, amusing, even cherished, but not trusted to spend five minutes alone. "They're in the house," he said patiently. "Except for Hal. He's getting ice cream. They want to have a party for me."

"Oh, jolly good! Am I invited?"

Who could stop you? Arthur thought. "Sure," he said. "They're probably ready by now, if you'd . . ."

But by then the old man was gone. In an instant, like the fire on the mountain, like the blue moment, he had simply vanished.

He's nearly ready, Taliesin thought as the boy looked for him. The old man was actually standing in the same spot where he had been

during his conversation with Arthur; it was just that he had chosen
not to be seen any longer.

It was for the best. Arthur was showing signs of teenage rebellion, or whatever they called it these days. Get a job, indeed! It
had been all Taliesin could do to keep from laughing aloud after
that announcement.

"Taliesin?" Arthur peered into the darkness once more, then
sighed and turned away. "Nice talking to you, too," he said, breaking a twig into pieces.

Oh, Arthur, Arthur. Taliesin stroked his beard, smiling. What a
long way we've come.

The legend: Uther Pendragon, disguised by the Merlin's magic to
resemble his rival Gorlois, enters Gorlois's castle and seduces his
wife, Ygraine. As payment for his part in the deception, the Merlin
takes the child born of that union.

The fact was that Ygraine, widow of the tribal chieftain Gorlois,
was forced to marry her husband's enemy Uther Pendragon after
her husband's death in battle. Uther had long lusted after both
Gorlois's rich lands, which abutted his own in the far south of
Britain, and his rival's beautiful young bride. By killing Gorlois,
he was able to take both prizes.

Eight months later, when Uther was on his way to becoming
the most powerful of the tribal chiefs—although far from the most
popular—a son was born to Ygraine. The child was puny. "Because
he was born early," Ygraine reasoned.

Uther was not convinced. Born early, indeed. He could count
on his fingers. It took nine months from conception to birth; the
child was probably Gorlois's spawn. And besides, he looked a weakling. If he lived to manhood, the boy would probably be sickly and
die young.

No. No, this was not the child Uther Pendragon wanted as his
heir. Three months after the birth, in the cold of November, Uther
announced his decision. The boy would be left to die on the sea-
swept rocks at the base of Tintagel Castle.

Ygraine's anguished cries of protest were met with stony silence
as the child was carried to the inhospitable shore and placed inside

a cave. In one final maternal effort, she begged Uther to call a holy man to pray over the child before it left the realm of the living. This small mercy was the least he could do for her, she reminded him scornfully.

Uther was glad to comply. After all, the isle of Mona, where the druids lived, was more than a week's journey away. By the time a holy man reached Tintagel, the child would already be dead, and even a druid's magic could not raise him. So at Uther's command, a lady-in-waiting was dispatched toward Mona.

It was by sheer good fortune that the lady had not ridden a quarter of an hour when she encountered a druid on Tintagel's very grounds.

Actually, it was not so unusual an event as it might seem. The druid was Taliesin, former bard and noble bastard, whose half brother was Uther Pendragon. Taliesin had been sent by the chief druid, a woman known only as the Innocent, ten days before to pay respects to his brother and his new wife on the birth of their child.

He had lingered along the way; Taliesin had never gotten along well with his powerful but rather stupid sibling. During their youth, Uther had reveled in finding ways to torture the frail and sensitive Taliesin, even though it had always been understood that Uther would inherit all their father's property. As a young bard, Taliesin had been summoned occasionally to sing ballads extolling Uther's greatness in battle, but he was never particularly well received, possibly because even Uther's dull mind could perceive that Taliesin's songs of praise were less than heartfelt.

The druid had heard only through gossip that his brother had married; he hadn't been invited for the wedding festivities. And so it was with some misgiving that the Innocent had sent him off to bless the child of this union.

"Has it even been born yet?" Taliesin had waffled. "That is, they don't seem to have been married very long." He hadn't questioned the Innocent's assertion that a child had been born, even though no one else seemed to know of it. The Innocent knew everything.

"The child is alive, and in need of you," she had said, her blank eyes boring into him.

"Yes, well ... thank you," he'd concluded unenthusiastically. The druids at Mona were permitted very little time with their birth families. Taliesin had certainly never objected to this; he had no one to visit anyway. "Actually, though, in our preparations for the Winter Solstice—"

"You will miss the celebrations," the Innocent said flatly.

Taliesin's last hope faded. "Very well," he mumbled, and took off at a snail's pace toward Tintagel.

Of course, after he'd encountered the lady in the woods, who had slid off her horse to kneel before him and kiss his hand in gratitude, he saw the Innocent's hand in the matter.

"Please, sir!" the lady shrilled. "My lady begs you to pray over her small babe, that it may not suffer as it passes into the Summer Country!"

Taliesin felt a hot pang of pure rage as he put the pieces of the puzzle together. The child was born small, just has Taliesin himself had been small, and therefore an object of contempt for the brute sensibilities of Uther Pendragon. He remembered the times when Uther had led him into the woods and abandoned him there, laughing as if it had all been a huge joke when Taliesin came back days later, hungry and filthy. Those forays had not only given him an excellent sense of direction, but had taught him how to live in the open countryside—a skill which put him in good stead with the druids when he came to join them.

"I will give the child my prayers and more, lady," he answered, and moved ahead without waiting for her.

As he was on foot, the woman was sure she would overtake him on the way back to Tintagel, but he seemed literally to have disappeared. The lady-in-waiting spent several hours calling and looking for him. When she finally returned to the castle, perhaps, she thought, to be rebuked for losing her mistress's last hope for her baby's soul, she found the druid already in Ygraine's chambers.

But of course, she thought. He is a druid. He travels by magic.

For several minutes Taliesin stood by silently while Ygraine wept with gratitude over the baby he had brought back to her and which was now suckling at her breast.

"He is warming now, my precious boy," she murmured. "Uther thought he would die in an instant, but my son is stronger than he looks."

Uther can sit on a thorn, Taliesin thought, but remained still.

Suddenly Ygraine looked up, her eyes still red and brimming with tears. "You have to take him," she said. "Please. You can do this. Take him with you to whatever strange realms in which you dwell. He can become a druid. It will be better, at least, than death."

Taliesin couldn't help smiling. Ygraine's plea was so urgent and heartfelt that he felt no offense at her words. Worldly people held the druids in awe and fear, as if they were demons. For her to choose what she believed to be a terrifying life for her son rather than death revealed her attachment to him.

"Don't worry, my Queen," he said gently. "I shall not take him to Mona. He wouldn't be accepted there, in any case." The only children permitted on the island were those born to the druids themselves, conceived during the Great Sabbats.

"No, I did not mean—" She reached out a desperate hand to him.

"Shh. I will take him with me. But he shall be raised in the home of a nobleman, in keeping with his true station. Then who knows? One day perhaps he will succeed Uther."

Ygraine looked down at the child. "No, I do not believe Uther will ever recognize this child."

And who says Uther's opinion will matter a fig? Taliesin thought. Still, it would be necessary to tell him about the child. Too many people already knew that the baby had been brought back to the castle. If Taliesin were to leave so soon after his arrival without mentioning the child, Uther would be suspicious. And it would take no more than a suspicion to send Uther into a rage that might harm Ygraine and her servants. The druid understood tyrants: The best way to keep a secret from a man like Uther was to tell him just enough to bore him.

And so Taliesin approached him the next day. "I was coming to visit you, brother, when I chanced upon a baby lying naked on the rocks," he said, sounding bewildered.

Uther rolled his eyes. "And what did you think it was, you superstitious fool, a sea spirit?"

Taliesin laughed lightly. "Perhaps."

"I suppose you made up a song to it."

"No, actually, I brought him inside."

Uther slapped the table in front of him with his fist. "Idiot! That was Ygraine's bastard. I was trying to get rid of it." His eyes bulged with anger as he stared at his illegitimate half brother. "No point in raising a by-blow runt that no one wants," he added maliciously.

If his words wounded the druid, he made no sign. "The child's nearly dead already," Taliesin said. "I'll take it with me and bury it in the woods if you like. That would spare your wife some little suffering, at least."

"And it would spare me the bother of having to listen to her." Uther grinned. Taliesin thought he looked like a slavering dog, his yellow teeth bared beneath his unkempt beard.

"Very well. I'll go straightaway."

"I thought you were coming to visit."

Taliesin raised his chin. "Shall we both listen to the queen's lamentations, then?"

Uther scratched his beard. "I suppose that'll be the case. All right, you can go. Perhaps you'll come back afterward. Write a song for me or something."

"I'm no longer a bard, brother. I could pray for you, though. Conduct a day-long ritual to cleanse your soul. You'd have to fast for a week beforehand, of course."

"Er . . . Fine. That is . . ."

"If I have time. I have some pressing duties in the east."

"Then surely you must attend to them, Taliesin," Uther said heartily, although his eyes were already scanning the room for a distraction. "And don't forget the bastard. Bury it somewhere far away from here. I wouldn't want Ygraine to . . . while hunting or something . . ."

"She'll never find the child, I assure you," Taliesin said. "Nor will you."

"Good. No marker will be necessary."

"I understand, my King."

Appeased by his half brother's recognition of his superiority, Uther nodded beatifically. The interview was over.

Within the hour, holding a hollow gourd containing a milk-soaked rag, the druid Taliesin, who would one day be known throughout the Celtic world as the Merlin, last of the great magicians, set off into the forest with the future king of Britain.

And not just any king, the old man thought. Arthur of the House of Pendragon had become the greatest ruler the Celtic world had ever known. On that day in the year 488, when Taliesin bore away Uther's unwanted infant, he took the first step toward the salvation of Britain.

The island had been left bereft after the Romans' abrupt departure. "Defend yourselves!" the governor had admonished in parting.

Defend against what? the educated among the abandoned Britons asked. For there was more than foreign invasion to fear. Starvation, disease, and ignorance would send a civilization back to the Stone Age more easily than a conquering army. What was to become of the Roman-built cities without Roman supplies to maintain them, and Roman-trained administrators to run them?

A hundred years before Arthur Pendragon began his journey into destiny in the arms of the druid named Taliesin, Britain was in many ways worse off than the savage hinterlands of the Picts to the far north; for while the Picts had never lost their tribal ways, the Britons had become sufficiently Romanized to have grown accustomed to such trappings of civilization as flush toilets, heated homes, paved roads, and professional armies.

These, the wise among them realized, were gone forever, along with the Romans' efficient government and superb methods of organization. If Britain were not to fall into utter chaos and ruin, someone had to take charge.

And this was where the real problem lay.

For it was not in the makeup of the British Celts to accept leadership easily. They had fought the Romans for fifty years before submitting to the empire's benign yoke. They were a tribal people, with ancient and unbreakable ties to family and clan. During the nightmare years after the end of the Roman occupation, the clans rose again to prominence.

There were ten of them: ten tribes which functioned as separate kingdoms, constantly at war with one another. Even if there were terms of peace between neighboring clans, skirmishes over cattle rustling and sheep stealing were almost daily occurrences.

Added to this confusion were the increasingly frequent invasions by Saxon warriors, who were looking not only for the dogs and goldwork for which the Celts were famous, but for land.

Why did the Britons need so much land, the Saxons argued. Since they were always killing one another off in their clan wars, they would never have enough people to populate the island, anyway. Besides, the Britons' lack of unity made the place vulnerable by sea in all directions. And so, as the ten tribes of the Celts fought among themselves over a stolen pony or a disputed hayfield, the Saxons sharpened their weapons and cast their eyes toward Britain's white shores.

It was into this world that Arthur came of age. During his rule, he accomplished a feat that any man would have believed impossible: Without using coercion or the shedding of blood, he united the ten tribes of Britain into a single nation, and brought about its first flowering.

And then he had died, prematurely, unfairly, wrongly. He left no heir. When King Arthur passed into the Summer Country, the nation he had created with his brilliance and his decency sank back into despair and ruin.

The Saxons took over then, and changed the very face of Britain. Within the span of a few generations, the English people ceased to resemble either Celts or Romans, but became something entirely different, speaking a new language and practicing customs their ancestors had never known.

The Celts, who had occupied the island of Britain since the time of the oldest legends, who had maintained their identity and their ancient religion through four hundred years of Roman rule, ceased to exist. And their last great hero, Arthur, High King of

Britain, passed into the realm of legend, remembered only in stories told to children.

I could not allow that, the old man thought. His spotted hands were clenched into fists; his whole body trembled. Even now, he felt the same overwhelming anger he had experienced when he had touched Arthur's cold, bloody corpse after the battle of Camlun.

It had not been time for Arthur to die, Taliesin thought, tasting bile. The king had been cheated of his life through sorcery and evil.

And so he would get back that lost life. The Merlin would see to it.

It had been an unreasonable wish, even for a druid of Taliesin's standing. He had studied for more than twenty years on the island of Mona under the aegis of the great blind witch known only as the Innocent. During his years at Camelot, he had served as chief adviser to the king and had been awarded the title of Merlin, or Wise One.

Among the common people, Taliesin had been a wizard, pure and simple. They believed him capable of performing any magic from transforming men into chickens to taking away the sun. Such claims were untrue, of course, although a trained druid—which Taliesin the Merlin certainly was—knew how to do a number of things that might easily be interpreted as magic by those who were not so well educated. He could chart and predict lunar and solar eclipses, for example. He understood the dynamics of flight. He had a vast knowledge of herbs and their healing properties, and knew almost as much about poisonous plants as the women of Orkney, who were famous for their ability to kill without trace.

But he had never truly performed any feat that might unequivocally be termed "magic" until that blinding, rage-filled moment when he knew—simply knew—that he must make the impossible occur:

Arthur Pendragon must be brought back from the dead.

And so the Merlin set the magic into motion. He did not know how long it would take for the magic to become strong enough to work, but whenever that was, he would be ready. Someday, when the stars were right, the king would return to fulfill his rightful destiny.

The first thing the magic required was Taliesin's own life.

This he gave willingly. His life for the king's? It was not even a consideration. Taliesin went into a cave and said good-bye to his days as a human being. What he would become after this death was something other, something bigger, something much more difficult to be.

But he did not know this at the time. All he knew was that he was weaving a spell, a great spell, that would bring a hero back to the world of the living—a world that was as much in need of heroes as it had been sixteen centuries before.

CHAPTER TWO

WALKING THROUGH THE ROCK

Every light in the old farmhouse was lit. When Arthur walked into the kitchen, there was a roar of welcome from the men.

"By my balls, boy, where have ye been?" boomed Kay, rising as high as he could before reeling back into his chair. The contents of his tankard sloshed over his shirt.

The uncles had never heard of sobriety where they came from, and could not fathom why anyone would desire to be in such a state. Their view of alcohol was to drink as much of it as possible whenever the opportunity arose.

Some of them were truly prodigious drinkers. Kay was among them, as was an equally large Welshman known to his fellows as Dry Lips, and the diminutive but perennially thirsty Curoi MacDaire.

MacDaire's other half—though he would have fought any man who dared even to bring up the subject—was a huge and shaggy Irishman named Lugh Loinnbheimionach who spoke little, thought less, and fought like a baited bear.

"Pour young Arthur an ale, Gawain!" Kay ordered. "'Tis not every day a man celebrates his coming into the world!"

A thin, melancholy-faced man dressed in green army-surplus fatigues drew a beer from a squat metal keg which occupied the bottom half of the refrigerator.

"Nay, nay," said MacDaire. "For the lad's birthday, he'll be needing something a wee bit stronger." He poured some colorless liquid from an industrial-size mayonnaise jar into a water tumbler. "Try this potcheen. I made it myself." He winked, holding out the glass. MacDaire's potcheen was more than 180 proof, and had nearly blinded Lugh a few years before during a particularly festive Christmas.

"No, thanks." Arthur waved the drink away good-naturedly.

MacDaire sighed. "You've got to stop drinking water sometime, lad," he said with a shake of his head.

A handsome young man named Fairhands put down the autoharp he had been playing and took the glass out of MacDaire's hands. "No point in wasting it, then," he said before downing the contents.

Fairhands was one of the younger members of the group, along with Bedwyr, who, at the age of twenty-four, maintained and repaired every piece of machinery on the farm, hook-handed Agravaine, and Tristan, whom women loved. A few years older than these, whom the elder uncles considered children, was Geraint Lightfoot who, true to his name, usually patrolled the far borders of the farm and was therefore rarely in the company of the others.

Dry Lips wiped foam from his mouth. His head, slick bald and shaped like a dum-dum bullet, shone beneath the incandescent light. "By the by, lad, whilst you were taking the air, did you happen to notice the Merlin?"

Arthur smiled, startled. "You saw him, too?"

A roar or laughter went up from the group. "How could you miss him?" Curoi MacDaire said. "Up on that mountain, hopping about like a Pict."

"Aye, and as lacking in clothes," Kay added.

"Thought he'd come for you," Gawain said quietly. He looked steadily at the boy.

"Yes, I . . . I talked with him." He did not add, "At least I think I did."

"Ah, then he'll be about," Fairhands said, picking up his auto-harp and strumming a lively tune upon it. "The bard's a-come, the bard's a-come," he sang.

A tall man with sandy hair and the bearing of a prince sniffed disdainfully. "Bard!" he muttered. "Sorcerer, you mean."

"Oh, be still, Launcelot," Kay said, waving him down.

Launcelot was the eleventh uncle. He belonged with neither the group of hard-drinking senior farmhands nor the younger crowd, nor with Geraint Lightfoot, traveling constantly around the outskirts of the land. Launcelot had always held himself apart, with different, higher standards than the others. He never drank to excess. Indeed, the degree of restraint that he exhibited toward the triple lure of beer, ale, and mead was surpassed only by one other.

"Hal says the Merlin's no sorcerer," Fairhands said, his sensitive face looking hurt. "He's a great magician, though. The greatest wizard in the world."

"He's Satan incarnate," Launcelot groused. "Whatever Hal may say."

Hal was the leader of the group. He drank no alcoholic bever-ages, which was one of the things that made him an oddity to the others. One of many things.

"Now, now," Kay admonished. "There's no need for getting your pecker bent about it."

"It makes no difference to Hal that the old man is a pagan and a practicioner of black arts," Launcelot said.

Kay tried to speak reasonably. "That's as it should be. Not every-one's a Christian like you, you know."

"Do not call me that." Launcelot's eyes were downcast. His shoulders slumped. "I am not worthy to be called 'Christian.' "

All the young men stole glances at one another. Agravaine rolled his eyes. Launcelot had been annoyingly holy back when they had been warriors. As a farmer, he was even more annoying.

"Well, then that's settled," Curoi MacDaire said, breaking the silence. "Potcheen?" He held out a glass. Launcelot shook his head.

"Pity," MacDaire said, tossing the liquid down his own gullet. He exhaled with a wheeze and a smile.

"Hal is the sorcerer's special companion," Launcelot muttered. "I fear he walks in the path of darkness."

Kay thumped his fist on the table. "Bloody Mithras," he growled, "will you stop your hangdog complaining? Hal is doing no such thing. Just because he's your son—" He was cut off by the swift slam of a kitchen cabinet.

Dry Lips spilled the ale he was pouring into a large tankard. "By the gods, what was—"

Suddenly the place was aclatter with the noise of cupboards opening and slapping shut of their own will, of doors blowing open, of the pots and pans that hung behind the big iron stove crashing against the walls. Even the cinders in the fireplace whooshed upward.

And then a meek knock at the door.

The men roared with laughter. It was a joke, a joke that only ghosts understood. Because the old man didn't need doors. He could have appeared on the kitchen table in a puff of smoke and riding a dragon if he had wanted to.

"That'll be His Nibs now!" MacDaire shouted.

Arthur opened the door. There was no one on the other side.

The men laughed again. "He wants us to look for him," Dry Lips observed.

"Aye," agreed MacDaire, draining his glass. "But for the search, we'll first need another round of stout."

Arthur stepped outside. He shivered, though the night was warm. Above, the full moon had sailed above the trees. "No, that's not it," he said. His neck prickled. "Something's happened," he said, turning back toward the men. "Where's Hal?"

"In town. At the store," MacDaire said. "We need ice cream."

"And stout," Dry Lips complained, banging his tankard on the table. The others followed suit. Since none of them was frightened by the prospect of death, neither their own nor anyone else's, Arthur's unease was incomprehensible to them.

Launcelot put his hand on the boy's shoulder. "Don't worry about them," he said gently. "There's not a one on this earth can harm that wicked old man, so much the worse, and he'll be watching over Hal."

On his way home from the 7-Eleven, Hal Woczniak hit a pedestrian with his truck.

At least it appeared that way. He hadn't heard or felt anything, only seen the old man tumbling end over end above the hood of the pickup and coming to a halt in a kind of squat directly in front of the windshield.

Hal slammed on his brakes and shot out. "Oh God, oh God, oh . . ." He straightened up. "You!"

"Quite," the old man said crankily. "Don't bother asking how I am. I suppose if I'm not dead, that's good enough for you."

"No, it's just that . . ." He helped the old man off the front of the truck. A crowd was beginning to form. "I'm sorry, Taliesin. I don't know how I hit you. Are you all right?"

"I'm fine, and you never touched me with your filthy machine," Taliesin said, yanking his arm away from Hal's grip and straightening his clothing, which consisted of a plaid flannel shirt and a pair of bib overalls, topped by a sheepskin jacket. "How do I look?" He turned in a circle, preening.

"Er . . . I don't see any blood, if that's—"

"No, no. I meant my appearance. I'm trying to fit in."

The crowd, sweating from a hundred-degree day, was whispering. They had never seen the old man, but they knew Hal. And they knew about the boy he was hiding.

"Get in," Hal said. "People are getting interested in us."

The old man scowled at the onlookers. "Haven't they anything else to do?"

"Well, I did almost kill you," Hal said, getting into the truck.

"Nonsense. I just materialized in the wrong place."

Hal glanced at him sideways. "Materialized?"

"The old term is 'walking through the rock.' The first of the great lessons of magic. It's based on the theory that most of what you'd call matter is really empty space—"

"I don't know what in hell you're talking about."

"Walking through . . ." Taliesin waved him away irritably. "Oh, never mind. You wouldn't understand, anyway."

"Are you saying you just . . ." He gestured toward the hood of the car. ". . . materialized?"

"That's exactly what I said," the old man snapped.

"Why?" Hal was bellicose. "Why would you materialize in front of my truck?"

"Miscalculation. Theoretically, one should be able to will one-self to the middle of Picadilly Circus. Of course, one might end up in front of a truck there, too. Or even in the truck's engine." He chortled. "A little wizard humor," he said, poking Hal in the arm with a bony finger. "Ah, well, we all have things to learn."

"I wish you'd learn them someplace besides the parking lot of the Seven-Eleven," Hal said.

For the hundredth time that week, he wondered if it was time to get Arthur out of Jones County. The locals had begun to take an unhealthy interest in Hal and the gang of odd Englishmen who occupied the old rambling farmhouse on Black River Road. Several of them, on behalf of one church or another, had come visiting, "to see about the boy."

It was all about Arthur, of course. Arthur was the reason for them all being there, their reason for being, period.

Two weeks before, a delegation from the local school board had come to check on Arthur's progress with home schooling. It had been an unnecessary visit, and perhaps an illegal one, but Hal had let them in nevertheless. He had shown them Arthur's text-books and papers, and explained the computer program which Ar-thur himself had devised to provide a structured school day. Then they had spoken with Arthur. When they left, they were con-vinced that the boy was unusually bright and being taught at a pace in keeping with his abilities.

The board members were convinced, but Hal knew that others would be coming. After four years, people were beginning to rec-ognize that a celebrity was living in their midst. A celebrity or a renegade.

Arthur's unsought fame was based on an incident that had occurred some four years before, at the scene of a freak accident in New York City in which an entire apartment building collapsed into a sinkhole. Standing in the wreckage, with television cameras from every station in the city trained on him, Arthur had made a speech announcing the dawn of a new era in which people's fears would be eradicated by a level of spiritual understanding previously unknown on earth.

Hal winced even now to think of it. What had possessed the boy to say such a thing? He was sure that Arthur had not planned it, probably hadn't thought about it at all. The words had just come tumbling out of his mouth while the cameras rolled and Hal plotted a quick route out of the city.

It was funny, Hal thought now. Four years ago, when September 11th was only a date and not a synonym for world-scale panic, you could get away with something like that. A fourteen-year-old kid with an entourage of twelve mystery men could tell the world that a new day was dawning, and then they could all leave the city without being arrested, or worse.

Four years ago, the world had been a much younger place. Arthur's impromptu television appearance had not sparked feelings of fear or danger: On the contrary, his message of peace and hope—a message which Arthur himself could no longer remember—began an underground ripple among the city's youth that grew, in the unique way of teenage fads, into a nationwide phenomenon.

By the time of the Jones County school board's visit to the farm, the phenomenon was just beginning to come to the attention of adults, and then only because their children were thoroughly conversant about Arthur. That is, Arthur, which was to say *their* Arthur, the secret herald of a new time whose speech delivered on that summer night was played and replayed on computers set up in bedrooms covered with posters of Britney Spears or Korn. For them, Arthur was the messenger of the New Age, or perhaps the emissary of an ancient one.

Arthur? their parents would ask, smiling indulgently. That doesn't sound like a very macho name, does it? Sort of like Microsoft, ha ha.

And their kids would look at them blank-faced, inwardly enraged, frustrated, knowing. Because Arthur was the perfect name for him, the only name, Arthur, King Arthur, come back to fulfill the legend that he would return to finish out his reign.

And he had come back as one of them.

The photograph of him that appeared in *Teen People* magazine graced the schoolbooks and lockers of girls from every region of the United States. Hundreds of web sites were devoted to what little was known about his mysterious life. His short speech was broken into sound bites which were printed and published as pocket-sized books which young people carried around and quoted from. Stores were bombarded with demands for all things medieval, from fantasy clothing to replica shields and swords. "Celtic" became the buzzword from which whole new industries grew.

Psychologists passed this off as another fad, a momentary—if widespread—infatuation like poodle skirts, Mohawk haircuts, or pierced navels. What made the infatuation so persistent was the fact that the subject of it seemed to appear and vanish within the same instant. One Arthur Blessing, whose school pictures matched the image of the person who had spoken so meaningfully on television, had gone to public school in Chicago until the fifth grade, when he and his aunt, who was his legal guardian, both disappeared inexplicably.

According to the media, which went on an immediate feeding frenzy after the boy's appearance on television, no records existed for either of his parents. And, as anyone under the age of twenty well knew, Arthur vanished from the face of the earth immediately after his stunning speech. Gone without a trace in the midst of a gang of twelve motocyclists. ("The knights," wrote one keen-eyed observer. "The apostles," wrote another.)

Although Arthur was not aware of the extent of this blossoming underground publicity, Hal was, and took on the preservation of the boy's anonymity as his mission. Arthur never left the farm. On the home-schooling documents, Hal had identified him as Arthur Woczniak, his son.

Still, people talked. In the past year, young people had begun to congregate at the driveway leading to the farmhouse. Occasionally a bold one even came to the door, requesting Arthur's auto-graph, which was always declined. Once a girl named Cecilia Marks, who was the daughter of the mayor of Seidersville, South Dakota, ten miles to the north of Munro, actually broke in through Arthur's bedroom window and kissed him full on the mouth.

After the girl was sent home, her father looked mightily for grounds upon which to sue Arthur and his uncles, but since his daughter had admitted freely to the break-in (and had rhapsodized to the entire student body at Jones County Senior High about her success in kissing the boy), the mayor was forced to drop whatever charges he had planned to press.

"King Arthur," he shouted to his wife as he threw down a double martini. "Cecilia thinks she kissed King fricking Arthur!"

The mayor had no idea that he was telling the truth, that the country's teenagers were right, or that his daughter had just be-come the most popular girl in the county.

"So where were you trying to materialize?" Hal asked.

"When? Oh, just now? I was hoping for your house. I got fairly close on one of my tries—made it to the field—Arthur was there, by the way. And just before I landed on your lorry, I'd almost made it into your kitchen. Unfortunate, that. I was hoping to join in the merrymaking."

"Instead, you got me," Hal said.

"Quite. Oh, well, we'll be there soon enough. I presume you are merrymaking? Er, not you, of course," he said offhandedly. "You never do. I meant the knights. Because of the boy's coming of age."

"They're always merrymaking," Hal said glumly, remembering an incident two weeks before when Dry Lips and MacDaire were ar-rested for engaging in swordplay on the loading dock at the local Wal-Mart. A month before that, a neighboring farmer nearly shot Lugh for swinging a fifty-pound mace at his prize Holstein. "They've been so merry, we're on the verge of getting evicted."

"Ah. High-spirited lads, eh?"

"They're idiots. Trying to pass them off as South Dakota farmers is like pretending that Attila the Hun is the Tooth Fairy. And don't call them knights. It took me three months to get them to refer to themselves as uncles."

"Oh, yes. Uncles. You see, you're training them marvelously."

Actually, the uncles were rather good farmers, not that it mattered. Taliesin had given Hal enough money for them all to live on for several more years, whether they worked the farm or not.

"But I hate it!" Hal cried. "Do you understand? I'm from New York City, for crying out loud! I don't know beans about farming. I trained to be an FBI agent—"

"And nearly committed suicide." The old man patted Hal's shoulder. "Believe me, Hal, this is a better life for you."

"Bullshit! I didn't sign on to baby-sit eleven ghosts—"

"Ah-ah," Taliesin said, wagging his finger. Uncles."

"Whatever," Hal roared.

"Yes." The old man met Hal's eyes. "Whatever they are, my friend, Arthur needs them." He put his hand on Hal's shoulder. "And you. You know that, don't you?"

Hal was silent. He still often woke in the night thinking that what he believed to be reality was in fact only a dream from which he was just then waking. For a few groggy, confused moments, he could believe that he was an automobile mechanic in the Inwood section of Manhattan or, better yet, still with the FBI in the days before his slow descent into ruin.

But then the confusion would clear, and the truth would fall on him like cold snow. He was not a mechanic; he was not a federal agent; he was no longer even a drunk. What he was, in fact, was the caretaker of eleven souls from the fifth century who had been brought into being to serve a young boy who once, lifetimes ago, had been their king.

"Yes, I know," Hal said finally.

"It won't be for much longer." Taliesin's voice was gentle. "It's almost time."

Hal turned sharply to face him. "Arthur just turned eighteen today."

"Yes, I know. That's old enough."

"For what? He doesn't know how to do anything yet."

"He'll remember."

"I meant in this world," Hal said roughly. "He needs to go to college, learn a trade, meet a girl, have some kind of a life—"

"No time for that, I'm afraid," Taliesin said crisply. "Too much work to be done."

"Such as what?"

"Well, I couldn't say, old chap. I'm not a fortune-teller, you know."

CHAPTER THREE

THE JOURNEY BEGINS

The old man entered in spectacular fashion, beginning as a vapor curling languorously through the floorboards of the farmhouse and finishing by standing, fully formed, on top of the dining room table as the knights shouted their approval.

"I say!" Fairhands said, beaming. He poked Launcelot in the ribs. "You see? The greatest magician in the world."

"He's standing in the cake," Launcelot said dryly.

The old man looked down. Beneath his wizard's robe adorned with stars and crescent moons, his mud-caked work boots grew out of what had once been a whipped cream cake inscribed with a birthday greeting in red gel.

"Dash it all," Taliesin mumbled.

Hal sighed. The ice cream was leaking through the paper bag onto his arms.

"Did you get it?" Bedwyr asked, tossing his bowl-cut blond hair. He was the only one in the room who had noticed Hal.

"Yeah. Relax." Hal took a magazine out of the bag and tossed it to him.

Bedwyr retired with it immediately to an armchair in the far corner of the living room and opened it to the stapled section in the middle. On its glossy cover was the title *Vintage Motorcycle* superimposed over the image of a 1971 Harley FX Superglide Night Train.

Although the young man's official capacity was that of Master of Horse, Hal had persuaded Bedwyr to change his allegiance to motorcycles upon the knights' arrival in the New World. Given the young man's natural understanding of things mechanical, he had fallen utterly in love with the first Harley whose engine he exposed, and had carried on an *affaire du coeur* with the species ever since.

"Hi, Hal." Arthur walked over to him as the others helped Taliesin down off the table. "Are you all right?"

He tried to sound casual, but Hal knew that the boy was worried.

In the years since he and Hal had gone into hiding, Arthur had begun to exhibit a sixth sense about danger. Perhaps it was because they had encountered it so often; or maybe it was only the natural development of a talent the boy had been born with. Either way, the sense, Arthur's "knowing," as he called it, had been growing more acute.

"One of the old man's stunts, that's all," Hal said reassuringly. "I thought I'd hit him with the truck, but . . . well, there he is, stepping out of your cake." He inclined his head toward Taliesin, ringed by men who had once been the Knights of the Round Table.

Arthur laughed. "It looked like a pretty disgusting cake, anyway."

While he was helping Hal dish out the ice cream (the knights, who had never tasted such a thing during their previous incarnation, could not get enough of it), he watched the old man in the next room. It was a great relief that Taliesin had actually come, and had not been, after all, a figment of Arthur's imagination.

"This is all hard for you, isn't it," Hal said quietly.

Arthur looked up. "What? What do you mean?"

"This." Hal gestured with the ice cream scoop. "The guys, the old man . . . The cup."

"We got rid of the cup."

"That doesn't mean it never existed."

Arthur bent over his ice cream again. "I kind of wish none of it had ever existed," he said.

"You and me both."

"I mean, it's not that I'm not grateful to you. . . ."

"Cut the crap, Arthur. Most of your life has been spent trying not to get killed. It's been lousy, and we both know it."

"It would have been lousy if you hadn't been there," Arthur said, acknowledging Hal's sacrifice in staying with him as his guardian and protector for the better part of a decade.

Hal waved him away. Sentiment made him uncomfortable. "I just wish there'd been another way," he said lamely. "I've tried to write to your aunt Emily, but all the letters came back. I just don't know where she is."

"She may not be alive." Arthur did not look up from his task. The last time they had seen Emily Blessing was in the dining room of a hotel in Lisbon, Portugal, nearly four years before. He had seen only the barest glimpse of his aunt—his only living relative—before a fire and its aftermath of pandemonium broke out. The three of them had become separated then, and by the time Hal and Arthur found one another, Emily had disappeared. "It was a pretty bad fire."

Hal didn't answer. He had loved Emily Blessing. It was for her—and Arthur, and himself—that he had stopped drinking, brought a halt to the self-destructive lifestyle of a man who'd had nothing left to live for. He had saved their lives, and they, in turn, had saved his.

Had Emily ever known that? he wondered. Had she ever believed that their one night of love had changed Hal forever, that he hadn't intended to leave her, that he had taken her nephew away because the boy was in danger, that he hadn't told her about it so that the danger would not spread to her?

No. No, of course she wouldn't believe that. All Emily would know was that she had given herself to a man who had left her without a word, and in the process abducted the child she had raised from infancy.

"What do you think will happen to us, Hal?" Arthur asked so quietly that he was barely audible.

After a long pause, Hal answered, "I don't know."

"Taliesin wants to take me on a vision quest."

"What for?"

Arthur shrugged. "I suppose he wants me to see for myself."

"See what?"

"Who I was. Or will be. He says I need to know about my future." The ice cream in the dishes arrayed before them was melting rapidly in the August heat. "Hal?"

Hal looked up.

"If I . . . left . . ." Shyly he looked over to Hal to see his reaction, but the older man's face was carefully blank. "Not that I would, but if I did . . ."

"Go on."

". . . could I change the way things are supposed to turn out?"

Hal looked away. "Maybe," he said.

"Is there such a thing as destiny?"

"I'm not the guy to ask things like that."

"Other people . . . other people's lives turn out the way they do because of their own decisions."

Hal nodded slightly. "I guess."

"Then why don't I have any say about my own life?"

Because we're special, Hal wanted to say. Because we came from another time, cryogenic masterpieces, except that it was our souls that got preserved, not our bodies. You were born to be king, and I was born to protect you, and that's all been decided by forces way beyond anything we can control. "Eat your ice cream," Hal said.

Arthur ignored him, wiping his forehead on his sleeve. "I don't even know if it's real anymore."

"What do you mean?"

"All of it. This." He opened his hands. "I mean, sometimes I just don't know. It's all so weird that I wonder if the uncles even exist. If Taliesin exists. Even you. Maybe this is just some delusion of mine, and I've made you all up."

"You wish," Hal said.

Arthur tried to smile. "Yeah."

He looked so fragile, Hal thought, as if he could fly apart into pieces like confetti. "Oh, Christ," he said, throwing down the ice cream scoop. He hugged the boy fiercely. "Nobody should have to live like this."

"Just tell me it's real, and I'll believe you."

"No," Hal said. "Because that won't mean anything." He held him at arm's length. "And don't ever believe anything just because someone tells you." He handed Arthur a spoon and a dish of ice cream and propelled him out of the kitchen. "Do what you've got to do, and don't tell me or anyone else," he said.

"Sturgis!" Bedwyr exclaimed, leaping out of his chair, waving the magazine in his hand.

He was so large, and so loud, that the other knights ceased their noisy guzzling of the half-melted ice cream and turned toward him in annoyance. A lone twang from Fairhands's autoharp disturbed the sudden silence.

"Well, what is it?" Kay snapped. "Some sort of stinging bee?"

"Sturgis," Bedwyr repeated, grinning. "This!" He laid the magazine flat on the table and pointed to a two-page spread of a small-town street packed solid with bikers and their motorcycles. "The Sturgis Motorcycle Rally. A great tournament," he said solemnly. "It takes place over a week, and that week has begun."

"A tourney," Launcelot said in wonder. "Is it a far journey?"

" 'Tis not even a day's ride," Bedwyr answered, his face flushed with excitement.

Dry lips picked up the magazine and brought it close to his face. "The steeds appear to be most excellent," he said. All of the knights rode motorcycles now, thanks to Bedwyr's tutelage, and took as much pride in the appearance of their machines as they had in their mounts.

"Steeds!" MacDaire exclaimed, laughing. "Are ye blind, man? Look at the women! I swear, this one's bare-breasted!"

Lugh crowded next to Dry Lips to leer from behind black beetle brows, grunting in agreement.

"And that!"

Kay snatched the magazine out of Dry Lips's hands. "By Saint Patrick's smelly balls, she's a beauty."

A dribble of saliva dropped onto the page. There was a moment of silence as Lugh covered his mouth sheepishly.

"Fiend!" Bedwyr screamed, lunging for Lugh. "Your drool has befouled my picture!" Lugh leaped out of the way with surprising agility, backing into the table, from which he grabbed a candlestick and held it in front of him in preparation for combat. Bedwyr unsheathed his dirk.

Hal threw up his arms. "What'd I tell you?" he shouted to Taliesin. "They're morons."

"Stop, stop, stop!" the old man spat, coming between the two combatants. "Good heavens, no wonder Hal's disgusted with the lot of you. You've the manners of goats!" He cast a hard eye on Lugh, who was still gripping the candlestick.

"Would it please you to be a goat, Lugh?" Taliesin asked softly.

Lugh set the object down at once. Most of the knights still believed that the old man, like all the Merlins trained by the magical druids, had the power to turn ordinary men into whatever beasts caught their fancy. "No, sir, I would not like that," Lugh said, patting the candlestick for good measure. It was perhaps the longest sentence ever uttered by the man. Lugh did not like to waste his limited mental resources on talk, but apparently felt that the situation called for extraordinary measures.

"Very good," Taliesin said. Lugh retreated to a corner. "Go on, Bedwyr."

The Master of Horse straightened, shooting a disdainful glance at Lugh. "I was considering, sir, that it might be a pleasant diversion for us to attend."

"Indeed. Well, that would be your decision. And Hal's, of course. He's in charge."

Hal's eyes were closed in dread.

Fairhands strummed his autoharp in delight. "Come joust, fine knights, and taste the wine. . . ."

"These be not knights," Launcelot said, sneering at the photograph, "but evildoers of the worst sort."

"So much the better!" Kay shouted, raising his glass.

MacDaire clapped Arthur on the back. "Come, Arthur, 'Twill be the first tourney for you in sixteen hundred years!"

"He won't be going along," Taliesin said. "We've plans, the boy and I." He gave Arthur a wink.

"You mean, we're going to the mountain . . . now?"

"No better time," the old man said. "Go fetch a blanket. The rest of you, go on about your business."

Arthur stood up. Across the room, his eyes met Hal's. He wanted to go to him, to say good-bye.

But he did not have to say anything. Hal knew perfectly well that, despite whatever plans Taliesin had made, the boy would not be coming back to the farmhouse in Jones County.

It was time.

CHAPTER FOUR

THE HEALING WATERS

DAWNING FALLS, NEW YORK

Far away from the farmhouse in Jones County, South Dakota, on the northern ridge of the Laurel highlands, flowed a body of water known to the locals as Miller's Creek, named for the family which had built a house over it in the early 1880s.

No one had paid any attention to Miller's Creek until a few years ago, when a member of the Dawning Falls Gardening Society noticed the exquisite condition of the land on either side of it. Although it only ran above ground for a few hundred feet, its banks were lush with grass fragrant as perfume. Flanking the creek were fields of flowers and tangled vines of wild, sweet grapes. Huge warrens of rabbits honeycombed the soil nearby. Beyond it, long past the point where the creek ran underground, the tall trees of a great pine forest dropped cones the size of pineapples.

But the landscaping around Miller's Creek was not what drew more than five thousand people to Dawning Falls each day. They came because something about the water contained the miraculous power to heal.

It healed flesh wounds, hereditary diseases, bone deformities, cirrhotic livers, weak hearts, skin rashes, tumors, blood clots, enlarged prostates, swollen glands, and hyperactive thyroids. It alleviated migraines, nausea, menstrual cramps, erectile dysfunction, gall bladder disease, and a thousand other ailments.

There had been not thousands, but hundreds of thousands of documented cases of people who had been confined to wheelchairs, dependent on walkers or canes suddenly standing in astonishment after drinking or even touching the water that flowed from the stream, and then walking away unassisted. Children who had been brought to the water blue and nearly lifeless left it skipping. The elderly emerged from Miller's Creek still old, but free of pain. At night, deer maimed by hunters found their way to the water and then, brought back from the edge of death, bounded whole again into the pine woods.

What was more, nothing could taint the purity of the water. On one occasion, a man who was obviously deranged threw a container of what he claimed was rat poison into the creek. The area was closed and a sample of the water, as well as the now empty container, was taken immediately to a laboratory in Corning for analysis. The results showed that the container had indeed been filled with rat poison, enough, in fact, to kill thousands of people. The water, however, tested absolutely devoid of toxins.

The creek had not always exhibited this remarkable property. Four years before, when the land upon which it ran was sold to an idealistic young New Yorker named Zack Diamond, it was no more than a narrow, marshy strip of water running beneath a tumbledown frame house assessed at twelve thousand dollars.

Diamond, who bought the land as agent for an eccentric British gentleman named Taliesin, had been charged with the task of protecting a singular artifact: This was a pitted, misshapen, handleless cup of greenish metal which, depending on whose hands it was in, could bring either great good to the world, or great evil.

The young man had hoped that his were the right hands. With Taliesin's permission, he pulled up the floorboards of the house and dug straight down until he reached the running creek. Into it he placed a concrete block containing the cup, covered the water with a layer of flat rock, then filled it all in again with earth and replaced the floor. As a result, all the water in Miller's Creek flowed over the cup before ascending to its short overland outcropping.

He knew well what the cup could do. It had saved his own life. It could, he believed, save the lives of countless others.

And so its magic was offered free to anyone who came to Miller's Creek. Despite the warnings of early cynics who claimed that anything this good had to be a hoax from which someone was making money, the miraculous water turned out to be neither apocryphal nor profitable, for the young man or anyone else. The only restriction was that no one was permitted to take any of the water away. It was, Diamond felt, the only way to maintain the simplicity of the healing waters, and the cup as a sacred, if hidden, relic.

For he knew what the cup was, and why he had to keep it away from himself and everyone else. It had been healing wounds on earth for thousands of years, mostly in secret, and mostly in the service of evil men. In fact, it was an enormous irony known only to a select few, including the dismayed Mr. Taliesin, that the only two people in all of human history who might have been able to keep the cup without being corrupted by it had both willingly let it go.

One of those men was Jesus of Nazareth. The other was Arthur Pendragon.

And the cup, which might have kept either of those individuals alive for all eternity, had been known as the Holy Grail.

Gwen Ranier watched, unnoticed, as her mother smiled into the mirror. "Honey!" she called, arranging a coral-colored silk hibiscus flower behind her ear. "Hon . . . Oh. I didn't see you standing there, angel." She lifted a limp hand to her heart. "How's this look?" She turned around, fixing Gwen with the full wattage of her smile.

At forty-six, Ginger Ranier was still abundantly beautiful. She wore her dark hair long, pulled back like a girl's. On anyone else, the effect might have looked like a fading woman trying to hang on to a vanished youth, but Ginger was able to carry it off. She was shapely, well groomed, and her face, naturally exotic with wide-set, amber-colored eyes and a sensitive aqualine nose, was enhanced by expertly applied makeup.

"You almost can't see the bruise," Gwen said.

"What did you say?" her mother shrilled.

Gwen shook her head sullenly. "Why don't you cut your hair?"

"Oh, so that I can look like you?" Ginger asked. Her voice was soft, but her daughter felt the barb.

"You're a prize, Mom. A real prize."

For a moment the two women stared at one another's reflections in the frilly boudoir mirror. They could not have looked more different. In contrast to her mother's studied youthfulness, Gwen appeared to be much older than her seventeen years. Her eyes were circled with a thick rim of black pencil. Her lips were black, too, although sometimes she lightened them to a deep eggplant color for daytime wear. Her hair, also dyed black, was short as a boy's and spiked straight up, causing her to look as if she had just been electrocuted. Her earrings, silver and black beads, hung to her shoulders like long dog ears.

"You should talk," Ginger said. "You look like a freak."

"And you have a nice day, too," Gwen said, turning away.

"Hey, I'm sorry," her mother called. "Please come back."

Gwen turned back with an exaggerated sigh. "Only if you get rid of that stupid flower."

Ginger took the hibiscus from behind her ear and twirled it thoughtfully between her fingers. "We're so different," she said.

"Duh."

"Why do you dress that way, honey?"

"What way?" Gwen asked, feigning innocence.

"Oh, come on. Scary, like."

Gwen made a face and wiggled her black-nailed fingers at her mother's reflection. "You think I'm scary?"

"No, I think you're wonderful. Smart and kind and good to me, probably better than I deserve. You've never complained about any of the crap I've made you put up with. And you're a super artist, too. You really have talent."

"But . . ." Gwen said, arching her eyebrows, waiting.

"But you make yourself look weird."

"God." Gwen snatched the flower from her mother's hands and threw it in the wastebasket. "Are you doing this so we won't have to talk about how you look?"

Ginger took a deep breath. "Could be. But I'd still like to know."

Her daughter smiled. "Well, that's honest at least." She took a long look at herself in the mirror, then shrugged. "Maybe I want to look like this so that people can look at me without seeing me."

Her mother looked blankly into the mirror for a moment, then smiled. "I think that's too deep for me," she said.

Gwen smiled back. "That's okay."

"We can talk about me now," Ginger said humbly. "What's wrong with me, I mean."

She sounded so innocent, like a child waiting for punishment, that Gwen wanted to put her arms around her.

She had always been, in some respects, her mother's mother. Ginger was an artist; that was always the reason she gave for failing to provide Gwen with things like lunch money, clean clothes, or a resident adult. "There's nothing wrong with you," Gwen said.

Ginger was still staring into the mirror. "Do I look . . ." The words seemed to hurt her as they emerged from her lips. "Well . . . *old?*" A whisper.

Gwen had been holding her breath, but at her mother's question, delivered with such blushing shame, she nearly laughed aloud. Old! If her mother only knew the names people really called her!

Ginger was a sort of icon among the local women and their daughters. With her long dyed hair and rouged cheeks, she was everyone's favorite object of scorn. Who's Ginger sleeping with now? Oh, no one, dear. Haven't you noticed—she hasn't had a black eye in months!

It used to hurt Gwen beyond measure to hear these remarks about her mother. Her mother, who was, actually, not bad for a mother. She was loving and gentle and kind to everyone, including animals. Over the years she'd found dozens of injured dogs, cats, birds, raccoons, turtles, and even a badger, which she'd nursed back to health.

The only one Ginger couldn't seem to keep out of harm's way was herself. But Gwen knew her mother wouldn't understand that in a hundred years.

"It's just jealousy, baby," Ginger had said so often that it had become a kind of mantra. "Those wrinkled old bags just wish they could look like me."

She was, in fact, a virtual miracle of regeneration and good genes. Her nose had been broken at one time, as had a cheekbone, a forearm, a finger, and several ribs. Whenever one of the earthy paramours with whom she was fond of mating took out his frustrations on her with his fists, Ginger had run to the battered women's shelter with Gwen in tow. She was always wild-eyed and weeping, her nose streaming blood, her perfect makeup smeared grotesquely, her eyes swollen, beginning already to blacken, her lips thick and stippled with cuts, her body bruised.

But she had never filed charges. Not once, not even against one man who had almost killed her. He was the father of her child, she explained, forgetting that she used that explanation for all of them. In truth, the real father of her daughter had been quite respectable, a student from Cambridge University in England, passing through Dawning Falls on vacation.

But that had been nearly eighteen years ago. Ginger never talked about him.

The day after each of her encounters with the wild side of love, Ginger would once again be smiling, her long hair shining and lovely, her makeup perfectly applied over the bruises and cuts.

She had not been to the shelter in some time now, and for nearly a year had not become involved enough with a man to invite him to live with her and her daughter in their small rented house.

For Gwen, that had been a tremendous relief. The men had always frightened her. The men, and their fists, and the blood on her mother's face. In the past year she had finally begun to relax in her home.

But her mother had taken up with someone again. She could

tell. The flowers, the careful makeup, the faint streak of blue over her cheekbone, the slight swelling. "No, Mom," Gwen said dully. "You don't look old."

The relief on Ginger's face was visible. "Well, that's a blessing," she said. She picked the flower out of the wastebasket casually, as if the wind had blown it there. Held it up to her experimentally. Looked at her daughter's reflection with puppy eyes, as if asking Gwen's permission. Finally she set the flower down. "Okay, I'll leave it off if that'll make you happy," she said.

"And cut your hair."

"John likes it," Ginger said, tossing the long curls.

The gesture disgusted Gwen. "John?" the girl asked, remembering another lover of her mother's with the same name. When she had made the mistake of mentioning him to a classmate, the girl had asked if "John" was the man's name, or his relationship to her mother.

Ginger stood up and straightened her skirt. Her eyes did not meet Gwen's. "He's very nice, really. I've been thinking about letting him move in for a while."

Gwen froze. "What?"

"Well, it wouldn't be for long. He's a little down on his luck, and—"

"You mean he doesn't have a job," Gwen said.

"He could help out around the house. Fix that leak in the roof. We could sure use some help with that, couldn't we?"

"How many times has he hit you?"

Ginger's hand went to her face. "That was just an accident," she said. "He didn't mean anything. John's really a sweetie."

"How long have you known him, a week?" Gwen demanded. It had, indeed, been a week. "Please don't let him move in, Mom."

"Look," Ginger said with a smile. "I can take care of myself."

"Then you don't need him!" Gwen felt her shoulders begin to tremble and her voice quaver. Not another one. Oh, God, not another man in our house.

"I mean I can control the situation," Ginger said evenly. "I'm not going to let anybody use me for a doormat, believe me, Gwen. Now we're going to go over to Miller's Creek. John's not from around here, and he wants to see if the waters'll get rid of some scars he got in the service. You can come, too."

Gwen ran her hand over her eyes. "Why would I want to do that?"

"Just so he can meet you, honey." As an afterthought she added, "And you can give him the once-over, too."

"If I don't like him, will you tell him he can't live here?"

Ginger hesitated for a moment, then smiled. "Sure," she said, taking her daughter's hand. "It's you and me, baby girl."

"Yeah," Gwen said, feeling her eyes start to fill.

"What's the matter?" Ginger asked.

"Nothing." Gwen wiped her eyes with the back of her hand. "Go ahead and wear the flower," she said softly. "Never can tell when Mr. Right's going to come along."

CHAPTER FIVE

EVERYDAY MIRACLES

Miller's Creek—that is, the section of the creek that attracted so many visitors—was actually a very short stretch of water. It came up out of the ground just north of the frame house which stood over the buried cup, then meandered for three hundred feet or so before disappearing again, to emerge next as a swamp in the middle of the woods. The house, and consequently the creek, was near a two-lane macadam road which had been known for the past century as Germantown Pike. Across the Pike was a huge parking lot to accommodate all the visitors to the creek. It had been built over a field of wildflowers. Some of the field remained on the far side of the lot. Beyond that lay the town of Dawning Falls proper. The street on the far side of the wildflower field was, in fact, the location of the battered women's shelter which Ginger Ranier and her daughter had visited so often.

Glancing toward the creek from her place in the long line winding toward it, Ginger unconsciously touched the bruise on her cheek.

"This way, please," a young volunteer said, urging her along. The volunteer was a pretty young girl Gwen's age. She was, actually, one of Gwen's classmates, although neither acknowledged the other.

The volunteers were a big improvement on Zack Diamond's original setup. He had thought only to offer the water to the public; he had not anticipated the huge crowds the water would draw.

The creek itself had become a muddy, slippery mess almost as soon as the place opened to the public. Now, even though a wooden deck covered the entire area of what had once been the frame house's front lawn and a double rail running the length of the creek had been installed, Miller's Creek was still a problem for the large numbers of disabled persons who visited it.

For this reason, a bevy of helpers was recruited from local churches, businesses, charities and, during summer months, among the high school population.

Gwen Ranier was herself one of the volunteers, a fact that astonished most of the administrators at Dawning Falls High. She certainly did not appear to be the sort of student who typically offered her time in community service.

"Was that one of your friends, dear?" Ginger asked in a voice that approximated what she thought good mothers should sound like.

Gwen laughed mirthlessly. "Girls like that don't have friends like me."

"Well, maybe—" her mother began, but she was distracted by John, the man of the moment, who was squeezing her buttock.

Gwen turned away, disgusted. The man was so recently sobered that he still reeked of alcohol, his hair slicked back after a morning shower, his skin pasty, his eyes red and unused to the early hour. Despite Ginger's rhapsodic enthusiasm for him, Gwen recognized him as the latest in a long string of losers who had come to violate her mother and her home. When he looked back at her, she stuck her finger in her mouth and pantomimed vomiting. He made a face. Gwen gave him the finger and left the line.

"Don't go, honey," Ginger said. "Please. I want to try the water. It's been here all this time—"

"Go ahead," Gwen said. "I'll wait for you. Don't lose your place in line."

Ginger smiled. "Thanks," she said, rushing back to John's side. She tried to put her arm through his, but he shook it off.

John didn't like Gwen, Ginger thought, disappointed but not surprised. Most of her boyfriends didn't take to the girl.

But that hadn't all been their fault. Gwen had never made an effort to get them to like her. And then, inevitably, they had ended up being cranky with Ginger for burdening them with a surly teenage girl.

Ginger wished she could explain to them that Gwen was really a good girl at heart. She just didn't know how to make people like her, that was all. One of Ginger's basic beliefs was that, if you were a woman and you wanted to get by in life, you had to get people to like you. Especially men. You didn't want to antagonize men, because they could cause God-knew-what kind of trouble for you if they wanted to. They could take you to the stars, but they could dump you in the garbage, too, so you'd better make sure you were on their good side. That put you in control.

Throughout all of Ginger's relationships with men, no matter how abusive or humiliating those experiences had been, she had always boasted to Gwen that she was really the one in control, because she knew how to get back on a man's good side.

Unfortunately, Gwen did not show signs of knowing how to handle men. She certainly hadn't known how to handle her mother's boyfriends. It was getting to the point where Ginger was embarrassed to introduce her daughter to anyone, because more often than not Gwen would sneer at them without a word, roll her kohl-encircled eyes heavenward, and saunter away, leaving Ginger to make lame explanations about teenagers.

Gwen did have one thing going for her, though: She could draw. Some of her sketches were pretty good. Ginger knew, because she, too, had been able to draw well at one time.

At Gwen's age, Ginger had been offered a scholarship to Cooper Union, one of the best art schools in New York City. Unfortunately, she got pregnant. Three years, a baby, and a number of emergency room visits later, Ginger was once again unwed, and Cooper Union was no more than a name.

Ginger felt herself blushing. Hot flashes, she told herself, but she knew better. It was shame, red-hot and unforgettable.

To turn down a scholarship to Cooper Union! What might she have become?

Nothing, she thought dimly. *I probably wouldn't have made it anyway.*

Gwen was every bit as talented as her mother, but even less ambitious. She wouldn't even apply for the scholarship, Ginger thought with dismay. And with her attitude, no one was likely to offer her one if she did.

As they neared the front of the slow-moving line, John removed his shirt, revealing a dramatic line of nine deep scars across his stomach. "Machine gun fire," he explained, displaying his torso to the staring crowd. He pointed to a large tattoo of the Marine insignia on his right arm. " 'Nam," he intoned.

When they finally took their places at the creek, John made a show of splashing water all over himself and everyone around him. "Got to make sure I get enough," he said.

Ginger put up her hands, trying to protect her hair from the spraying water. "John, please—"

"Hey!" He was looking down at his belly. Then, dripping and sodden, he turned toward the crowd, and a gasp of amazement went up around him.

"Praise the Lord!" someone shouted.

"Amen!"

Not a trace of the nine deep scars remained. John laughed and shook hands with everyone in the line who was willing to touch him. "Well, don't that beat all," he said, thumping the unbroken expanse of skin across his stomach. "I'd say I need to get me a beer after that." He tugged at Ginger's arm. "Come on."

"Wait a minute, sweetie," she said, dabbing water prettily on her wrists and behind her ears, as if it were perfume. With a swift gesture she swept some of the water across her swollen cheekbone. "There we are!" she said, patting her hair in place.

"That was frickin' unbelievable!" John said, putting on his shirt as they walked away.

A pretty blond woman gave him a wink. He kissed the air in her direction.

Ginger pretended not to notice as she took a compact out of her purse and scanned her face with it. "Oh," she said, faltering.

"What is it, baby?"

"Oh, nothing. Just stumbled over a stone or something." She smiled as she replaced the compact.

Gwen walked over to them, peering to get a look at her mother's face. "Mom, let me see—"

"Goodness, but it's getting hot out here!" Ginger exclaimed, rushing past her daughter over the boardwalk. "John, honey, I think I'll just go back home now, if you don't mind."

"You can go anyplace you want, but I'm getting me a beer." His glance wandered back to the blond woman.

"Certainly. You go ahead. I'll see you later."

"How are we supposed to get home?" Gwen shouted after John's back as he loped off. "Jerk."

"It's all right, honey. We can walk."

John was making a beeline toward the blonde.

"Looks like your boyfriend has a short attention span," Gwen said. Her mother barely glanced up. "Well, you can't keep them on a leash, can you," Ginger said perfunctorily, her heels clattering against the wooden flooring, her skirt billowing.

"Mom, wait a minute."

"What?" Ginger asked irritably, out of breath from her sprint away from the creek.

"Let me look at you."

"Oh, don't be—"

Gwen took her mother by both arms and stood facing her head-on. The bruise over Ginger's cheekbone was still there, even more prominent now that some of her makeup had been rinsed off by the water. "It didn't work," she said, puzzled.

Ginger tried to twist away. "I probably just didn't put enough on," she said. "Doesn't matter, anyway. It's only a bruise."

Gwen continued to stare at her.

"Come on," Ginger said, pulling her daughter with surprising strength down the hill.

CHAPTER SIX

UGLY WOMEN CAN DANCE, TOO

Ginger Ranier had known that the water did not heal everyone. That fact had been known almost as soon as its healing power was discovered. The question was why. Why did it work on some, and not on others?

Among those who achieved perfect wellness after visiting the water were young people, old people, sick people, people with injuries, people of all races and all beliefs, atheists and zealots, drunks and addicts, the hopeless and the saintly, bulimics and overeaters, carnivores and vegetarians, people who had been kept alive by drugs, and people who had never visited a physician.

The same mix of people were left unaffected by the water.

This led to all sorts of speculation. New Agers proclaimed Miller's Creek to be a vortex of extraterrestrial vibrations. The movement of the planets was their explanation for why the water might cure one twenty-year-old woman's case of multiple sclerosis and not another's, or one brother's cleft palate while leaving the other afflicted. Almost every religion had some sect or other claiming the water's healing as the exclusive property of their particular deity. A surprisingly large number of people voiced the opinion that the government was behind the phenomenon in some way. These people insisted that, despite the fact that use of the water was completely free of charge, hardworking citizens were in some way paying for it all in the end. And, predictably, there were those who proclaimed it all to be the work of the devil.

Had the water affected everyone in the same way, Miller's Creek might have been accepted by the Catholic Church, or even by the medical establishment, as a bona fide place of miracles. But the fact that many who came to the waters in good faith left unhealed and heartbroken (including a number of small children with pathetic disabilities) caused both the media and the general public to slough off the place as a fraud or, at best, a psychosomatic "cure" for the gullible.

As a result, the flow of visitors, while always heavy, did not require any major changes to the simple setup. And after an initial flurry of media attention, the press ceased to maintain an interest in the authentic but inconsistent miracle of the water from Miller's Creek. This was disappointing for the young man who had purchased the land, because it had been his hope that the healing water would serve as the cornerstone for a great center of metaphysical study. To keep his dream alive, he found it necessary to spend almost all his time traveling the country soliciting funds to pay taxes on the property, keep up insurance policies, and maintain a minimal staff of two to oversee daily operations.

Miller's Creek's two employees were a night watchman, to ensure that people did not remove the water from the creek, which would eventually cause a drought in the pine forest downstream, and an administrator working out of the ramshackle house on the property to take care of the myriad details of a nonprofit enterprise.

In this, the owner had been lucky. The night watchman, Enrico Santori, was a local septuagenarian whose grandson was the chief of police of Dawning Falls. Miller's Creek was patrolled every hour of every night from six in the evening to six in the morning.

And the administrator was a woman whose prodigious powers of organization kept everything running so smoothly that one would not have guessed that there was any work at all involved in keeping a shrine visited by millions of people each year. Her name was Emily Blessing.

Ms. B, as she preferred to be called by the local populace, had appeared in Dawning Falls seemingly out of thin air, and looked like everyone's idea of a small-town librarian. Perched on her nose were a pair of black-framed, mannish glasses that were so old that they had actually become more fashionable than they had been when new. She always wore her hair parted in the middle and pulled into a severe bun on the back of her head. Her wardrobe reflected a sense of style so undeveloped that a number of women in town speculated that Ms. B might be a renegade nun.

They were wrong. What she had been, back in the days before her life became so utterly, unalterably changed by circumstances she still did not fully understand, was a prime mover at the Katzenbaum Institute, a think tank devoted to exploring the implications of science on society. She had been an intellectual, a scientist, and an atheist. She had also been the reluctant guardian of a child she had never wanted, a child she had lost one day, whose loss had made her radically reassess her life.

Most of the populace of Dawning Falls neither knew nor cared about her background, however. What was interesting about Ms. B was that she had come to Miller's Creek covered by a twisted mass of scar tissue that ran from the base of her right ear all the way down her arm, and that it had never gone away.

Emily Blessing was the first person to have been unaffected by the healing waters.

"I'm a reminder to everyone who visits here that the miracle doesn't always work," she told Gwen Ranier's high school class in the same crisp, matter-of-fact manner that she explained the molecular structure of the curative water or the history of other "miracle" sites around the world. Part of Ms. B's job was to drum up volunteers to clean the grounds around the creek.

After hearing her speak, Gwen went to the makeshift office at Miller's Creek the next day to volunteer. She had returned every week since then, mostly for the chance to speak with Ms. B.

Gwen admired the woman's factual, unemotional approach. After the teary, fairy-tale world in which she had been raised, Gwen's head nearly spun from the freshness of the air around this woman of ideas.

And there was another reason Gwen liked to spend time around Ms. B. The woman never commented on Gwen's appearance. Most people had a quite strong reaction to her. Either they were afraid of her, or they found her disgusting. But Ms. B seemed to notice nothing about her but her mind.

"Why do you suppose the water helps some people and not others?" she asked Gwen pointedly on the first day she came to volunteer.

The girl had looked around awkwardly, her kohl-rimmed eyes reluctant to light on either Ms. B's face or her scarred body.

"Look at me," Emily snapped. "These marks are from burns. They're part of who I am. You don't insult me by seeing them. You insult me by wanting not to see them."

Gwen blinked. She had spent her entire life around people who had wanted her to be different from what she was. She gulped and met Ms. B's eyes.

"Again," the woman said. "Why do you think the water heals some people and not others?"

"Why do you want to know?" Gwen countered, folding her arms defiantly over her chest. "Are you looking for advice?"

Ms. B's eyes widened, then crinkled into a deep, quiet smile that Gwen recognized and appreciated. "No," she said, "I am not, thanks all the same. Actually, I am interested in learning how you think. If you think."

Gwen inhaled sharply. She had not frightened the woman with her attitude. Ms. B had not grown suddenly insecure and ordered her out of her presence.

"Well?"

No one had ever spoken to her this way. As if what she said mattered, if only as an intellectual exercise. "Some people think the water's magic," she said tentatively.

"Do you?"

"I don't know. It might be. That is, it may only work if you believe it does. Deep down, that is. Some people act like skeptics, but they really believe. Or want to."

"Do you think I don't believe?"

Gwen shrugged. "I don't know. I can't think for you, Ms. B."

Emily sat back. Gwen felt—knew—that she had gone too far. She liked this woman. But, as usual, she had blown all possibility of making contact with Ms. B by a useless show of bravado.

"I . . . I didn't mean that," she said, feeling stupid.

"Mean what?" Ms. B asked crisply. "That you can't think for me?" She cocked her head. Her expression was that of someone engaged in an interesting conversation. Which was to say, she was not smiling, but neither was she visibly angry. "I would say that, with that comment, you have shown me that you possess a teachable mind."

Two hectic spots of color rose in Gwen's cheeks. "Can I come back tomorrow?" she asked.

Emily Blessing smiled. "Anytime," she said.

That evening, Emily thought about children. She had heard about Gwen Ranier and her unfortunate mother, and could see for herself the direction the girl's rebellion had taken. Mothers were of paramount importance to the development of their offspring, she thought, whether they did anything or not.

She stayed awake all that night, as she did many nights, fighting off the memories of another child. For Emily had once been offered the chance to be a mother, even though her body had not borne an infant. She had once had a boy to raise. And she had failed that boy utterly.

The last time she saw Arthur had been four years before, in a hotel in Lisbon, Portugal. She had only caught a glimpse of his face before the fire that would nearly claim her life had broken out. He was there, waiting to see her, and she was walking over to him, nervous, anxious, excited. . . .

They had never met. The fire had swooped into the room like an army of avenging angels, spreading destruction and terror in a heartbeat. The ceiling had fallen; the people inside the building had run, screaming, in all directions. Emily had fallen and been trampled by the mob. She woke up days later in a hospital room, looking like some nightmare beast.

Afterward, during the long months of her painful recuperation, she had seen Arthur on television, delivering some sort of apocalyptic message. But Emily had paid no attention to what he said. It was enough to know that he was alive. She had reached for the phone then, determined to find him somehow. He was alive! Arthur had made it out of the fire without a scratch.

She put down the phone. Yes, she thought soberly, he was alive. And he had chosen not to find her.

She could not blame him. Emily was not Arthur's real mother. She had come to be his guardian by default after her sister had been thoughtless enough to die before her child was weaned, and there had not been a single day during the first ten years of his life that she had not resented having to care for him.

Oh, she had taught him. Arthur had been bright beyond words. He had picked up every scrap of knowledge his aunt would bring him. But nothing he did could make up for what Emily had considered the derailment of her career. The Katzenbaum Institute did not make allowances for its scientists with young children at home. In spite of her brilliance, she was bypassed for the big projects, demoted to the second tier of players, removed from the inner circle.

For this she blamed the child. And though she had dutifully kept her humiliating job as a second-rate employee of the institute in order to support the unwanted infant who had been dumped into her lap, she had never held him in her arms, nor sung him a lullaby, nor dried his tears. In the early years of his disappearance, she had wondered if he had missed those things.

Of course he had, she told herself a thousand times since he had gone.

Still, he had not left out of hatred for her. The fact that she had been a terrible mother was actually quite coincidental to his necessity to leave. There had been people who would have harmed Arthur if they had found him. Going to the police had not been an option. If it had not been for Hal Woczniak, Arthur surely would have died long before the hotel fire in Lisbon.

Emily had given up trying to get Arthur back. She understood that he was special, more special than anyone knew except for Hal. The boy belonged with him.

She had never explained that to either of them. That was going to be Emily's gift to them at the hotel in Lisbon: She was going to let Hal know that he had done right by the boy. She was going to tell Arthur that she knew about the cup, that he wouldn't have been safe with Emily, that the circumstances in which they had found themselves had made ordinary life impossible.

And that she loved him. But the fire had rendered all that impossible.

Now, everyone who had been after them was dead. And the cup, that magical, wicked thing that had come to Arthur Blessing during the tenth year of his life and made sure he would never have a normal life again, had been safely hidden at last.

Hidden to others. Perhaps all others. But Emily knew exactly where it was.

It was in Miller's Creek.

CHAPTER SEVEN

THE GODS AT PLAY

She had known it since she first read about the healing water in Dawning Falls. The first articles, humorous stories about gigantic pumpkins and dairy cows that produced extraordinary quantities of milk, began to appear shortly after Arthur's surprise appearance on television, after which he had vanished without a trace.

The second spate of articles was about an unassuming young man named Zack Diamond, who had recently bought the land containing Miller's Creek. Skeptical journalists had pointed out that the so-called healing properties of the water had begun to occur right after Mr. Diamond had taken ownership of the creek. Some sort of moneymaking scheme was suspected, but a thorough check on Diamond revealed a young man of high ideals whose single oddity seemed to be that he had undergone a near-death experience during a catastrophe involving a building collapsing into a sinkhole in Manhattan.

As soon as she learned that, Emily traveled immediately to

Dawning Falls and walked without knocking into the tumbledown frame house built on Miller's Creek.

"Oh, hi," Diamond had said as he looked up from a two-foot stack of papers on a desk made of a hollow-core door laid over two empty file cabinets. Books and notes to himself were scattered all over the room as if they had been blown about by the wind.

Diamond himself was far younger than Emily had expected, and there was nothing in his manner to indicate that he was in any way knowledgeable about business, which was the sad truth. Motivated only by a desire to help mankind, Zack Diamond was obviously inadequate to the task of running what was quickly becoming one of the biggest tourist attractions in the eastern United States.

"Just a . . ." He became momentarily engrossed in something he was reading, then looked up, suddenly seeming to remember the woman standing in front of him. "Um, the water's outside," he said, noticing her scars. "Help yourself."

"I am Arthur Blessing's aunt and legal guardian," she said without preamble. "Did you kill him for the cup?"

Diamond looked at her as if someone had just knocked the air out of his lungs.

"Well, did you?"

"No! He didn't want it. I mean . . ." His mouth opened and closed in frustration. "No," he repeated quietly. "He's fine, as far as I know."

"Where is he?"

"I don't know," he said honestly. "If I did, people might be able to find out by torturing me. So I don't keep in touch."

Emily stared at the man for a moment. He was afraid. She did not have to verify her suspicions about the cup. By his silence, Zack Diamond had confirmed everything she had wanted to know.

"Look, whoever you are—"

"I'm who I said I was," Emily explained, her voice more gentle than it had been. "I'm not a spy, and I don't want to take the cup from you, if that is your suspicion. If you have it, then it's because Arthur wants you to have it. And I rather like what you're doing with it." She looked around the cluttered room. "This office, how-ever, is another matter."

Diamond smiled sheepishly. "I can't afford any help yet."

"You will. Meanwhile, I can help you to organize this mess." She looked down at her scarred hands. "I haven't anything else to do with my time, anyway."

Diamond faltered.

"You're wondering if you can trust me," Emily said, writing down the phone number of the boardinghouse where she had rented a room. "Let me know know when you've made your decision." She turned to leave. "Just one more question."

Diamond looked at the papers clutched in both of his hands. "Yes?"

"Is Hal still alive?"

At Hal's name, Diamond's brow relaxed. "You know Hal?"

"I do," she said simply.

"He's alive. He's keeping Arthur hidden."

Emily smiled. "Hal's good at hiding things," Emily said. "Better than you. Why didn't you just keep the cup to yourself?"

Zack swallowed hard. "I wanted to do some good," he said. "And . . . and I was afraid to be alone with it."

She nodded. "I understand." She held out her hand. "Emily Blessing," she said. "If you want to reach me, I'll be—"

"I want you to work here," Diamond said. "For no money, and no guarantee of ever getting any money."

"Agreed," Emily said. "Until I decide to leave."

"Okay." He shook her hand. "Er, you won't—"

"I won't tell anyone."

"Thanks."

"You could still be killed, though."

"I know."

"And I could be lying."

"I know," Diamond said.

Emily sighed. "I think I'd better get to work," she said. "You're hopeless."

Within a month, the administrative office of Miller's Creek was running smoothly. The following month, Diamond received a large donation from the father of a young girl whose bone cancer had gone into complete remission after an encounter with the healing waters. It was enough to pay Emily a modest salary for the next year. After that, Zack Diamond was called to speak all over the world about the miraculous water of Miller's Creek, and Emily Blessing was left to run the place alone.

She never told the young man that she had gone to the creek on the same day she had first come to see him.

Emily Blessing had never been a vain woman—her mind had always been her best feature—but when she heard the gasps of those who had been miraculously healed at the creek right in front of her, when she watched people fall to their knees in prayerful gratitude, when she saw an old woman's goiter shrink before her eyes and the fingers at the end of a five-year-old boy's withered arm move, she had been filled with hope for herself.

Before she went in to see Zack Diamond, she had waited in the line for hours, ashamed that she was putting off the task she had traveled a great distance to do, but feeling compelled to feel once again the healing warmth of the cup.

For she had come in contact with it before. Long before the cup had found its way to its underground place in this unsophisticated town, when it was still an object known to men who were willing to kill for it, Emily had been shot point-blank in the middle of her chest and left for dead.

She had been past all hope of survival when the cup had touched her. That was all it had been, a touch, yet it had been enough to heal the massive wound from the inside out, leaving nothing but smooth skin and a blood-soaked blouse.

The cup, like all miraculous objects, had caused so much trouble that Emily had been glad to learn that it was gone forever. And yet now, waiting her turn in the line of pilgrims, hope surged through her body, her heart pounding as she drew closer to the healing waters, her face flushing, her hands trembling with excitement.

And then her turn came to touch the magic water, to splash it on the grotesque scars that had transformed her from an ordinary, forgettable woman into a pitiable monster whom people avoided because they did not know where to look when they talked with her. She poured the water on herself, she drank it, she held it to her throat like a poultice as others behind her craned their necks to watch the expected miracle of her transformation.

But there had been no miracle. Emily had known from the first moment that the cup was not working for her. There was no warmth. The last time she had been touched by it, her whole body had vibrated with its intense power.

But not this time.

For a moment, the entire crowd at the creek gasped and moaned with dismay at Emily's unchanged appearance. But their concern was soon superseded by their desire to experience their own healing, and within minutes she found herself completely edged out, standing alone outside the periphery of the group as they once again shouted in amazement at the miracle water.

Maybe it's not the cup after all, she thought, shaking with disappointment. She knew that the cup worked. It had worked on her before.

A woman rose out of a wheelchair and walked through the parted crowd with tears streaming down her face. "It was warm!" she cried. "It was warm, like a living thing."

Like a living thing. Yes, that was how the cup had felt before, those years ago, warm and living.

Emily made way for the woman, who walked past her as if she did not exist. There was no room in the hearts of the faithful for reminders of failure. The secret of Miller's Creek was indeed the cup, and the cup still worked.

Just not for her.

She gathered her strength, steadying herself as others filed past her without a glance, pretending she did not exist. Then she wiped her face with a tissue, threw back her shoulders, and walked into the building where Zack Diamond sat at his desk surrounded by papers.

Now, four years later, she no longer wept over the scars that covered her body, just as she no longer wept over the loss of Arthur, or her guilt, or her broken love for Hal, who had left her without a word of good-bye.

She had a job and lived her small life, and tried to accept those things as enough.

A week after Ginger Ranier's disappointing pilgrimage to Miller's Creek, her daughter Gwen came to visit Ms. B.

"The water didn't work on my mother," she said, thumping a tattered scrapbook on the corner of the desk.

"Hmmm." Emily was absorbed in double-entry bookkeeping. There had been a number of sizeable donations that month.

"It wasn't a big deal, though. She only had a couple of bruises. They went away by themselves."

"Good."

"And her boyfriend never came back."

"I see."

"He was a brainless prick."

"Are you trying to shock me?" she said without looking up.

Gwen laughed. "Just seeing if you were paying attention."

"Well, I'm not, unless you come up with something at least mildly interesting."

Gwen folded her hands. She bit her lips.

Ms. B looked up. "Yes?"

"It's just . . . well . . . That is, I have a question, if you don't mind answering it."

"I will if I can."

Gwen took a deep breath. "It's about the water," she said. "The water from the creek, and how it doesn't work . . . on some people."

"Like me," Emily said.

"And my mother," Gwen added quickly. I'm thinking more about her."

"Okay."

"Do you remember when we talked once about how magic might only work if you believed in it?"

"Not always," Emily said with a half smile.

"I know. Because my mom does believe. She really does. But it didn't help her." She squirmed in her seat. "My point is, I don't think it's a belief in magic that makes the difference. It's something else."

Emily raised her eyebrows. "Such as?"

"Such as maybe it's feeling that you—I mean her, my mother—feeling that she doesn't deserve to be healed."

Emily swallowed, looked away.

"I'm saying that maybe some people just can't accept it, that's all." Her face was strained. "I wasn't talking about you, though."

"I see," Emily said hoarsely, feeling uncomfortable with how personal the conversation had grown. "Was there anything else?"

Gwen looked crestfallen. "No," she said. Then she added: "I'm working today."

"Good," Emily said brightly. "I'll see you later, then." She went back to her bookkeeping, her jaw clenched tightly.

Gwen recognized the dismissal. As she rose, she made a small, apologetic gesture that succeeded only in knocking the scrapbook off the desk. It landed with a resounding slap. Several pages spilled out and scattered beneath the desk.

Emily looked up in annoyance.

"They're just some drawings, Ms. B," Gwen said as she scrambled on her hands and knees to pick up the rough, yellowed papers.

Emily's irritation vanished in an instant. The shabby scrapbook looked as if it were thirty years old. It was probably the only paper the girl had, she realized. One of the pages rested against her shoe. Emily reached down to retrieve it.

It was a charcoal portrait, quite good. The subject was a girl with dark hair bound intricately by a netting of fine thread.

"Why, it's superb," Emily said. "Really, Gwen, your talent is such . . ." She squinted at the drawing. "She looks familiar. Who was your model?"

"I dreamed her," Gwen said. "Last night. I don't remember what the dream was about, exactly, except that there were three people, two girls and a boy, and one of them said something about healing, and how it was like love, it wasn't enough that it was given, but it had to be accepted, too." She blushed. "That's where I got the idea for . . . for what I said."

Emily picked up another of the portraits.

"That's the second one I did," Gwen said. "I got up at five o'clock in the morning and started drawing, so I wouldn't forget what the faces looked like."

This, too, was a young woman's face, framed by flowing blond hair. Wearing a long gown of what looked to be coarse fabric, she stood in a posture of supplication, her arms upraised before a large stone on which had been placed ritual items: the skull of a bird, a shell, a flowering branch. In her hand was a dagger, pointed skyward.

"This is interesting," Emily said.

"I don't know why she's holding a knife."

Emily brought the sketch closer to her face. Though the figure was smaller than the first, the features of the face were very detailed. "Why, it's you," she said.

"It is?" Gwen bent over the sketch. "I didn't plan it."

"Remarkable." Emily turned the page back to the first portrait. "Of course. This one is your face, too, minus the extreme makeup."

"But I dreamed them both. Plus the third one. It's underneath."

"It's entirely possible that you dreamed them," Emily said, glad to be on less emotional ground. "In fact, it makes perfect sense. These are aspects of yourself you're seeing, this rather fairy-tale princess persona, and this, a priestess of some sort." She smiled as she lifted the paper to reveal the third drawing. "They're wonderful, Gwen, and as examples of your technique—"

She froze. The spittle in her mouth dried as she moved her fingers slowly over the sketch of a boy on the brink of manhood.

"Well, you can't say that's me," Gwen said. "I really don't know who it is. I've been through all my music magazines. He's not in a band, I don't think, and I don't watch much TV. Ms. B?"

Emily was still staring at the portrait, transfixed.

"Ms. B?"

"I know him," Emily rasped. "His name is Arthur."

CHAPTER EIGHT

PINTO

He had been born John Stapp. That was the name on his school and prison records, but everyone knew him as Pinto. He liked the name: Pinto. It was a kind of horse. He didn't know much more than that, even though he'd grown up in Montana, but he'd always liked the sound of it.

Pinto wasn't in Montana now; hadn't been since he broke parole in '94. He doubted if anyone was still looking for him there, but he wasn't going back. He never stayed very long in one place, anyway. His longest stretch, outside of doing time, was in Pittsburgh, Pennsylvania, where he'd hung with a gang called the Vandals in a bar called the Mad Dog Café.

A succession of owners had tried to take over the Mad Dog, make it into a respectable place, keep out the bikers. But no one could keep out the Vandals.

The Vandals were a righteous gang, with colors and discipline, almost like the army. Pinto felt at home with them. He liked the discipline. If somebody had to get whacked, he'd whack them. He did what he had to do, and if people didn't like it, they could leave. Or else he'd kill them.

He'd ridden his first motorycycle with the Vandals. Now, heading westward on Route 40 out of Ohio astride a Harley Hell Bound Pro Street Custom, which he'd taken off some jerk kid outside of Tijuana, Mexico (on whose body Pinto had discovered nearly four hundred dollars taped to the inside thigh), he felt as if he'd always known how to ride. And he was wearing Vandal colors, purple and green.

He didn't always wear colors; just when he wanted to. He wanted to now because colors would give him status at the Sturgis Motorcycle Rally, where every biker from the Atlantic to the Pacific spent the first week in August. A lot of the bikers were stone fakes, doctors and lawyers who went to Sturgis to pretend they had dicks. But there were some there who knew what was happening. They knew what it meant to be a Vandal. They gave the colors respect.

But still, he didn't wear them all the time. That would be too much like following a rule, and Pinto didn't follow anything. Once a fellow Vandal named Banger had criticized him for not wearing the colors. Pinto had responded by cutting through the man's nostril with his pocketknife.

Pinto didn't like rules, he'd explained to Banger after the wound healed and they were tight again. He liked the discipline, he'd whack whoever needed it, but he wasn't about to follow anybody's dumb-ass rules. Sometimes he was a Vandal, okay? Through and through, purple and green down to the hair on his ass. And sometimes he'd just as soon take these guys' heads off with his teeth. He'd said he hoped Banger understood that point.

That was why he hadn't hung around Montana after doing time. Too many rules. Well, what did those parole geeks expect him to do, get a job at McDonald's? Or how about selling shoes down at the mall, yes, ma'am, I'll see to little Junior's footsies right away, yes ma'am. Shit, he was on the road an hour after he got out of the joint.

Never got stopped either, until that last thing in Pittsburgh at the Mad Dog. It had started out cool, nothing serious, just smashing some bottles because the latest owner was this righteous ass-hole, said he wouldn't serve them, had his finger on the alarm as soon as the Vandals walked in the door. So they knew the cops were coming, and they would have been out of there in a couple a minutes.

There was just Banger—he and Pinto were tight again by then—smashing a few bottles around, and Metalhead kicking the jukebox, and Fisheye, he was feeling up this girl, some slut probably liked it anyway, when this asshole bartender who owned the place decided he was like the Lone Avenger all of a sudden and pulled out a shotgun.

That was when things started to get serious as far as Pinto was concerned, because the shotgun was pointed right at him, even though he wasn't doing anything except trying to get a beer from the cooler. He only defended himself, pulling out a knife and throwing it so that it landed, *thwuck*, right in the bartender's eye, and then Pinto grabbed the shotgun out of the guy's hands while he was still standing even though he was dead, and then Pinto shot the girl, and then Fisheye, the Vandal who was feeling up the girl, started to get belligerent, so Pinto shot him too, nasty mother, and then the other two were all over him like white on paint, so what could he do.

He shoved his hand, straight-arm, into Metalhead's throat. He'd learned that in prison. Saw some big black lifer from Alabama do that once in the latrine. The lifer had probably been paid for whacking the guy, since he didn't seem pissed off while he was doing it. He'd been a Marine in Vietnam, Special Forces or some-thing like that. They taught those crazy bastards all kinds of shit. Anyway, this one wasn't young, must have been pushing fifty, but he was one strong inmate. He'd shoved his hands into that white guy's gullet so easy, it was like he was fixing the dude's collar.

And so Metalhead went down, which left only Banger standing. He started to to back away with his hands making that motion that people do when they're scared shitless, like "there, there." It made Pinto laugh.

"Think I'm going to kill you, too, Banger?"

Banger forced himself to smile, even though his face was all white and he was probably taking a righteous dump in his pants at the time, and he said, "No, no, man. You're not going to do that. We're friends, okay? Like brothers. And the cops are coming. Come on, we got to get out of here, you know?" And then he looked at his hands and saw that they were shaking, so he balled them into fists like he was ashamed to look at them.

It was that gesture, that little shame thing, that tipped the scales against him in Pinto's eyes. He took two steps over to where the dead bartender lay with the knife sticking up out of his eye, and he pulled it out. "Yeah, okay, let's go," Pinto said, and he watched Banger grow a couple of inches shorter as the breath sighed out of him with relief. Pinto wiped the blood off the knife with a cocktail napkin. Then he grabbed a handful of yellow goldfish crackers and ate them while he took the cash out of the register.

"Come on," Banger said. He was getting bigger again. Pinto had always liked Banger. He came from Utah or Colorado or something, one of those pretty states. And he was pretty himself. He had long hair down to his waist. Girls always liked how he looked. If he'd wanted to, Banger could have been like those guys in TV commercials. He had all his teeth and was really good looking. But he didn't really have any balls.

Pinto knew that now. So he walked slowly and deliberately in front of Banger when they got to the doorway because he knew Banger wouldn't say anything, even about Pinto taking the money and not offering him any, and then he turned around in a quick, graceful movement and sank the blade of the knife between Banger's ribs, right into his heart.

Their faces were so close that it was almost funny. Banger must have been eating candy or something, because his breath smelled like peppermint. When Pinto pulled out the knife, some blood dripped onto his hand. It felt hot.

Pinto walked out of the Mad Dog Café singing Foreigner's "Hot Blooded," chuckling at the clever play on words as he wiped the knife off onto his jeans. Six hours later, heading west on Route 40, two days away from the Sturgis Motorcycle Rally, he was still singing the song, steering with one hand as he strummed with the other, as if playing a guitar, against the blood-caked denim along his thigh.

CHAPTER NINE

STURGIS!

Every year during the first week of August, some four hundred thousand motorcyclists from every state in the union descend upon the small town of Sturgis, South Dakota, for a seven-day nonstop party on two wheels.

It began in 1938, when a local businessman and enthusiast of the new sport of motorcycling invited a few of his friends for a retreat away from their day-to-day lives. Now, six and a half decades later, the principle still holds true. Once a year, all manner of people from every walk of life—farmers, accountants, dentists, drifters—shed their quotidien skins to become Bikers, with a capital B.

Enroute to Sturgis, Bedwyr, who had made a lifelong mission of the study of motorcycles and their owners and had painstakingly taught himself the vocabulary of the American road, shared his newfound knowledge with the other knights. According to his theory, there were five main categories of Bikers: Tourists, Old Greasers, Clubbers, Colors, Doc Bikers, and Hot Dogs.

The Tourists were, generally speaking, family men. They traveled, often in packs, on large road machines loaded with camping gear and food. Often they were accompanied by wives or girlfriends of long standing as they made their way around the country during their precious vacation days from work.

Old Greasers, more often than not, did not work, except for occasional odd jobs when making a living became absolutely necessary. Even then, as their employers would soon learn, their work was secondary to their biking plans. For a Greaser, a weekend of hunting in northern Minnesota or the last fine day of fall in Kentucky will supersede all deadlines.

Clubbers belonged to organized groups, with laws, bylaws, and sublaws. They funded scholarships, brought Christmas toys to orphanages, helped out in soup kitchens, and formed glee clubs.

The Clubbers' evil twins, the Colors, had no laws, and their idea of glee often involved terror. These were gang members, tribesmen who adorned themselves with the colors of their tribes. Their main lines of work were drug dealing, theft, and hired murder. It was universally acknowledged that when Colors appeared, the party was, for the most part, over.

Doc Bikers, by contrast, were the aristocrats of the motorcycling population. These were professionals—doctors, lawyers, college professors. While others of their ilk were flying airplanes or pursuing other expensive hobbies, the Doc Bikers took pseudonyms like "Spike" or "Broadway" and zoomed off on their forty-thousand-dollar handmade vehicles in butter-soft leathers to enjoy their weekend identities.

The worst combination of Bikers possible was the Doc Biker/Colors mix. Egalitarian though the Sturgis Rally may be, there was an unspoken law, especially among Doc Bikers, to stay as far away from Colors as possible.

Finally, Bedwyr explained, came the Hot Dogs, or as the nation's young people referred to individuals of this stripe, wieners. They were generally young, generally good-hearted, generally foolish, occasionally stupid. They loved speed. Their main ambition in life was to impress girls. They liked to drink beer. Most Hot Dogs were robbed of their bikes and other possessions at least twice during their first decade of biking, after which they usually settled down to become Tourists, Old Greasers, or bus riders.

Whatever their category, though, the Bikers at Sturgis were, almost always, men. Men with their women, perhaps, or men alone, or men bonding in an unmistakably heterosexual way with other men . . . However they combined, men were at the core of every activity in Sturgis. The Rally was a male function, a tribal gathering as ancient in its underlying principles as a Roman battalion or an Aztec priesthood. Because Sturgis was not about motorcycles, not really. It was about Machismo.

Here the trappings of civilization, the masks of social evolution, were cast aside. Money, position, academic degrees, family pedigree . . . These were of no consequence in this place at this time in the testosterone-heavy summer of the year, when the measure of a man could be found only in the strength of his arm and the power of his will. The usher in church with the clean fingernails and a smile for everyone transmogrified during this week. He became one of the Bikers, wild and dangerous men who challenged one another in contests of strength and skill and the ability to hold one's liquor, men whose motorcycles were symbols of their own raw and potent sexuality.

And their women, displayed like spoils of war, were proud to belong to them, for they, too, had shed their skins. Stripping off the veneers of housewives and mothers, of career women and pink-collar workers, of sweet girls and sensible women, they transformed themselves into babes, biker chicks, sex machines, objects of desire to be displayed and coveted. They wore their hair unbound and flowing, their clothing tight. They enticed. They lifted the atmosphere with their beauty and charged it with their ripe sexuality. The very air became an incendiary mixture of gasoline and leather, alcohol and heady perfume. The women sent out a signal: Try and win me. And their men sent another: Touch her and you're dead.

Most of the time, no one tried. That restraint, too, was part of the macho mystique. No one but a true Hot Dog would openly invite disaster from men covered with chrome studs, fueled with confidence and beer.

Unfortunately, all of the Knights of the Round Table, after their miraculous transfer from the Middle Ages to the first years of the twenty-first century, became Hot Dogs.

Hal first knew that something had gone wrong when he saw one of his charges walking down Lazelle Street with a woman slung over his shoulder. It was Lugh, carrying the spiked mace with which he had nearly attacked the neighbor's Holstein back in Jones County, and for which he had been arrested and temporarily jailed. Never overly bright, even in the days of King Arthur, Lugh's transition to the present time had perhaps been among the more awkward. He simply did not understand, or care, that one should not take what one wanted just because one was physically able to do so.

Lugh, of course, was physically able to take just about anything. But he was an honorable man, at least according to the mores of the ancient and semibarbarous Celts, and so would never attempt to steal anything of real value. A man's horse, for example, was utterly safe with Lugh. In fact, had anyone attempted to steal a horse (or motorcycle, as Lugh did understand that they fulfilled the same function), he would certainly have killed him, and in as bloody and painful a fashion as the gravity of the crime warranted.

But to take liquor or food when there was plenty to be had? Why, this was nothing resembling a wrongdoing. Indeed, for a man to deny these necessities to his fellow was, as far as Lugh was concerned, a mark of ill breeding, and hence deserving of at least a strong thump on the nose.

And as for women . . . Well, there were certain things a man just couldn't help. It wasn't as if they were good plain women minding their spinning; no, these were beauties with red lips and clothes that let you know just what they had to offer. The one slung over his shoulder, for example, was wearing a pair of black jeans with two ovals cut out of the rear. Her cheeks, plump and rosy-white as pillows, had caught Lugh's admittedly limited imagination and had not let go. Come to me, they taunted. And he had answered the call.

The woman in question did not appear to be particularly displeased with the situation. She even smiled as the crowd parted to let them through. It was a warm day, and the sun bounced off the white perfection of her buttocks. There was many an appreciative comment as they passed. Lugh beamed with pride and satisfaction.

"What are you going to do with her?" someone called out.

Lugh only grinned while emitting a low rumble of anticipation.

"Oh, no," Hal muttered as he took in the scene, trying to think of the course of action that would result in the least amount of pain and injury. As he was deliberating, a cadre of motorcycles revved up less than a block away and peeled out toward Lugh and his captive.

Hal felt his heart sink. The bikers were all, to a man, wearing red bandannas. Not colors, exactly, but there was no doubt in Hal's mind that they were decidedly not Hot Dogs. "Put her down, Lugh," he shouted as he ran to place himself between Lugh and the bandannas. "Do it now," he added softly, "while we can still walk away."

"Why would I want to do that?" Lugh answered, genuinely puzzled. Then he saw the men approaching and grinned, his smile breaking the black bushy expanse of his beard with a row of broken brown teeth. He gave the woman's bare rump a lusty pat.

"Aye, and a beauty she is, too, Lugh," chimed in Curoi MacDaire, rubbing his hands together in anticipation of a rousing bare-knuckle fight.

Although MacDaire was considerably smaller and smarter than Lugh, he was still more a fighter than a thinker. The two of them, come together from Ireland, could cause more trouble than all the rest put together.

"Cut it out!" Hal shouted above the noise of the gathering crowd. "Get him out of here, MacDaire!"

"Ah, you'll be jesting now," MacDaire said. "This is nowt but a little exercise to work up a thirst, don't you know."

The woman on Lugh's shoulder giggled. "You talk cute," she said.

MacDaire cocked his head. "How could we disappoint the lass, I ask you?" Then he ducked, just in time for Hal to take the first blow square on the jaw. He missed everything that happened after that.

CHAPTER TEN

BRUNCH WITH THE DOC BIKERS

While the skirmish involving the knights and the bikers in the red bandannas was backing up traffic nearly to Sturgis's Main Street, four Doc Bikers were settling down to a late breakfast eight blocks away.

They actually were doctors, all four of them from hospitals within a ten-block radius in Chicago. Once a year for the past three years, they left their BMWs and Jags in the parking garage and burned rubber away from the city with strains of "Born to Be Wild" thrumming through their brains.

The house in Sturgis where they stayed was a modest ranch with petunias in the flower bed and dime-store ceramic statuettes of cherubs and kittens perched on little corner knicknack shelves in every room. The focus of the living room was a reproduction of a painting of a clown. On the opposite wall was a mounted fish whose mouth, when activated by changes in light, opened and closed while a computer chip implanted in its innards produced a voice singing "For He's a Jolly Good Fellow."

The weekly rental for this dwelling was roughly equivalent to that of a five-star hotel in Paris.

For many of the local residents, who fled from the encroaching motorcyclists as if they were hordes of locusts, renting out their homes during Rally Week provided enough income to last the rest of the year. They could, in fact, have charged double the going rate. As it was, most of the bikers who attended slept on the ground in sleeping bags. Some brought tents and stayed at campgrounds anywhere within a hundred miles of the rally. A very small number stayed in the few hotels and motels in the area, and then only if they had booked their rooms several years in advance. But only the richest bikers—the ones with Italian leather chaps and special cell phone cases built into their handlebars—got the houses.

One of the Doc Bikers, an anesthesiologist named Barry Cohen, was cooking eggs and sausages while the others moved about in various states of readiness for their first day at the rally. The table, like the rest of the furniture in the house, was in the Early-American style, and was decorated with orange plastic flowers, salt and pepper shakers shaped like chubby pilgrims, and a game purchased from a truck stop featuring golf tees stuck into a triangular piece of wood. It was a weird setting for men accustomed to gadgets and style. Another of the doctors—a young neurologist with a future worth watching—sat absorbed in the tee game, his perfectly coiffed hair falling into his eyes.

"Is someone going to set the table, or do you just want me to tip the frying pan into your mouths?" Dr. Cohen asked.

"I've just got one more move," the neurologist said, shifting the tees in the game.

"I'll do it." A tall man wearing a vest of Australian lambskin opened the cabinet near the window. "Ed, get us some juice."

"Ed?" the fourth man said, pretending to be offended.

The tall man rolled his eyes. "Sorry. I meant Sandbag."

"Sandman." Ed—in his alternate life a cytopathologist, chained to a microscope in a laboratory—had announced the previous day that he had taken a biker name. It was common practice, even among Doc Bikers, to take a special name for the road. It was an initiation of sorts, an entrée into the macho mystique.

"Oh, right." The tall man slapped his forehead. "Sandman. Sorry."

"Very funny."

"So pour some juice, Sandman."

"*Si, mon capitaine!*" Ed saluted.

"Geez, even the dishes are repulsive," the tall man remarked, turning a scallop-edged plate with a design of brown flowers in the center of it. "Where do these people . . ." He frowned. "What in the hell . . ." He put down the plate and strode toward the door.

Cohen looked out the window. "Oh, man," he said with a sigh. "Will you look at that."

Outside, a scruffy biker with a week's worth of beard and mud up to his knees was urinating in the petunia bed.

"Tom'll get him out of there," Ed said. Indeed, even as he spoke, the tall doctor in the beautiful leathers came into view in the window's frame. He gesticulated to the scruffy biker, indicating without a doubt that he wanted the man to leave at once.

The biker was strangely unmoved by being discovered and thus confronted. He zipped up slowly and then turned with a swagger to face Tom, who was much taller than he was. Deliberately, he ground his foot into the petunias.

"Tough guy," Cohen said. Ed laughed.

Then Tom reached out with his long, elegantly clad arm and grabbed the lapel of the little man's leather jacket. He managed to make the biker lose his footing momentarily, but the fellow didn't fall. Instead, with a snarl, he pushed Tom back with both hands.

"Oh, he's getting touchy now."

Cohen turned off the stove. "Maybe we should call the police."

"Over a guy pissing in the yard?" Ed rolled his eyes. "Tom can handle this, okay? Besides, there are four of us."

"Yeah, you're right, I guess," Cohen said. Both figures were now out of sight of the window.

"Can you imagine what the local cops would say? 'Yep, reckon you city slickers couldn't lick an ice cream cone, har har. . . .' "

At that moment there was a loud thump as the front door slammed open and both men hurtled inside.

Their positions were reversed from the scene in the window: This time the short biker held Tom by his lapels. By his throat, really. With one hand. And Tom's eyes were registering stark terror because in the biker's other hand was a .45 semiautomatic thrust right up to Tom's Adam's apple.

For the first time, the neurologist looked up from his tee game. "Oh, my God," he whispered.

Cohen inched toward the wall phone.

"Get away from that," the biker said.

As soon as Cohen retracted his hand, the biker fired the gun point-blank into Tom's eye. The wall behind him, thick with blood and brain tissue, shook. Several ceramic figurines wobbled and fell to the floor. Then, releasing Tom's body, he trained the barrel of the .45 on the other three.

"Howdy," he said as a slow smile spread across his face. "Name's Pinto."

He fired the second round into Cohen's forehead.

When all four of the occupants of the house were dead, Pinto looked irritably at the blood-spattered breakfast. He was hungry, but no way was he going to eat anything off that table. He headed for the door, then thought better of it. The cost of food at the rally was sky high. He went back into the kitchen, discarded the first layer of sausage patties, then picked up the rest in one hand. Eating the pile like a sandwich, he sauntered back to his bike and headed toward the rally.

CHAPTER ELEVEN

FUN TIMES IN HELL

The fight in which Hal had been knocked cold on the street had fizzled out quickly. It was still early in the day, and the bandanna'd bikers soon discovered that they were more interested in slaking their thirst than in recapturing the damsel in the transparent jeans, who did not seem overly distressed, in any case.

Within twenty minutes, both Lugh and Curoi MacDaire were sharing a drink with them in the cavernous vastness of the Full Throttle Saloon while the woman whose bare bottom had started the dispute selected tunes on the jukebox. Momentarily exhausted, none of the participants in the fracas had enough energy left to do anything with her except to admire the woman as she swayed with the music, displaying the creamy white moons that had launched the day's events.

"Tonight," the huge, red-bearded leader of the bikers in bandannas panted, raising his bruised fist in the air, "we got the wet T-shirt contest!"

The room rocked with whistles and shouts and a loud stomping of feet. Lugh, who had no idea what the man was talking about, nevertheless put his arm around him and made noises of approval while chewing a strip of beef jerky.

He liked the red-bearded man. Even though the man was an outlander from this strange place that the knights had been forced to inhabit, he at least behaved like a true man. That was what had most befuddled Lugh about the New World: The men here appeared to take pride in behaving like perfumed eunuchs.

Everywhere he went, Hal—who was himself rather too peace-loving for Lugh's taste, although he had proved himself in battle more than once—was constantly upbraiding him for what Lugh considered normal behavior. Fighting, drinking, lusting after tarts . . . Hal disapproved of all of these. Even such commonplace activities as boasting, singing, or competing in games of weaponry were frowned upon by the man they were bound to follow as their leader in this place.

In this aspect, Hal was even more stern and joyless than Launcelot—a feat which Lugh and the other knights would once have not believed possible. At least with Launcelot, a man was entitled to do what he deemed necessary to bring wrongdoers to justice. Hal would not even countenance that. Launcelot's attitude could be explained by the fact that he was a Christian, but Hal went even beyond that.

Through the window he could see Launcelot still kneeling over Hal. His nursing was not necessary—Lugh and Curoi MacDaire had dragged Hal into the shade—but that was Lance's way. Besides, in some way that involved the dread Merlin and fearful magic, Launcelot and Hal were of the same blood.

So that would account for why the two of them were inclined to act like old women, one worse than the other. Lugh would never say such a thing, of course. Early on in life, he had found it better for a man as physically imposing and verbally limited as himself to say as little as possible under most circumstances.

Through the tavern window, Launcelot saw Lugh raise a glass with the red-bearded man. Launcelot shook his head in disapproval.

It was unseemly for the knights to associate with the citizenry so intimately. Still, Launcelot could see the affinity between those two. The red-bearded fellow, like many others in this gigantic fair of headless, mechanized horses (which were, according to Bedwyr, not called horses but *hogs*), was a welcome change from most of the men in this place where Merlin had transported them with his magic.

It was the magic, Launcelot thought, that was so hard to get used to. That, and the idea that, against his will, he was alive again.

Launcelot had died a violent and less than honorable death.

The year was 524, two years before the death of Arthur Pendragon. Once the cleanest and most modest of the Round Table knights, Launcelot had died filthy, naked, and mad. He had by then been living alone for years in the forest near the Pictish border far to the north of Hadrian's Wall.

He had never recovered from the events concerning the queen. Launcelot's exile, which he had hoped would help him to forget his fallen state, had instead sharpened his memory, causing him to suffer every moment of every day for his inadvertent betrayal of his king and friend.

In the end, he threw himself off a cliff.

Death came virtually instantly. Aside from the long, terrifying fall toward the boulder-strewn stream below, it was painless, which was why he had regretted it as soon as he jumped.

Launcelot had wanted his death, like his exile, to serve as penance for his sins. But in the end, neither had seemed a sufficient punishment. While he tumbled toward death, he thought of the others who, unlike him, had died bravely in battle, bearing the pain of their mortal wounds until such time as the Angel of Christ came to claim their souls. He had been called the greatest of all knights, but in his own mind he was the most lowly, a view punctuated by the ignominy in which his life ended with his coward's fall to oblivion.

But oblivion had not come, at least not of the permanent variety. There had been an angel, to be sure, a being more magnificent and loving than Launcelot had ever imagined. His ghost, rising from his broken, stinking body, had wept in speechless gratitude at the sight of the genderless spirit who had come to take him to his God.

And that was as far as it went. He ascended, not to the Christian heaven he had anticipated so fervently, but to a sort of holding area, where he found himself alone and mute, surrounded by a thick white fog as if he were a carved figurine encased in wool.

I'm in hell, he thought, noticing that the angel had vanished. Of course he was. Suicides didn't get to heaven. That, too, had been part of the penance. To suffer not just on earth, but also for eternity. To commit oneself to the flames of damnation for all time.

Yet even in this, Launcelot felt a sense of failure. This was not torture. It was not paradise, certainly, but never could one construe this state of blankness, of comfortable, inert nothingness as anything resembling the punishment he deserved for cuckolding the king of England!

And then he saw a face through the fog, and heard an old man's voice droning. . . .

His heart sank. It was the Merlin! That damned meddling pagan magician was chanting some kind of spell, something so wicked that Launcelot could hear it even through the veils of death and time. Was the old man himself dead, he wondered. If so, why was he here? Surely a sorcerer deserved the most fiery sort of hell. If this place was too good for Launcelot, he thought, then surely it was too good for the wicked Taliesin.

His head was spinning, speculating. Perhaps this was some sort of pagan afterlife. Yes, that would be a suitable eternity for a failed Christian like himself, wandering among the heretics. But then, he mused, what about those who had not found the true way because it had not been introduced to them? Had the heroes of ancient times also come here, he wondered. Was this the resting place of those great warriors who had not known of Christianity?

He pulled himself up short. But that could not be, he thought wildly. Could his ancestors possibly be here with him, him, the failed one, here? In hell? That would be an outrage! His great-grandfather Dulac, who had served as a general under the great Vercingetorix . . .

"Oh, do be still, Lance!" the Merlin said crankily.

"Where are you?" Launcelot demanded. "You may not cast a spell on me!"

"I most certainly may. Now be quiet."

In fact, there was very little Launcelot could do. He was, in addition to being dead, not really even speaking, except in the telepathic manner of spirits. Only the Merlin, concentrating now in the extreme way of wizards, could hear him, and heathen beast that he was, the old man was not in the least concerned with Launcelot's immortal soul.

"Consider this your penance, if you must," the Merlin said as the white woolly fog began to swirl. "It's all to serve a good purpose, though."

It was the strangest sensation for Launcelot, as if he were traveling through a dimension other than space. He perceived—without actually seeing, hearing, or feeling—the other knights moving closer to him. He felt a kinship so profound that he believed his heart would break.

I am not in hell, then, he whispered in his mind.

"No," the Merlin answered.

"Alas. I do not deserve to be in heaven."

"No doubt," Taliesin said. "But have no fear. This is hardly heaven. You and the others are just being held until you're needed."

"What others? Needed for what?" The white fog around Launcelot twisted into vibrating spikes.

"Oh, calm down. By Mithras, what a worrywart you always were!" The Merlin made a *tut-tut*ting sound. "The others are the knights of the Round Table. And you'll know what you're being held for soon enough."

"They're all here? With me?" He thought silently, *In hell?*

"For the last time, it's not hell!" the old man snapped. "Ask the others."

"I don't see any others."

The Merlin exhaled a long, exasperated breath. "That is because you are dead," he explained patiently. "Your eyeballs are rotting somewhere in the Scottish Highlands. Find another way."

Launcelot cast his mind about, sniffing with his soul-senses like a dog.

"There you go," Taliesin said.

"My son Galahad. He's not here. Perhaps he's not dead."

"Not anymore," the old man answered cryptically.

"I beg your pardon?"

"He was dead. But he's been sent back."

"You can't do that!" Launcelot said, aghast.

"Of course I can," the old man bristled.

"It's unnatural!" Launcelot sputtered, then fell silent, trying to control his grief and fear. "Did he die young?" he asked at last. "Galahad, my son?"

There was the slightest hesitation before the Merlin spoke. "He did. He died when he found the Grail."

"He . . . He actually found it?" There was something close to ecstasy in Launcelot's voice.

"Yes."

"Then the king . . ."

"No. It didn't help, really. Arthur died anyway. In battle. Gawain and Kay went with him. Lugh, too. It was the end of all of them," he added softly.

Valiant knights who died honorably, Launcelot thought, forgetting that thoughts and speech were the same in the state of being in which he found himself.

"But the bravest of all was Galahad," someone else spoke up. It sounded like Fairhands, who had always been as beautiful as a painting, and blessed with the gift of music. "He went back, you know."

"To wait for the king." Another new voice. Bedwyr, Master of Horse.

"I thought the king was dead."

"We're all dead," Curoi MacDaire said with a chuckle. "But Arthur's going to come back. It's the prophecy, don't you know."

"More pagan magic," Launcelot muttered.

"Galahad's gone ahead to wait for him." This from Geraint Lightfoot, who added, "It should have been me. I'm the fastest of the lot of you. I'd run the length and breadth of the whole world to find him."

"It should have been me," another said. It was Agravaine, known to his enemies as Cat's Claws because of the hook that had replaced his severed hand. "I wouldn't have minded going back. Even if I didn't find the king, I'd have had two good hands."

"Well, that's why you weren't picked, isn't it?" boomed Dry Lips. "Galahad will find the king, just as he found the Grail. Aye, and he's earned the privilege, too. No one loved Arthur so well as that one."

Certainly not I, thought Launcelot, *though I'd wished it with all my—*

"Oh, shut up," Merlin snapped. "Do you really have to feel guilty even after you're dead?"

The others laughed. Now Launcelot knew that he truly was in hell. Still, he admitted grudgingly, it was good to hear the voices of his old friends. "How long has Galahad been back?"

"Four lifetimes," Merlin said casually.

"Four whats?"

Taliesin sniffed. "Since I don't know exactly when Arthur's going to come back, someone has to wait for him."

"And what's he been doing these four lifetimes, besides waiting for the king to be born?"

"Oh, I don't know," the old man said peevishly. "Whatever they do. Let me see. They're calling this year 1258, I think. Ah, yes, he's a baker in Turkey."

"A baker!" Launcelot shouted. "My son, finder of the Holy Grail, greatest of all the knights of the Round Table, a baker?"

"There's only so much a wizard can do," Taliesin explained defensively.

"A baker of turkeys," Lugh said in amazement.

"Calm down, Lance."

"Who are you?" the knight seethed.

"It's Tristan. I understand these things."

Launcelot's thoughts made a strangled sound. "You don't understand anything beyond what's kept between a woman's legs! A baker!"

Tristan went on calmly. "But that's how it works, Lancelot. We aren't always knights. Sometimes we go back as bakers. Or cobblers, or farmers, or thieves . . . or even women."

"I have not been a woman!" Dry Lips bellowed.

"You're the woman, Tristan!" Kay shouted.

"Where's my sword?"

Lugh chortled. "If I was a woman, I'd like a pair of great fat teats and an arse all pink and shiny." No one paid any attention to him.

"By the horned balls of Cernunnos!" thundered Kay.

The Merlin took in a long, exasperated breath and left them there, in the corner of the Summer Country that he had taken for his spell, for another seven and a half centuries.

In the meantime, Galahad waited. Lifetime after lifetime he returned to wait for the king he had vowed to serve for all eternity. He was not aware of the waiting, of course, at least not on the level of human consciousness. The bond he had with Arthur had been forged on another plane altogether.

So while the soul of the man who had been Galahad, son of Launcelot and true champion of Arthur Pendragon, served as a sentinel for the return of the once and future king, his human self carried on quite autonomously.

In addition to his life as a baker, Galahad also lived as a blacksmith, a fishwife, an astronomer in the court of Wenceslas of Prague, a mason who died in a fall off a scaffold while erecting the great cathedral at Rheims, a horseman under Kublai Khan, a Japanese geisha, a beggar in India, an Arab mathematician, a Mexican hairdresser. . . . There were so many lives, and in each of them there was a feeling that he had been unable to put into words, a feeling of lack that had followed him throughout every minute of every life. He waited so long, and with so much disappointment, that at the end of the twentieth century, when he was living as an American FBI agent, he threw it all aside one day and got drunk. The sensation was such a relief that he decided to spend the rest of his life in that condition.

Perhaps that was his higher self giving up. Or perhaps that is just the way of the gods. Because it was during this lowest of moments that Galahad—who was now a New Yorker in his mid thirties named Hal Woczniak, ex–federal agent, part-time automobile mechanic, and career alcoholic—met a child with red hair and a soul that he recognized, after sixteen hundred years of searching, as that of his master.

To make things easier, the boy's name was Arthur.

Galahad—Hal, now—slipped back into his role as Arthur's champion so easily he hardly knew it was happening. There was a boy who needed help . . . and then the unfolding of the extraordinary events surrounding the boy . . . and then a dream, or what seemed like a dream, in which Hal realized exactly who he was.

It was here, in this dream-that-was-not-a-dream that the knights first appeared to him, in the castle of Camelot as it had been when they had all served as soldiers under Arthur the King. Because their souls and consciousnesses were still bound up in Merlin's spell somewhere in the fog of the Summer Country, all that appeared to Hal in his vision were the outer shells of the knights, the gossamer remnants of their physical selves. They were ghosts, without words or laughter. But slowly, in fits and starts as Hal grew close again to Arthur, the knights also reappeared in the flesh.

This was the Merlin's great spell, the Second Magic, that made it possible for the great king to return to the world of men as he had been, surrounded by good men and true, so that his vision would have a chance to succeed.

But there was a difference. The knights, returned now to blood-pounding, lusty life, were not at all the same as Hal. They were pristine, plucked straight from death to wait in the mists of Avalon for their leader's return like fragile Christmas ornaments packed away in tissue-filled crates. Hal was in a different, new body, the latest in a long string of used-up selves, wearier than he had once been of the delights life had to offer, not so eager anymore to fall again into the fray.

He had, in short, become a sort of father to all of them, and the task was tiresome. Though he would never permit himself to admit it, there were times when his ancient soul wished it could return to the days of the Round Table, when the world was young for him and adventure lay thick as perfume in the air.

It was this thought that was flitting through the synapses of his brain when Hal Woczniak came to on the sidewalk outside the Full Throttle Saloon, with Launcelot bending over him in concern.

"Hello, Da," he said, though he would forget having said it as soon as he fully regained consciousness.

Launcelot smiled.

Then Hal turned his head to see a man walking past. Hal had not seen the man before; he had become aware of Pinto's presence through another sense.

He had smelled the blood on him.

CHAPTER TWELVE

THE COFFEEHOUSE GANG

PIERRE, SOUTH DAKOTA

Despite extreme security measures, Titus Wolfe breezed through the airport without a hitch, just as he had passed smoothly through customs at JFK. He was an ideal passenger, tidy, quiet, courteous to his fellow travellers, charming to the staff.

The first class hostess had placed a matchbook from the hotel where she would be staying on his dinner tray. Inside the cover she had written her name.

Titus smiled as he tossed it into the waste can. He never carried any extraneous papers on him.

The incident was not uncommon. Women found Titus, with his sharp good looks and elegant British accent, irresistible. Everything about him was "just enough"—he was thin without being gaunt, muscular enough to look good naked, but without the narcisisstic overdevelopment of a bodybuilder, and his face had features that were both interesting and pleasant—clear blue eyes, a chiseled nose, soft blond hair that, when struck by light, shone with a trace of silver at the temples—yet he was not by any means "pretty." These qualities, along with his cultured speech and impeccable wardrobe, made Titus Wolfe appear to be the epitome of the perfect British aristocrat.

He was not.

He was, in fact, one of the most wanted criminals in the world.

To call Titus a terrorist would be an oversimplification: Terrorists generally work either for themselves, from a demented sense of amusement or justice, or for a cause. Titus's job description fit neither category. At the moment, he was a mercenary jack-of-all-trades working in the interests of Libya, but his loyalties would shift with his next paycheck.

Near the men's room at the airport, he opened a locker with a key he had carried with him from Tripoli. The locker contained a molded plastic suitcase that perfectly matched the small carry-on with its innocuous contents which he had brought on the plane.

In the suitcase were the components of a cluster bomb designed to blow up a nuclear silo at the F. E. Warren Air Force Base in Cheyenne, Wyoming. If successful, the result would be the destruction of much of the American interior, including the centers of grain production and cattle.

It would be a difficult assignment, Titus knew. Difficult, and probably lengthy. Since the World Trade Center incident, men in his profession had been forced to work much more slowly and carefully than he had in the past. There was no longer any room for error, and the old days of shooting one's way out of a difficult situation were over.

If there were to be one slip, one question, one misstep, the operation would be suspended. He would hide, he would wait for a better time. It was not unusual these days for Titus to spend weeks on a single assignment, even if that was nothing more than a simple assassination.

This one could take months. In time, he would complete his work, but it was to everyone's benefit—including his employers, who now paid more than double what they had before the latter half of the year 2001—that Titus remain uncaptured and alive.

———

Titus rarely thought about the consequences of his work anymore. His goal was to do the job, get out alive, and collect his pay. It made no difference to him that his work always resulted in loss of life, and often in war. He no longer cared if he believed in the ideas of those he served. It made utterly no difference to him anymore if what he did was considered heroic or evil. That, he had learned, was simply a matter of whose side one was on. Titus himself no longer belonged to any side.

It had not always been so.

There had been a time when he would have contemplated the destruction of a hated global power like the United States with lusty relish. In his youth, he had spent many a drunken night denouncing the corrupt governments of the West with the circle of intellectual freethinkers he had found at university. They were righteous idealists then, those shining young men who risked their freedom—and in most cases, their lives—by talking treason in London's dark places.

They called themselves the Coffeehouse Gang. There was little enough coffee, to be sure, but it had sounded better than the truth, which was that they were drunk most of the time.

It had seemed like one long party, from his school days through the early years working for British intelligence. He had felt so clever then, wriggling into the service under the tutelege of a Soviet mole!

There had been others like him, young agents working as doubles from the very beginning. Since they had all met as university students, most members of the Coffeehouse Gang were disaffected aristocrats experiencing the thrill of what they believed to be independence, striking out in shame against their own backgrounds of privilege. Only Titus had felt the harsh inequality of England's unofficial but undeniable caste system at first hand.

Reared in a coal mining village in Yorkshire, he had turned at an early age against the British government and its indifference to the poor. First, he watched his father die coughing blood from his blackened lungs at the age of thirty-four. Then the mine was closed, leaving not even the filthy work that had killed him available to his children. In desperation, Titus, his mother, and her seven other children who had managed to live through infancy moved to the city of Leeds where, until her death, his mother worked in a factory making rubber tires.

By that time, Titus was in his last year at school. He had managed to remain an excellent student despite his difficulties at home. At his mother's death, when the rest of the children were shipped off to various orphanages and foster homes, he stunned the authorities overseeing his case by getting accepted to Cambridge on full scholarship.

That he would even apply to such a place was a shock. He ought to work, the social services woman told him. Then he could put a little something by, take care of his brothers and sisters.

But he had not listened to her. He went instead to the university, got a job in the dining hall for living expenses, and then got a second job in a pub in the civilian sector. He made no attempt to fit in with his "betters"—his elite classmates with their public school backgrounds whom he occasionally overheard imitating his countrified speech—but concentrated instead on his studies. He tried not to think about his brothers and sisters growing up in institutions while he himself, though ragged, made his home inside the ancient and hallowed walls of this bastion of the English upper class.

As it turned out, he never saw the other members of his family again.

He might have, of course, if things had gone differently for him. Titus had had a vague idea of helping them all as he made a career for himself in law or business or whatever avenue might open to him. He knew too little about the world outside his own small and impoverished experience to have a clear vision of what he wanted. He only knew what he didn't want, and that was to go to an early grave the way his parents had, with nothing to show for their miserable lives except sooty lungs, empty pockets, and an unspoken curse for the government in their broken hearts.

But the events in his life took a strange turn then. And, like all major occurrences, this turning point seemed at the time to be nothing of great consequence. It was, in fact, a perfectly ordinary meeting, one of those pseudo-social gatherings at the home of one of his professors. That the don was, and had been for nearly fifteen years, an agent of what was then the Soviet Union, was unknown to Titus. Nevertheless, that fact would color the rest of the young man's life.

The professor's name was Darling. Lucius Darling, né Dubrovny, had probably been one of the most effective moles the Soviets ever produced. He was a born teacher, and his charm and charisma had served his country from the moment he was placed in Cambridge by his masters.

Darling was older than his forged birth certificate indicated. He was already an established agent when he was sent underground to become a recruiter for the cause of world communism among the English intelligentsia. As his career in academia grew, so did his parallel life. By his retirement, Darling had brought more than fifty new agents into his sphere. Fifty British subjects, all devoting their lives to the welfare of their Sovereign's enemy.

Among them was Titus Wolfe.

The meeting in question took place in Darling's home. Darling was an extremely popular professor, whose class on world social structures was one that every underclassman clamored to attend. Those who were accepted—there was a brief interview to determine which of the interested students would be permitted to take the class—enjoyed a certain prestige among the student body. But the greatest honor was to be invited to the don's house, to participate in civilized conversation over tea and scones and the occasional glass of sherry.

Darling picked Titus out of the crowd almost immediately. During a classroom discussion about the condition of the working poor in England, a young nob with distant royal connections had drawled disdainfully that no one suffered from poverty in Britain since the advent of the National Health Service and the dole, paid for by productive citizens bearing the burden of one of the highest tax rates in the world.

Cheeks ablaze, Titus, until then a silent, timid sort of fellow, by Darling's assessment, stood up in the middle of class and began shouting, in the rich, archaic brogue of a true Yorkshire peasant, a tirade of epithets at his classmate. When he was done, he picked up his books and stormed toward the exit.

"No, no, no," Darling said soothingly. "You've won, dear fellow. Everyone in this room, including your hapless if insensitive target, has been startled to attention by the force of your conviction. The next time you speak, whether they agree with you or not, they will listen to you. Don't run away from that, Mr. . . ." He looked vaguely at his roster.

"Wolfe," Titus said.

Darling smiled slowly. "Wolfe. A passionate name. Lean and hungry. Don't leave us, Mr. Wolfe, I beseech you. There are many here who need your presence among them."

The students in the room laughed good-naturedly. The professor had dispelled the tension with a few lighthearted, well-chosen words. Titus sat down.

And Lucius Darling made a mental note to himself: This one doesn't even have to be turned.

Later that same week, over tea and scones, Darling drew out Titus's simmering hatred of the system which had fostered the great chasm between himself and the other boy in the class (conspicuously uninvited) who had spurred his verbal flash fire.

Then gently, deftly, over the years the professor fanned those flames, surrounded Titus with other, older students who shared his views ideologically if not experientially, tutored him in subtle, palatable ways, saw that he lost his telltale Yorkshire accent, and slowly—very, very slowly—introduced him to the possibility of working for justice from the inside of the system that oppressed it.

He suggested that Titus allow himself to be recruited into Her Majesty's Secret Service.

Darling had done his work so well that when Titus finally learned that he was already deeply involved with the Soviet spy apparatus, he was not only not particularly surprised, he did not connect Lucius Darling with his situation at all, convinced instead that it had all been his own idea from the beginning.

Such was Darling's genius.

In Moscow, Darling had been honored in absentia by his peers and superiors in what remained of the KGB. Darling himself never left the United Kingdom. After the collapse of the Soviet Union, there seemed to be little reason to return to Mother Russia, particularly since by then he knew absolutely no one in his homeland and had virtually forgotten his native language.

Nevertheless, he still served his distant masters in an area apart from his now benign professorial duties. One of the lesser known facts about the beloved university don, even among those who knew his real calling, was that Darling was a crack shot. He had, in fact, taught Titus the art of shooting, once it became clear that the boy would be of greatest use as an active field agent.

And so Titus never knew that one of his teacher's ongoing tasks, a job Darling did not enjoy but performed flawlessly, always with the utmost care and secrecy, was to kill his students.

CHAPTER THIRTEEN

CRONOS

Professor Darling did not kill all of the earnest young men who had sat in his book-lined study drinking tea, of course. He had chosen his protégés so carefully that a majority of those he recruited remained loyal to the cause during their entire careers. But there were exceptions.

Some of his boys reverted to type after leaving Cambridge. Some of them wanted to forget the wild talk of their student days and return to their family estates. Some of them became disenchanted with communism, and no longer wished to sit in Parliament or run newspapers to further the cause.

These could not be permitted simply to walk away. One by one, each of them was eliminated by an assassin's bullet. In time the brighter recruits into the Coffeehouse Gang picked up on the fact that the weaklings among them were being culled like slow deer from a herd.

The name they gave to their unknown executioner was Cronos, after the Greek Titan who devoured his own children.

"Cronos is coming," they would whisper when one of their number tried to ease his way out of the Soviet box.

And Cronos always came.

He came even after the demise of the U.S.S.R., when the remaining members of the Coffeehouse Gang—those who hadn't been betrayed by some KGB officer or another looking to avoid the usual fate of a captured spy—were set adrift on their own. Eleven members of Darling's original fifty recruits had still been alive and working as double agents when the huge Soviet spy apparatus was dismantled. Titus Wolfe was among them.

Two of the eleven were named as enemy agents, and they were killed before they could talk. Some emigrated to Russia, where they were given new identifies and ordinary jobs. The others simply seemed to disappear.

Titus was very nervous during this time. He had been with MI-6 for three years, all the while delivering information to the KGB through a series of blind drops. With the exception of his control, who only spoke with him on the telephone, Titus had been offered no human contact with the Soviets. He was still considered too junior to be trusted.

His lack of standing was probably what saved his life. That, plus Darling's increasing awareness that, were all of his recruits sanctioned, the panicked KGB would be tempted, sooner or later, to give over Darling himself to the West in exchange for some favor or other. These were hungry times, and spies were always regarded as expendable.

On the other hand, Darling realized, he might be able to use the agents he had trained from boyhood for his own benefit. If he were careful about it, what was left of the Coffeehouse Gang could be made into an autonomous organization that Darling himself could disappear into. Everything was already in place: There were agents with boats and planes and untraceable automobiles; experts in forging and stealing necessary documents; agents in place whose job had been to provide safe houses around the world. All of them were running scared now, expecting to be executed or arrested. All would cooperate with Darling, he was sure, and would thank him for the opportunity.

And best of all, it could all be offered, for a price, to mercenaries, free agents, private concerns, and governments that did not wish to involve their own intelligence operations.

And so it came to pass: One day Lucius Darling, renowned professor of comparative literature at Cambridge, simply disappeared off the face of the earth.

Titus found out about it through his Russian contact, who telephoned him especially to find out if he knew anything of his mentor's whereabouts.

He said that he did not. Then he hung up the phone and returned to his apartment in Munich, where British intelligence—his official employer—had assigned him, and waited for Cronos to come for him.

To his surprise, he found Darling on his living room sofa. Titus's first thought was that he had finally learned Cronos's true identity. So great was his fear that at first he could not even understand the words Darling was speaking, but slowly they began to permeate the fog of confusion and panic that had engulfed him since his conversation with the Soviet agent.

"The Russians have too much of a hammer over you," Darling was saying in his clipped, kingly accent. "If they don't kill you just for your association with me—which they probably will—they'll want you to go over and kill Poles and Afghanis for them."

Titus was speechless. For a full minute or more, he opened and closed his fists, which had gone stone cold with fear at the sight of his former teacher. "I thought you'd come to kill me," he said at last.

Darling smiled. It was a strange smile, musing, rueful, resigned. "What a terrible thing," he said softly.

"That is . . . I didn't . . ." Titus waffled.

Darling waved him down with a gesture. "I can help you to disappear, if you'd like. Aside from that, I'm afraid you'll be on your own for a time."

"Disappear?" Titus asked numbly.

"We can stage your death."

"Could you set me up with someone?"

"Yes, of course. But you've got to be careful. We don't want to compromise the Coffeehouse Gang."

"No," Titus said. "Certainly not. Thank you, sir. I hope I'll be able to make this up to you one day."

In time to come, Titus Wolfe would make Lucius Darling a very rich man. But at that moment, when he realized that he would be living out the rest of his life as a man with no permanent identity, no career, not even a country to serve, he was terrified. He had been trained as a soldier in a cold war that had ended. As of now, he would be not a citizen of the world, but the world's outcast, belonging nowhere, living for no reason other than the fear of death.

His existence ended officially in the early hours of morning, when his car careered dramatically into the Amper River. The "accident" was a fairly simple matter to arrange: All it took was for the steering mechanism of his two-year-old BMW 540i to be set so that it would veer off the bridge without a driver.

Although there had been no traffic on the bridge itself at three A.M., when the occurrence took place, dozens of people saw the automobile's flying exit through the guardrail. Later, when the car was recovered, MI-6 was able to find enough traces of Titus Wolfe so that even without a body they could determine with some certainty that he had been in the car during the accident and had probably drowned. They also found the timed mechanism that had forced the car off the road. The secret service concluded that Wolfe's death had been the work of German terrorists who had discovered that he was a British agent.

Titus was given a military memorial service at the queen's expense. His youngest sister, who was working as a domestic in Manchester, was astonished when she was notified of his death to learn that he had been driving a car worth forty thousand pounds.

Professor Darling's parting words to him had been, "Go to Panama. In Colón, look for a boat named *Sea Legs*."

That was the last time Titus ever saw him, although he continued to work through Darling's byzantine network of contacts. Wherever Titus went, sooner or later he would receive a message through some member or other of the Coffeehouse Gang, which would lead him though a series of further calls, messages, and meetings, until the exact details of his assignment were made clear to him. Sometimes he met directly with his employer of the moment; at other times, he had no idea for whom he was working.

The system was a work of genius.

In Panama, Titus discovered that the captain of *Sea Legs* was a man named Richard Edgington. Several years Titus's senior, Edgington had been one of the brightest stars during the Gang's pub-crawling days. Supported by an indulgent and wealthy family, he hung around Cambridge for some time after his graduation, publishing tracts that condemned British foreign, economic, and domestic policy, and talking treason with the glib tongue of a natural orator.

Too visible and outspoken to work for either MI-6 or the Soviets directly, Edgington's function had evolved into serving as a sort of general getaway driver for his compatriots who often found themselves in need of fast transportation to another country.

It was a fairly lucrative business—a real consideration for Edgington, since his father had found out about his communist leanings and cut him off financially. He had been given the boat, however.

Sea Legs was a cumbersome, old-fashioned six-hundred-foot yacht decorated with brass and heavy teakwood trim. It had been a jewel back in the thirties, when Edgington's father had had it built, but through the years it had fallen into disrepair. By the time Titus Wolfe walked up its gangway, *Sea Legs* was such a wreck that it seemed incredible to him that the thing could even remain afloat.

But its looks were deceiving. Beneath its decrepit exterior, it contained an engine more powerful than any police vessel in open water. It had been provided by Lucius Darling, through a chain of contacts, as had nearly half a ton of weaponry, all of it carefully hidden inside the wallboards and flooring.

Most of the profit generated by *Sea Legs* as spy transport went to Darling, but Edgington augmented his income considerably by running cocaine and heroin between North and South America. In this way he had achieved not only financial independence from his family, but had actually become rather wealthy.

"Never had to work a day in my life for it," he said with amusement.

Titus told him about his own situation—about Darling's intercession and his decidedly vague prospects for the future.

"Well, the don did tell me what you've been doing for a living." He took two tinned beers off a shelf and offered Titus one. "I say, does a field agent do anything besides kill people?"

Titus felt his face reddening. He was unaccustomed to discussing any aspect of his work with anyone.

"I'm trying to see what you'd be good for, you see." He held out the beer again. Titus ignored it.

"You—you can help me?"

Edgington laughed. "My dear boy, didn't Darling tell you? We've all stuck together. All of us from the old days. We don't work together or anything like that, of course, although I do see quite a few of the old boys in the course of my travels. I imagine I'm the only one who sees any of the others. But we do keep in touch, do one another favors, that sort of thing. Quite valuable, actually."

"The . . . the whole Gang just slipped out from under the Russians?" Titus asked.

Edgington laughed. "Well, we didn't all take to your sort of work, old man, guns blazing and all that. We're not all in as much difficulty as you are." He took a long pull from the bottle. "Carsons, for example, works in the Department of Immigration. He can get you papers into or out of just about anywhere. And Henry—remember Henry, tall fellow—well, he's with the Exchequer. Access to all sorts of confiscated counterfeit money." He chortled. "Can you imagine, free money for the asking? No English currency, of course. That's burned straightaway. But no one cares about drachmas or pesos or yen. Comes in handy in a pinch, you can be sure of that."

"I see," Titus said, his mind reeling. "And all of them, the, the Gang . . ."

"They were all working for the Reds in one capacity or another, although usually indirectly, through Darling. Still, there's risk, especially now that the Soviet machine is folding up like a Chinese box. We've had to stay together. Saved each other's arses more than once, I can tell you."

"You're saving mine now," Titus said humbly.

"Oh, you'll pay for it," the captain said with a grin. "The Coffeehouse Gang doesn't let you ride free for long."

Edgington was able to find Titus work as a strong-arm for a Colombian cocaine exporter. His job was to kill people in the cocaine king's own circle who had become untrustworthy either through greed or power. An assassin's assassin. It was a supremely disagreeable job for Titus, but under the circumstances he could not afford to be choosy about what he did for a living.

For several months he languished in a sleazy hotel room in Bogotá, hardly daring to step outside except to perform his duties, and wondering how long it would take for his Colombian employer to get rid of him with yet another hit man, when he was approached by a rival drug lord who offered Titus the equivalent of fifty thousand British pounds to blow up a boat in Manaus, Brazil.

He never asked what was on the boat, or who it belonged to. He simply did the job, collected his money, and left for Miami the following day.

In time, he—or rather his work, which was extraordinary by any standard—became known among the most discreet and dangerous segments of nearly every civilized country in the world.

Titus himself, however, remained an almost perfect mystery. For one thing, there were no photographs of him. One of the few advantages of his growing up in extreme poverty was that his childhood likeness had not been preserved anywhere. And once he got to Cambridge, Professor Darling had ensured (so subtly that even Titus had not been aware) that his protégé was not photographed for any reason. He had been thinking of the boy's future as a Soviet spy back then, but Titus's anonymity was of even greater value in his new incarnation as a mercenary.

No one outside the Coffeehouse Gang knew his name, either. The Colombian and his closest henchmen, who all happened to be on the boat in Manaus when it exploded, had called him "the English." The Brazilians had not known even that much about him.

Before long, Titus's skill became so finely honed that no one even identified his jobs as the work of one man. Only in the late nineties, following a spate of bombings on behalf of a number of Middle Eastern concerns, did an American journalist speculate that the terrorist activities filling the newspapers over the past two years might be the handiwork of a single brilliant mind.

The journalist, through painstaking but stunningly erroneous research, even found a name for the hitherto unknown terrorist: Hassam Bayat.

Titus had been drinking coffee in an Algerian cafe when he read about his new identity. He had laughed aloud: It had taken the press the better part of five years to pick up on the clues Titus had left leading to his false identity, but some bumble-headed writer had finally taken his subtle bait. Soon every counterterrorist organization in the world would be looking for "Hassam Bayat"— an Arab. Once the ball got rolling, no one would look twice at a blond, blue-eyed Englishman with the right papers.

By the time he passed Rapid City, South Dakota, Titus Wolfe was getting excited. The initial phase of the Cheyenne assignment had occurred without incident. He was in the United States, his passport stamped, his presence unsuspicious. He had an appointment with the head of the purchasing department at the Air Force base to show some metal dies from a company in Minnesota. The real sales representative, with whom Titus had conversed in a bar two weeks before, was now decomposing in a Minneapolis parking garage.

It would be a good long drive to Wyoming in the stolen Cadillac—long enough to assemble and perfect the device he had picked up in the airport locker, and to practice with the new handgun that had also been waiting for him.

Titus didn't work quickly unless he had to. He always had backup plans, and backups for backups. For his current assignment, he had planned for so many contingencies that the possibility of actually accomplishing the mission on this try was fairly remote. Only a zealot concerned with getting publicity would sacrifice himself in something like a bombing. A professional of Titus's caliber would never move forward with a plan if even one element went awry, and his employers knew this.

After the mission—or, what was more likely, when the mission was aborted because a part of the plan was found to be faulty— Titus had made arrangements to be picked up in Alberta, Canada, within two days of the assignment. If this route of escape was not possible, he was to travel eastward to Atlantic City, New Jersey, within two weeks.

Whether the mission was successful or not, it would be up to him to stay alive for those two weeks.

They would prove to be two of the most difficult weeks of his life, and would begin with a chance encounter with a biker named Pinto.

CHAPTER FOURTEEN

HOGS IN BATTLE

STURGIS, SOUTH DAKOTA

"You a cop?" asked the man who smelled of blood. He was leaning against a rail outside a bar, where a constant stream of people flowed around the two of them.

Launcelot helped Hal to his feet.

"Look like one," Pinto added. He took a toothpick out of his pocket and examined it before placing it in his mouth. His fingers were stained with blood.

None of my business, Hal thought. Some criminal types could spot cops from a mile away. They were usually drug dealers, creatures accustomed to being tailed. It was hard to deceive them. But other sorts had the nose, too. Some killers. During his FBI days, Hal had encountered a few who'd made him as soon as he stepped into the room.

He had the same talent. Not with every crook, certainly—he'd go crazy if he got the vibe with every petty thief who crossed his path—but sometimes. When there was something off. With murderers, when the killer was the kind of sicko who needed to kill. Hal could sniff them out at a hundred yards.

Pinto was one of those.

"I don't like cops."

"Get lost," Hal said.

Pinto took a step toward him.

In the next moment, the door to the Full Throttle Saloon opened and the ten other knights walked out. They moved swiftly to surround Hal. Dry Lips sauntered implacably between the two men.

Pinto spat out the toothpick. Then, with a soundless motion of his wrist, a switchblade leaped into his hand, the blade pressed against Dry Lips's big neck.

There was the slightest of rustles as the others adjusted themselves for combat. Launcelot, Kay, Bedwyr, MacDaire, and Tristan drew their swords in unison, the shafts whistling softly as they exited their scabbards. Gawain and Fair Hands, both experts with the light spear, held their weapons in the air as if they had suddenly materialized there. Geraint Lightfoot drew a dagger, prepared to throw. Agravaine ran his tongue along the cold silver of the hook that had replaced his left hand. Lugh slowly dragged into view the ball-end of his favorite weapon, the unwieldy but thoroughly effective, at least at close range, mace.

"I think you'd better put down the blade," Hal said.

"How about I take his fat head off?" Pinto taunted, rubbing Dry Lips's bald head with his knuckles. The big man's eyes widened.

"Shouldn't have done that," Hal said a split second before Dry Lips lifted the biker into the air behind him by the crotch. Pinto flew into the street, landing headfirst in the wheel of an airbrushed Bourget 230 chopper, causing it to fall over.

The milling crowd stopped cold. The fallen motorcycle had made it personal for all of them. In an instant the knights had surrounded the perpetrator. Agravaine's hook was already inside Pinto's nostril and drawing blood.

"Leave it," Hal said.

Reluctantly, the men withdrew their hardware. Lugh looked

hurt. It was the sort of thing Hal was always doing. It made no sense not to kill the blackguard on the spot. It made them all look bad.

Then, slowly, the crowd parted and a three-hundred-pound Greaser with a Pancho Villa mustache and a tattoo on his arm bearing the legend "Pure Poison" over a skull and crossbones strode forward. "Which one of you knocked over my bike?" he demanded, the skull seeming to come to life as he flexed his muscles.

The knights stepped back to reveal Pinto on the ground, blood and mucus from his nose spraying over the flawless chrome of the Bourget.

"Be my guest," Hal said, offering the man a little salute. "Come on, let's get out of here."

Pinto raised his head. "I'll kill you, cop," he wheezed.

"This cannot be countenanced," Dry Lips complained as they neared the motorcycles. "I was deprived of my proper right to defend myself."

"Aye, he should have been allowed to kill the knave," MacDaire agreed. " 'Tis only seemly." The others nodded.

"You can't kill anybody, okay?" Hal said.

"But surely if the fiend's got a knife—"

"I'm saying it would make things complicated, that's all." Hal mounted and put on his helmet. "Look, guys, I know it's hard to walk away from a jerk like that, but I'm thinking about Arthur. He can't have any attention drawn to him, not yet."

"And why not?" Kay rumbled. "The boy's lived eighteen years as a child. It's time he showed himself."

"True enough," Tristan said. "He was at this age when he pulled the sword from the stone."

Hal blinked. "He was?"

"Aye. Eighteen, and by just a day or two," Kay confirmed. "He was my squire."

Dry Lips waved his hands in the air. "Arthur's nothing to do with this. That one over there was a smelly mole, and mine by right to tread on till his blood ran red."

"No," Hal insisted. "I don't want anybody to get killed, even him, understand? It'll just cause problems. Now let's go for a ride or something. By the time we get back to the rally, snot-nose'll be long gone. Okay?" He fastened the helmet and revved the engine. "Okay?"

Truculently the others followed suit.

God, but I'm getting tired of this, Hal thought for the fiftieth time that day. What happened to the days when he didn't have anyone to worry about except himself? He wasn't cut out to be a boy scout leader, especially with this gang of delinquents. "Move it out," he said, waving lackadaisically.

In his rearview he saw Pinto staggering away from the Bourget and its owner. The crowd was shouting encouragement: Clearly the man with the tattoo was a popular personage at the rally. Poor bastard, Hal thought. The guy who had called him a cop was a born loser if he ever saw one. He was half the size of the Bourget owner. And if he tried the stunt with the switchblade on that one, the crowd would knock him down and see that he never got up.

Still, he was tough. As Hal picked up speed, he saw the small man leap onto a motorcycle and peel away from the parking area with a screech of tires.

It took a moment or two for Hal to realize that Pinto was headed toward him. As the caravan of knights pulled onto a two-lane highway, Hal saw that the man behind him was pulling something out of his saddlebag as he rode.

It was a gun.

Oh, great, Hal thought, feeling a hundred years old. Just great. After the events of the morning, an impromptu gunfight was just what he needed.

He veered off the road onto the hardscrabble dirt. What everyone needed was time. Hal and the knights would just clear out for a little while, long enough to give the creep with the gun a chance to come off whatever bad high he was on.

In the distance, he saw smoke from the campfires in the makeshift tent villages that had grown up around Sturgis for Rally Week. Nobody would follow them out here, he thought.

He was wrong. The gunman was right behind them, gaining fast. As he drew closer to Hal, he aimed his weapon carefully. Then he fired.

It took Hal a moment to take in the entire scene. First, there were the knights, who were beginning to realize that all was not well. Too far from the campsite even to be seen, they were slowing down, confused, and generally making targets of themselves.

To make things worse, a cream-colored Cadillac was cresting a hill on a road cutting through the countryside where they were riding, its driver blissfully unaware that he was heading for what promised to be a first class disaster. And of course, behind him was the nut from the street in front of the bar, teeth bared and shooting his gun like Yosemite Sam. It was a big gun, too, from the sound of it, probably a .45 Magnum.

It was indeed a Magnum. It tore a hole the size of a dime into Hal's side as he tried to signal the others to turn back toward the town. He skidded out of control, falling off the motorcycle a second before it hit the ground. He was quickly losing feeling in his right arm. Blood was pouring from beneath his jacket onto the dry, yellow grass. And the nut was coming directly at him.

"Oh, man," Hal muttered. This was not a method he would have chosen to depart this life, shot by some fool at a motorcycle rally while the knights wandered off without a clue about how to live in the twenty-first century. "Hell of a thing," he slurred, beginning to feel stuporous.

Pinto was screaming like a banshee and aiming at him with both hands.

And then in the next instant, the gun was flying behind him, and the scream of victory had turned into a wail of confusion and pain. Pinto's right hand was moving up and down mechanically. Growing from the center of its palm was Lightfoot's dagger.

Stunned out of shock, Hal managed to roll aside as the gunman's bike moved over the spot where he had been a moment before.

Launcelot rallied the men into a charge. Eleven motorcycles came together in a single point. Fairhands and Gawain lifted their spears. Lugh swung his mace over his head with a whoop of delight. Six swords gleamed under the midday sun.

At that moment the Cadillac came over another hill. The driver's face was a mask of bewilderment.

No one paid attention to the car. By the time the charge was in full force, Pinto had pulled the dagger out of his palm, and his hand was now spraying blood in all directions. His face was virtually painted red with it, making him look even more ferocious as he careened blindly forward.

In the front rank of the charge, Gawain let loose his spear. It caught Pinto a glancing blow on his shoulder—just enough of a wound to cause pain. The second spear, belonging to Fairhands, missed the man entirely, hitting instead the windshield of the Cadillac, which shattered into a million shining crumbs, and then coming to rest at an angle on the left side of the driver's neck.

The Cadillac swerved wildly, heading toward Pinto and Lugh, who was immediately behind him. More out of panic than anything else, Lugh let fly his mace, which careened over the biker to land with a thud on the Cadillac's roof. At nearly the same moment, Pinto's motorcycle crashed into the side of the car just behind the stunned driver, who still had Fairhands's spear lodged in his flesh. As Pinto was ejected from the bike and shot neatly into the Cadillac's back seat, the driver began to cough up blood.

Through the final moments of this debacle, a siren and a cloud of dust from the direction of the town announced the presence of the authorities. For a brief moment, every head turned toward the approaching police vehicle.

Pinto was the first to move. Inside the car, he sat up, wiped the spray of blood from his eyes, and then yanked the spear-tip from the driver's neck. The man's blood was copious, but not spurting, and Pinto was familiar enough with wounds to know that he would probably live, at least for a day or so. He snaked his one functional, if bloody, hand over the gaping hole in the driver's throat to stanch the flow of blood.

"Get going," he growled. "Now."

A hundred thoughts ran through the driver's head at once, but all were superseded by the inescapable, if temporary, need to obey the psychopath who was holding his throat in a death grip.

Titus Wolfe floored the accelerator.

———

Fortunately for Pinto, the man in the cream-colored Cadillac was, despite his infirmity, an exceptionally good driver. Also, although he was unaware of this fact, the man had even more to lose if waylaid by the police than Pinto did.

In the back seat, next to Pinto's blood-stained buttocks, was the molded plastic case containing the one-of-a-kind components for the bomb that was created to destroy a nuclear missile base. Piercing the case with several four-inch spikes was a medieval iron mace.

It took Titus less than seven minutes to lose the local cops. They weren't the problem. The problem was Pinto, who had kicked the suitcase, mace and all, onto the floor in an effort to make himself more comfortable while he was performing crude first aid on a man he believed to be just another hijacked driver.

"For God's sake," Titus objected through a gush of his own blood. "Be care—"

"Shut up, shithead," Pinto responded, getting a firmer grip on Titus's throat. He felt uneasy, at a level of consciousness he did not quite understand, that the driver of the Cadillac did not appear to be as terrified as he should. He felt even more uneasy after the car skidded to a stop and a gunshot from the front seat thudded through the upholstery.

Pinto gave a little yelp as he looked down reflexively to see if he had been hit. In that moment of confusion, Titus whirled around, gun in hand—it was a small Beretta, an extra to be carried in one's sock, but capable of real damage at point-blank range— and stuck it beneath Pinto's chin.

"I think you had better be the one to shut up," Titus rasped, drooling blood.

Pinto screamed. It was a wild, charging battle cry such as Titus had never heard. All he could see for the moment was a close-up of Pinto's teeth—smelly brown tombstones going in all directions—while the Beretta was knocked out of his hands.

Later he would puzzle over that moment, wondering if he had lost his weapon to this psychotic ignoramus because of his injury, or because he had just never encountered anyone as crazy as Pinto before. Agents, even terrorist agents, operated under some sort of guidelines. They used reason. Even if they were willing to die during the course of a mission, they generally tried to stay alive. They talked, threatened, fought, deceived. They didn't just scream into your face.

A split second after Pinto knocked the gun out of Titus's hand, he dived into the front seat. Titus saw that coming, at least. He tried to break Pinto's nose, but by that time they were both so covered with blood that the heel of his hand, which was supposed to kill Pinto, instead merely slid off his face without even stopping the crazy biker from lunging at him. The gun discharged again, into the door, when Pinto's foot inadvertently got the trigger mechanism stuck on the seat adjustment lever. They both dived after it, crashing their heads together. Titus vomited blood into Pinto's lap. Pinto tried to kick him away. The movement of the seat caused the gun to go off several more times before finally coming loose from the lever and sliding beneath the passenger seat, where it was lodged too tightly for either of the men to retrieve.

All in all, they scuffled inside the car for less than five minutes, at the end of which both of them lay back, exhausted, slick with blood, and bruised in all their joints from striking the hard parts of the automobile.

"Idiot," panted Titus.

"Asshole," breathed Pinto.

Thus was born a partnership between two men whose destinies would come to be entwined, in the unlikely yet inexorable way of fate, with the legend of King Arthur.

CHAPTER FIFTEEN

DESTINY

PUMA MOUNTAIN, SOUTH DAKOTA

The sword's name was Excalibur, from the Celtic *caladbolg*, meaning "voracious."

It was magnificent, this hungry-bellied man-eater of a weapon, with its gold pommel studded with polished gemstones, its blade gleaming with its own cruel intelligence: a sword created, it was said, by the ancient gods themselves and given as birthright to the great king of the Celts.

"Can you see it?" Taliesin whispered.

In the black scrying mirror, dazzling now with moonlight, the sword stood shrouded in a film of what looked like smoke. "Yes," Arthur said, his eyes unblinking. "What's around it?"

"Rock."

"But I can see through it."

Taliesin's mouth closed into a thin line. "That's because it's a vision," he snapped. "You're looking not with the eyes of the senses, but of the soul. Don't be a dullard."

He struggled to maintain a stern expression, but inwardly the old man was whooping for joy. The boy was better than he had been four years ago, sharper, more intuitive, possessed of a capacity for vision and magic usually found only in trained druids.

Even Arthur Pendragon had not been able to see through a scrying mirror. The king had tried once or twice, at the Merlin's urging, but had quickly given up, muttering about feeling foolish.

But this one could see even through the rock!

"Concentrate," Taliesin said softly.

Arthur rubbed his hands over his face. "I'm sorry," he said, breaking the connection in the mirror. "I lost it."

The old man sighed. "It happens. Rest for a moment. The vision will come back." He leaned back, bracing himself with his long spindly arms. "Tell me, Arthur. Do you ever see this sort of thing on your own? That is, without trying?"

"I never try," Arthur said tersely, hoping that would be the end of the conversation.

It was true; he never tried to see beyond his normal senses. He never had to. Ever since the televised incident in New York, during which he had been in a kind of trance, episodes of uncanny clarity had been happening to him with increasing frequency. Mostly it had been small things: being able to find missing objects, or knowing when one of the farm animals was going to have trouble delivering its young. But there were stranger occurrences, too, such as the time a hired hand on the farm had died, and then had told Arthur in a dream where to find his family.

Or the girl.

No, not the girl, he thought, feeling himself sweating cold. The girl was not a vision. She was an indication of insanity.

Nameless yet familiar, she stole into his dreams and the timeless moments before sleep when everything seemed possible. She came again and again—not the vague, pneumatically breasted fantasy of a teenage boy who knew no females, but a rather conventionally pretty girl with gray-green eyes and the slender fingers of an artist.

She seemed real, achingly, blood-poundingly real to him, so real that there had been nights when he had waited for her to come, prayed that she would. And then they would have conversations, sometimes desultory and trivial, sometimes burning with importance, outrage, tears. She would complain about her mother, or talk about God. It didn't matter. Arthur just liked to hear the sound of her voice.

When he spoke, he would tell her his plans for the future, and it also did not matter that he knew his plans would never materialize, because by then Arthur realized that the girl was not real, that she was no more than an outcropping of his growing madness.

He had read that schizophrenia often manifested in the young, bringing to promising lives barely begun a horror which no human being should have to live through. The disease was characterized by florid and utterly believable hallucinations, both visual and auditory. . . .

It was her hair that informed him.

She rarely appeared with the same kind of hair. Sometimes it was blond and flowing, like a river of gold. At other times, the hair was hacked short, dyed jet black and sticking out in all directions. And there was a third version of this nameless, wonderful girl, too: a vision in veils and headpieces, or with long chestnut curls bound by ropes of gold and silver.

Yes, the hair. Only a lunatic would change the color of his dream lover's hair and never learn her name.

"Arthur?" The old man was peering into his face. "Do you want to tell me something?"

He inhaled sharply. "No. That is . . . No." His face turned toward the moon, enormous now, sitting fatly on the tops of trees beyond the mountain. "I just get confused sometimes." He spoke in a whisper. "It's as if I can't remember where I am. Maybe I'm still in there." He nodded toward the scrying mirror. "There, I mean."

"Oh, but that's good," Taliesin said. "It means the veil is getting thinner."

"Veil?"

"The veil between the worlds." Taliesin squatted on the rock, perfectly comfortable. "What you see is not merely another place, but another life."

"I know that." He looked away, muttering, "I also know that mental hospitals are filled with people who believe they're King Arthur."

"Now don't start that," Taliesin said. "Just because you're extraordinary doesn't mean you're mad."

The moon shimmered. Maybe the reason he was going insane was because he was constantly subjected to insanity, Arthur thought. If he could only go, just go, find a job, learn a trade, get a place to live, make some friends . . .

"Let me put it this way," the old man said, settling comfortably on the ground. "Every person on the planet has lived many times before. And most people remember those lives, or at least parts of them. How else would you explain a young Irish girl's fascination with Peruvian weavings, or a person in Iowa who is deathly afraid of water?" He smiled. "But they can't make sense of things because they won't allow themselves to believe the memories."

. . . instead of always listening to how he had been the bloody High King Grand Poobah of the goddamned Dark Ages . . .

"Although, if the truth be told, most of the time, it's probably for the best that humans don't remember. Doesn't do much good for a house painter to recall that he used to be the queen of Sheba, does it? Heh, heh." The old man smiled, savoring his little joke. "Anyway, it's different in your case. You see, Arthur Pendragon's life was unfinished. You were killed by magic. In the karmic scheme of things, the death didn't really count." He waved a hand in front of Arthur's blank face. "I say, are you quite sure you feel all right?"

Arthur forced himself to pay attention. "Yes, I'm fine." He took a deep breath. "So you're saying that because something interfered with his—that is, my—former life, and made me die before my time, I got another life to make up for it?"

"Just so. At the time, everyone knew you'd come back. Even the Christians, although I don't know how they reconciled that with their belief that people are permitted only one body through all eternity." He shrugged. "Odd new religion, that." He tapped the scrying mirror. "Let's continue, shall we? What else do you see?"

Arthur frowned as he stared into the smoky vision. "Nothing. Woods." He looked at Taliesin. "Where is this place?"

"Camelot," the old man answered with relish. The boy was perfect. "You're looking at Camelot, before the castle was built. The spot where the sword came from is very sacred. It's said to be the burial site of ancient heroes, watched over by the the Cailleach herself."

"The what?"

"The Cailleach. She's a goddess, very old, known sometimes as the Wild Hag. According to Celtic lore, it was she who made the very mountains of Britain."

"Did you worship her when you were a druid?" Arthur asked.

"Not really. She was too old, even back in the fifth century. No one knew much about her, not even what she represented or how she was worshipped in the time before time. No, the Cailleach is one of the truly ancient gods."

"Did she put Excalibur there?"

He shrugged. "Perhaps. No one knows. But it was put there for you." He smiled. "For the Great King."

Arthur closed his eyes. He was getting a headache. "Taliesin . . ." His voice caught. "Sir—"

"Yes, Arthur?"

"What if . . . well, what if I don't want to take up that life again?" Arthur interrupted.

The old man sat back, aghast. "I beg your pardon?"

"I mean, Arthur Pendragon was a great man, there's no doubt about that. He united the Celtic tribal kingdoms. Got rid of the Saxons. Brought order out of the chaos of post-Roman Britain. But . . ."

"But what?"

Arthur looked levelly into the old man's eyes. "That's the point. All that's been done. It doesn't need to be done again."

"What on earth are you talking about?"

"I'm talking about me, Taliesin! Arthur Blessing, Boy Nobody. Why can't that be enough?"

"Nonsense—" The old man waved him away with a smile.

Arthur clasped his hand. "No, don't dismiss me." He made sure Taliesin was listening before he went on. "Look, I appreciate all that you and Hal have done for me, but I think it's time for me to go."

"Go?" The old man was genuinely perplexed. "Go where?"

Arthur released his hand, smiled, shrugged. "Wherever," he said mildly. "That's how most people's lives go. They're free to choose what they want to do with their time on earth."

Taliesin looked stunned. "That may be true for them, but good heavens, child, you're the king of the Celts. You can't just go wandering off like some itinerant tradesman."

Arthur breathed deeply, trying to be patient. "Be reasonable, Taliesin. This isn't England, and it isn't the fifth century. What do you imagine I would I be king of? Jones County, South Dakota?"

"That's not for me to say, Arthur. Your destiny would determine that."

"But my destiny is what I decide it is."

The old man hesitated. "I'm afraid not," he said. "That is . . . it might not be as easy as you think to live as Arthur Blessing."

"Why wouldn't it?"

Taliesin exhaled noisily. "It's rather difficult to explain. That is, actually, it's nothing to do with . . ." His face reddened. "Oh, dash it all, Highness, Arthur Blessing doesn't exist!"

Arthur blanched. "What?" He tried to laugh, but the attempt was unsuccessful.

"Don't you see, you *are* King Arthur. Then or now, that is who you are, and all that you are. You came here to finish out that life, that destiny. And whatever you might do, that destiny would catch up with you."

"Are you saying I can never live a normal life, no matter what I do?" The boy looked stricken.

"Come now, you're acting as if you'd come down with the plague!" Taliesin said cheerfully. "It took a lot of magic to get you here, you know."

"Then undo it," Arthur demanded.

"Now see here. You're hardly mature enough to make a decision of his magnitude—"

"I said undo it!" Arthur shouted. "I want my life, my own life, whether you think it's worthwhile or not. Now undo whatever spell you put on me and Hal and the rest of them!"

A terrible silence stretched between them like a chasm. "I can't," the old man said at last. "That magic can't be undone. Centuries have passed. The lives of all the knights have been suspended. And Hal . . ."

Arthur stood up.

"Oh, do try to understand," Taliesin said, putting his arm on the boy's shoulder. Arthur shrugged it off.

"It'll all be fine, you'll see. . . ."

Arthur turned to face him, his eyes filling with tears and rage. "I always knew there was something wrong with me," he whispered hoarsely. "Something not quite normal. I thought I was just crazy. But this . . ." He backed away, stumbling.

"Arthur—"

"Get away from me!" He turned and ran down the mountain, tripping over loose rock, skinning his legs as he bolted away from the nightmare truth of his existence.

"Don't be a fool!" Taliesin called after him. "You have an opportunity never before granted to anyone! You can pick up your life where you left off, don't you see? You can live again!"

But the boy was not listening. He was running, still believing that he could run away.

The old man sighed. Humans, even kings, always had to learn things the hard way.

CHAPTER SIXTEEN

THE ARAB AND THE MORON

ST. FRANCIS HOSPITAL
RAPID CITY, SOUTH DAKOTA

The two FBI agents passed the object between them over Hal, who was sitting up in bed. "Object" was the word they had decided to use to describe the thing Hal had called them in for, the thing he had picked up near the spot where the cream-colored Cadillac had stopped.

It had been flung out of the car during the sixty seconds or so when everything had seemed to happen at once: Gawain's spear had hit the crazy biker on the shoulder, sending him spinning out of control until he struck the side of the Cadillac at almost the same time Lugh's fifteen-inch mace tore a hole through the automobile's roof.

What had occurred then, which no one saw, was that the mace had smashed open the locked case in the Cadillac's back seat. When Pinto hit the car, the now-opened case bounced upward and toward the point of impact, at which point the object—a small metal thing weighing less than two ounces and shaped vaguely like the midsection of a miniature trumpet—was propelled out the window at approximately the same moment that Pinto was being propelled in.

To anyone else, including the local police, the object would have been something of no concern, but Hal knew better. For one thing, it was made of extremely lightweight metal, with no rough edges, meaning that it had been worked and polished by hand. For another, it was made of a single piece. No welds. A die had been specially made to produce it. From those two facts, Hal was ready to deduce that there were very few of these objects around. Maybe only one.

"What do you think? Titanium?" One of the agents held the faintly key-shaped object up to the light.

"Something like that," Hal said. "Ben'll be able to tell you, if he's still in the lab."

The agent smiled. "Oh, he's still there, all right. They'd let the director go before him."

Ben was the man in charge of the FBI laboratories. He had been working in the lab since before Hal came in as a new recruit. Hal had been gone for more than ten years now. The agent who had been called into the hospital to talk to Hal had worked briefly with him long ago.

"So, you doing all right?" the agent asked awkwardly. It was common knowledge, Hal supposed, that he'd burned out like a rocket in the FBI and turned into every agent's worst nightmare: a drunk with no connections.

"Yeah, I've been okay," Hal said. In fact, those bad times had only gone on for a year or two. Then he had found Arthur Blessing.

But he could never tell this man who used to be his peer what had happened. *Oh, well, yes, while I was busy drinking myself to death, I ran into this kid who is the reincarnation of King Arthur, and everyone was trying to kill him because he had the Holy Grail with him, see, only now that's not a problem because the Grail's buried in a well in upstate New York, and the Knights of the Round Table have come back from the dead to look after him.*

Oh, yes. That would go over big.

"Say, didn't we see something like this once . . ."

"At JFK," Hal said, remembering. And then he knew: "It's a detonator," he said.

"Christ, yes. The bomb in the engine of the 747. It was one of the Arab's jobs."

Hal shrugged. "Never proven." The Arab only meant one Arab, the most famous Arab in the world to anyone involved in counterterrorism.

"Never caught, you mean," the younger agent said, loosening up in the presence of the two veterans. "And now he's in the States."

"Oh?"

The other agent gave his partner a look indicating that he had said too much in front of a civilian.

"So what's around here that anyone would want?" Hal asked. No one answered him. "Except for the nuclear silos at Warren," he remembered.

The older FBI agent took out his cell phone and dialed. "Bingo," he said, gesturing with two fingers for the detonator.

Hal handed it over. "The only problem with that theory is that the Arab wasn't on the field where I found that thing," he said. "No one was, except for my guys and that crazy trigger-happy cracker."

"And the witness," the younger agent said.

Hal tried to bring up the image of the man in the cream-colored Cadillac. Blond, handsome, thin-faced, expensive clothes . . . "The witness," he repeated slowly.

The older agent punched in the number he was calling again. "Goddamned switchboard," he muttered. "Hey, what was that guy's name, you remember?" he called out. "The Arab."

"Bayat," Hal said. "Hassam Bayat."

"An undisclosed number of Special Forces troops poured into Warren Air Force Base in Cheyenne, Wyoming, earlier today. Although the Air Force would not comment on the operation, several sources have speculated that the ultra–top security site has been targeted for destruction by international terrorist Hassam Bayat, who orchestrated last year's bombings in downtown London. . . ."

They found the detonator, Titus thought, feeling sick. When he had first discovered that it was missing, he had hoped that the small metal object would go unnoticed in a litter-filled campsite. But the Yanks, despite their continued blundering over the fictitious Hassam Bayat, got lucky.

Now the mission would be delayed by several months, and there was nothing for Titus to do, except get out of the country before the Feds traced him through the detonator.

He got up off the motel room bed with a groan and limped to the dresser on which he had placed his valise. Inside was a bottle of scotch—the one luxury he afforded himself while working, and for which he was now most grateful.

He poured himself a glass. It hurt to swallow, but the effect was worth it.

Pinto was running a shower in the bathroom. The stall would look like a pig had been slaughtered in it when he was done, Wolfe thought with a sigh.

It had not been difficult to convince Pinto that Titus himself was a fugitive from the law, and would therefore stay away from the police. He had made up a story about killing his wife somewhere in southern California. Pinto, in return, had boasted about the murder of the four physicians in Sturgis, a disgusting-sounding affair which would doubtless result in Pinto's execution.

Pinto was a common lout; he couldn't be trusted to do anything more than get caught. It had just been a matter of sheer misfortune that Titus had even encountered the creature in the first place.

Now, two cars and a hundred miles later, they had broken into a fleabag motel to clean themselves up. Titus had some spare clothing, so he would be able to throw away the bloody things he'd been wearing at the accident. Pinto, naturally, had nothing besides the shirt on his back, which was now in the shower with him.

Titus threw down a second scotch with irritation. Nothing had gone right. Absolutely nothing.

First, there was the detonator. Even if it were still in his possession, the bomb it was designed to explode would be impossible to assemble, since the other components had been rendered useless after being bludgeoned by a mace.

A *mace*, he thought with wonder. Who were those lunatics? Pinto swore he had never seen them before today.

"But one of them smelled like a cop," he had insisted.

The dolt. When asked if the fellow's smell was what had prompted Pinto to start a knife fight against a gang of twelve, he had only shrugged and shown his horrendous teeth.

Titus had wanted to pull them out of the man's head, one by one. If it weren't for Wolfe's injury, he'd have gotten rid of Pinto hours ago. The very thought of sharing a bathroom, even a bloody and temporary one, with such a cretin was enough to make him retch.

One of them smelled like a cop. Titus couldn't get Pinto's words out of his brain.

Was it possible that those fools on motorcycles were agents of some sort who had been waiting for him?

Of course not, he decided. Think about their weapons. Swords, spears, *pikes*, for God's sake! It had been like walking into a Shakespearean play. No, they couldn't have known anything. Literally. Titus had, he concluded, simply had the misfortune to encounter some sort of club for extremely stupid men.

By now, the authorities had probably found the car and determined that its driver had been killed and dumped somewhere. A search of the Cadillac's provenance would reveal that its owner, a merchant of surfing equipment, had vanished from Venice Beach, California, two months before. The discovery of the car would render that case closed and Titus a free man.

But then, someone had found the detonator. That changed everything. But Titus did not pursue the idea. There was no point in worrying unnecessarily, particularly since he was on his way out of the U.S.

He had given himself two avenues of escape. There was a car

waiting for him in northern Montana, in which he could cross over the Canadian border, if he wanted to leave now.

That option was out. If the Feds were sending troops in to Cheyenne, they would be watching the northern border.

The second escape route was much more complicated, and involved traveling across the United States, as well as three weeks of waiting. This was the backup plan Titus had devised in case things got sticky.

Well, it seemed they had.

The boat named *Sea Legs* would be docked at a pier in Atlantic City, New Jersey, at the end of the month. Richard Edgington would sail Titus to Panama on it. A roundabout route, but fairly safe, particularly since the mission at Warren had not even been attempted.

He would go by train to New York, then pass the time at a good hotel, perhaps the Pierre. It was small enough to be intimate, but lacked nothing. Even with the wound on his neck, he would be able to spend an enjoyable ten days.

At that moment, a photograph of a police sketch flashed on the television. Titus gasped as he recognized his own face.

"Police are looking for two men in connection with an episode of mayhem on the highways near Sturgis, South Dakota," the announcer said.

Only then did Titus notice that there was another face on the screen besides his own. He had no idea who it was.

Then he heard a low chuckling. It was Pinto, naked and dripping from his shower. "Them police drawings ain't never no good," he chortled.

"The one of me seems to bear a likeness," Titus said bitterly.

Pinto nodded. "Yep, now you mention it. Guess sometimes they hit it right." He looked over at the Englishman and laughed.

"Both men were wounded in the scuffle. One has an injured hand. The other sustained a wound to the neck," the announcer went on.

Titus touched the heavy gauze bandage beneath his chin.

"They think you was in on it," Pinto drawled, his eyes crinkled in amusement.

No mention was made of the fact that Titus had merely been driving by during the incident.

"Anyone spotting either of these men is urged to contact the FBI." A phone number flashed across the screen.

"Didn't I say the one was a cop?" Pinto gloated.

The FBI," Titus whispered. The lunatics with the swords had been agents, after all. And they had remembered his face well enough to put together an accurate composite.

"Which one was the cop?" Titus asked, abstracted.

"The one on the ground. Shot him through the belly," Pinto said.

"He'd be in hospital, then."

Pinto looked up, frowning for a moment until he understood. "Yeah," he said, grinning. "Easy pickings."

Titus examined his face in a mirror. He would have to do something about his appearance, and quickly. Some hair color, a beard, perhaps. A pair of drugstore glasses. He would need someone to obtain those things for him. And drive him.

His gaze rested reluctantly on Pinto, who lit a cigarette. Titus hated smoking.

"How is your hand?" he asked.

"Fine," Pinto answered. He had taped the knife wound. A pair of thin gloves would cover it. Not that anyone would recognize his face from the poor police sketch, anyway.

Titus rested his head in his hands. He had never had to rely on anyone before. And now, in his hour of need, fate had sent as his partner the most stupid, barbarous, unstable human being he had ever met.

CHAPTER SEVENTEEN

THE SUMMER COUNTRY

It was known to the ancient Celts as the doorway to the dwelling place of the gods, the Summer Country, with its endless flowering meadows and streams running with clear water.

Most entered the Summer Country through death. It was the place where the soul journeyed after it was freed from the constraints of the body. But there have always been those who knew how to get there without dying.

"Innocent! Innocent!" the old man called. He was awash in clouds, which he swatted away to reveal a green hillside dotted with shining white rock. He stumbled over one, stubbing his toe. "Damn!" he shouted. With a handkerchief, he blotted perspiration off his forehead. That was the trouble with keeping one's body. It persisted in doing living things like sweating and hurting. "Innocent!"

Shhh.

"What?" Taliesin looked around. He didn't see anyone. And

then, far off, nearly at the crest of the hill, he spotted a large gray she-wolf.

"Innocent!" he shouted, breaking into a pitiful, loping run.

Calm yourself, little bard. I'll come to you.

The wolf sauntered down the hill. When she reached him, her fur was decorated with snowdrops as white as its sightless eyes.

How do I look? she asked. Which is to say, Taliesin divined what the wolf was thinking. There was no sound.

"Er . . . Very festive," he answered. "I hope I'm not disturbing you, Innocent, but—"

Not at all. She sat down on her haunches. *Would you rather I were human?*

"Oh, I don't . . . Well, actually, yes. That would be rather nicer." He sat on a smooth rock and rubbed his toe. When he looked up, the Innocent had transformed into a wraithlike old woman with wispy white hair festooned with flowers.

"Oh. Oh, my." Taliesin smiled. She had looked just so when she was his teacher and he a young bard learning the magic of the druids. "Thank you," he said.

"And how is the great Merlin?" she asked, patting his knee.

He blushed. Taliesin was able to accept accolades for his power from anyone else. But with the Innocent, he still felt like a foolish boy dressing in his father's clothes. "I'm well," he said.

"The knights?"

"The usual," he said with equanimity.

"Ah." She smiled. "Tell me, then, little bard, what brings you here."

"Well . . ." He looked into her eyes. They were milk-white. As far as he knew, the Innocent had always been blind. In death, of course, she could have chosen to have eyesight, but she remained blind even here, in the Summer Country.

And why not, Taliesin thought. She saw everything anyway. Even now she was looking through him, not through her comforting, blank eyes, but through a thousand other avenues, through the very pores of her skin, it seemed to him.

"It's Arthur."

"Of course."

"He's . . . Well, it's difficult to put into words."

"Meaning it bruises your ego to say the plain truth."

"No, that's not . . ." He felt himself flushing and sputtering. "Oh, hang it all, he's run away!" He wrung his hands. "It's his age, I suppose. You know that in areas of the Far East, all teenagers are considered to be demented. Beloved but insane. Makes life easier for the families, no doubt . . ."

"Do stop babbling, Taliesin."

Downhearted, he forced his hands to be still. "I was explaining that he was nearly ready to begin his work—"

"Doing what?" the Innocent asked.

"Why . . . Whatever his destiny demands," Taliesin said.

"You mean cut ribbons, open factories, that sort of kingly thing? And that only if some existing monarch is willing to turn over a throne to the boy—"

"No," he said, astonished by his teacher's obtuseness. "He is King Arthur, the once and future king, cut down in his prime but destined to return to live out his glorious reign." He leaned forward as he spoke, enunciating each word clearly, as if it had been written in stone.

"My, my," she said. "That sounds terribly important."

Taliesin took a deep breath and spoke from the depth of his soul. "It is, Innocent. It is the most important spell I have ever undertaken, to bring Arthur Pendragon back from the dead, along with all his knights." He shook his head slightly, as if to emphasize the gravity of the matter. "It was, in fact, one of the Three Great Magics."

"Ah," the Innocent said, appropriately impressed.

On the druid island of Mona, the Great Magics were introduced to fledgling magicians almost as soon as they were accepted as students, yet after the required two decades of study, it was rare for any of them to have mastered the skill to perform even one.

They were difficult feats, to be sure: The First Great Magic, known as Walking Through the Rock, required the ability to be so still that the very atoms of one's body could merge with—and therefore pass through—solid objects.

The Second Great Magic, or Bringing the World into Being, was far more advanced. It involved no less than creating physical reality from thought.

This was what had brought the knights back from the Summer Country to take on human flesh. It was what had connected Hal, who had waited for centuries, with a recently-born Arthur. It had all been orchestrated sixteen centuries before, when the spell was begun.

This was the stunning achievement that was the Merlin's masterwork, the last spell of his earthly life, an accomplishment so extraordinary that when he awoke to spin the final threads of the spell, he found he was no longer a human being, but a true wizard.

The Third Magic, which, as far as Taliesin knew, no one had ever tried, carried the chilling subtitle of The End of the World. This Magic was discussed, but not taught, and students were strongly advised not to spend their lives conjuring a spell which would ultimately destroy everything they knew.

On Mona, the Three Magics were likened to the Fates of ancient Greek mythology: Clotho, who spun the thread of life, Lachesis, who wove the thread into cloth, and Atropos, who determined the thread's length and cut it when it was time. Walking Through the Rock was the initiation that created a magician out of a man; Bringing the World into Being allowed the magician, now fully formed, to practice his art and ascend to a higher level of knowledge; and The End of the World . . . Well, Taliesin thought, one didn't have to worry about that much.

The Innocent patted his leg. "Ah, well, don't feel too badly. You were doing your best."

Taliesin felt his blood rise. "My best! I beg your pardon, Innocent, but I have fulfilled—singlehandedly—the ancient prophecy about the return of the king."

She fixed him with her blank eyes. "And he was doing so well here in the Summer Country. The knights, too. I checked up on them from time to time." She winked at him. "Perhaps you ought to have spent more time practicing the First Magic, and left the Second until you had attained a bit more maturity."

Taliesin sputtered. "I . . . how . . ."

"Walking Through the Rock is always the beginning," she said.

"Walking Through the Rock is about transportation!" he shouted.

"Oh, you're wrong, little bard," the old woman went on gently. "To walk through the rock, you have to become the rock before you can move through it. You must, wholly and truly, become one with objects, other beings, with the very gods themselves. It takes nothing less, Taliesin. That is why it is one of the Three Great Magics: because all of the wonders of all the wizards in creation can be distilled into one of these three, and of the three the first, Walking Through the Rock, is the most necessary."

Talisin felt unappreciated and unfairly judged. No one else in all of history had ever brought a king back from the Summer Country.

"The second great Magic, Bringing the World into Being, grows out of the first. To create, to manifest the tangible from an idea, to bring form to pure energy, to bring to new life a man who had been dead . . . these come also from becoming. From understanding deeply." She cocked her head. "Do you understand deeply, O Merlin?"

"Yes, yes," he said, bored. Sometimes the Innocent worried an idea to death, like a dog with a bone.

"Then you understand why the boy did not want to live the life you gave him."

"He doesn't know any better."

"I see. And you do."

"Well, naturally I do," he said, puzzled. "I know the nature of the life he had—"

"But you talk as if Arthur lived only one life before this current one. That simply isn't true. He has lived many times, Taliesin."

"But his life as High King was the only one that mattered!"

The Innocent was silent.

"Oh, I know what you're saying," he admitted crankily. "Human beings are very attached to their lives, even if they're quite ordinary. They all like to believe that their trivial experiences are important." He stifled a yawn.

"Everything that happens is important," the Innocent said. "I wish you understood that, little bard."

She stretched on the bench, a frail old woman, impossibly old, and then leaped into the air on powerful haunches. When she alighted, twenty feet away, she had again taken the form of the she-wolf.

"Innocent, please," Taliesin said, but the wolf sauntered away without a backward glance.

"She treats me like an idiot," he muttered as he propelled himself back to Puma Mountain. He landed in the ashes of the previous night's fire. "Damn, damn, damn!" he said, brushing the soot off his robe. "Becoming the rock. Pah!"

In his rage, he nearly stepped on the scrying mirror which he had been using with Arthur before the boy had stormed off so unreasonably.

Arthur came into view almost immediately. "Hmmph," the old man said. He had half a mind to forget the ungrateful brat. "Hmmph," he said again as his gaze slid toward Arthur's image in the mirror.

The boy was still in the Black Hills, in what was called the Needles area of the rolling forest, where tall, slender rocks jutted skyward like daggers. He was hiking determinedly beneath the summer sun, wiping the sweat off his brow.

"You always were a stubborn child," Taliesin said.

Arthur scanned the horizon, trying to find his way.

"It won't do any good, you know," the old man said. "The knights will find you."

As if hearing what Taliesin had said, Arthur found a shady spot beneath an outcropping of rock and sat down.

"Jolly good," Taliesin whispered. "Now let me in, Arthur. Let me see what you're thinking."

The scene in the mirror was the same one that Arthur had conjured when the two of them had sat together on Puma Mountain. Taliesin recognized the lush terrain of the land on which Camelot had once stood. But again, they were seeing Camelot before Camelot, when the flattened summit of the hill on which Arthur's great castle would come to stand was still the ancient burial ground of heroes long forgotten even during the Middle Ages.

"Why do you keep going there?" the old man wondered aloud, though he knew Arthur could not hear him. "You're in the wrong time, lad! You need to move a few hundred years forward!"

This time, he noticed, the shimmering spectre of Excalibur was not present in the vision. There was only a big yellow rock in a clearing, with a young woman walking by.

"I say," Taliesin said, bewildered. "Who the devil is that?"

The young woman ran her hand over the smooth, barley-colored stone. She was dressed oddly, in a rough woolen shift tied at the hip by a cord of vine, but beautiful. Tall and slender, her long legs strode with an authority far beyond her years. The sensual features of her face were framed by a cascade of wavy red-gold hair held in place by a band of white moonstones across her forehead.

"The girl," Arthur whispered. The girl who had come to him so often in his dreams. She was back.

"What girl?" Taliesin growled agitatedly. "I've never seen her before in my life."

"Brigid," the boy said as he fell deeply into trance. "Brigid, yes. Yes."

What he felt for her was love, pure, strong, aching love, in his body, his thoughts, his heart, a love so deep it seemed to him that he had loved her for a thousand years.

He had, in fact, loved Brigid for as long as he could remember. They had been children together. He had carried her across the river when it had been too deep for her to cross. He had made her gifts all his life: armloads of flowers picked at night and left in a dried pumpkin shell filled with water in front of her family's hut. Fish he had caught, still wriggling on the line.

And jewelry. He had always collected stones, wood, amber. Pretty things that he could string onto vines, cord, bone, things for her hair, her waist, her neck. He had learned how to forge metal, and though most of what he made were weapons, there was always enough time and material left over to make something beautiful for her.

The circlet she wore over her brow had been a gift from him. Three strands of milk-colored stones were mounted on thin wires of copper, with a larger stone hanging between her eyes, in the place of the Second Sight, which she had. It had taken him nearly a year to refine the copper to the point where he could make wire from it, but the time had been worth it. The stones shone against her skin like light made of water. Like moons.

As he strode near her, she held out her arms to him. Her lips parted in a smile of welcome. He met them with his own, entwined his arms with hers, touched her body with his. He felt whole now, as if he had been walking around with only isolated pieces of himself, and the rest of him had just grown in place to make him complete.

Yes, he thought, *I have known you forever. . . .*

"I've brought you something," he said. He took a long leather bag which hung over his shoulder by a strap and removed its contents.

What it held was a sword, although the word did not adequately serve to describe the object. It was a sword in the the way that a diamond was a stone. In truth, although its shape was that of a sword, it looked like nothing else on earth.

Its hilt, crafted of gold and silver and bronze and copper, was fashioned into the form of a coiled snake. Over the body of the snake were embedded gemstones which he had polished over the course of many months: lapis, rose quartz, onyx, malachite, spotted jasper, bloodstone. For the eyes of the snake, he had placed two rubies, very rare, for which he had traded a fine iron sword to a traveler from a distant land.

Unlike most swords, which were made of bronze, or even the new, famous black swords invented by Macsen's grandfather on the hilltop known as the Tor where they lived, this sword's blade was silver-colored, and light as wood. Anyone wielding it would not be swinging a heavy iron bludgeon, but a precision edge designed to function like a sharp knife.

"Macsen," Brigid breathed, running her slender hands above the deep, perfect metal of the blade. "You have made something wonderful."

"My grandfather helped," Macsen said, smiling. His grandfather had been the greatest swordmaker in Britain. Until his death, he had worked with his grandson to perfect what he had called the sword of the gods, this sword, Excalibur.

1275 B.C.E.

The old man first got the idea for it during his travels. "Travels" was how old Macdoo referred to the seventeen years he spent in slavery.

He had been taken during some long-forgotten foreign incursion, and put on a ship to a faraway city called Mycenae in a land so highly advanced and so alien that Macdoo might as well have been on another planet. He was set to work in a foundry, at first burning his hands and lungs at the filthy task of smelting the raw ore that was to be made into bronze for the weapons which were produced in huge quantity for the use of the Mycenaean army.

During the nearly two decades that Macsen's grandfather spent in this place, his owner, the armorer, grew old. He came to rely on the sturdy and pleasant young fellow more and more. Eventually he taught Macdoo everything he knew about making swords.

Toward the end of the armorer's life, with his own sons long dead in battle and no one to tend him except for the slave who had served him for so long, he shared with Macdoo a secret he had guarded jealously for many years: the secret of iron.

He had made only one such sword in his life, and given it as a gift to the king of Mycenae; but the king was sickly and frail, and could barely lift the heavy black sword. Embarassed by his own weakness, he had dismissed the armorer with little fanfare. Afterward, the sword had been relegated to a storehouse somewhere, never to be used again.

But the armorer knew its value. To those who could wield it, the heavy but nearly indestructible iron sword would vanquish every enemy. As a dying gift to his faithful slave, he passed on the process of the iron sword's manufacture before setting him free. The generous Greek had thought to provide Macdoo, who was no longer young, with a way to earn a living in his adopted homeland, but the Briton had no intention of remaining in the complex, cosmopolitan atmosphere of urban Attica. He was going back to the Tor on the island he would always call home.

It took him another six years to reach his destination. By then he was nearly forty, an age seldom attained by anyone, let alone a slave who had spent a lifetime at hard labor. There were few in his village on the Tor who remembered him. His wife had died of fever many years before. His daughter, who had only been one year old when he was taken into slavery, was now a widow herself, with an eight-year-old son and two younger daughters to raise alone. She had been glad to take in the old man, especially because he possessed a skill prized among all, the ability to make weapons of war.

Throughout the sparsely populated island of Britain, metal-working had been in a primitive state before Macdoo's arrival. Daggers and short, thrusting-type longer weapons were made by various methods here and there, but their hilts came apart from the blades easily, and in many cases the blades themselves broke on impact the first time they were used.

Macdoo's bronze swords, with their sophisticated tangs and rivets, changed all that. Demand for them was so great that men would often travel great distances in order to barter for one of the prized weapons. But his masterpieces were the iron swords he developed during his twilight years. The "black swords of the Tor," as they came to be known, became so prized that none of the precious blades were permitted outside the settlement. If a man wanted to own a sword of iron, he would have to move with his family onto the Tor.

By the time old Macdoo could no longer work the forge himself, he had taught his grandson everything he himself had learned about swordmaking, and one thing that he had not yet learned.

"There is something beyond iron," he confided to Macsen one winter night as he felt the chill of death breathing in the room. "I know it to be true, though I have not had time to try it."

"Try what, grandfather?" Macsen had asked.

"To purify the metal. To burn away everything in the ore that is not perfect, and use only what is left. It would be a perfect sword, Macsen. A sword of the gods."

"What . . . what would we call it, this sword made of a metal beyond iron?"

"Call it Excalibur," old Macdoo had commanded. "In the tongue of the Mycenaeans, it means 'voracious.' "

"Voracious?" Macsen asked, smiling. "A hungry sword?"

"Hungry for blood." The old man's eyes twinkled. "Men like their women sweet, but their swords vicious."

And from that day, Macsen worked to create, from his mind and his sweat and the strength of his arm, the sword of the gods, which he now presented to the woman he loved.

THE BLACK HILLS, SOUTH DAKOTA

Arthur gasped as the vision of Brigid vanished from his mind. "Hal!" he cried, looking around helplessly at the silent hills. Hal was in danger. Arthur did not know how he knew that. Nor did he know where he was, how to reach Hal, or who might help him.

There was only one person who could, of course. To summon him, Arthur would have to swallow his pride and admit his weakness. And betray his location.

But it would be for Hal. The premonition had been strong; he knew Hal would die unless he was taken from where he was.

Standing erect, Arthur opened his arms wide and shouted a cry of supplication that rang through the swordlike rocks of the sacred hills:

"Merlin!"

With a small smile, the old man touched two fingers to his forelock as he began to fade away. "At your service, Highness," he whispered.

CHAPTER EIGHTEEN

FACE-OFF OVER MOUNT RUSHMORE

RAPID CITY, SOUTH DAKOTA

Taliesin materialized in the boiler room of St. Francis Hospital, grateful to all the old gods that the Innocent had not been present to see him.

Somewhere along the line his concentration had wavered. The problem with magic was that it was so bloody exact. The focus required was such that it would literally kill most people. Why, he thought, if it hadn't been for his training on Mona . . .

What am I thinking? he realized as he made his way through the basement toward the elevator, feeling with his senses for Hal's presence in the building.

It did kill me. I spent sixteen hundred years being dead.

His thoughts drifted to the Innocent and her unenthusiastic comments about his accomplishments. "Some people appreciate nothing," he sniffed.

Hal was in room 503. He was sitting up in bed, watching television and eating the waxy yellow flesh of a chicken. Taliesin shuddered.

"What are you doing here?" the old man demanded, his hands on his hips. "Besides fattening yourself up, that is."

"Glad to see you, too," Hal said, turning up the volume on the TV news.

"No broken bones? No addled brains? I thought this was an emergency."

"I took a bullet. Flesh wound. I should be well enough to leave by tomorrow. Who told you I was here, anyway?"

"Arthur."

Hal looked over, frowning. "Arthur? How'd he know?"

"By using his mind for something other than staring at an inanimate object," he said irritably, snatching the remote control out of Hal's hand. He pressed several buttons to no effect. "How the devil— Oh, my."

The remote fell out of his hand.

Suddenly the old man looked as if he had eaten a worm. Hal followed his gaze to the television screen.

"On a lighter note, police have arrested eleven men who claim to be the Knights of the Round Table," the news announcer said as the camera focused on a group of large, loud men in various states of inebriety being surrounded by uniformed police. "Yesterday evening, the as yet unidentified individuals were apprehended while attempting to scale Mount Rushmore. Their plan, according to a spokesman, was to carve a fifth face into the side of the mountain."

The camera now shifted to a shot of Lugh Loinnbheimionach, wild-haired and sporting a leather jerkin open to the waist, climbing meekly into the back of a police wagon. In the background were the carved likenesses of the four Presidents, brightly lit against the night sky.

"Whose face would have joined the ranks of Washington, Jefferson, Lincoln, and Teddy Roosevelt?" the newscaster asked, grinning. "You guessed it: King Arthur's."

Hal made a strangling sound. "I'm going to kill them," he said, hobbling from his bed to the bathroom, where his clothes were hanging on the door. "Take their necks in my bare hands one by one, and—"

"Oh, no," Taliesin said. He was at the window. "They're right outside. The police station must be nearby."

"Good," Hal said. "I'll turn myself in as soon as they're all dead. Ouch." He touched his wound gingerly. "At least Arthur's all right."

"Well . . ."

Hal looked up. "He is all right, isn't he?"

Taliesin cleared his throat. "I'm sure he's fine. It's just that . . . Well . . ."

"Where is he?" Hal bellowed.

"I'm afraid he's somewhere in the Black Hills. On something of a . . . a walkabout, you might say."

"Alone?"

"Yes. That is—"

"Jesus," Hal muttered. "You, too."

"Now, really—"

"Just save it, okay?" He stumbled out of the room and limped toward the elevator.

Fortunately, Taliesin could move far more quickly than Hal.

They had intended no wrongdoing. Curoi MacDaire made that clear from the beginning. In fact, they had followed Hal's orders to the letter after the debacle with the gun-toting biker. As soon as the lone police car left in pursuit of the Cadillac bearing Titus Wolfe and Pinto, the knights had escaped into the hills and remained there, determined to behave like good citizens until Hal's return.

It was not until long afterward—several hours later, in fact—that the men, bored and uncertain about what to do in Hal's absence, wandered into a roadside tavern called the Tally Ho Bar, where they learned from a rack of picture postcards about the American marvel called Mount Rushmore.

"Who might these blighters be?" Dry Lips asked after the tenth round of ale.

"Kings, I'll wager," Tristan said.

"But they've no crowns."

"Aye. 'Tis America, remember."

Dry Lips nodded sagely. "What say you, barkeep? Be these kings, whose faces are carved into the rock?"

The bartender looked up momentarily from the sink, where he was washing glasses. "Sort of," he said, noticing that they were all carrying weapons. "Presidents, kings . . ." He glanced at Dry Lips's narrowed eyes. "Same thing, I guess," he finished gamely.

The knights passed around the postcard in silence. Finally Gawain, who rarely spoke, said the words that all of them were thinking: "Arthur's face should be up here."

There was a moment of electrified hesitation in which the men's eyes shifted intensely from one to the other. Their jaws clenched. Their hands caressed the hilts of their swords. Then Kay banged his fist on the table, shattering the quiet.

"That's settled, then! We'll put the great king's image on the mountain!"

A cheer went up. "Where would it be going?" Bedwyr asked passing the postcard to Fairhands, who was the most artistic of the lot. "Here, do you think, between these two blokes?" He pointed to the space between Lincoln and Roosevelt.

"Perhaps at the end," Fairhands replied. "Here, beside this fellow with the big nose." He pointed to the carving of George Washington.

As the knights rose as a man and lumbered toward the door, their swords clattering, the bartender set down his cloth with an air of annoyance.

"Someone planning to pay for those drinks?" he asked the group at large.

"Of course," said Curoi MacDaire, grinning. He swaggered forward and tossed a small leather bag to the bartender. "And a fine ale it was, my good man!" With a salute, he followed the others outside.

The bartender opened the bag. Inside were eight quarters.

With a curse, he picked up the phone and dialed the police station.

———

They were enjoying an afternoon of song in the Pennington County jail when Taliesin appeared, furious, with their bail.

It seemed that the knights had hardly begun the climb up the south face of the illuminated mountain when they were surrounded by police and taken promptly into custody. Despite the hyperbole of the police reporter who accompanied the arresting officers, the knights had not really done much wrong besides underpay the bar bill at the Tally Ho. They had not begun to climb the mountain (although they had been vocal in their intention to do so) at the time of their encounter with the police, and so could not be charged with either being a public nuisance or disturbing the peace. In the end, their weapons—and the objects they carried in full view could only be loosely interpreted as such—were confiscated, their debts at the Tally Ho satisfied with a fistful of twenty dollar bills which the Merlin produced, and they were, at least temporarily, set free.

"I suggest you ride into the mountains as soon as possible," the old man said, "before Hal makes a scene on the street."

"Is he here?" Launcelot asked.

"He was nearby, in one of those places where they saw off your limbs."

"My son!" Launcelot choked.

"It's quite all right. He was leaving when I had to come to the aid of this sorry bunch." Launcelot looked abashed. "My thanks to thee, Wizard," he said humbly. "Might we be of help?"

"You've helped quite enough already, the lot of you," the old man snapped. "Just keep these fools in check. Now be off with you."

"Not so fast." Hal lumbered up beside them. He was grimacing and holding the wound on his side.

"You have an injury," Launcelot said.

"And you're going to have one, too," Hal began, but a handheld camera moved into his line of vision.

Since news of the arrest first broke, a number of reporters had made the connection between the antics of the strangely attired Britons on Mount Rushmore and the accounts of four years before concerning a young boy with miraculous powers who disappeared one night in New York City.

"Aye, he ought to have his face up there on your mountain, that's what I've been telling ye," Curoi MacDaire was pontificating into a microphone. "Do you not know who the boy is, then?"

"Who?" the reporter prodded.

"Peter Pan," Hal said, shoving the camera and microphone away.

"Peter who?" MacDaire asked pleasantly.

"Get moving," Hal said.

Taliesin gave a map to Launcelot. "The boy's here, more or less," he said, pointing to an X in the Black Hills region. "Do you think you can get these fools there without being televised or imprisoned?"

"I can," Launcelot said, stoic in his shame. "But . . ." He glanced over at Hal, who was sweating profusely.

"Take him with you."

"Wait a minute," Hal protested, but the old man made a dismissive gesture. Launcelot put his arm around Hal and led him firmly toward the motorcycles. "You'll be riding with me, then," the big knight said gently.

"No, no." Hal screwed his eyes shut, trying to focus. His voice was growing weak.

"*Hist*, Galahad," Launcelot said.

Hal followed without another word.

At a discreet signal from Launcelot, the men slowly left the parking area, the noise of their motorcycles diminished in the pandemonium of the street.

"Sir, do you know anything about the missing boy?" The handheld camera was now focused on Taliesin.

"What?" he asked irritably, pushing the camera out of his face.

"Four years ago, a boy named Arthur Blessing was kidnapped off the streets of New York City by a gang of motorcyclists—"

"For heaven's sake, it was nothing of the kind!" he sputtered. "No one was kidnapped. The boy was only . . ." He saw the reporter's eyes gleaming with anticipation. The man had slanted the story in order to get him to talk.

"Go on," the reporter urged.

With a squeal of frustration, Taliesin raised his fist, as if he were about to strike the reporter, then stomped away into the crowd.

The reporter tried to follow him, but couldn't find the old man anywhere. A moment later, the motorcade roared down the highway leading out of town.

Titus Wolfe looked out the hospital window at the motorcyclists vanishing down the road.

He had just missed him. It could not have been more than twenty minutes ago that the man who had identified Titus to the FBI had occupied this very room. The floor nurses had not seen him leave.

It was uncanny, Titus thought. Hal Woczniak had known he was coming.

Simply uncanny.

"Sir, may I help you?" a tall nurse with suspicious eyes asked.

"I was just watching the crowd outside," he said pleasantly, automatically ridding himself of his British accent.

His hair was colored dark and cut so that he appeared to be balding. He wore colored contacts as well as glasses, and in his mouth he kept a small device to alter slightly the configuration of his teeth. The result was astonishing: Even his mother would not have recognized him as the man in the FBI sketch.

Titus turned to leave, allowing the nurse to see the bandage on his neck. This was the one place where a wounded man would not look out of place.

CHAPTER NINETEEN

THE SECOND MAGIC

By the time Hal and the others left Rapid City to find Arthur and bring him back to the fold, Taliesin was feeling ragged. He had Walked Through the Rock so many times in the past two days that he was no longer certain that he even had a body to dematerialize anymore.

Nevertheless, as he had no desire to remain surrounded by the loutish members of the press who were congregated there in such profusion, he knew he had to make one more effort.

As the reporter slogged after him, firing rude questions and generally making a nuisance of himself, Taliesin moved his hands in the ancient silent language of druid magic called Ogham, and tried to quiet his mind. That was the difficult part. His lessons with the Innocent had taken place on Mona, where silence was the norm and even talk was discouraged. Here, in the middle of motorcars and cheap music from every doorway and people shouting everywhere, going into one's inner silence required all his powers of concentration.

Sinking, releasing, leaning farther into the magic as his hands moved in the untranslatable alphabet of Ogham, he prepared, first, to leave his body, and secondly, to maneuver the molecules of his body around the molecules of whatever obstacle he might encounter on his journey, and to do it all at the speed of thought.

He left his body easily. Most people who became druids knew how to do that before their twenty years of study even began. The second step was more delicate: It was the painstaking process of slowing his life force to the vibration of rock while concentrating, distilling his energy, directing the mass of moving atoms that was his body as if it were a handkerchief he was transporting telekinetically. Easy, easy, keep the mind clear, not the smallest fragment of thought must interfere with the process, right, move steadily through the rock, ignore the objects, clear, clear . . .

Brigid.

The name fell like an anvil on Taliesin's fragile transitional state. He came crashing into reality in the middle of the Oahe River, ten feet in front of a fifteen-ton barge filled with garbage.

The old man screamed; the barge struck him head-on at twenty-five knots. Within sixty seconds he lay floating in the jetsam in the wake of the vessel, quite dead.

"Good heavens," he said, looking aghast at his lifeless body as it drifted, surrounded by empty milk cartons and orange peelings, behind the garbage boat.

"Well, get it out of there," came the Innocent's voice.

Taliesin looked around in hopeful anticipation, but there was nothing to see. Without a body, he simply floated in the void between the worlds. "I say, I'm back in the Summer Country."

"It is the usual place for the dead," she said.

"Oh. Quite. Er, the body. Do you suppose it's—"

"Good as new," she said as Taliesin suddenly appeared, clothed in his old flesh and dressed in a dry robe of iridescent stars on a blue background.

"Why, thank you," he said, touching his head. "Barely a dent."

"It's just an earth suit," she explained. "Easily mended. Still, one should take proper care of one's things."

"Indeed," he said. "I became distracted. Most distressing."

"You should be long past that sort of mistake, Taliesin. How could you allow your concentration to break so utterly?"

"Oh, I don't know," he said, irritated at being chastised yet again by his teacher. "I was tired. I've had a busy day, and it was a difficult transfer. And . . . Oh, yes. The name."

"What name?"

He cast about. "Brigid. Yes, that was what set me off. I remembered the name Arthur called when he was daydreaming—"

"I beg your pardon? You encroached on the boy's thoughts?"

"Well, I did have to find him . . ." he waffled. "All right, yes, I did."

"You're worse than the worst parent," she said coldly. "No wonder he's left you. You take his future away from him, and then monitor his thoughts. For shame."

"Dash it all, I was only . . ." He closed his eyes and tried to calm himself. "Never mind that," he said. "The point is, he was seeing Camelot before it was Camelot. He'd seen the same thing while he was with me. Except that in this new vision, a woman appeared. Someone I didn't know."

"Heaven forbid," the Innocent said dryly.

"But don't you see? There wasn't anyone named Brigid in Arthur Pendragon's life. Unless you count the ancient goddess Brigid, of course. But this wasn't goddess. It was a flesh and blood person. A yellow-haired woman. And he knew her. He kissed her, Innocent."

"So?"

He hesitated. When he spoke, he did not meet her eyes. "So I would like to go there."

"Ah," she said. "Now I understand. You wish to learn the magic to take you to this place."

"This *time*," he corrected.

"Yes," she said, smiling. "It's part of the Second Magic, you know."

"I know," he said, biting his lip.

"As I told you, Taliesin, the Second Magic springs from the first. You must become, you must believe, long before the creation can take place. First it is created in the mind. And so you must see it there."

"Yes," he said softly, his eyes closing.

"Do you see it?"

"I do. Perfectly."

"Good," the Innocent said. "Now create it for me."

His eyes opened, blinking. "But that's what I don't know how to do."

She looked dismayed. "Can you make it small?" she asked, holding out her cupped hand. "Like one of those pretty glass globes."

He frowned. "Well, perhaps," he answered uncertainly. Then, straightening his shoulders and clearing his throat, he began.

Becoming very still, going into a place of profound concentration, the wizard called upon the elements to mix by his will in his hands, molecule by swirling molecule, a clear glass globe. "Careful," he whispered, fixing its reality in place, knowing that for a few moments, before his mind fully accepted the globe as existing, it might cease to be.

"Very good," the Innocent said sweetly. Then, with a casual wave of her hand, the globe grew beyond the dimensions of Taliesin's hand to encompass both of them and then slide beyond the horizon of a landscape filled with pine trees and boulders, where a castle of white limestone rose out of the morning mist.

"Good heavens!" Taliesin exclaimed. "Where are we?"

"Inside the globe."

Taliesin gave a small involuntary squeal of delight. "This is what I made?"

"Yes," she said. "This is the past you created."

"Look," the old man said, pointing in the distance. "There's the stronghold of King Leodegranz. He owns Camelot at the moment."

"Really?"

"It's an old graveyard," he said. "As I was telling Arthur . . ." He shielded his eyes and pointed toward a little rise in the distance. "I say, there's someone now." He dashed up ahead, panting and wheezing. "Blast it all, that's not the girl," he said.

The Innocent caught up with him. "The girl in Arthur's vision, you mean?"

"Yes. This one's got dark hair."

"Of course," the Innocent said. "That is Guenevere."

"What?"

"You created the past you wanted," she said softly. "I told you that was how it worked."

"Damn!" Taliesin looked out over the rolling green hills so full of promise. "It was a lovely time, though, wasn't it," he said, almost to himself. "A lovely, lovely time . . ."

CHAPTER TWENTY

THE SWORD IN THE STONE

IMBOLC, THE FESTIVAL OF BRIGID
FEBRUARY 2, 506 A.D.

Guenevere walked quickly over the frost-covered ground, her cape
pulled tightly around her.

She had been coming to this spot since her childhood. It was
her special sanctuary whenever she wanted to be alone, or not
alone, or surrounded by magic. For there was real magic here.

Guenevere did not talk about it with her family, since they were
followers of the New Religion, which frowned upon magic, and
called it demonic. And among those who followed the old ways,
there were few who took the magic seriously. Even the Great Sabbats like Imbolc, days once revered as times of high magic, had
been degraded into little more than excuses for festivals. Indeed,
it was now quite out of fashion even to admit one was religious.

Her father, King Leodegranz, took pride in being a modern man.

Any talk about magic or the ancient gods was dismissed as foolish superstition.

Leodegranz hadn't always been so hard-headed. It had been he, in fact, more than his wife, who had taught Guenevere the stories of the fierce Celtic gods, making them seem so real that his young daughter could all but see them standing before her.

"And why not?" he would say, laughing, when his wife objected to his lurid tales of gods and goddesses changing the world through their magic.

"Because you make them seem like real people," she answered, only pretending to be annoyed.

"As well I should!" Leodegranz shouted. "For I do believe they were all real at one time, as real as you and I."

"Real people who could do magic?"

"Perhaps a little. Or maybe they were just clever. At any rate, they were remembered, and then the legends grew around them."

His wife really was shocked now. "The gods as real people! Such sacrilege!"

Leodegranz laughed. So did Guenevere, to please her father, but she remembered his words. The gods as people? Actual living people, who lived as we all did and suffered from the cold and wind and got knobby with old age? Was it possible? The wild, powerful deities of the Old Religion—Cerridwen, Arionhod, Gwion, Morrigan, perhaps even the Cailleach herself, real?

But then, Guenevere thought, how did they become gods?

She arrived at the place she had come to think of as her chapel. It was a copse of smooth grassland, roughly in the shape of a circle. In the middle of it was a huge rectangular boulder made of yellow rock. With a little imagination, one could think of it as a place where the ancients might have gathered to summon the gods and borrow their magic.

She had come to pray to Brigid, who was one of the great Triple goddesses, embodying the three aspects of woman: maiden, mother, and crone. Once the very soul of Celtic Britain, Brigid had suffered from the incursions of the Romans and, later, the Christians. Now, like many of the traditions that grew from ancient religious practices, the only vestige of Brigid's veneration was the festival of

Imbolc, also called "Brigid's Day," in which all the nobles within a day's ride would gather to watch the goddess, in the form of a snake, emerge from the cold ground, thus signaling the beginning of the end of winter.

Of course, since even in those times England had almost no snakes, one small garter snake was prudently cared for year round for the express purpose of releasing it on Brigid's Day to the cheers and applause of the onlookers. If it was a fine day and the snake cast a shadow, then it was said that winter would be late in leaving; but it the day was overcast, those present—and freezing—would be heartened by the knowledge that spring would soon be coming. Either way, a boy from the kitchen was sent out as soon as the crowd dispersed for a day of stag hunting to locate the snake and put it back in its cage, to feed on pantry mice until the following year.

For the women, Brigid's Day held other fascinations. A pilgrimage was usually made to all the wells in the area, since on this day the water was supposed to be capable of healing sickness. A pitcher of water from one of the wells was brought inside the dwelling and used to cool fevers, cleanse wounds, and particularly to ease inflammations of the eye. In exchange, the women left bouquets of snowdrops, gathered in the morning, at the bases of the wells.

But for young girls, the most important part of Brigid's Day was the night before when, during sleep, one was supposed to dream of one's true love.

This was a tradition that bore no weight whatever with any women of the nobility, since they never had anything to say about whom they were to marry; but among the peasants, it was still common practice for girls to braid together the chunky, lopsided-looking rush crosses and then hang them by the hearth as prayers to Brigid to grant them a glimpse of their heart's desire while they slept.

Guenevere learned about it from one of the cooks, who showed her how to hold the straw and whisper the ancient prayers into the fragrant rushes.

"Will I see the man I'll marry?" the girl had asked excitedly the first time she made one of the crosses.

"Like as not," the cook had answered. "And if not this year or the next, keep asking of the Goddess to show you the face of your love, and you'll see it, this I promise."

"Did you see your husband's face, cook?"

"Aye, that I did. And it was a right handsome face at the time, it was." She sighed. "Alas, he lived only twenty-four years."

Guenevere practiced sighing with her. She decided it felt very womanly.

Now, standing before the great yellow rock in the sacred clearing, she sighed again.

For the night before, as she slept beneath the rush crosses she had woven each year since the family cook had taught her how, the Goddess had indeed granted Guenevere a glimpse of her true love.

She had not recognized him, although that was often the way with dreams. She would not even have recognized herself, except for the fact that she simply knew that she was both the dreamer and the one being dreamed about.

The dream had taken place on this very spot. She was sure of it, because she had seen the big yellow stone in her vision. She had run her hand over its smooth coolness and felt its power surging through her.

"Imbolc," she had whispered. In the old tongue of the Celts, it meant "in the belly," or the quickening of the year. On this day, spring let itself be felt. Beneath the snow bloomed the white flowers that signaled the promise of a new season of life. The world was pregnant, and spring was in her belly.

And the person whom Guenevere was in her dream had rejoiced with a sense of awe and reverence.

"Imbolc," Guenevere said again, trying to summon those same feelings. She smelled the sweetness of the air, the gentleness of the breeze, still cold but mild now, flowing in the wake of winter's passing. She knelt beside the yellow rock and touched it reverently. What came off them into her hands and body was a feeling of inexpressible bliss. Tears sprang to her eyes. She closed them.

And then he came to her. She was back in the dream, remembering with such intensity that it seemed to be occurring all over again, down to the last molecule of scent. He came, tousle-haired, grinning, filled with love for her.

His hands were fairly small, with long thin, fingers. They were the hands of an artist, even though they were callused and usually covered with burns from working with molten metal. These hands he held out to her in love, and she welcomed his embrace.

Then the dream had ended, abruptly and for no reason. Guenevere had awakened in the black of night, longing, longing for those hands that had held her so surely.

And then she remembered where she was, and who. She was the daughter of a noble, and therefore had no right to choose her own mate, or even to dream of him. Her father, Leodegranz, had already betrothed her, in fact.

The suitor he had selected was Prince Melwas of Orkney, a fairly handsome but decidedly stupid fellow from a region so far away that after her marriage to him, she would probably never see her home again. Orkney was cold and barren and windswept, and its inhabitants famous for their joyless taciturnity.

Guenevere's father had no wish to see her married to a man known universally as a dolt, but a bond linking the two kingdoms would have great advantages for Leodegranz. In addition to providing him with allies against the invading Saxons, such an association would strengthen both chiefs in any bid they made for the vast land holdings left by Uther Pendragon.

Uther had died some months earlier without leaving an heir, and the result had been almost immediate civil war. Each tribe made its own claims to the territory stretching from the southwestern shore of England inland to the place of the mysterious standing stones of the Giant's Dance. With Britain in such chaos, Leodegranz had no choice but to trade his only bargaining chip, his daughter, in order to survive during the coming years of tumult.

Since Guenevere understood this, it was with some guilt that she stood here now, in her sacred place, with the intention of invoking the ancient goddess Brigid. She simply could not marry Melwas, especially not after her dream. She had seen the face of the man she loved, and even though she had never met him—

indeed, she was not even certain that he existed at all—she wanted no other man in her life.

Turning around slowly, her eyes closed, her hands raised in the ancient pose of supplication, she called out: "Brigid, great transformer, protector of women, you of the clear sight who has brought a vision of my true love to me, I call upon you to beg your help on this your day of greatest power...."

She did not know where the words came from. They just flowed out of her on a stream of emotion, resonating throughout her body and filling the sacred circle until the air was thick with magic.

"Bring my true love to me, you who are my mother and my friend. Make this a union that will harm none, but will bring joy and satisfaction to all, especially to my father, who has need of me...."

Just then she spied something shining in the brambles, shining so brightly that she was blinded by the flash of it. The thicket was very dense, and it was impossible even to see light behind it, so the sudden sparkle was more than mysterious. Momentarily forgetting her prayer, Guenevere picked up a stick and tried to part the thick thornbushes wide enough to get a better look at the gleaming thing behind it.

To her astonishment, the wiry branches cracked as if they were made of dry twigs. The stick in her hand, which was not particularly thick or heavy, chopped through them like the sharpest axe, until, standing before the object which had reflected such strong light, she dropped the stick and stood, awestruck, with trembling hands.

For before her, stuck into a piece of yellow rock just like the one that marked the middle of her circle, was a magnificent sword with a jeweled hilt and a blade that looked as if it had been made of pure starlight.

Backing up, feeling her heart beating wildly in her chest, she ran back to the castle to summon her father.

"Look!" she shouted, pointing as she ran toward the thicket. A number of men followed behind, amused. It was unseemly for a gentlewoman to run so excitedly, but young Guenevere was so ardent that even her mother's stern admonitions meant nothing to her. "Hurry, Father!"

The noblemen with him had come for the hunt following the short ceremony of watching the snake dart out of its cage, and were in a jolly mood. "Ho, Leo!" one of them called behind him to the portly and puffing chieftain. "I'd say young Melwas had better practice his paces if he's to catch that daughter of yours on her wedding night!"

Leodegranz was not laughing. Inwardly he was blaming his wife for raising such a daughter as Guenevere, who would mortify her family for the sake of a girlish lark. It occurred to him that, demon that she was, she may even have done this as a protest against marrying Prince Melwas. He knew she hated the idea. An effigy, perhaps, Leodegranz thought with mounting apprehension. Oh, Gods, what would he do if Guenevere had set up a scarecrow in a field with some object that identified it as Melwas?

He felt his bowels loosening. That was what came of having an only child who was a daughter. She had been spoiled from the beginning. She had no respect—

The chieftain nearly tripped over the men in front of him, who had come to a sudden halt.

"By the gods!" someone said. It was Lot of Rheged, the most ambitious of the ten kings of Britain. Already his hand was reaching out as he moved as if in a trance through the thicket toward the gleaming sword.

"The thing's not yours by right," said old Cheneus, who was by far the oldest of the tribal chiefs. He had kept his head long enough for the hair on it to grow white by being not only a good warrior, but a fair negotiator as well. "It's Leodegranz's land we're on."

"Aye, mine and the Cailleach's," Leodegranz huffed. "These are the ancient graves of Camlod we're trodding upon. 'Tis the gods themselves placed that sword in the thicket."

"More than a thicket, Father," Guenevere said. "It's stuck into a great rock."

At this, all the men rushed forward into the brambles, heedless of the thorns. But again, the thicket broke to pieces with a touch.

As the men moved through it, bits of thornbush and vine, dry as ash, flew about them in a virtual cloud.

Lot was in the lead, and broke into a run as he heard the others behind him. "It's no more than a sword," he said stoically, "and it'll go to him that takes it." With a small cry of triumph, he reached it, stumbling, and clasped both hands around its hilt.

But the sword did not budge. Lot tried again, grimacing, the veins in his neck standing out and he strained to remove it from the stone.

"This is someone's idea of a joke," he said irritably, drawing a dagger from its sheath around his waist and stabbing it roughly around the blade. "This is some kind of mortar, no doubt, with the sword placed inside it as a novelty. Is this your doing, Leodegranz?"

"It's not mortar," the chieftain answered. "Any fool can tell the difference between mortar and a rock. And get that dagger away, Lot. You'll break the bloody sword."

At that moment, the dagger snapped in two, the tip flying up to cut a deep gash in Lot's hand. With a curse, he stepped back.

"Father, look," Guenevere said, kneeling as she brushed lichen from the base of the rock.

Near the ground, where the stone had been broken, was a faint etching, nearly worn away by time, of a circle surrounded by radiant lines.

"A sun," old Cheneus said quietly. "Ancient symbol of the great king Macsen."

There was a stunned silence for some time, in which the chieftains barely breathed as each took in the meaning of the old chief's words.

Macsen was a legendary hero, a great warrior who had, it was said, once united all of England under his mighty sword. So great were his fighting skills that stone fortresses trembled at the very sound of his name, and the inhabitants of villages took to the hills at his approach.

In fact, such a leader had not existed; England had never been united under a single ruler, though many had tried. Even the most superstitious of men knew in his heart that the story was not possible, because he himself, his family, and his tribe, would never submit to a high king who ruled over the ten chieftains, no matter how powerful he was.

It was the nature of the independent Celts to rebel against all authority. That was why Britain had never submitted to Roman rule, despite centuries of domination. The English had accepted their lot, perhaps, but they had never, ever considered themselves to be Roman; and the instant that the Romans left, the Britons reverted to their old ways, even though many of those ways were patently inferior to the Romans'.

Nevertheless, in the weird circumstance in which the petty kings now found themselves, gathered around a mysterious stone on which was engraved a very old likeness of a sun, and from which, inexplicably, grew a magnificent sword, it did not take much for them to reconsider the merits of the Macsen story.

"No one knows what happened to his sword," someone volunteered into the silence.

"The gods kept it," someone else answered.

"And hid it until they were ready to choose a new high king."

"Aye," Cheneus said. "And they're ready now."

There was a massed, audible intake of breath. Yes, they all knew it. The gods were ready, and so were the kings. In the wake of the Roman occupation, England had become too difficult to rule in the old ways. The island was no longer simply a collection of farms and tribal strongholds. Great cities had come and gone, leaving in their wake a plethora of blessings and curses: Roads, bridges, new entertainments; and also disease, crime, decay, pollution, mass poverty, slavery, and war with invaders from lands outside of England as well as the ongoing battles among the tribes themselves.

The leaders of these tribes called themselves kings, but each of them knew what they really were: relics from a distant time who were unable to cope with the problems of an entirely new society. What was needed was . . .

Well, a miracle.

A miracle in the form of leader who could somehow make the whole country work together to keep the Saxons from conquering and obliterating England.

But who would consent to such a man? Which of the petty chiefdoms would give way and pay homage to another? And how long before the winning chief, the one to be deemed the high king, turned on the others, seizing their land and waging war for his own personal gain?

Only a leader appointed by the gods themselves would do.

And the gods were speaking now.

One among them, only one, would rise to save the ancient land of the Celts.

Leodegranz cleared his throat. "Well, it is my land," he said gruffly. "I imagine that makes the sword mine."

Cheneus shook his head. "Not unless you take it from the stone."

One of the young chieftains from the east pushed his way through the small crowd. "Or I do," he said, gripping the jeweled hilt. Then, shouting, "Christ be with me!" he held his breath and pulled so hard that one could see, even beneath his tunic, the bands of his muscles cording.

But he too failed.

"If you don't mind," Leodegranz said with great dignity, waving the young man aside. With a sniff of disdain, he placed his stubby-fingered, rather soft hands around the hilt. Secretly he thought two things: One was that, since he was clearly the one chosen by the gods to rule over the other kings, the sword would come out easily for him. The second was that the intricate metalwork of the hilt was damned uncomfortable.

After he withdrew, perspiring and embarrassed, and the others took their turns, old Cheneus gave him a wink. "There's no shame in not being able to take that sword, Leo," he said kindly. "As long as you remember to serve the one who does."

There were disgruntled noises all around. Even now, though they all believed they were in the midst of a miracle, the petty kings did not like the idea of giving over their power to anyone else. But the wiser among them knew that the only hope for them all lay in unity.

"We'll let the others try when they arrive," Leodegranz said, squinting up at the sun. "They'll be coming shortly."

The younger nobles squirmed and murmured. Each of them wanted a second chance at removing the sword. Lot actually did grasp it again, only to let it go with a series of muffled curses.

"What if the one who pulls it out is someone like Melwas?" the young king of Northumberland asked. "Must we then serve a fool?"

Leodegranz bristled. "Melwas is to marry my daughter!" he blustered.

"Unfortunately," Cheneus said, "that won't make him less of a fool."

Guenevere, long silent, could not quite suppress a rather unladylike laugh.

"But if he pulls the sword from the stone, I'll serve him nonetheless," Leodegranz said stolidly.

"Well, I won't. Unless I approve of this person who is to be our king, I'll challenge him with the full force of my army." This from Northumberland.

Lot struck a haughty pose. "That's true for me as well."

"It'd be true for you if the man were Macsen himself," Cheneus said dryly.

CHAPTER TWENTY-ONE

EXCALIBUR'S SONG

Not far away from the ancient graveyard where Guenevere had discovered the great sword, the household of another noble was making ready for the short journey to the lands of King Leodegranz to celebrate the festival of Brigid.

"Damn this thing!" Ector shouted, throwing his crossbow across the hall, where it hit the stone wall and splintered.

He winced. The bow was a copy of an old Roman weapon, and had never balanced well, but now it was beyond repair.

"Use mine, Father," his strapping son Kay offered.

They were both big men, of the type of Celtic stock which visitors often described as gigantic. Fair, ruddy-skinned, and prone to fits of temper, Ector and his son cut a swath wherever they went, although both were known for their good-heartedness and loyalty.

Even now, with Uther Pendragon dead without an heir, Ector, who served as head of Uther's army, had made no attempt to take over as king. He maintained iron discipline over his troops, whose loyalty had always been more to Ector rather than Uther, but used them only to keep away would-be usurpers.

He took Kay's bow with a grunt. "Don't know why we have to go to this blasted festival in the first place," he muttered. "The troops need drilling on holidays, too."

"We'll have a good time, father," Kay said good-naturedly, pulling on his jerkin. Though it was so cold in the moldy old stone house where they lived that the two were surrounded by a cloud of their own breath, neither of them noticed.

"Where's the damned food?" Ector boomed.

"I've got it, sir," his foster son called from the doorway.

"Well, don't be all day, Arthur. Get my sword."

"And mine," Kay added. "Since that's what I'll be using to hunt the boar."

Ector chuckled. "That I want to see," he said.

When Arthur brought his sword to him, Ector ruffled his hair the way he always did, as if he were patting a good dog. "By the gods," he said, his gaze following his own arm to the top of the boy's head. "Look how you've grown."

"Aye," Kay said with a wink. "Arthur's only a baby from the neck up now."

The boy blushed. He took Kay's remark as a compliment. Arthur had always admired Kay, whom he thought of as an older brother, since he had no recollection of ever living anywhere else. Ector made sure that the boy knew that he was only fostering with them, which meant that he had another family elsewhere, and that it was a noble one, since no one but nobles followed the practice. Unfortunately, he could not tell Arthur who his family—or even his father—was, since he did not know.

It was an exceedingly odd arrangement, and more than once Ector had cursed the druid who had brought the baby to his keeping. To add to the knight's burdens, Ector's wife had died two years after Arthur's arrival, leaving only himself and the twelve-year-old Kay to look after the child.

Ector was a soldier, accustomed to living roughly, and did not relish the idea of playing nursemaid to some druid foundling. That had become clear to Ector fairly early. If the boy were really the son of a noble, or even a petty king, as the holy man who brought him had indicated, then surely Ector would have heard from the family within two years. But there had been no word, either from the tribal chiefs or the druids at Mona.

A little sorcerer, no doubt, Ector had thought bitterly as the infant had toddled about the stone hall. The boy was probably some druid bastard conceived during one of their weird doings at the full moon. Ector pictured himself feeding and clothing the boy for twenty years, only to be rewarded by being turned into a frog. And there was nothing to be done about it, for to cross a druid was the most dangerous thing one could do. A man—any man, even a king—could do no more than kill you. But everyone knew that the druids of Mona, the great Merlins as they were called, the magical ones taught by a witch with no eyes, could pluck the very stars from the sky if they wanted to.

No, he would do exactly as the druid had instructed.

And so Ector raised the boy like his own—which was to say, in the manner of a soldier with no taste for luxury and little thought of homely comforts. If the child was as sickly as the druid had said he was, Ector thought, he'll die anyway. Even the druids could not fault a man if his child succumbed to the myriad deaths that lay in wait for tiny souls.

But the boy thrived in the austere atmosphere of Ector's world, and soon both he and his son found themselves completely taken by the little boy who had come into their lives. Arthur was bright, hardworking, and always cheerful. When Kay, because of his size and strength, had begun to practice with the army—a privilege which was afforded to no other boys his age, and therefore a source of great pride—he had brought the four-year-old Arthur with him to watch. And afterward, while he was practicing, Arthur served as a wildly appreciative audience, cheering his brother as Kay went through his paces with his wooden sword. There was no jealously between them, and indeed, for all their lives, the two men would remain fast friends.

As for Ector, very early on he ceased to wonder or even care who Arthur's real father was. The boy was welcome in his home and his life.

And so it was that on this day, on the morning of the festival of Brigid in the year 506, that the three of them set out to hunt wild boar on King Leodegranz's lands. They had delierately missed the ceremony of Imbolc, which Ector considered to be one of the sillier traditions of the aristocracy, of which he was not a member.

"Damn fools," he muttered as they approached the site of the ancient graveyard of Camlod. "The bones of great warriors are in this ground, and these fat kings are standing on them so they can watch a garter snake." He spat in disgust.

"Look on the bright side, father," Kay said pleasantly. "We're lucky to be invited. We never were before."

"Well, somebody's got to represent Uther, I suppose," Ector said. Both Kay and Arthur could detect the smallest hint of pride in his voice. They looked at one another and smiled.

"And don't forget, Arthur, you're to be squire to both of us."

Arthur beamed. It was a great honor, but typical of Ector, to bring along his foster child to such an occasion.

"Damn and blast, they're all standing about," Ector said, picking up the pace. "I hope they're not waiting for us." Sweat popped on his brow as the stocky man marched up the hill in military double-time.

At the crest of the hill, however, he found not a gaggle of rich men wasting time before a hunt, but a hushed and reverent assembly gathered around a sword which apparently grew out of a piece of solid rock.

"By Mithras," he said under his breath.

One of the princes—young Melwas, he thought it was, the pup with the soft face and vicious eyes—was kneeling before the sword, while King Cheneus of Dumnonia stood over him, incanting like a druid.

"Whoso pulleth this sword from this stone shall be rightwise named king of all England," he said.

Ector stopped short. "What?" he said aloud, his hands on his hips.

Several of the kings gave him a hard stare. Melwas ignored the interruption, rising serenely to grasp the sword's jeweled hilt. He gave a mighty pull. Spittle flew from his rubbery lips. His fair face grew instantly red and shiny.

"Damn it!" he shouted finally, releasing the thing with disdain. "No one can get that out of there! It's some kind of joke."

Old Cheneus gave the young man little more than a pitying glance. "Whoso . . ." he began.

"Oh, shut up!" Melwas snapped.

"Can anyone try?" Ector said suddenly.

A number of heads swivelled toward him. "Not you, if that's what you mean," Melwas said, still red-faced and irritable.

"And why not?" Cheneus asked, his chin jutting out.

"Ector?" Lot of Rheged said. "He's not a king."

"But he's got Uther Pendragon's army under his thumb, by the gods," King Leodegranz whispered to Dorcas of Northumberland, who stood beside him.

Dorcas nodded in agreement. "King or no, that one could wage war on us all if he gets a mind to, make no mistake."

"I'll not be led by a commoner!" Melwas shouted.

"We agreed that the gods would decide the matter," Cheneus said.

"Aye." Leodegranz waved the prince down. "It was agreed by all, including you. This is in the hands of the gods."

By this time Ector was quite embarrassed, having spoken before he'd had time to think. He hadn't meant to presume to be the equal of the kings; he'd simply wanted to try his hand at taking the sword from the stone.

"Go on, Father," Kay said, grinning. "You can do it." He bent toward Arthur and added, "He's surely the strongest of this lot, I'd say,"

"And the smartest," Arthur whispered, and they both laughed.

"Oh, well, no," Ector waffled good-naturedly.

"Please, sir," Leodegranz offered graciously, extending his hand.

Cheneus gathered himself into his new wise elder persona. "Whoso pulleth this sword—"

"Very well, very well," Ector said with relish, rubbing his hands together as he approached the sword.

"Do you suppose this is real?" Kay asked.

Arthur shrugged. "Perhaps it's part of the festival of Brigid."

Kay reddened. "If they've done this to mock my father, I'll . . ." His jaw clenched as Ector pulled and tugged, his barrellike arms bulging with effort.

"I cannot," Ector said at last, with the dignity of a soldier who had done his best.

Kay's body tensed, waiting for laughter, but there was none. "I suppose it was all right, then," he said.

"I'd like my boy to try," Ector announced from the rock.

Cheneus raised his eyebrows. Melwas and Lot scowled, but no one voiced an objection.

"Me?" Kay was stunned.

"Go ahead," Arthur prompted.

Kay stumbled toward the sword. With Ector beaming behind him, he tried to pull it from the rock.

And failed.

Afterward, he rubbed his sore palms. "Father," he said quietly, "do you suppose Arthur—"

Ector shook his head. He had ruffled enough feathers already. He wasn't about to rub the kings' noses in muck by proposing a teenage druid foundling of unknown parentage as their leader. "Come on down, Kay," he said. "We'll leave this matter to the nobles."

But below, something had happened. As Arthur watched Kay mount the hill, the sword embedded in the rock began to sing. It was an eerie, otherwordly sound, a song of distant stars, keening, mournful, surpassingly beautiful.

And then the sword spoke its name to him. One perfect word: *Excalibur.*

Arthur gasped. He looked around, certain that everyone had heard it, but not one face showed any response.

No, there was one face. Only one.

It was the girl's, Leodegranz's daughter, Guenevere, who had been standing silently near her father. At the moment when the sword spoke its name, she had lifted her head and her eyes had locked into Arthur's with a recognition both of them felt in the deepest part of their souls.

"Excalibur," he whispered; and as he did, Guenevere's lips formed the name along with him.

They are mine, Arthur thought. He blushed. He had no right to think any such thing. And yet he knew it to be true: Both the sword and the woman were meant to be his.

They belonged to him as much as the blood in his veins and, even then, he loved them both as much.

CHAPTER TWENTY-TWO

LONESOME ROADS

Emily began to choke on her chicken salad as soon as she saw the old man on television.

It was the same one, she was sure of it, the strange old man with the phony name.

She stood up, still hacking, and gestured toward the TV set. The waitress behind the counter paid no attention to her.

Taliesin, Emily thought as she strode across the restaurant, her napkin pressed to her lips. Yes, that was it, Taliesin. The name Merlin the Magician was supposed to have called himself in the legend of King Arthur. She had picked up on that as soon as she had met the old coot. Englishmen always assumed Americans were illiterate.

He had told her that he was a curator of the British Museum. Naturally, when she had called, her inquiry had been met with some amusement. Taliesin, you say? No, madam, I'm afraid there's no one here by that name.

What shame she had felt at being taken by such a blatant hoax!

But by then, of course, it had been too late. Arthur had already gone.

The television, still nearly silent, showed the old man frowning as a reporter spoke. Emily reached up and turned the volume up to full.

"Four years ago, a boy named Arthur Blessing was kidnapped off the streets of New York by a gang of motorcyclists. . . ." the reporter was blaring.

"For heaven's sake, it was nothing of the kind," the old man answered. Then he gave the newsman an exasperated look and stormed away into the crowd. The reporter tried to follow him, but apparently lost his quarry.

He disappeared, Emily thought.

She had seen him do it before. Vanish, right before her eyes. He had done that just before Arthur went off with Hal.

"The motorcyclists, who are apparently from England, would not reveal the whereabouts of the boy whose mesmerizing appearance on a news telecast covering a sinkhole in midtown Manhattan four years ago caused a nationwide uproar. Some who heard young Arthur Blessing speak believe that he is mentally ill and has been abducted. Others are convinced that the entire performance was a hoax. And yet others have speculated that the boy is some sort of messiah, after stunned viewers witnessed one of the most remarkable . . ."

"People are trying to eat here, you know," the counter waitress said. Casting Emily the dirtiest of looks, she set down a macaroni and cheese platter and then turned down the volume on the television to zero. The picture switched to footage of a fourteen-year-old boy standing amid the rubble of a collapsed building.

At that moment Gwen Ranier entered the diner. The sketchbook in her hands fell out of her hands to the floor. "Ms. B," she said, her voice quavering.

"What is it?" Emily asked irritably.

"Him," Gwen said, pointing at the television. "That's him. The one I dreamed about."

"Yes, I know," Emily said.

"Is . . . is he in some kind of trouble?" Gwen asked.

Emily swallowed. "I don't know," she said, and walked past her out the door.

The girl followed her. "Where are you going?"

"I'm going to get him back," she said.

She called the *Christian Science Monitor,* a publication which she felt would not seek to exploit her and Arthur, and promised an exclusive interview with herself in exchange for one favor: a reporter was to get a message to Hal Woczniak as quickly as possible.

The message said only:

Come immediately to Dawning Falls. Bring Arthur. Emily.

The rest of the message, which was that Emily had been searching for her nephew for eight years and that she would make sure that Hal was arrested and sent to jail on a more or less permanent basis unless he complied with her request, was tacit.

"He's . . . he's coming here?" Gwen asked. She had been sitting across from Emily as she conducted her business with the newspaper.

"I hope so," Emily said. She looked at the girl. "What did he say to you?" she asked.

"What?"

"In your dream. The one in which you saw his face."

Gwen turned the pages of her sketchbook carefully. "I had more than one dream," she said. There were at least ten drawings of Arthur, as a small boy, a teenager, and as a man older than Arthur Blessing was now. In all of them he wore odd clothing and his shaggy hair looked as if it had been cut with a knife. "I've seen him again and again," she said softly, looking at the portraits. "But each time he says the same thing."

"What's that?"

"That he's coming back for me," Gwen said simply. "He's coming back."

By the time they reached Buffalo County, South Dakota, Hal and the knights thought they had lost the last of the diehard news people. It was important that they be able to pick up Arthur and return to the farm unnoticed, unless they were prepared to pull up stakes yet again. If necessary, they would have ridden in circles for the next week; but the media had given up after less than fifty miles.

For the past several hours, the only vehicle that had shared the road with them had been a U-Haul with a baby carriage tied to its roof. Finally, a few miles west of Fort Thompson, they stopped at a diner so that the knights could eat and Hal could assess the damage done to his wound by the rigors of the road. His bandage was sodden with blood. Although he said nothing to the others about it, Hal was feeling every mile they had traveled since Rapid City.

He was sitting alone at the counter when the reporter from the *Christian Science Monitor* approached him.

"Christ, the guy in the U-Haul," he moaned.

"I've brought you a message," the man said, handing over the note he had copied, word for word, from his editor, who had copied it word for word from Emily Blessing.

Hal read it without expression.

"Is there a response?" the reporter asked eagerly.

Hal read it again. *Come immediately to Dawning Falls.*

She was alive. His heart was pounding. Emily had made it out of the burning hotel, after all.

He licked his cracked lips. "You going to print this?" he asked.

"Yes, sir. That's the deal. If I get it to you, we get to print it."

Then everyone and his brother would know where Arthur was. Who he was. Hal wondered if Emily knew what she was letting herself in for.

But then, he told himself, it wasn't as if she didn't have the right. She was Arthur's legal guardian, whose nephew had been taken away by a virtual stranger. It was a testament to Emily Blessing's good sense that she had not instituted a full-scale manhunt years ago. If she had, all three of them would have been dead by now.

Her timing was good. Better than good. Arthur was finally safe from the men who had been after him. What he wasn't safe from was publicity. In that, Emily might be able to help him more than Hal could. The knights were a target that could not bear much scrutiny.

And, like it or not, Hal's place was with the knights. They could not survive without him. Arthur could. Arthur would, in fact, be far better off if he were away from Taliesin's schemes and the knights' uneducable barbarism. With Emily, Arthur would one day be able to reclaim his life. And it would not be the vague and grandiose future the old man was so certain lay in wait for Arthur, but the normal future of a normal American, with a wife, a job, and the opportunity to think for himself. Arthur had never wanted more. He had certainly never wanted to be the reincarnation of a legend.

"There's another thing," the reporter said. "Miss Blessing said to tell you about her . . ." He looked down, embarrassed. "Her face. She thought you might not know."

"Her face?" Hal asked. "What about her face?"

The reporter swallowed hard. "I . . . um, well, I think she was in a fire or something. She's pretty badly scarred."

Hal felt himself go cold. She had burned. Burned, and he hadn't been there with so much as a kind word. How long had she been in the hospital? How often had she wondered, while she waited for the skin on her face to grow back, if Arthur was alive?

"Are you okay?" the reporter asked.

Hal looked up, startled. "Yeah," he said. "When's the story going to run?"

"Tomorrow. It won't be front page, though."

It wouldn't have to be, Hal knew. By the time they arrived, Dawning Falls would be a circus.

"Consider it your fifteen minutes of fame," the reporter said in an attempt at jocularity. "Now, if I might have a few words with you about—"

"Just get out of here," Hal said. "Please." Lugh, Dry Lips, and Agravaine stood up at once, brushing the crumbs from their mouths.

"Sure," the reporter said, moving swiftly toward the exit.

"We've got a new destination," Hal announced. He told the knights that they would be traveling eastward to deliver Arthur to his aunt in New York state.

"But the boy belongs with us," Kay objected.

"He belongs where he'll be safe," Hal snapped. "We can't do that for him anymore."

As he signaled for them to leave, he felt a curious sensation, something he had not felt in years. Not since he sat next to a woman in a yellow dress and tried to tell her that he loved her.

He wondered if Emily still had the yellow dress. He wondered if she had any recollection of that day, when there was so much possibility that Hal had truly believed that he might finally be, for the first time in his life, in the right place at the right time.

Who was he kidding, he told himself. From the cold tone of her message, Hal knew that Emily still regarded him not only as the kidnapper of her nephew, but also as the man who had betrayed her love.

Because he had. Their love was one of the things that had to be sacrificed to save the boy.

He touched the bandage beneath his shirt. A thin film of blood came off on his palm. The trip would be hard, but not impossible. They would arrive in Dawning Falls, hand over the boy, and say good-bye to them both.

That would be the impossible part.

Yet that, too, he would manage, he thought. He was doing this for Arthur. Because it was the boy's time now, not his own. Hal's time was long past.

Arthur trekked desultorily through the butterscotch-scented wilderness of ponderosa pines that made up the otherworldly forest of the Black Hills. Using the sun as a compass, he tried to maintain an easterly direction. Although it made no difference where he went, he wanted to avoid traveling in a circle.

Hal was no longer in danger, of that he was certain. The old man had helped; he always did. Had he heard Arthur's call? He probably had not needed it, anyway: Taliesin knew everything.

Arthur Blessing doesn't exist, he had said. According to the old man, Arthur had only been born to finish out the life of a king who had died sixteen centuries before. He would have no life of his own, no destiny other than what waited for that vanished, moldering king. Whatever you might do, that destiny will catch up with you.

But if that were true, Arthur thought, if his life was no more than a construct created by the old man in order to continue someone else's life, then why would he even want to find himself? He would be happy living as King Arthur Pendragon, wouldn't he? He moved on. Taliesin was wrong. He had to be. However Arthur had come into being, he was alive now, and he belonged to no one but himself. He repeated that over and over, trying to make himself believe it. But he knew that was not quite true.

Because the incident in New York was not the only time he had acted without quite knowing what he was doing. It was just the only time others had been aware of it. Several times during his life Arthur had seen people who had turned out not to be present at all, or had held conversations with people who had not existed outside of his imagination. On one occasion, he had even believed that he had communicated with the dead.

It had been a part-time farmhand who had died suddenly from a bee sting. The doctor in the emergency room said that the man, a Vietnamese refugee named Tran, had died of anaphylactic shock even before the ambulance arrived. It had been a terrible situation made worse by the fact that Tran had had no ID on him at the time of his death. No one knew where the man lived or who would claim his body.

Because the knights could not be trusted to exercise any sort of sensitivity in the matter, Hal had enlisted Arthur's help in making a street-by-street search of Murdo, the biggest town in Jones County, for someone who knew Tran. It had been the first time Arthur had been permitted off the farm since their arrival, and he had hoped to justify his new freedom with some success in the search, but neither he nor Hal had turned up anything.

Then, nearly three weeks after the death, long after Tran's body had been buried in the county graveyard, Arthur had a dream in which the deceased Mr. Tran told him that his family lived in

Minneapolis, Minnesota, at the Sterling Apartments on Hudson Avenue, and that he would require what he called a "prayer doll" in addition to the pay that was owed him.

Among Tran's personal effects were several items that were out of the ordinary, including a minuscule fan trailing pieces of folded colored paper and a tiny pouch made of gold cloth, but nothing resembling a doll. Arthur even looked inside the pouch to see if a doll might be inside, but found nothing except a mat of goat hair.

To say he had his doubts about this vision would have been an understatement. For one thing, Tran had spoken to Arthur in perfect English—a feat the living Tran, who knew only a few hundred words in his new language, could never have managed. Nevertheless, Arthur took Hal's truck in the middle of the night and drove 217 miles to the Sterling Apartments in Minneapolis, where he found a Vietnamese family named Tran living on the basement level. The nine residents of the apartment included Tran's mother, Minh, who worked in a candle factory within walking distance and spoke a little English.

Arthur had tried to communicate the news of Tran's death to her in simple but compassionate terms. He told her that her son's body had been decently buried and that his grave had been decorated with flowers in the American way.

"How you . . . know?" Minh had asked, unable to find more exact words for her question. But Arthur had understood.

"I had a dream," he said, and she had accepted this explanation.

After giving her the hundred twenty dollars owed to her son for his labors on the farm, he produced the plastic bag containing Tran's personal effects. Minh took it with trembling hands and looked inside.

"Is there a doll in there?" Arthur asked quietly, his face red with embarrassment.

Minh looked up through tear-glazed eyes. "Doll, yes." She held up the fan with its braided construction-paper tail. Then, sniffing, she picked up a pen and drew two lovely almond-shaped eyes beneath the fan, transforming it into the likeness of a dancing girl wearing a headdress.

"Face getting wear off," she said, trying to smile.

Arthur puzzled for some time about Tran's visitation. He never told anyone, and confronted Hal's questions about the unauthorized use of his truck with stony silence. In time the knights had convinced Hal that Arthur had simply wanted to kick up his heels; but Arthur had never explained.

It was not that no one would believe him. The knights would, without question. He could have told them that Elvis had come back in a rhinestone spaceship and they would have believed him, such was their loyalty. Even Hal, who had a lot of sense, managed to discard it when it came to Arthur. It was as if he, of all the people in the world, were somehow not subject to the laws of nature. If Arthur said something, then it must be so.

Perhaps this was why he had not told the knights about his clairvoyant dreams: because they would have believed him even if he were lying.

Nor could he attribute episodes like the one with Tran to simple insanity. That was the easy explanation, of course, the first level of weirdness in the multilayered parfait of impossibilities that was Arthur Blessing's life. If he ever wanted to learn the truth about himself, he knew, he would have to look beyond the pat answer of madness.

But if he weren't mad, Arthur thought, then what of the girl?

She had been coming into his thoughts more frequently than ever in the past few weeks. In her golden-haired guise, he even knew her name: *Brigid*.

Brigid. His nostrils flared at the mere thought of her name. *I will love you forever.*

How ridiculous! He shook his head. He had never even met this person.

And so he could only surmise, with great bitterness and resentment, that Brigid was a memory of the Other.

That was how he had grown to think of the glorious King Arthur whom Taliesin and the knights and even, at times, Hal, believed was so wonderful. Arthur Blessing did not find him wonderful. The Other had taken his life and his future away from him. It was as if had been adopted by people who had lost a son, and insisted that he behave exactly the way their beloved lost child had. He, Arthur Blessing, did not count in this strange universe of magic and timelessness. Nothing he liked, did, thought, said, wanted, shunned, or feared mattered a damn to any of them. Not only did they think he did not exist; they were dead certain of it.

But he was not. Not certain at all.

Beyond Jones County, beyond Puma Mountain and the Black Hills, was a whole world where no one cared if King Arthur had returned from the dead or not. There were, he would bet, a good number of people who had not even heard of King Arthur. Among them he would only be Arthur Blessing, and allow the Other to die and remain dead.

In the distance he heard a low, familiar rumbling. At first he tried to run, to seek a hiding place among the tall rocks. He ran into the shadows, covering his ears to block out the sound. But it only grew steadily louder, as he knew in his secret heart it would.

Whatever you might do, that destiny would catch up with you.

It had been foolish to think he could run away. Wherever he went, he would always be found. He would never escape the Other. He had been created to live out the life of another man, and nothing he could do would change that. The magic was just too strong.

As the first motorcycles pulled into view, he stepped out from behind the rocks and waited. Bedwyr waved, genuinely glad to see him. Curoi MacDaire and Lugh both greeted him with upraised fists as they roared nearer.

Only Hal, who stopped some distance away and removed his helmet, looked less than delighted.

Arthur walked the length of the motorcade to him. "Did Taliesin tell you where to find me?" he asked dully.

"Yes," Hal said. "I'm sorry, kid. It was worth a try."

Arthur mounted the motorcycle behind Hal. He did not speak again until after the incident that sealed Arthur's fate forever.

CHAPTER TWENTY-THREE

THE LOAVES AND FISHES

After the media blitz in Rapid City, the press became a permanent fixture on the motorcade. Occasionally Launcelot would cast a baleful glance at Hal, asking the unspoken question: *Why are you doing this to Arthur?*

This trip was in total defiance of Taliesin's directive to keep the boy in the midst of the knights, and he would be furious. Nevertheless, the knights could no longer assure Arthur's anonymity or safety, and Hal was prepared to face the old man. His only thought now was to get the boy to Dawning Falls, New York, without incident. As the news helicopter circled overhead, Hal knew that even this simple task would be more difficult than it seemed.

No one had expected Arthur's fame, which had flared into being one night four years before and then died away to nothing, to suddenly rekindle. It seemed that all America was suddenly terribly interested in the comings and goings of an eighteen-year-old boy.

Some were already calling him a new messiah; others denounced him as Satan, come with an army of evildoers on motorcycles.

It had always been like that with Arthur, Hal reflected. Through no fault of his own, the boy seemed to find his way into the very soul of his civilization. Arthur thought of himself as an ordinary American kid, and Hal had done his best to maintain that identity for him, but he had always been plagued with doubts about who Arthur Blessing really was.

Ever since he met Arthur, it had seemed that Hal's life had been pushed along on some predestined plan. He had thought only to keep the boy safe, to keep him anonymous, but that had not been possible. Arthur himself had told the world about his extraordinary past, which had reached beyond this lifetime, beyond this millennium. And now, strangely, instead of dismissing him as a charlatan or a fool, the boy was being believed, for good or ill.

It was all as if everything that was happening was meant to be.

Hal tried to dismiss these thoughts. Despite what Taliesin believed, Hal had always operated under the assumption that Arthur was nothing more than an ordinary kid, and that he deserved the same chance for happiness that every other kid had. And now everything seemed to be conspiring to take Arthur's anonymity away from him, pushing him into a role he had never consented to play.

Hal did not like the buzzing helicopters or the television cameras that followed them on their route, or the reporters that swarmed around them like insects whenever they stopped. He did not like the protesters with their placards calling Arthur names, or the screaming faithful, holding up talismans as they passed, or the infirm reaching out to them in desperation, as if the exhaust from their motorcycles could heal them of their ailments.

He looked back at Arthur. What had this boy done to both of their lives? What had he done, by doing nothing other than being born?

Launcelot's hand touched his elbow. Ahead of them lay a crossroads marked by an abandoned one-room church. This was where the crowd had gathered to wait for them.

They filled the four corners of land abutting the crossroads, sitting in folding chairs, playing cards, drinking beer from coolers scattered around the ground. They peered out of Airstreams and

Winnebagos, sheltering their eyes from the sun, or wiped the sweat from their faces with grimy cloths. Music from dozens of different radio stations competed discordantly as the knights approached and the crowd moved inexorably onto Route I-90 heading toward Sioux City.

Hal tried to swerve around them, turn around, but several hundred more seemed to dart out of the hillsides as they rode, making it impossible to escape.

Ambush, Hal thought. His eye caught Launcelot's. The knight was thinking the same thing. Were these people armed? Was the best course of action to abandon their bikes and fight? Overhead the helicopter swooped lower.

Hal was relieved. A massacre was less likely if the killers knew they were being recorded by television cameras. He signaled for the men to stop and told Launcelot to protect the boy. Then he dismounted, took off his helmet, and walked toward the waiting crowd.

They were poor, they said. Poor people gathered from the hard streets of Chicago and the other big cities of the Midwest, and from the shacks and rusted trailers of the countryside. A movement had begun in Chicago, where the magic of television had told them Arthur had been born, and the poor had come to welcome him home.

"Give us a miracle!" someone shouted, and after that the cry was almost continuous.

"He can't . . . listen, everyone . . ." Hal held up his hands, but it was no use. The crowd, hot and thirsty in the summer sun, did not want to hear what he had to say.

They wanted Arthur. They wanted a messiah, to make them happy. Beyond them, and on the other side of the mob, traffic had begun to back up. A lone horn sounded, followed by another.

Hal looked back at Launcelot, who stood with the others cross-armed on the highway in a protective circle around the boy. The pavement around them steamed with ground heat; the air around them waved, making the circle of muscular men seem like a mirage.

And then, out of the mirage, like a figure from a dream, walked Arthur.

The crowd broke into wild cheers. Some headed toward him, but the others held them back.

"No," Hal moaned, moving instinctively toward the boy, but Arthur held up a hand to stop him while he walked confidently forward.

Hal hesitated, then obeyed. The mass of people seemed to be managing itself, leaving space around Arthur.

Anxiously, Hal ran his hands through his hair. Every nerve in his body was on full alert. This was precisely the situation he'd hoped to avoid: having Arthur surrounded by a mob of people demanding that he make their wishes come true. All in the middle of a snarl of traffic on the hottest day of the year, while television cameras moved in from all directions to capture every moment of the debacle.

Arthur raised his hands, and the crowd quieted. But before he could speak, a breeze began to blow. An audible sigh of relief rose from the people standing on the hot pavement. The waves of heat that had given the knights a surreal appearance vanished. Then, within less than a minute, the sky darkened and filled with fast-moving clouds.

Hal moved back to join the knights. He planned to disperse them through the crowd. They all knew that their prime directive was to protect Arthur at all costs. Hal did not like to see the boy so vulnerable.

"Bit of luck, this weather, eh?" Curoi MacDaire said, gesturing skyward with his eyes. "Could have got ugly, this lot."

Indeed, the crowd was now comfortable and good-natured, no longer insisting on a miracle, but waiting courteously for whatever was to come.

But what could that be? Hal thought, panicking. Whatever he might have been in another life—and even now, even with the presence of the knights and Taliesin's wizardly, Hal was still not certain that any of that meant a damn, anyway—Arthur was not even a man yet, let alone a king. These people were expecting too much.

He gave Launcelot the word to move the men into the crowd slowly, so not to frighten anyone. They did, gradually widening the circle around Arthur, who was still standing with his arms upraised and his eyes closed.

And then, in the silence, a soft rain began.

"Thank God," Hal said. People were unlikely to riot in the rain. They would soon disperse, and the whole thing would be over. It was time to think about an alternate route, though, Hal noted.

Launcelot was staring at him. "What's up?" Hal asked.

The big knight said nothing, but his eyes never left Hal's.

"You're not thinking . . . Arthur didn't do this, Lance. Keep yourself together."

At that moment a truck carrying twenty thousand bottles of designer water which had just been bottled at its source in northern Illinois crested the hill. The truck's driver, completely unprepared for the tangle of traffic in what was usually an empty stretch of road, stomped on the brake and skidded out of control on the rain-slicked pavement. He careened squarely into the back of another truck, a semi filled with North Atlantic smoked salmon. The point of impact was the refrigeration condenser, which immediately turned the metal container of the semi into an oven. To make matters worse, the semi had jackknifed to the side, crashing in turn into the vehicle immediately to its right. This, too, was a truck, a bakery truck whose back doors flung open as hundreds of bags of America's Best Bagels flew out into the crowd.

The recipients of the bagels jubilantly raised their prizes in the air, and an atmosphere of jollity immediately took hold.

"The food literally rained down from the sky," a smiling television reporter said into a camera, trying to speak loudly enough to be heard over the incessant claxoning of the halted cars. The reporter in the helicopter announced that police were on their way to detangle the traffic, but already the irate drivers were leaving their cars to threaten the assembled pedestrians, and particularly Arthur.

It all might have become awkward again, had it not been for the driver of the salmon-carting semi, whose curses rose above the rest of the din as he threw large salmon carcasses out of the sweltering truck.

"Pigshit!" he howled. A motorist who had just exited his car to complain caught a fish in his arms. It was fragrant, but not yet stinking.

"Lox!" he shouted.

A bagel-bearer rushed toward him.

Thus did the feast begin. Before long, everyone, including the horn-honking motorists, was partaking of what the reporters called "manna," but which really would have been a quite standard deli breakfast with the addition of a *schmear* of cream cheese. The man carrying the bottled water donated his entire load, having been directed on the phone by the company's vice president of marketing to do so. With all the television cameras in attendance, the generous gesture would advertise his company's product more effectively than a massive campaign.

It took the police more than an hour to clear the traffic. Even so, hundreds remained on the sides of the road, watching the young man who had never moved nor spoken a single word. Even the police, following some instinct about crowd control, had not touched Arthur Blessing.

After the roadway was clear, Arthur walked back toward the circle of motorcycles. It was still his custom to ride behind one or another of the knights, as he had since he was a child. Although it was never spoken, whomever Arthur chose to ride behind felt as if he had been conferred an honor. The knights all stood beside their bikes, eyes forward, hoping that he would choose them. Fairhands, the youngest of the lot, stepped forward as Arthur approached.

"Take it, Highness," he said. "I will ride behind you, or with one of the others."

Arthur smiled genially and straddled the seat. "Thank you," he said.

The crowd parted for them as they left. In their wake was a sea of waving hands.

Launcelot lagged behind, paying no attention to the people who followed him as he walked toward the abandoned church. They were shouting questions at him, questions about Arthur, no doubt, although their words were no more than muted sounds to him.

All he saw, all he knew or felt in the rawness of his bones, was the church.

It was a humble enough structure, to be sure, with its flat-painted, finger-stained doors and its spindly aluminum cross sticking out of its rooflike an antenna; but to Launcelot, it was a wonderful building. He had seen great cathedrals during his time in twenty-first century America, but they had meant no more to him than the gigantic skyscrapers of Manhattan. That was to say, they did not touch Launcelot's view of reality.

He had accepted the fearsome oddities of the New World with the resignation of a man who was being punished for a great sin. For that was what he felt himself to be, an audacious, blackhearted example of human degradation who had been relegated to a special hell.

All the world—no, worse than that, all of history—knew what he had done with the queen, the wife of the king to whom he had pledged his life. He deserved to suffer for that, and he had. His punishment had been to submit to the magic of an evil sorcerer who was leading him through an alternate world of unimaginable horror. There were buildings big as mountains here, and headless horses with mechanical hearts. There were places like the great stone block from which Hal had been rescued, where one's arms and legs were routinely sawn off. Under the ground were huge rumbling snakes called subways that devoured anyone foolish enough to venture down the many stairways leading to the netherworld.

And yet in the midst of these dreadful surroundings, he occasionally saw things that made him remember his life on earth with painful piquancy.

Such was the Church of the Lord's Fellowship, which stood at the crossroads where so many had gathered to see the young king. It resembled a church Launcelot might have seen during his own time, a grand church compared with the beehive-shaped wattle huts where most of the Christian holy men in Britain lived. This church could not have existed in Britain, of course; but in Gaul, where Launcelot had spent his boyhood, the Christians had made deeper inroads. There were great churches like this in Gaul, where thirty or forty people at a time raised their voices in prayer to the invisible God who had lived as a man and died in humility and pain.

The sight of it had filled him with awe from the first. But then, after the miracle of the loaves and fishes . . .

That was something that still puzzled him. The others had not noticed, naturally; most of them were pagans with no knowledge of the New Religion. But Launcelot was a Christian, the only one of the Round Table knights to have come converted into Arthur's service. He was familiar with the story of the Messiah who had fed multitudes.

What he did not understand was why it had happened again, and here, of all places. Launcelot's Christ was a distant being, a figure from centuries past who had lived in a faraway, almost myth-ical land. That these people would try to reenact the biblical story with Arthur at its core seemed to him to be both sacrilegious and bizarre.

Hesitantly he approached the entrance to the church. There was so much he needed to know, so many questions. Why had they all been brought to his place with Launcelot? Some of the knights, like young Fairhands, had done no real evil at all in their lives. Had he been summoned from the Summer Country simply because he had known a sinner like Launcelot? Was God so unfair?

And Arthur. What on earth was Arthur doing here, and at such an age? He had been a great king, yes. And his pulling the sword from the stone had become the stuff of legend. But why had he come back? To produce miracles replicating those of Christ?

Whose work was this, God's or Satan's?

Launcelot needed to pray. He reached for the door.

It had been bolted with a metal device. *Not for you,* the door seemed to say to him. The church would accept sinners, but not suicides.

No, of course the doors would be locked, the knight thought. This was hell, and God did not dwell here.

Launcelot mounted his motorcycle and roared down the road to join the others.

CHAPTER TWENTY-FOUR

A STAR IS BORN

In Grenoo, Louisiana, Mary Faith and Ruth Ann Newcastle looked over at one another from above their glasses. Mary Faith turned down the volume on the television.

"The loaves and the fishes," she said.

Her sister patted her white hair pensively. "Do you think it matters that it was Jewish fish?"

"Jesus was Jewish," Mary Faith said.

"Oh, dear, yes." Ruth Ann fanned herself with the *TV Guide*. "What do you suppose it tastes like?"

Mary Faith sniffed. "Wouldn't know, and wouldn't care to know," she said.

On a farm near Jacksonville, Texas, an African American family consisting of five adults and ten children all got on their knees.

"Hallelujah," the matriarch said. Her name was Martha.

Her youngest son, Roland, an entertainment lawyer who practiced in New York City, had been about to refuse to participate in

Martha's call to worship, but his wife had smiled and touched his elbow. Go ahead, her eyes told him. She's your mom.

"Thank you, Jesus," Martha intoned.

"Thank you, Jesus," the others repeated.

"He's not Jesus," Roland said. "His name is Arthur, or some damn thing. Yes, Arthur, as in King Arthur, which he thinks he is. I can't believe we're all here on our knees in front of the television set adoring some Marjoe white bread con artist."

His mother narrowed her eyes at him. "Don't you start," she rumbled, her massive forearms flexing beneath her shawl. She looked back at the television.

"Shut up, Roland," his brother Tony said placidly. Tony had remained in East Texas to work the farm. He weighed 450 pounds and bench-pressed over six hundred.

Roland grew silent.

"The Messiah don't have to be black," Martha said.

"If he was, he'd be sent to jail," Roland muttered under his breath.

"Shut up, Roland," Tony said.

In Minneapolis, Minnesota, Minh Tran bowed three times before the prayer doll left to her by her dead son. The boy who had brought the doll to her was in need of her prayers.

Slowly she rolled her ivory prayer beads between her palms and began the long chant whose words had been transliterated centuries ago from ancient Sanskrit writings.

Minh did not understand the words of the chant, but that did not matter, since the words and their meaning were of no importance. It was the sound of the prayer itself that held the magic. Through her chant, she would set up the vibration of a holy thought that would travel through space and envelop the quiet American boy who had once driven so far to tell Minh that her son had died.

Before she began the ritual of the chant, she had been watching the television, on which the boy had appeared, surrounded by a nimbus of light. Minh had only seen such a light once before, when she had been a very young child in Saigon.

The light had appeared around a monk who was buying a papaya from a street vendor. Minh had watched him shyly from around the corner of a building. He spotted her and smiled as she ducked behind the crumbling stones. In those days Minh had been afraid to speak to anyone. She had awakened one morning to find her mother lying dead, her face red as a demon's and her tongue cut out. Minh had fled, screaming, and for three days she had lived on the street, hiding from whomever might have come into the apartment where she and her mother had lived and then taken nothing but her mother's tongue.

By the time she saw the monk, she was dizzy with hunger. And so she was surprised and delighted when she peeked again from behind the building to find the papaya, freshly cut and waiting for her.

After she ate the papaya, the monk, who was still a young man, picked her up and carried her to a weeping woman whom Minh would come to call her mother, although she would always remember that her real mother had died without her tongue, and that no one had ever found out who had killed her, or why.

All of Vietnam was in chaos then, with soldiers and businessmen and criminals from everywhere filling the streets of the city, getting drunk and finding women and laughing, while just outside the perimeter of lights they were cutting one another with knives and shooting bullets into village children. Some said that the Americans were the barbarians; others, the French. Still others blamed the northerners, who had embraced the ways of the Chinese and turned their backs on sacred things and the ancient Buddhist chants.

But the monk had believed that they were all wrong, that everyone who lifted a hand in violence insulted the gods and brought shame upon all humanity.

At least that was what he said before he sat down in the middle of the Street of Plum Blossoms and recited the short poem that was the summation of his life and thoughts. Later, Minh would understand that he had chosen that particular street for his final act of humanity because the flower of the plum tree blooms even in snow, but she never heard the poem, because the woman to whom she had been given turned away then, sobbing loudly and trying to cover Minh's eyes and ears as she ran down the street with bouncing short steps.

But before she was taken out of sight of the monk, Minh saw the glow around him once more, and it was brighter than before, a halo of light that nearly blinded the girl as she watched the young man in the process of accepting his death.

When she heard the *thwoop* of flames as the monk immolated himself and the gasps of the other people on the street, Minh turned around and for a moment, before the weeping woman pressed Minh's face into her chest to prevent her from watching, saw the monk sitting calmly in the midst of a gasoline-fed fireball. But the aura around him was stronger than ever then, diminishing even the flames that surrounded him.

Since that day Minh had chanted for him, sending the sound of her prayers to whatever realm the monk now dwelt, believing him to have been one of the true holy beings alive at any given time on the plane of earthly life.

But for today, she would chant for the boy who had brought rain and food to the people on the road. Because he, too, had a wide aura of light around him. Like the monk in Saigon, his life was burning too brightly, and would soon be extinguished.

Titus Wolfe watched the last minutes of the broadcast from the bar of the Bluejay Motel. At the far end, near the restrooms, Pinto played intently on a pinball machine.

Pinto had left him reasonably alone. That was something in his favor. He spoke little, and fended for himself. Titus had no idea where Pinto got any money—stole it, he supposed—but he seemed to have some, at least enough to feed himself. Titus saw little of him during the evening, when he himself stayed in the motel room, out of sight until his wound healed. Pinto only returned to sleep, smelling of beer, and Titus asked no questions.

Meanwhile, Titus's entire appearance had changed. Aside from his dark hair with its artificial bald spot, his moustache, and the overbite provided by the dental appliance in his mouth, he had also made a point of eating as much as he could. Already the contours of his normally sculpted, almost gaunt face had filled out a little. Nothing changed one's appearance like weight gain. Within three months he would be unrecognizable.

It would take at least that long for the panic in Cheyenne to die down. That was all right. There was plenty of time to get back to the missile silos. The important thing now was to get out of the country.

But that, too, would have to wait. *Sea Legs* was not scheduled to dock in Atlantic City for another two weeks. Titus had confirmed the pickup through an internet connection with the Coffeehouse Gang made at the public library. The captain of the boat would not jeopardize his operation by changing his schedule. It was up to Titus to avoid capture until the appointed time.

Fair enough. Who was the Fed, he had wanted to know. The one who had been shot and hospitalized.

The answer had come within four minutes: Hal Woczniak, former FBI agent. During his truncated hospital stay, he had met twice with current agents.

Titus did not ask for any more information. The Coffeehouse Gang would already know that Woczniak had given Titus's description to the Feds. Now they would be watching Titus. The FBI would not catch him alive, he knew. Lucius Darling and his network would never permit that.

So it was important that he make the rendezvous with *Sea Legs*. But that was two weeks in the future. Between now and then, a great deal could happen.

He was about to order another drink when the television screen filled with the image of a huge crowd assembled on I-90. The scene showed a motley group of people, some chowing down on the salmon and bagels that had spontaneously been offered, some on their knees and in a state of bliss.

"Assholes," a patron of the Bluejay Lounge said.

"Yeah, some people'll do anything for a free meal."

"They want to be on TV, that's all it is."

Then came the angry motorists, the frustrated policemen, and the men on motorcycles who looked nervously toward the boy who was at the center of it all.

"And him!" a bleary-eyed fellow working on his third boiler-
maker huffed, pointing to Arthur Blessing's image on the screen.
"You'd think the little shit was God Almighty, the way they go on
about him."

"Drugs," someone offered by way of explanation. "Got to be on
drugs."

"Yeah. Kids today, you can keep 'em."

"Oh, they're all into it."

As the traffic began to disperse, one of the boy's motorcycle
escorts walked over to him and stood silently. It was Hal.

The Fed, Titus thought. And then: *Is the FBI protecting this boy?*

The newscaster was giving the destination of the entourage as
Dawning Falls, New York. Oddly, Titus, who had spent little time
in the United States, knew the town.

He had spent a few weeks there during his Coffeehouse Gang
days. A rich classmate at Oxford had once taken him along on
holiday to Manhattan as a lark. There Titus had met a beautiful
young artist—she'd had an odd name, something to do with food,
as he recalled—who had kept an arsenal of humorous stories about
the small town where she had been raised.

Meeting her had been the end of Titus's association with his
fellow student and benefactor. The sod had turned out to be a
poof, anyway, and was spending his evenings buggering boys in
Greenwich Village. Titus had left Manhattan within two days of
his arrival to sport with the pretty girl in the anonymous little
village she had described so vituperatively. In her charming apartment above the local bakery, they had enjoyed an idyllic fortnight.

The girl had possessed the one quality which Titus deemed es-
sential in a woman: She had expected nothing from him. It had
been understood from the beginning that Titus (who had given
her a false name, as he usually did in these circumstances) was
only interested in a bit of fun and would be gone from her life
quick as a blink, and the lovely lady had accepted those terms. He
had liked that about her. Oh, what the devil was the bird's name?

Now apparently there was something new in Dawning Falls, he'd
heard from the TV reports covering the teenage messiah—the
Yanks would do anything to make their blood pump a little fas-

ter—some sort of magical well where all your dreams came true. An incredible fantasy, he thought, even for a country where greed was the national pastime.

Ginger, that was it. Ginger something or other. Beautiful black hair. She painted portraits or something. And had been great in bed. She'd probably gone on to marry the town banker or some such. She would be a portly matron by now, with a dyed helmet of hair and three chins.

The next item on the news was about the ongoing search for the terrorist known as Hassam Bagat. The FBI had received information that the terrorist may recently have been in the vicinity of Rapid City, South Dakota.

Titus shivered. They knew. The Hassam Bayat nonsense was for the press. Their former colleage, the one who had seen Titus's face, had told them to look for a blond Caucasian who would almost certainly try to disguise his appearance.

He would have to get out of the Midwest now. Pinto was a liability, but Titus still needed the thug to drive.

Calm, calm. It would be fine, he told himself. This was a big country. It would not be so easy to find him. There was, after all, only one man who could link Titus's face with his occupation.

Hal Woczniak.

Titus felt his heart beating. How difficult would it be to kill one man on a motorcycle?

The FBI were doubtless following the former agent. They had removed him from the hospital as soon as they realized how easy it would be to kill him. And they would expect an attempt on the road.

But what about afterwards? From what he had just seen, this boy messiah was picking up new converts by the minute. By the time he reached Dawning Falls, there would be thousands of people crowding into the town to catch a glimpse of him.

The boy would be the one the Feds were watching then, not his bodyguard. Besides, there would be too many people about to guarantee anyone's safety.

Especially against a man with the skill of Titus Wolfe.

He looked up over his glass, caught Pinto's eye, and made a

small gesture with his head. Pinto left the pinball machine immediately and headed for the door.

Useful, Titus thought. Pinto would still be useful for a time. As he rose, he cast a final glance at the television. Hal was still visible in the corner of the screen, mounted again on his motorcycle, looking around slowly and suspiciously.

God, why couldn't I see he was a Fed? Titus berated himself. The man couldn't have been more obvious if he were wearing a sign.

Oh, well, it hardly mattered now. He tossed a few dollars onto the bar. Within a few days the man would be dead, and Titus would be on his way to Panama.

Hal looked ahead at Arthur, who seemed to be handling the bike without a problem. Fairhands, riding behind the boy, gave the thumbs-up sign. With a signal, Hal sent two of the knights to ride at the head of the phalanx. There was no way Arthur was going to be point man. Not with all the nuts Hal had seen since this journey began.

And it was only going to get worse. What the hell was going on, he wondered. The thing with the bread and fish was a coincidence, for God's sake. People were ready to believe anything.

But what had really been strange was Arthur's behavior. It was as if he had expected it all to happen.

Maybe Arthur had even enjoyed it, Hal thought. He was a kid who had been virtually locked up for years with a bunch of doofuses who treated him literally as if he were the king of the world. Maybe it all just went to his head.

But Hal knew that wasn't true. Arthur never did anything to court attention. It just came to him because he was special, and always had been.

Hal hated living like this. He hated what was happening, hated it so much that every day he thought about just walking away from it. A part of him believed what Taliesin was always telling him, that all this madness was just part of Arthur's destiny, and that whatever happened was meant to happen, regardless of what Hal said or did. There were times when Hal looked at each winding, empty road with longing, picturing himself peeling off the pack and finding his way to some hick town where he would get a job in a garage and forget he ever knew a kid named Arthur Blessing.

But he never did leave. Every day, when he made the decision to stay, he felt himself growing sick with anxiety.

But he stayed.

CHAPTER TWENTY-FIVE

THE PROCESSION TO THE
SANCTUARY

Some people were actually waving palms. More than a thousand of them had come to the Sanctuary at Dawning Falls. Some had made pilgrimages of hundreds of miles just to see the boy whom the press was calling the new Jesus.

"I don't like this," Hal said to Launcelot as they rode into town.

Launcelot looked about him, astonished. "Is it not enough that the boy is their king?" he asked.

"I don't know whose idea this is, but it isn't going to do Arthur any good," Hal said, riding forward to search the crowd.

There were going to be crazies among this bunch, Hal knew. Any issue smacking of religion brought out the fanatics on both sides of the issue; but a story about a teenager who acted like Jesus Christ was going to attract every lunatic within a hundred-mile radius. Before long the churches were going to start objecting—and not to the press, who started it all, but to Arthur himself. That was how the media worked. They stirred up what they called controversy and others called hatred and then, when the people in the center of the story were thoroughly ruined, they lost interest and went after another story.

The problem was, just about everyone here was some kind of nut. How was he going to tell the benign nuts from the violent ones?

Had he stood face to face with Titus Wolfe, Hal would not have judged the man to be either a benign or a violent nut. He looked, in fact, like ninety percent of the males there. He was dressed in jeans, a Buffalo Bills T-shirt and a baseball cap worn backward. He wore sunglasses. His feet were shod in white sneakers. He held a can of Coca Cola.

He had already been inside the old farmhouse which served as the administrative office for the Miller's Creek enterprise. It had not been difficult to get in. The lone security guard—a very old man—had not even seen Titus slip away from the crowd gathered at the well and walk up the back stairway to the upper floor of the building.

The place had not offered any clues about either the boy or the so-called healing water. Not that Titus had expected to find any. Any information worth knowing would not be kept in some ramshackle building without so much as a burglar alarm. Inside, there were no expensive paintings on the walls, no gift shop. The office itself held no more than a couple of cheap desks and typist's chairs, some metal file cabinets, an old electric typewriter such as could be bought in any pawn shop for twenty dollars, and a few molded plastic chairs for visitors. Hardly the thing to attract thieves.

It probably would not even have mattered if he had been discovered, although he made sure to exit the place unnoticed. The place was so loose. The woman who was acting director was outside waiting for the boy—the one Titus had come to think of as the Christ Child—with a bouquet of flowers and a welcoming committee.

He spotted Pinto near the back of the assembled crowd, his arms crossed in front of him. As Titus watched, Pinto slowly made his way toward the roadway where the boy and his motorcycle escort would be approaching.

Titus had done a fairly decent job of cleaning him up. Pinto now sported a small goatee. His hair had been cut neatly, and he was wearing a plaid shirt in place of his usual filty leathers. Titus had told him to keep his mouth closed, literally. As long as no one saw his teeth, Pinto would be difficult to identify.

The gun and silencer he carried were concealed inside his boot.

Pinto watched Hal from a safe distance, although he thought he could discern the cop-smell of him even from where he stood. He knew how to avoid the notice of those in authority: The point was not to move much. Cops looked for moving things—hands, eyes, scared feet on the run. It was important to stay cool, still as a statue if you could do it, casual if you couldn't. He kept his hands in his pockets. Titus had told him not to smoke or chew gum, and he was uncomfortable with that, but he could keep it up long enough to do this job.

It wouldn't take long, and there was a wad of money in it. Titus had bucks, that was for sure. Pinto supposed he could just kill him and take it, but why bother, if the English prick was willing to share it so willingly? Besides, the guy was a good car thief. They'd gone through six or seven already. It didn't take Titus but a minute to boost one. He had a gizmo, some electronic thing, and didn't even need to hotwire, although he could.

The guy definitely had his amazing aspects. Like how he changed how he looked so totally, and inside of a half hour, except for the eating. Hell, who thought about *eating* to change your looks? But it worked. He wondered how fat Titus would be by the end of summer.

They wouldn't be together that long, though. There was something about Titus that was . . . well, dangerous. That was a funny word, Pinto thought, coming from him. Oh, he was dangerous, too, no question about that, Pinto was plenty dangerous. Just ask any cop who'd ever met him. But Titus, he was something else. So smart, yet he'd still kill his own mother between dinner and dessert. That was why it wasn't worth it to try to rip off Titus. Better let him pay you. He was good for it.

Out of the corner of his eye he saw Hal. The pig was looking around in that cop way, mean-eyed, obvious.

Well, that wasn't going to last much longer, Pinto thought, holding still. Before long, those pig eyes were going to be staring straight up at the blue sky.

The press had begun to refer to the house, for reasons known only to them, as the Sanctuary. It was hardly that for Emily, who waited miserably in the spot appointed to her by the mayor's office. The Chamber of Commerce had assembled a wooden platform with steps for her to stand on. A local radio station had given her a bouquet of three dozen roses to present to Arthur upon his triumphant entry into Dawning Falls.

The roses were overwhelming. After ten minutes of sweltering in the August sun with her arms tired from the sheer weight of the flowers and their heady scent in her nostrils, she was about to toss them onto the ground when she spotted Gwen walking through the crowd toward her.

It took Emily a moment to recognize her. The girl had washed off her freakish makeup, and pulled her hair back with a headband of green grosgrain.

"Gwen!" she began "What . . ."

"Don't, Ms. B." Gwen's cheeks were blazing with embarrassment. "I've already been through this with my mother. I just didn't have time to do my face, okay?"

Emily smiled and shook her head. "Fine. Do you think you could take these roses? My nose feels as if it's full of bees."

Awkwardly Gwen climbed on the platform and scooped the flowers out of Emily's arms. Even her clothes were different, Emily noticed. Instead of her usual black T-shirt, Gwen was wearing a pretty blouse with ruffles and pintucks. Over it she wore a long green silk duster that covered her jeans.

"This was my mom's," she said, plucking at the duster. "I found it in an old box in the attic."

"It's lovely." Emily touched the girl's hair. "You look like a beauty queen."

"Especially with these," Gwen said, holding up the flowers.

Emily smiled wanly. "Aren't they awful?"

"This whole thing is awful," Gwen agreed. "That's why I came. I thought you might need moral support."

"I need a brain transplant," Emily moaned. "How could I have allowed this to get so out of control? Look at these people!"

"Smile, girls!" A photographer took their picture.

"Please go away!" Emily had tried to sound cold and commanding, but her voice had quavered.

Ever since the *Christian Science Monitor* had run the story about Arthur's destination, the media had been relentless. Apparently the combination of Arthur's mysterious past, his abduction by foreigners, the healing waters of Miller's Creek, and the legend of King Arthur were irresistible news fodder.

And, of course, there was Emily's face to add yet another dimension to the story. Arthur's long-lost aunt was never more than a footnote to the news stories about the miracle-making boy, but her appearance seemed to be a subject of concern to the media nonetheless. The major papers and television networks tried not to show her likeness, since the image of such an ugly woman ran counter to all the romantic things they were inventing about Arthur. The tabloids, though, enjoyed smearing pictures of Emily's melted-mask features over the pages of their publications. "Messiah's Monster Mom," read one particularly coarse—and inaccurate—headline.

The townspeople of Dawning Falls had gone to great lengths to express their support for Ms. B, who had long ago ceased to be a freak in their eyes. Nevertheless, the attention they gave her was painful. As she stood on the platform waiting for Arthur, she had to force herself to keep her head held high as an endless stream of strangers with cameras took her picture.

She deeply regretted having made the deal with the *Monitor,* and not just because of the exposure she had brought to herself. She was sorry she had made such a demand of Hal, who had been doing an excellent job of safeguarding Arthur from the certain harm of publicity. Realizing the position in which she was placing her nephew, she wished she had never begun her search for Arthur in the first place.

He had never been meant to stay with her, she thought, too late, feeling sick in her heart at the danger in which she knew she was placing him.

"The boy whom the faithful are calling the new messiah is headed for Dawning Falls, the small town in upstate New York which is the location of what some believe to be a healing spring," a reporter was saying into a microphone nearby.

Messiah?

The whole idea of it was ridiculous, more than ridiculous. How could anyone even think such a thing? She remembered Arthur as a little boy, with scraped knees and fevers. A normal boy.

Normal, but not ordinary. She bit her lip. Because she had always known that Arthur was not like other children. From the beginning there had been something of the ascetic about him, something pared down and finely textured, as if the world could not stick to him.

And then the cup had come into their lives. The cup had started everything.

Arthur had found the cup when he was still a child. Together they had discovered its miraculous properties. He had never wanted it, though, despite the power it might have conferred on him. That was why the cup was now at the bottom of a well encased in cement.

Because no one else should have the cup. Its power was too strong. A lesser being would be tempted—no, more than tempted, because its pull was irresistible—to use the cup for selfish ends. Oh, its owner would vow at first to use it only for good, for the welfare of all humanity. But in the end, whoever owned the cup would want it for himself. That was its nature, and the nature of human beings.

Two signs came into view above the heads of the milling crowd. One read SATAN. The other, ANTICHRIST.

Emily turned to Gwen. "How did you get here?" she asked.

"Bike."

"Could you . . ." She hesitated. "Do you think you could do a favor for me?" Emily was blushing. She did not like to ask favors of anyone.

"Anything, Ms. B," Gwen said.

"I'd like you to meet Arthur before he gets here. They'll be traveling eastbound."

Gwen looked down Germantown Pike. It was all but impassible, jammed with people as if it were a fair. "No problem," she said. "What do you want me to tell him?"

"Just to be careful. I didn't expect . . ." She opened her hands. ". . . this."

Gwen felt a wave of pity for the woman. Standing in front of all these cameras had to be hard for her. Her personal reuinion with her nephew had snowballed into some tacky festival. All the place lacked was a marching band, and the only reason it wasn't blaring right now was because Emily had nearly screamed in horror when the mayor had mentioned it. "Don't worry about anything," Gwen said, tossing the roses into the crowd, where one of the tourists took it upon herself to distribute the flowers among the assemblage. "It'll all be over soon."

As Gwen pedaled her bicycle past a mile or more of endless, crawling traffic and parked cars, she realized that Ms. B's fear that Arthur would be shocked by the crowd at Dawning Falls was naive. He was used to crowds.

This is how he lives, she thought, shuddering. Surrounded by hordes of people whose behavior he had no way of predicting. For every well wisher, there was somebody who thought he should be dead. But they all had one thing in common: They wanted something from Arthur. Something: happiness, amusement, maybe only the cheap thrill of being where the media was. Some insisted on full-fledged miracles; others called for no less than Arthur's death.

It must have been like this to be king, she thought, and then felt silly. She had heard the stories in school about how Arthur Blessing was the reincarnation of King Arthur—it was the sort of thing girls talked about in hushed tones, with big eyes and tossing hair.

Stupid girls. Gwen had never shown her drawings to any of them. They would have said that she'd copied Arthur's face from his image on television. They would have made photocopies of them and hung them in their lockers, as if he were some rocker in an MTV video.

But the fact was that she hadn't copied his face from the news, or from anywhere else. It had just come to her, as she had told Ms. B, in a dream. Ms. B herself didn't quite believe her, either, she knew. Gwen's story just didn't stand up to scrutiny.

Yet it was the truth. She had never seen him before she had drawn his face. And when she had finally seen Arthur on television, she had recognized him, and not just as the face in her drawing. She had known him as surely, as deeply, as she knew herself.

That was why she had kept her face bare of makeup today. Like this, she resembled the other drawings, the portraits of the women, to a startling degree. If she had recognized Arthur so easily, Gwen wondered, perhaps he would recognize her, too.

That's the most stupid thing of all, she thought. Recognize her from what? He was a celebrity. His picture had appeared in *People* magazine. She was a loser high school girl in a hick town. Arthur Blessing wouldn't recognize her. He wouldn't even notice her.

Nevertheless, she had promised Ms. B that she would try to talk with him, and she would. At the sound of approaching motorcycles, she propped up her bicycle between two parked cars and waited. Then, when the entourage came into view and the spectators stepped out of their cars to wave or display their signs and placards, Gwen walked out into the middle of the road to face Arthur head-on. If he was going to ignore her, she reasoned, he would at least have to make the effort to avoid hitting her.

Arthur swallowed nervously as he rode past the rows of parked cars along the highway. They had been present every mile of the way since the incident on Route 16.

He didn't like being treated like a hero. He hadn't done anything heroic, for one thing. On that occasion—the "First Miracle," as the newspapers were referring to it, as if he had miracles spilling from his sleeves like magicians' scarves—Arthur had meant only to ask all those people to please go home and stop thinking that he was anything other than an eighteen-year-old farm boy.

What happened after that was as much a mystery to him as it

had been to everyone else. While he was walking toward the crowd, he had felt an irresistible compulsion to stop in his tracks. It was almost as if a hand had physically restrained him from moving.

That was all. He was aware of nothing after that. He had no recollection of raising his hands skyward, or of closing his eyes, or even of remaining in the same spot for nearly an hour. As far as he knew, he had just stopped for a moment, the briefest pause. It was almost as if he had fallen asleep. He could even still recall a faint recollection of dreaming—not the dream itself, but the bare ends of the dream, like the barest brush of birds' feathers.

A sword had been in his hand. The sword, Excalibur, the magic one. It had hummed and throbbed like living steel as he had pulled it, pulled it from . . . what? A body? Its scabbard?

No, of course, he recollected. The stone. It had to have been the stone.

A memory of the Other, ringing through his physical brain. How long would it be before all of his memories became those of the Other, of the great king come to live again? How long before the king's life took over, and Arthur Blessing ceased to exist altogether?

These were the thoughts going through his mind when he saw the girl standing in the middle of the road.

Instantly those thoughts vanished. At the sight of her, it suddenly did not matter a whit whether his memories belonged to himself, to a dead king, or to the man in the moon. It was the girl, the girl who had come to him in a thousand dreams and visions, standing before him.

He swerved so badly that Fairhands, sitting behind him, nearly fell off. When he raised one hand, indicating that he wanted the group to halt, the knights automatically formed a protective circle around him before turning off their engines. Then Arthur dismounted and walked toward Gwen.

For a moment they said nothing. The warm breeze carried her scent toward him, and he closed his eyes, allowing her fragrance to wash over him.

"I've brought a message. . . ." she began, but as he took her hands in his, her words seemed to be both inadequate and redundant.

Through her touch, Arthur saw a series of faces, all different, all beautiful, all hers. He heard the music of her voice, speaking words of languages that no longer existed. She moved closer, touched his face with her own, brushed her hair against his eyes. She sighed, softly, a tender breath, catching deep in her throat on buds of passion.

In the circle surrounding them, an amateur photographer ducked into the space between Kay and Gawain and snapped a picture. Without a moment's hesitation, Kay struck the photographer on the forehead, and the man reeled backward. But the circle had been broken. Slowly, the onlookers lining the highway began to move in.

"Arthur," Hal said in warning.

Gwen broke away from him. "Your aunt wants you to be careful," she said. "The town has made a big deal out of your visit. It's crowded. And some of the people don't like you. Some of them . . ."

The knights were circle in more tightly. Gwen looked around, frightened.

"Let's go," Hal said. Gwen backed away.

"Wait," Arthur called. "Who are you? How can I see you again? Where—"

But the knights were pushing him toward the motorcycles, their leathers squeaking as they formed a phalanx around their king.

The girl was gone.

Fairhands took over the controls of the Harley. Hal led the group through the crowd, which had already reached the stage where they could become dangerous. Several hands reached out to touch the motorcyclists. Some of them called Arthur's name. "Touch me, too!" a woman shouted.

Launcelot, pulling up the rear, looked back to see if he could find the girl again. She was there, standing still as a statue. He knew her, of course, although he had never seen her so young.

Young enough to be my daughter, he thought. He crossed himself, his cheeks blazing with shame.

Forgive me, Guenevere.

CHAPTER TWENTY-SIX

RIGHTWISE KING OF ALL ENGLAND

Arthur hardly noticed the burgeoning crowd that grew steadily as the knights approached Miller's Creek. All around them horns blared and people cheered, but he heard only three words that ricocheted through his mind like circling birds:

She is mine.

He pulled the sword from the stone on the occasion of Beltane, or May Day.

Old Cheneus, who had appointed himself a sort of éminence grise concerning the sword which was embedded in a rock in Leodegranz's thicket, had decreed that the only attempts at extricating the blade which would be deemed legitimate would be those performed in full view of other nobles on sanctified holy days. Some, like Lot of Rheged, grumbled; but then, he would grumble in any case. Most, however, agreed that this was the best course of action, and discouraged those who might try to remove the sword by unethical means.

This meant that after the initial discovery of the sword at Imbolc, no one else could attempt to take the sword until Ostara, the spring equinox. And after that, since no one had succeeded then, the entire community of nobles was forced to meet once again at the next holiday, Beltane.

By this time, the assemblage of petty chiefs and their favorite sons was quite impressive. King Leodegranz's reputation grew considerably just by virtue of hosting all these events. At Beltane the nobles brought along full entourages to cheer them on during their turn at the sword, so that the entire hillside was swarming with people. Commoners came, too, including children, musicians, jugglers, and even food vendors from the local villages who saw an opportunity to sell their wares at highly inflated prices.

In the short months since Imbolc, it became known that no man could really remove the sword from the stone; and so the feast days slowly became just that—opportunities for people to get together in a festive atmosphere. It was like the days of old, before the Romans came with their metal roads and flush toilets, when the land was everything, and the Greater and Lesser Sabbats celebrated the changes in the land. Festivals like Beltane were in the Britons' Celtic blood, calling them to ancient revelries, taking them all back to the simpler times, not just before the Romans, but before even the Druids, when the most ancient of gods, who were always female, opened the earth to magic and permitted human beings to be a part of that magic.

And so it was that when Arthur—who was, really, little more than a boy, and one of unknown lineage at that—took the sword from the stone, there was immediately a sense of ancient magic about the act.

To be sure, when it happened it was as if all of the air had vanished off the earth.

No one had been paying much attention. Ector and his son Kay had been trying again, as they had twice before. No one among the nobility wanted either of them to be made high king, since Ector had not inherited any chiefdom. But then, there was the question of Uther's army, which was loyal to Ector now. And so if he or his son managed to take the sword, the others would be forced to at least consider Ector.

Most of the nobility refused even to consider this possibility. They took the attitude that whatever gods were in charge of this odd procedure of acquiring a high king surely would not place a commoner in such a position.

So it was that very few of the celebrants were watching when Ector, in a spirit of goodwill, allowed his foster son, Arthur, to have a go at the Great Sword of Macsen, as it was then being called.

"Go on there, lad, let's see what you can do!" Ector said bluffly, nudging Kay's belly with an elbow.

Kay gave a loud and uncouth shout which caused Cheneus and a few of the others to look over in disdain. What could be expected from the offspring of a common soldier, their tight lips and veiled gazes seemed to say. And who was that walking up to the sword, someone's squire? Something would have to be done. The whole affair was turning into a mockery. Ector was bad enough, but now . . .

Excalibur, Arthur whispered as he reached for the sword's hilt. For the smallest moment, the briefest flicker, he raised his gaze. In the crowd was Guenevere, King Leodegranz's beautiful daughter whom Arthur felt as if he had known forever. Her lips were moving. They were forming the same name which he himself spoke:

Excalibur. The magic sword. She knew it.

And she knew him.

With a sudden intake of breath, Arthur pulled the sword cleanly, effortlessly, out of the stone and held it aloft in silent triumph.

The first gasps silenced the noise of the festival so effectively that only the scattered calls of birds broke it. Arthur stood in the silence, transfixed in it, feeling only the rightness of the sword in his hand and the sight of the woman whose eyes had never left his.

Now it begins, he thought.

———

No one bowed to him. After a few minutes, when those who had been watching were able to catch their breath and those who had not were able to comprehend the magnitude of what had just occurred, Cheneus stepped forward tentatively. He examined the opening in the rock from which the sword had been taken, looked carefully at the blade still held aloft in Arthur's upraised hand.

Arthur said nothing. His eyes never wavered, but remained fixed on the rapt gaze of Guenevere. In both their hearts, they were already bound as surely as if they had been married.

"He has taken the sword without impediment," Cheneus announced in his creaky voice. "And so I do declare this man, whose name is . . ." He looked to the boy dubiously.

"Arthur," the boy said.

"That's all?" Cheneus whispered. "You've no family name at all?"

Arthur did not answer.

Old Cheneus sighed. ". . . whose name is Arthur, of the house of Ector—"

"The house of Pendragon," came a voice in the crowd. A druid whom no one had noticed amid them lowered his cowl.

"By Mithras, it's the one brought him to my house those years ago!" Ector exclaimed. "Pendragon, you say! Is the boy Uther's own son, then?"

"He is," the druid answered. "Left in your care for safekeeping all this time."

Lot of Rheged pushed his way through the crowd. "I'll not serve Uther's bastard, nor any other nameless whelp!"

"He is not a bastard, but Uther's true and only son," Taliesin said, cold-eyed. "But that is of no matter, for he has taken the sword in the manner set forth by the gods, and you will serve him!"

Lot spat on the ground.

Ector immediately reached for his own sword, but the druid stopped him. "What say you, Arthur?" the wizard challenged.

For a moment Arthur could only stand gawping. The magnitude of what had just happened was beginning to register. How was he to speak now? What would he say?

"High King indeed!" Lot shouted scornfully. "That one's no more fit to rule than a barnyard cur. He can't even speak!"

"I can speak," Arthur answered, and the sound of his voice captured everyone's attention. He looked around at the crowd, studying each face. Some were encouraging, most were dubious, a few were overtly hostile. But they were all listening.

"This occurrence is as strange to me as it is to you," he said in a clear voice. "Nevertheless, it has occurred. I have won the sword according to rules which which were made by you, not me. If I had been raised as a nobleman, perhaps I would abdicate, thinking this to be some gross mistake. But I was raised not as a nobleman but as a soldier, and when a soldier is given an order, he obeys it." He raised the sword high. "This sword is my order. I do not know which god has issued it, but I am prepared to carry it out."

Ector's chest swelled with pride. "He speaks the truth," Kay said, squaring his shoulders.

"Only a high king can unite us against the invading Saxons!" someone called out. "It doesn't matter who that is."

"Actually, that's right," Old Cheneus agreed. "A high king only needs to keep the peace between the rest of us."

"We can keep our own peace," Lot said hotly, "without the help of an untutored child!"

Several people shouted Lot down. He turned on the crowd with a snarl. "Idiots! Is the high king to be some powerless, landless spirit, then? Who do you think will get Uther's kingdom and army?"

"The army'll go to whoever I say it goes to," Ector said in a rare moment of bravado. "You can make any laws you want, but Uther's army listens to me at the moment, and I'm going to tell them to follow the boy!"

"Look to your head, then," Lot threatened. The crowd began to get noisy.

"King Leodegranz!" Arthur shouted, silencing the assembly once again.

Leodegranz stepped forward, uncertain of how to address the young man. "I am he," he said at last. It seemed a safe thing to say.

"I wish to ask for your daughter's hand in marriage!"

Leodegranz staggered backward, and the crowd burst into disquiet again. Only two remained still and focused: Guenevere, who smiled in surprise and delight, and Arthur, whose love for her poured out of his very eyes.

Then, from out of the stillness came a wail of protest. "No! No! No!" It was Prince Melwas of Orkney striding forward with his fists clenched and his fleshy face contorted into a pout of heroic dimensions. Some of the ladies in attendance smiled behind their hands at the sight of him. Always known as something of a spoiled child, Melwas looked particularly infantile today. His curly gold hair bobbed up and down as he walked, drawing attention to his red cheeks and hunched shoulders. He looked for all the world like a child holding his breath in order to get his way.

"Princess Guenevere is betrothed to me, fool!" he shouted so loudly that his voice broke. "King Leodegranz's daughter and kingdom are mine. If you wish to challenge my right to them, you will have to fight both me and my army!" He placed his hands on his hips and smirked.

No one smiled back. Lot looked at Melwas from under his frowning brows, considering. Orkney was a backwater. Melwas's army—if they would even follow the young pup, since the prince's father was still alive—was composed mainly of farmers conscripted right out of the fields, and fishermen caught between boats. Hardly a match for Uther's well-trained troops.

Lot calculated the risk to his army if he participated with Melwas in battle against the boy Arthur and the army that would be his. Uther's men would not be at their best under the so-called leadership of that untried boy, but they could still do Lot a great deal of damage, particularly since Lot would have to march his men nearly five hundred miles to engage in battle.

No, he reasoned, perhaps not. He would fight Arthur "Pendragon" one day, but that day would not be in the immediate future. He gave Melwas one last contemptuous look, then turned his back and pushed his way back through the crowd.

Melwas's stricken eyes followed him. They registered panic. He had counted on Lot's assistance.

Ector watched the scene with undisguised amusement, then turned to Arthur to see how the boy administered the coup de grâce to the already defeated Melwas. To his surprise, however, Arthur took pains to save the young prince's pride.

"As high king, I will serve you, Prince Melwas, not fight you. I promise we will preserve our kingdoms, and the peace of Britain. We will speak privately of this matter, and a resolution will be reached." Arthur nodded once, solemnly, and Melwas, thinking that Arthur meant to buy him off with a large tract of land, was appeased.

Of course, Melwas did not remain happy for long. Despite the quite generous gift of land that Arthur gave him in exchange for his unwilling bride-to-be, Melwas did ambush Arthur in an act of war less than a month afterward.

It was the first of many skirmishes with the petty kings. In time, Arthur came to view these as tests of the validity of his kingship, and did not hold them against the kings who tested him. In fact, his handling of these battles—not just his victories, although he won them all, but also his settlements after the victories—was eventually the mortar that kept the petty kings loyal to him for so long. Arthur never took their land, or their women, or their crops, or humiliated the kings for going against him. Instead, he fought with them, and after beating them, he permitted them still to rule over their tribes in the manner they had always done.

At last, when the kings knew they were safe and that their ways would be respected, they came round to accepting the light yoke of a high king, even one so young as Arthur Pendragon. Slowly he gained their respect. And with time, Arthur became known as a just, fair, and enlightened leader of free men.

But in the beginning of his reign, begun so strangely with a sword placed by the gods in an ancient graveyard, Arthur had yet to prove himself to the arrogant nobles who considered themselves to be his betters.

The first test came in the month of June. The odd situation which had occurred at Beltane was accepted, more or less, but with an uneasy silence. The kings had all agreed to a high king, after all, and had further agreed that this king, who would bind the rest of them together, would be chosen by the Sword of Macsen. Arthur had taken the sword and accepted the responsibilities of high king. It was now simply a question of whether or not the nobles would be good to their word.

For a long time, several weeks, no one spoke about it at all. Everyone was waiting for someone else to resolve the situation.

Arthur, mentored now by the Merlin on matters of power and politics, and by Ector on matters of war, had no time to worry about the indecisiveness of the petty kings. Merlin had told him to anticipate battles with most, if not all, of them, but harbored no doubt whatever that Arthur would claim the high kingship in deed as well as name.

"It is what the gods have decreed," he said blithely. "Those fellows can try to go against that, but it will be of no use. Therefore you'll not waste your time trying to convince them to make you king. You are king; that's all there is to it. Everything else is detail."

The only other person Arthur saw during those days was Guenevere. Neither Taliesin nor Ector approved, naturally. This was not the time to be mooning over a woman: They both made this perfectly clear to him. And they both reiterated it to themselves every time he gave them the slip and rode to King Leodegranz's castle to pay his respects to the young woman whom he was determined to make his queen.

Leodegranz himself was growing used to the idea that Arthur really was going to be high king. Although he had not officially given his blessing to the couple, he had never much liked Melwas, with his soft, milk-fed piglet looks, and the more he saw of Arthur, the more he grew to believe that perhaps his headstrong daughter had been right to follow her heart. And so he permitted the two young people to see as much of one another as they wanted, providing they were properly chaperoned. Chaperones were quite the thing in those days, owing to the stylishness of the New Religion, Christianity, whose adherents believed that the lusty old ways were uncivilized and vulgar.

"He's being stuffy because he wants to be modern," Guenevere said as they trotted their horses across a meadow. "You know, in the old days, couples who wanted one another simply took their pleasure." She said it very matter-of-factly, although she could not disguise the deep blush that came to her cheeks. Guenevere, though devoted to the old ways and the Old Religion, had been raised a modest semi-Christian, steeped in guilt and shame. She had often listened to the servants, who had no such new ideas, talk in their unpretentious way about love and sex and death, and wished that her family were not so keen to take on the subtle foreign values which denounced nearly everything pleasurable as forbidden and intrisically wrong. Yet those values still ran deep within her, despite her efforts to be a "natural" woman.

"I imagine that would stop Melwas," Arthur said, smiling.

"Well, why should women come to marriage as untouched virgins?" she demanded. "Men certainly don't."

"It's because men like to know who their children are."

"Uther didn't know who you were," she rejoined. "And look, you're going to be high king."

"I *am* high king," Arthur corrected, although his tone was as easy and natural as if he were saying that he was red haired.

"Then I'm right," Guenevere said.

Arthur smiled. "Just right," he said, watching her blush again.

Then, in the space of a heartbeat, the moment shattered. The blush on Guenevere's face whitened to a terrified pallor as her horse suddenly shied and threw her into the air; and Arthur could only look on helplessly as she fell, screaming, to the ground.

CHAPTER TWENTY-SEVEN

A VALIANT KNIGHT AND TRUE

Sometimes the world shatters all at once.

Within ten seconds, it seemed, the knights had dropped their motorcycles and swarmed over Arthur like a thick leather blanket, while a woman's voice screamed, "Someone's been shot!" over the din of the crowd.

Arthur could smell the blood. "No," he whispered, feeling cold.

Launcelot clapped his hands over Arthur's shoulders and moved with him as if they were two snakes winding toward the shelter of a tree where Hal lay, his legs twisted beneath the front wheel of his Harley. Around them, the crowd exploded into a scatter bomb of noise and movement as people ran in panic.

"Oh, no," Arthur moaned. He tried to get to his feet, but Launcelot held him down. "Hal!"

Hal gave no response. Blood trickled out the side of his mouth and dropped slowly onto the asphalt.

With a violent jerk, Arthur freed himself from Launcelot's grip. Bedwyr, who had lifted the motorcycle off Hal, moved aside in deference. There was nothing he could do, anyway. Their brother, whom they had all known as Galahad in another life, was clearly dying.

Arthur knelt beside him. Cradling his friend's head in his lap, Arthur looked around with helpless, terrified eyes.

"The water!" a woman exclaimed. It was Emily Blessing, pushing through the panicked mob to get to the creek. "I've got the water! Let me through!"

The only receptacle she could find to carry the water was her shoe. As she held it to Hal's lips, Emily tried to block out the images of Hal that flashed through her mind like a moving montage. Hal, sitting behind them on a bus in England, his face so handsome that Emily had been afraid even to look at it; Hal looking at her across a table in a restaurant; Hal lying naked beside her while she thought she would burst with happiness . . .

"Hal," she said softly. "Hal . . ."

He was not responding. "Hal!" she said again, her voice beginning to strain.

"It doesn't always work," she heard someone say behind her.

"Don't believe it ever could bring back the dead," an old man said sonorously.

"Shut up!" Emily shouted. "He's not dead!"

The water pooled in Hal's mouth.

"Should have worked by now," someone whispered.

Emily's hands were shaking so badly that water spilled wildly out of the shoe. A hand reached out to steady her. She looked up to see Arthur's face.

"Oh, my God, what have I done?" she squeaked, tears streaking down her face.

"Don't cry, Aunt Emily," the boy said, taking the shoe from her and setting it on the ground. He took her hand. "It's going to be all right."

A whisper ran through the crowd, growing to a murmur that rippled through the gathering like shock waves. A woman standing behind Arthur pointed a trembling finger at Emily. Then her eyes rolled back in her head and she fainted.

Emily closed her eyes. It was her face, she knew. Even now, all they saw was her face.

"I'll call an ambulance," she said dispiritedly, starting to rise. "The water . . ."

"No." Arthur held her hand more tightly. "Stay here." Then together, they held their hands over Hal's bloody chest.

Hal was spinning, weightless, tumbling through a tunnel, faster, faster in the darkness, feeling very light and not at all frightened. He couldn't quite remember what had happened—it all seemed so trivial and so long ago.

"Someone's been shot!" he'd heard a voice call.

"Hal!" Arthur's voice. Had Arthur been shot? No, no, it couldn't be, that would just be too much of a failure. . . . But of course it wouldn't be Arthur. Arthur had come back to be king. It was he himself, Hal, who was no longer needed.

He felt better at that. Yes. He had brought the boy through the first dangers in those early days when Arthur had just been a child. He had collected the knights to protect him. He had fought in single combat as Arthur's champion.

Yes, his time was done. And he had done well.

You were valiant, knight, and true, Arthur had told him during one of those surreal moments when the kid knew exactly who he was and what he was doing here.

That had always been the tough part. Every time Hal would convince himself that it was all bull, that either the kid was demented or he was, there would come a moment of clarity in which Arthur revealed the strange and wonderful creature he was: a being half from another time, who had come back to finish out his life.

It had been hard sometimes when Arthur would speak, and what came out of his little kid's mouth were things that only a king would think about. And harder still during the times when Arthur realized that his life was not his to live.

Could they have changed that? Could Hal have helped the boy to grow into himself, or King Arthur, or something between the two?

Oh, how he wished he could watch Arthur grow up!

But he must be out of danger now, or Hal wouldn't be dying. That was good.

Very good . . .

And then two very warm hands were on his chest, hands that seemed to vibrate with something like light. The vibration was so strong, so ferociously bright, that Hal would have shaken them off if he could.

"The water . . ." Emily's voice.

Emily. He didn't think she was beautiful when he'd first met her. She'd been so schoolmarmish. And she hadn't liked him much, either, which came as no surprise. It was astonishing, actually, that anything had come of that at all. She had been so . . . well, not disdainful so much as afraid. Yes, that was it. She never seemed to notice that she was too good for him. It was almost as if she thought he was too good for her. Crazy lady. She had been afraid to open up, and he had been so filled with self-hatred that he barely spoke to anyone.

And yet they had found one another.

For a time. He had screwed that up, naturally. The only woman he ever loved, and he had left her with the impression that he wanted nothing to do with her. Good work, Hal.

But that was all behind him now. All of it. Emily, the kid . . . all of it receding into the distance, behind him now in the tunnel.

Except that those hands were vibrating like a jackhammer, and it seemed he was drowning. Water everywhere, in his mouth, up his nose . . .

Just travel in here, in this tunnel, toward the light. Beautiful light. Living light, like what came out of those hands. Living.

And now here was a meadow, oh, yes, just like the place he used to dream about when he was a kid growing up in a tenement in Inwood, in the part of Manhattan past Harlem where nobody went who didn't live there. A meadow in Technicolor green, with sheep. And there was his old dog, Pinky, God, she was an ugly thing but he loved her, and people were here too, waving to him, his mother with her head still all right, as if it hadn't been smashed under the wheels of that car, and others, but he was moving by so fast he could hardly make out who they were. . . .

And then the light seemed to press into him as if it were feeding him or something, feeding him with nourishment that came from the light itself. It was the first time Hal could recall in his entire life when everything felt perfect.

Are you ready? It was a voice but not a voice, perhaps his own voice, but probably no voice at all, unless it was God's voice, but then he couldn't even tell if it was male or female, that voice. What did it want to know? Was he ready? Ready for what? Oh, it was all so annoying with those hands practically spinning his head off with their vibrations, pulling on his chest, pulling, pulling him back, no, no, don't go . . .

And before he knew it, it was too late. The voice was gone. The light was gone. There was a deep pain in his chest, but that was going, too, going into those comforting hands. . . . And then a single tear, like a kiss, touching him. Hal opened his eyes. Arthur's face. But of course, they were Arthur's hands.

And Emily's tears, drowning him in love.

"You're beautiful," he said. Inexplicably, she picked a shoe up off the ground. It was an old lady shoe, her shoe, probably. Emily never had any taste in clothes. "Are you going to hit me with that?" he asked.

Two more tears fell silently from her wonderful, welcome face, and then she was gone, lost in a sea of faces that seemed to swallow her up like mist.

In her place were all the knights: Lugh and Fairhands, and Curoi MacDaire giving him a wink. "Aye, you'll be doing fine now, lad," he said. "Soon as we can find a tavern."

Bedwyr looked immensely relieved. "Are the bikes ready?" Hal asked. Bedwyr nodded gravely. So did Agravaine. Gawain and Kay, looking like Laurel and Hardy, both tried to smile, with each looking sillier than the other. Tristan showed his perfect teeth in a dazzling smile, while Geraint Lightfoot shrank into the muscular shadow of Dry Lips who was, in fact, smacking his lips right at this moment.

Launcelot, silent, somber, his eyes filled, as they always were, with the questions that only his soul could answer, completed the circle around him.

Except for Arthur, who had not raised his hands from Hal's chest.

"Your hands," Hal said. "That's what—"

"The water healed you, Hal," the boy said. Then he fainted.

Immediately a buzz began and spread out in all directions. "His hands! It was the boy's hands!"

"A miracle!"

"Arthur," whispered Hal, getting up onto one elbow. The knights were picking the boy up. Hal looked to Launcelot. "He's not—"

The knight shook his head. The boy was all right. It had just been the excitement, Hal told himself, the close quarters. . . .

"A miracle!" Others took up the chant.

"The second miracle!"

Hal stood up.

"Touch me!" a woman shrieked. "Please, I'm sick, I need it. . . ."

"The messiah . . ."

"Lay your hands on us, we beg you!"

"Touch me!"

The crowd started to draw in toward Arthur.

"Get the kid away," Hal ordered.

A police officer moved into the circle. "Ms. Blessing told me to tell you she's got a house for you," he said. His eyes widened as he saw the bloodstain on the front of Hal's shirt.

"Where is it?" Hal asked. "The house."

The officer stammered out the address. "Are you all right, sir?"

"Yeah, I'm fine." As an afterthought, Hal checked the wound on his side that he had received earlier. It was nonexistent.

The policeman was still looking at him. "I said I was fine," Hal repeated. "Where's Emily Blessing?"

"I don't know, sir. If you could come with me—"

"Give me a minute," Hal said. He moved swiftly toward Launcelot, who was carrying Arthur. "Keep him covered," Hal said to Launcelot. "Don't let anyone touch him. We're getting out of here."

The knights moved quickly through the crowd. As Hal followed them, a loud murmur rose up around him.

"Look at that!" someone whispered. "His shirt's still bloody."

"Was it the water?"

"No, it was . . ."

A man reached out to touch the blood on Hal's clothing. Hal swatted the hand away as if it were a crawling insect.

". . . the messiah . . ."

"Messiah . . ."

"Messiah . . ."

CHAPTER TWENTY-EIGHT

WHAT CHILD IS THIS?

"He's not the Messiah, for Christ's sake!" Hal stormed as the knights entered the house.

The old man was sitting on the sofa in the living room. His head was in his hands.

Hal sat down beside him with a sigh. "All right, get it over with," he said. "I shouldn't have brought him here. It's been a disaster."

Taliesin was silent.

"It just seemed that after what happened in Rapid City, we wouldn't be able to keep Arthur hidden," Hal said.

"You were right," Taliesin said wearily. "Unfortunately, your journey here was one of the most publicized progressions in history."

"Yeah." Hal rubbed his neck. "Guess so."

The old man sniffed. "Do you suppose you could change your clothes? You smell like an abattoir."

"Oh, excuse me," Hal said. "Blood sometimes is the result of getting shot in the chest. A minor consideration, though, in light of the larger problem of hygiene. Hardly worth a mention."

"Now, now, let's not be childish. You knew the cup was in the well. There was never any real danger."

"The cup didn't work."

Taliesin frowned. "What did you say?"

"I said the cup didn't work. Or the water, anyway. They say sometimes it has no effect. Maybe since I've used it before . . ."

"If it didn't work, how are you alive?" the old man asked.

He was not being sarcastic. It was a serious question, and Hal knew it. The air between them crackled with tension.

"It was Arthur," Hal said. "His hands. I felt his hands pulling me back."

For a moment, neither of them breathed. When Taliesin finally spoke, it was as if he were talking to himself. "What is he becoming?" he whispered.

Hal's face went blank with the realization. Then he stood up, furious. "Don't you know?" he shouted. "You're the one who arranged all this!"

Taliesin closed his eyes briefly, trying to compose himself. "I hadn't expected Arthur to . . . to change so much. That is, the incident on the road with the, er, food . . ." He put a trembling hand to his brow. "And now this . . ."

"Did you really think he'd be the same person he was sixteen hundred years ago?" Hal spat. "He's already lived that life. He needs another. His own life, not this perversion you've dreamed up."

"It's the only one there is!" the Merlin rasped. "That was the magic, to bring about this life, in this way. I paid for that magic with my life. I have nothing more to give."

Hal stood motionless, looking as if he were going to punch the old man. Then he turned away. "Jesus," he said, raking his fingers through his hair. "Jesus," he said again. A long moment passed between them. "How much time has he got?"

"What?"

"He's living out King Arthur's unspent life, isn't he? How much more of that life has he got? He's already eighteen years old."

"I ... I can't say." Taliesin licked his dry lips. "I never thought ..."

"Well, we'd better start thinking. Because sooner or later, somebody's going to try to kill him."

The old man blanched.

"That bullet I took could just as easily have hit Arthur."

"Hal, don't talk this way. Please."

"Will my shutting up keep it from happening?" He turned away in disgust. "You selfish old goat," he said.

"Selfish!" Taliesin shook with anger. "I gave my life for this magic, don't you understand?"

Hal whirled back to face him. "What I understand is that you stuck a wonderful kid with the butt-end of someone else's life, and it's turning bad."

"It's not turning bad. He's working miracles."

Hal's eyes were cold. "And guess what happens to miracle workers?" he asked softly. "What do you think we do with our messiahs?"

He walked out.

Taliesin leaned his head back on the sofa, feeling sick. Hal was right. Horribly, startlingly right. Arthur's time on earth would only be as long as his namesake had left after he died.

And the blood was already starting to flow.

Emily ran inside her house and leaned against the locked door, weeping.

It was the shock of the situation, she told herself. First, seeing Hal lying in a pool of his blood, then having him come to life again in front of her.

But it was neither of those remarkable occurrences that caused her to run away from Miller's Creek. It was the woman who had pointed at her with a look of horror in her eyes, and then fainted.

Fainted. Emily's face had apparently been so hideous that the woman had fainted at the sight of her.

And then Hal, critically injured, trying to make her feel better by calling her beautiful.

She thought she could bear anything, Emily thought, feeling

herself shaking. She had steeled herself for any reaction from Hal. She had anticipated shock, revulsion, pity . . . she could have handled any of those. But not what happened. When he had called her beautiful, his words had been like a knife in her heart.

He had been grateful, of course. The water had saved his life, and she had brought the water. Perhaps, in his half-conscious state, he had even believed her to be beautiful for a moment, before he saw her as the grotesquerie she truly was.

She covered her face with her hands. How her heart had shattered with that single gunshot! When Hal had fallen to the ground, she would have given her life to make him whole again. And she had, she had brought the water, though it had taken a while for it to work. . . .

Something was odd, she noticed. Something . . . She looked at her hands.

The scars on them were gone.

And on her arms. She touched her face again. It was smooth, the heavy ropes of her scars undetectable. With a cry, she leaped up and ran to the bathroom, which contained the only mirror in the building.

"Oh, my God," she whispered as she stood before the dirty glass. Her face was completely unmarked. She touched her smooth cheeks, unable to believe the sight.

"Oh, my God," she said again. She took her hands away from her face and looked at them.

It had not been the water that healed her. Of that she was absolutely certain.

It had been Arthur's hands.

Gwen walked back slowly to her house, where her mother was nearly beside herself with excitement.

"Honey, I've been watching you on TV!" she exclaimed. "Why, that boy—the one they're calling the Messiah—he acted like he knew you! I mean, he held your hand and everything!" Her eyes were sparkling. "Oh, tell me what it was like!"

Gwen stopped in the middle of the room. "That's what you noticed?" she asked incredulously. "A man was shot, and then was healed without a mark, Mom. Did you miss that part?"

"Well, of course not," Ginger said. "But that's what Miller's Creek does. That was no big surprise to those of us that live here."

"Oh," Gwen said. "The surprise was that a boy held my hand."

Ginger sighed. "Here we go again. All I'm saying is that you might be more excited. Out of all those girls he could have, he picked you!"

"He didn't pick me," Gwen explained irritably. "I was sent out to give him a message. He doesn't even know me."

"But he must have liked how you looked . . . or something." Ginger eyed her daughter dubiously. "Didn't you wear any makeup at all, honey?"

Gwen closed her eyes in exasperation. "No, I didn't. You didn't used to like my makeup, remember?"

"No, but . . ." She smiled gaily. "Well, maybe he likes the natural look."

"Jesus," Gwen muttered.

"What have I said now?"

"Nothing. Nothing at all." She walked to her room and closed the door. "As usual," she muttered.

She stood in front of her dresser and examined the face she saw in the mirror. What a dishrag, she thought. She must have been insane to go out looking like this, naked, exposed, her face showing her every emotion.

Still, as much as she hated to admit it, her mother had made a point. Arthur Blessing had seemed to choose her. He had looked into her eyes and then held out his hand to her with an urgency and truth that Gwen could not help but feel. And her response to him had been just as genuine. For the moment when their hands touched, she had felt something unlike any other experience in her life.

She had felt safe. She had felt as if she belonged.

What bullshit, she thought. She probably just looked easy, like her mom. The guy probably planted the photographer in the first place. Give the little hick girl a break. Make all the old folks think what a nice boy he was.

"Bullshit!" she said out loud, sweeping all the items off her dresser. "Bullshit!" Then she laid her head on her arms and cried.

CHAPTER TWENTY-NINE

THE SUITOR'S REVENGE

Almost to the end of her life, Guenevere had no idea why her horse had been so frightened that it threw her. She had felt the animal's fear, of course; it had rippled through the mare's body like a wave.

She had barely seen the two people before the mare bolted. And they looked innocuous enough, Prince Melwas and his sister, Morgause, who was still a small child. The mare had never minded people, and was in fact rather fond of children, unlike many of the beasts in her father's stables.

Only decades later, on her deathbed, did Guenevere understand the depth of Morgause's power. She had been born with it, a true witch. Long afterward, everyone who had been involved with her—that is, those who were somehow left alive—came to recognize its depth.

Merlin thought about her a great deal in his old age. It filled him with guilt that he had not tried to influence Morgause while she was still young. Had she received the training and knowledge given to others of her ability, she might have become as great a magician as himself. She might have developed her power to the point where, along with Merlin, she might have helped stem the tide of foreign invasions and the constant war that they brought.

Together, they might even have been able to revive the Old Religion, with its values of peace and spiritual mastery, so different from the new ways that men were coming to embrace, ways in which death was the final arbiter of right and wrong. According to the new ways, the man—and there were only men, no women— who remained alive after single combat became the one whose point of view prevailed. This idea, and all the others that sprang from it, would never have taken hold in the Old Religion, where winning and justice were not necessarily the same thing.

And so the Merlin chided himself for not giving Morgause a chance to learn from him in the way he had learned in the days of the great druid centers. Toward the end, though, he entertained another idea: that perhaps Morgause, with all her ability, was not a creature of the Old Ways at all, but rather the embodiment of the new, an evil masterwork born to destroy everything she touched, a living sword.

Morgause eventually brought them all down, even Arthur. But she had begun with Guenevere. Begun and failed. The girl's inexperience was undoubtedly the reason why Guenevere had lived. Had Morgause been even a little older, Guenevere's death would have been assured. All of the others had been.

Morgause never made the same mistake twice.

At the time she had set herself to the task of killing Guenevere, Morgause was only eleven years old. She was beautiful, sweet-faced and rosy-cheeked. Even as Guenevere tumbled through the air from her screaming horse, there was a part of her mind that took in the sight of the lovely little girl and thought, *What a sweet child!*

Morgause hadn't planned for the mare to shy. She hadn't even planned, at the time, to kill Guenevere. But the shying horse and the sight of Guenevere lying unconscious on the ground were so satisfying to her that the idea soon became inevitable.

Melwas, in a goodwill gesture by Guenevere's father, had been invited, along with virtually everyone from the house of Orkney, to spend the summer on the luxurious estate of King Leodegranz.

The truth was that the chiefdom of Orkney was remote, primitive, and impoverished. Although the chiefs liked to call themselves "kings," their kingdoms were little more than tribal settlements, not much changed from the Celtic clan holdings of a thousand years before. The Romans, though hated, had brought advances to Britain; but when the Romans beat their hasty retreat from the island because they themselves were under attack, Britain had reverted to its old ways.

The more progressive of the chiefdoms—generally, those which had to deal regularly with invasions from Saxon warships—kept in some contact with the outside world. But the inaccessible rural strongholds, like Orkney, had gone back to primitive ways in all respects, from using spears rather than swords as weapons, and eschewing more sophisticated forms of economics in favor of the old barter system. The only reason Orkney had not been gobbled up by another chiefdom was because it was worth so little.

Its chief, King Octa, never left the borders of his lands except for the occasional night foray into neighboring strongholds for the purpose of stealing horses. Since Orkney had changed very little during the Roman occupation, Octa remained the kind of tribal head that his ancestors had been, insular and isolated, surrounding himself with his warriors, spending his evenings drunk, attending to the simple needs of his people. For all events that required more political solutions, he sent young Melwas.

The prince, soft, foolish, utterly unlike his father in almost every way, would not have made a good warrior in any case. Perhaps Octa sent him on political missions in the hope that Melwas would bring Orkney into the modern world when he succeeded him. More likely, he just wanted to get his embarrassing son out of his sight and hoped that he would father another son before he died. At any rate, that was why the other kings of Britain were forced to regard Melwas as one of them, and why Leodegranz felt obligated to extend his hospitality to the Orkney contingent for as long as it was desired.

This, as it turned out, was a considerable length of time. Melwas, who had already been sufficiently bribed for the cancelled marriage with Guenevere, had been growing accustomed to the things that gold could buy in the richer kingdoms when he was called home to Orkney. Melwas's father, far from expressing displeasure at his son's failure to wed the daughter of King Leodegranz, was delighted at this new and bloodless way of robbing distant strongholds, and demanded that Melwas return, taking as many people from Orkney as he could get away with. No point in feeding a lot of extra mouths, Octa reasoned.

So Melwas's entourage, which included all of the old and un-attached women and most of the children in his father's circle of acquaintance, came in mid spring to the fertile lands of King Leo-degranz to show that there was no ill feeling between the two kingdoms, and there they remained, feasting nightly, until the latter part of June. And they would have remained even longer, were it not for Guenevere's fall from her horse and Morgause's murderous impulses.

It began innocently enough. Melwas, shocked—though slightly amused—at the sight of Guenevere flying through the air screaming, offered to help.

"I have women here with me," he said, motioning to a gaggle of sturdy females with forearms like bull shoulders. Rather than remain in Leodegranz's dank castle, these women had built their own thatch-roofed huts on the grounds, where they kept to themselves and demanded that their meals be brought to them in an unending stream of oxcarts. "They are healers," Melwas said. "They will see that the princess suffers no ill effects from this."

Arthur was at a loss. He had judged Melwas to be a dullard long ago, and did not care to see Guenevere in his keeping. On the other hand, no one else was in the vicinity. Guenevere was not capable of riding back to the castle, and the women of Orkney did seem to be formidably competent, so he agreed.

"I'll accompany you back to the castle," Melwas offered heartily. "Guenevere is in good hands. She'll probably be better by morning." He clapped a hand on the young king's back. "And meanwhile, you and I can have a few ales, eh?"

Arthur was trying to find words to get out of spending any more time with Melwas than necessary, when the young child-princess from Orkney spoke up. "If you please, brother, won't you stay alone with me for a moment, please? There is something of gravity that I wish to discuss with you."

The girl was so somber and pretty and intelligent, it was nearly impossible to imagine that she came from the same bloodline as the oafish Melwas. She resembled a serious little bird of some kind—silent, thoughtful, never demanding to be the center of attention, and so detached from whatever events swirled around her that one would think she lived in her own little world. She was not at all like a child, though.

"Go ahead," Arthur said affably. "Actually, I've got to get back to Ector's, anyway."

"Oh," Melwas said, pouting. "Pity." He scowled at little Morgause. "Well, what is it?" he fumed as Arthur rode away. "It's important that I make a good connection with the high king, you know."

"You have Guenevere," Morgause said in her serious, adult way.

"Well, I don't really have her. I mean she's here, but she's hardly—"

"Take her back to Orkney."

Melwas rolled his eyes elaborately. "And why would I do that?" he asked in a singsong.

"To hold hostage," Morgause replied. "You can say that you took her because your honor was broached."

"By what? Her wanting to marry Arthur Pendragon? Can you blame her? He's the high king. He's—"

"You can demand Leodegranz's kingdom in exchange for her."

Melwas laughed out loud. "Is this the sort of thing you think up while you're brewing potions with those hags? For your information, the army of Orkney isn't a tenth of what Arthur and Leodegranz together can drum up."

"Anyone who tries to invade our stronghold will have to go through the hill pass. Our men can pick them off one by one as they try to get through. Then you can make a bargain for Guen-evere's life."

Melwas tried to laugh, but his spittle dried in his throat. "A hostage . . . Good gods, you're serious, aren't you?"

Morgause didn't answer.

"What if they won't bargain?"

The girl shrugged. "Then you can marry her," she said softly. "Or kill her."

Unconsciously, Melwas backed away. He loved his half sister, but there had always been something about her that frightened him. Her beauty, perhaps. Or her coldness. Or, even then, her power.

Morgause was a bastard, spawned by one of the witch-women his father kept around him. To be sure, Octa had always been more comfortable with them than he had with his wife, Melwas's mother, Branwyn, who had come to him in marriage through an alliance between Octa and her father, the chieftain of Strathclyde. The poor woman had trembled and shaken through the entire wedding feast, so repelled had she been at the barbarism of Orkney and its king.

From the beginning of their marriage, Octa had referred to his wife as "the white girl," referring to the pallor of her skin, which he found unattractive and weak-looking. He had stayed with her only long enough to conceive a son. After Melwas's birth, the chief went back to his women, who all practiced the Old Religion, freely offering him their bodies as well as producing potions for ailments and luck and casting spells against enemies and various demons.

Branwyn found them all appalling. She never adjusted to life in Orkney, and her only pleasure seemed to be in telling young Mel-was tales of the delights of more civilized places. She sewed clothes for him that were utterly unlike the leather and hopsack garments worn by her husband and the other men in the tribe: shirts with billowing sleeves, made of fabric as soft as a maiden's hair, sent to Branwyn by her family in Strathclyde, and tunics of brilliantly dyed cloth.

The warriors—for all men in Orkney were warriors—looked at

the boy askance, but dared not speak against him. As for Octa, he only shrugged and left his wife and child alone, presuming that they were made of finer stuff than he, and not caring much. When the time came, he thought vaguely, he would make a warrior of his soft, rather fat son. Meanwhile, there were the lusty healer-women who concerned themselves with his body and his spirit.

One of them bore him a daughter just after the death of his wife. He moved the woman into his stronghold to perform the tasks Branwyn had taken on. She would hoot with derision at how little there was to do there, and poke Melwas in his stomach with her finger, telling him how flabby he was, and hold up her own little girl as an example of what a child ought to be.

Melwas hated the woman. To make matters worse, she decreed that Melwas's job henceforth would be to serve as young Morgause's nursemaid. To him had fallen the task of changing the baby's soiled wrappings and seeing that no harm came to her. The young prince protested, but his father only waved him away.

"It's what you're good for," he said in a drunken haze.

"Oh, it's not so bad," Morgause's mother told him as she swaddled the baby tightly and then hung her by the wrappings on a hook on the wall. "I'll be back to feed her. You just change the cloths when she starts to drip." She walked out of the room, then returned, shaking her finger at Melwas. "And bind her good and tight, mind you. I don't want her falling off."

After she left, Melwas could only stare at the baby hung up on the wall like a moosehead. It was the custom, even in the civilized kingdoms, as his mother had told him. Babies died too easily. To become attached to a newborn was to ask for heartache, as well as the displeasure of the gods. Most were not even named until they were two years old.

Melwas himself had been spared this fate, however, as Branwyn had been so lonely and neglected as a young wife that she had gone against all common sense and allowed herself to indulge in the company of her baby. Fortunately, she told him, her son had lived. Had he not, her bizarre method of child-rearing would undoubtedly have been blamed for his death.

Now he was ten years old, alienated from every other male in the tribe, including his own father, untrained in any skills necessary for a warrior, less valuable even than the dogs used for hunting. Absolutely the only being of his acquaintance who was considered to be less useful than Melwas was this red-faced infant hanging on the wall.

He took her down. Gently, cooing softly, he held her in his arms. The baby gurgled.

"I'll be your protector," he said, kissing the infant's downy head. "We'll be outcasts together."

That was not, however, to be the case, for even though Morgause and her mother lived in the fortress with Octa and Melwas, from the age of four she spent her days at the women's quarters, where she learned the ancient arts of healing and sorcery. She proved to be quite adept, perhaps the greatest natural witch the women had ever seen, and therefore gained an early reputation for herself, becoming anything but an outcast.

But Melwas was another story. Shortly after Morgause left to learn from the women, the young prince had begun training to succeed his father as chief, although he showed little talent in the arts of war. Octa was so disappointed in Melwas and in his own misfortune at being unable to father another, better, son, that he barely spoke to the boy. Overall, it was a miserable experience for Melwas, made worse by the fact that without Morgause, there was absolutely no one who wanted to spend any time with him.

The break came from an unlikely source: trees. Although Orkney had little to offer in the way of goods, it was rich in timber. The Romans, who had felled nearly all the trees on the once wooded island of Britain, either by building or by burning, by the time they left, had never journeyed to the far reaches of Orkney. It had simply been too much trouble. There were no roads, and the hill passes were narrow and invited ambush by the barbaric tribesmen who dwelled there.

By the time of King Leodegranz's offer of his daughter Guenevere's hand in marriage, lumber was at a premium. With the ever-growing incursions of the Saxons, settlements grew into strongholds of stone and wood. Stone lasted longer, but it took years to build a fortress of stone. Wood was needed, and Leodegranz was willing to sell his own daughter for a forest of big trees.

So when Octa sent his seventeen-year-old son to claim his bride, Melwas took Morgause with him.

"She'll probably be awful," he confided about Guenevere.

"Then we'll poison her," Morgause suggested.

Melwas had laughed. "Stuff some white berries down her throat at dinner," he said.

The girl had smiled in the enigmatic way that she had, with a small, lovely movement of her lips, but no hint of mirth in her eyes. "I've got something much better," she said softly. "Everyone will think it's her gut. My mother showed me how to make it."

Melwas frowned, remembering that his own mother had died of a burst gut.

"She only learned the other day how it's made," Morgause added quickly. "Anyway, if you marry the princess Guenevere, Leodegranz won't make war on you," Morgause said, looking over at the tent where Guenevere had been taken to be nursed by the wise women. "And if you kill her, you can give her fat greedy father some trees in compensation. He'll be so happy to get them that he'll forget all about his stupid daughter."

"Oh, I don't think she'll die," Melwas said abstractly. "After all, she was only thrown from a horse."

"I suppose not." Morgause arched an eyebrow. "You can never tell, though. She seems as if she'd be easy to kill."

CHAPTER THIRTY

THE FACE OF EVIL

The next morning, Arthur and Leodegranz rode out early to fetch Guenevere back to the castle. They had both agreed the night before that the princess would be best off staying off her feet after a bad spill.

"She'll be fit and rosy-cheeked, you'll see," the king said confidently as they trotted toward the dismal huts of the Orkney contingent. "Ghastly women, those," he added in a whisper, as if they could hear him. "Eat like pigs. Hello!"

He cupped his hand beside his mouth and shouted again. "I say, is anyone about?"

Not even a dog emerged from the huts.

"Odd. You wouldn't think them the sort to sleep so—"

"They're gone," Arthur said quietly, feeling a shiver. He dismounted and drew his sword before examining the huts.

"Is Guenevere . . ." Leodegranz dared not ask the question.

"They've taken her."

The old king closed his eyes. "Thank all the spirits. I thought perhaps they'd—"

"She'll be all right. We'll catch up to them."

It took Arthur less than three hours to assemble all of Leodegranz's and Uther's troops under Ector's command. He'd sent envoys to the neighboring petty kings, but all of them found some excuse for delay.

"Bloody cowards," Ector fumed, saddling his horse.

"That isn't it." Arthur looked over over the troops. They were seasoned and well trained. More than a match for the barbaric Orkneyans, if they could catch them before they reached Octa's stronghold and the treacherous northern hills. "They want to see how I handle things. If I make a fool of myself, they'll attack me themselves."

"Aye, that snake Lot of Rheged will be glad to lead them, too."

Arthur gave a philosophical shrug. "If I fail against the Orkneyans, I'll deserve whatever they give me."

"Now, boy."

"But I won't lose Guenevere. No matter what else happens, I'll get her home." He said that with such conviction that Ector knew it was the truth.

"The Orkneyans are tough men, but they haven't any decent weapons. Octa's got them all carrying spears. He must keep them in caves, like beasts."

"They've got good horses, though."

"That they have," Ector conceded. "But a lot of baggage. And women."

Arthur was thoughtful. "I don't think their women hold them back much," he said.

Ector grunted. "No, not by the look of them."

Arthur made a quick check of the troops. "Find me ten of your fastest riders," he said. "And give them all the best weapons."

The old soldier looked appalled. "Are you going into battle with but ten fighting men, then?" he asked, his hands on his hips.

"Yes," Arthur said. "You'll lead the rest at a more measured pace.

But you'll have to be quick, too. We'll hang on as long as we can. But we've got to stop Melwas."

"Melwas!" Ector spat on the ground. "Arthur, you're the king now, and I'll do what you ask," he said, his jowls trembling. "But by Mithras, I swear if you fall, I'll roast young Melwas on a spit and have him for my dinner."

Arthur grinned. "You do that, Ector."

Melwas and his entourage made excellent time. They might well have reached Orkney without incident if it hadn't been for one mistake. He had not taken sufficient care to watch his younger half-sister, Morgause. Because of this lapse, he did not realize until it was nearly too late that Guenevere was dying.

The princess had recovered from her fall within hours; that had not been the problem. When the Orkney women moved out, swift and spare as warriors, Guenevere had to be bound and her wrists tethered to her horse to prevent her escape.

"What are you doing? Where are you taking me?" she had demanded.

The women, who hours before had comforted her with fragrant compresses and soothing teas, now wordlessly wound ropes around her waist and neck so that she could only breathe if she sat perfectly erect. If her horse stumbled, she would be strangled.

"Can't you loosen her bonds a little?" Morgause asked, her eyes filled with pity for the poor princess.

"The master says keep 'em tight," one of the women answered.

The little girl touched Guenevere's hand, already chafing under the rough rope. "I'm sorry," she said in a whisper.

"Thank you for your concern," Guenevere said. "I shall remember your kindness when I am free."

Morgause turned to mount her own horse. It had been her idea, not her brother's, to tie Guenevere up like a trussed pig. It would make the journey much more difficult for the princess who, Morgause knew, could not have kept pace with the Orkneyan riders under the best of circumstances. Soft southern women like Guenevere never rode harder than a canter. By that evening, the princess would feel like a piece of wood.

Morgause kicked her horse and shot forward.

That night the Orkneyans stopped for less than an hour to water their horses and eat a meal of hard bread. They were accustomed to living rough while traveling, at top speed and with few provisions. From their sloth and drunkenness as guests of King Leodegranz, everyone thought the contingent from Orkney to be slow-witted, slow-moving hayseeds, especially with such a high percentage of women in tow. But the women of Orkney rode as well as the men, and fought as well, and killed far better, because they knew the arts of poison better than any people on earth.

There was a saying that circulated around the noble houses of Britain: To kill a criminal, cut off his head; to kill your enemy, run him through with a sword. But to kill your mother-in-law, you must send for a woman from Orkney.

Guenevere watched them as they sat around the fire, bolting their bread and laughing like soldiers. She herself could barely maintain consciousness. Her wrists and neck were rubbed raw from the ropes that bound her, and her back was sore from the breathtaking pace at which she had had to travel. Whenever her horse had slowed enough to give her a chance to breathe, someone came up from behind with a mighty smack on the animal's rump to send it galloping again.

The princess was too tired to eat. She accepted a little water, which mixed with the sweat and dirt on her lip and tasted of salt. There was a burn on her skin from the relentless sunlight during the long ride. At one point, she fell asleep while sitting up, and crashed headfirst into the cinders around the fire.

"Set her back up," one of the soldiers ordered. "Don't want to burn the little lady bald, do we?" There was much hooting and laughter in response. Guenevere felt two hot tears trickle down her face, and because her hands were tied, she could not even wipe them away. All she could do was to close her eyes and pretend she was elsewhere.

"I've brought you something for your skin," the girl named Morgause said softly in her ear. "Don't give me away."

Guenevere looked straight ahead while the child rubbed some strong-smelling but soothing unguent on her rope burns.

"I'm tying some cloth around your wrists, too, so the ropes won't touch your skin."

The princess began to sob in gratitude.

"You'll be all right," Morgause said. "They just want money from your father. I can give you something for your pain, too."

Guenevere blinked.

"It's not very strong. Not enough to make you sleep or anything. They give it to women in childbirth. It will make the journey more bearable."

"How . . ." Guenevere croaked. "How long?"

"Oh, quite a long way, I'm afraid. Another two days."

That was a lie. They planned to be in Orkney by dawn.

"I'll give it to you in a drink, if you wish."

Guenevere hesitated for a moment. Then she nodded her head. A moment later the child was holding a brass bowl to her lips. "Drink it all," Morgause whispered. "Quickly."

The concoction was foul tasting, but Guenevere obeyed the child and consumed it. And just in time, because one of the elder women saw her and yanked Morgause away by her arm.

"Hey, what are you doing giving drink to her? She had her turn."

"I'm sorry, Lady Goodbody," Morgause said, using the ancient form of address. She slid her lovely green eyes toward Guenevere. There was gratitude on the princess's face. The potion was working.

By the time they remounted, Guenevere was feeling much better.

A half hour later, she fell off her horse and was dragged twenty feet before someone could stop the animal and cut the rope that was strangling Guenevere.

"What did you do?" Melwas hissed.

Morgause shrugged. The other women moved away. One gave the sign of the evil eye.

Guenevere lay on the ground, her skin so pale it was almost blue.

"You've poisoned her, haven't you?" he accused.

"She needed to rest."

"She could have rested in Orkney! We'll be there in another three or four hours. Or we could have. I haven't any idea what we'll do now. Why, Arthur and half of Britain will be waging war on us." He turned away, but was too filled with anger and fear to leave. "Why on earth did you do such a thing, Morgause?

The child looked up at him with her lovely, somber face. "I wanted to see what it would do," she said innocently.

Melwas backed away slowly. He realized at that moment, and never forgot until the moment of his death, that his half sister was that rarest of beings, a true monster.

It was a strange drug. On the outside, Guenevere appeared to be all but dead. Her skin was ashen, her breath indiscernable. But inside her mind, images swirled stronger than any dream: images of someone she knew was herself, although the woman she saw looked nothing like Guenevere.

1275 B.C.E.

She was tall, with long fair hair that fell in waves almost to her knees, and wore the plainest of robes. Standing before a great yellow stone, she held aloft a sacred knife made of obsidian.

"Attend me, ye greater and lesser spirits!" she began, and the knife in her hands seemed to glow. "I am Brigid, priestess of the Cailleach. My voice speaks the words of the Goddess; my body is Her form in life. With the authority of the Great Hag do I call upon you. . . ."

It felt so familiar, the invocation of the spirits. She had spoken the words many times since she had been accepted, at the age of fifteen, to serve the Cailleach as one of Her priestesses.

The Cailleach, the Watcher, was among the most powerful of the ancient Celtic gods, and the Tor was her special place. Some believed that the hag goddess had once, long before the advent of man, lived on the Tor. There were tales, passed down through countless generations, about how she had created the mountain and the lakes with a stomp of her mighty foot, and filled her apron with boulders to bury those unfortunate enough to have come into her orbit. She was said to have transformed men into wolves, who served as her minions and brought her sheep that she would devour, whole, to keep up her colossal strength.

But even the gods can grow lonely, and one day, according to legend, the Cailleach felt the need to be with others of her kind in the god-world of the summer country. And so she invited a tribe of good people to inhabit her special place on earth, with only one condition: Her memory was to be kept alive through a sisterhood of priestesses, special women who had been born with the Sight.

"But how shall we find such creatures?" the humans asked. The gift of the Sight was rare, and sometimes frightening. Clans did not speak of these special ones. Often they were killed as children.

"You are to search all the land for them, and you shall bring them here, to the Tor, and provide them with safety and shelter and food. You will treat them with respect and reverence, and anyone who harms them will die in agony. In return for your care, they will give you good counsel, and will keep the magic of the Tor strong. Promise me these things, and you may live here in peace and prosperity forever."

The people agreed, and bowed down to the goddess. As a reward for their obedience, she created the great yellow stone on the Tor's summit to be the eye of the Watcher, and then engraved upon it her own sign, the sign of the dawn, that would ensure the people's protection from evil.

That had been untold eons ago, years beyond counting; yet all of the priestesses knew the story of how their order had begun, how the first of the great prophetic holy women had been brought to the Tor as young girls and how, in consequence, the people of the mountain had prospered and grown rich, and had never forgotten their covenant with the Cailleach.

Brigid was special, even among these special ones, for she had been born here on the Tor, the first among the villagers to have been born with the Sight.

Others with her gift had been born, of course; they were the daughters of the priestesses, who were permitted congress with anyone they desired, provided they did not marry. This was because a priestess, who embodied the physical form and voice of the Goddess, was required to be absolutely free. To be bound to a husband like ordinary women would necessitate making compromises, and to do this would be to deny her connection with the Goddess and hence her psychic power.

Therein lay Brigid's problem. Unlike the gifted children of the priestesses who, boys and girls alike, were raised from birth to be servants of the Cailleach, and unlike those with the Sight who journeyed from distant places in order to be among their own kind on the Tor, Brigid had a family. Until the age of fifteen, when she was chosen to live among the priestesses, she had helped her mother with the babies and fallen asleep on her father's knee and run through the woods with her brothers and sisters. And she had known Macsen.

Macsen, so kind, so protective of her, Macsen who had carved stones into the likenesses of birds and squirrels for her, who had loved her almost from the moment they were born, whom she had loved in return.

It had always been assumed that Brigid and Macsen would marry. He was the grandson of the great swordmaker Macdoo, who had travelled to the far side of the sea and returned with the secret of the black swords that had made the Tor as famous as its clairvoyant priestesses. Macsen was as skillful as his grandfather, and everyone knew that one day he would inherit the forge and, with Brigid by his side, take his place in the proud community of the Tor.

Brigid had wanted that to be her future. She had wanted it so much that she had not mentioned that she knew the outcome of events before they happened, whose babies would be lost at birth, which men would not return from battle. She had told no one that she possessed the Sight, though the burden of it was almost more than she could bear.

But through it all she had Macsen and the sure promise of their life together. That was enough. His love made up for the discomfort of containing a gift that strained to be freed.

It was enough, that is, until the gift decided her fate for her.

———

Brigid's father was going to die. She saw it all in a horrible vision that was so strong she did not even notice that her hands were burning over the cook fire. It was her mother, not herself, who screamed and pulled Brigid away from the flames.

"Brigid!" her mother called, bringing her out of her deep night-mare trance. "Your hands! Look—"

"On the far side of the lake, where the men will go to hunt boar tomorrow, the earth will open up and swallow them." she said. "Father will be among those who die there."

Her mother's hand flew to her mouth. "What are you saying!" she whispered.

"Tell him," Brigid insisted. And then she ran to warn Macsen.

Macsen had obeyed her without question, but her father had not. "Don't be foolish," he said good-naturedly. "We're not plan-ning to go anywhere near the lake."

"The boar will lead you there," she cried, pleading. "Please listen to me. Tell the others, I beg you."

But Brigid's entreaties were ignored. Her father left the next day. Her mother cast her gaze away from her daughter's, hoping that the girl's prediction was no more than foolish talk. That af-ternoon, as her father and his friends first spotted the boar that would lead them to their deaths, Brigid went to the priestesses of the Tor.

"Ask the Cailleach to spare my father's life," she begged. "If she will grant me this boon, I will join you here, and forego my life."

"We have lives, too," the high priestess said gently. "And if you have seen this vision, and it is true, then you are already one of us." She pointed to the great yellow stone with its carving of the sun. "Call the Cailleach, Brigid," she ordered.

The boar led the hunting party on a merry chase through the forest before the animal disappeared.

"Ah, well," Brigid's father said, taking a drink of his wife's fine beer, "the light's going. Suppose we'll have to make do with these paltry rabbits, eh?" He laughed. The take of rabbits and squirrels was one of the best of the winter.

"You can content yourself with rabbits, old man," one of the younger hunters said, pointing toward the lake. The boar they had been chasing, exhausted and thirsty, was walking warily toward the water.

"Ah, he'll be too quick for—" one of the men began, but at that moment the boar let out a bellow as its hind leg disappeared under the snow-covered ground.

"It's gone through the ice of the lake!" the young hunter shouted, elated by their good fortune. "Help me get him, quick, before he goes under!"

The men dropped everything except their weapons and ropes and ran toward the flailing beast.

Brigid's father felt his heart sinking as he finally, too late, remembered his daughter's words. "Stop!" he shouted to the others. "That's not the lake the beast fell through, it's the land! Look, it wouldn't have gone out onto the lake to drink, you great bloody fools! Come back! It's not safe for you!"

He wiped the sweat from his forehead, and felt the cold air against his skin. "Come back!" he called again, but he knew they could no longer hear him.

The boar fell through first, with a squeal. And then the white-crusted earth seemed to crack wide open, gaping black beneath the white, as the men tumbled, screaming, to their deaths.

Brigid's father watched it all, sobbing aloud.

After the priestesses had consecrated souls of the lost men, Brigid went to them.

"I have come to keep my promise," she said. Music, high and sweet and secret, seemed to be coming from the great altar stone,

"The Cailleach's song," the holy woman said. "Can you hear it?"

"Yes," Brigid whispered, trembling. "I have always heard it. I am one of you." Then, weeping, she collapsed on the yellow stone as if she had been longing all her life to touch it, her fingers tracing the crude engraving of the rising sun, her spirit listening to the song of the Cailleach sounding through her, transforming her, making of her body an instrument of the goddess. "This is where I belong."

Some distance away, Macsen the swordmaker hung his head.

———

That had been half a lifetime ago. Now, at the age of thirty, Brigid was herself high priestess, preparing to consecrate a special gift to the Goddess: a sword that looked as if it had been made from moonlight. The black iron swords from Macsen's forge were the finest in the land. They had brought victory to the Tor's warriors and wealth to its inhabitants. In a single generation, Macsen had advanced the art of swordmaking by a hundred years. But this sword, this gleaming unique being of a weapon, was beyond anyone's imagining.

He was approaching the altar with it now. The women gasped at its beauty, at the deep silver of its blade and its gold pommel encrusted with gems; the men regarded it with something akin to sadness. Nothing so perfect should have to be sacrificed, they thought, each of them wishing that they could, just once, hold the magnificent object in their own hands. With it they would be invincible. In battle, it would come to life for them, hungry like its name, voracious, *Excalibur*.

Macsen would not meet Brigid's eyes. He had made the sword for her, she knew, just as he had made delicate and beautiful jewelry for her. It had taken him many years to create, but he had never faltered in his devotion to it, just as he had waited each of those long years for Brigid.

When she had told him she was to enter the house of the priestesses, he had not objected. "You'll come back," he had said, certain that his love would be enough to break whatever bonds she was forging with the holy women.

"I cannot," Brigid had said. "It is my duty to serve our people as priestess. I cannot be your wife."

"Then I'll wait until you can," Macsen answered.

And he had. He had waited for fifteen years. He had not married, nor courted another woman in all that time. He had used those years, instead, to craft his masterwork.

He knelt, holding the sword out to her. "For your goddess," he spat.

Brigid regarded him. She knew how proud he was of the sword, how much it meant to him. "Why are you giving this up for sacrifice?" she asked.

His gaze rose to meet hers. "So that she'll give you back to me."

She stiffened. "My vow is for a lifetime," she said.

His jaw tightened. It was the only movement that betrayed his heartbreak. "Then I will wait for the next," he said. "I will wait until the gods themselves fall and die, if I must. But I will have you, Brigid. You are mine."

She stepped back, aghast. The villagers murmured. Some fled, expecting the Great Hag to send demons on horseback to destroy them for Macsen's blasphemy.

"And I am yours," he finished in a whisper.

The sword wavered in Brigid's hands and almost slipped out of her grasp. "Do not attempt to bargain with the mighty ones," she rasped.

"See if she'll accept my bargain."

Brigid's eyes blazed at the sacrilege while her throat constricted with love for the man who had waited for her with such foolish steadfastness.

"I will offer the sword," she said at last.

Then, holding it high, she summoned the elements about her: air, water, fire and earth. The wind grew, howling, blowing her hair about her. The sky darkened and rain fell, cold, punishing, pouring so hard that she found it difficult to breathe. Lightning flashed across the sky, crackling with its white flame of liquid light. Finally the earth itself seemed to tremble. The altar stone rose up, as if straining to leave its place in the ground and go sailing away like a leaf.

Then Brigid spoke. Rather, words came out of her mouth, but the voice was not her own. Hollow and wispy, as if the sounds issuing from her had traveled through a universe of time and space to reach her, she delivered the Cailleach's message to the young man who had crafted the sword of the gods.

"This gift is worthy," she intoned. "But you do not give it freely."

The observers held their breath. Even among the powerful priestesses of the Tor, this was no ordinary occurrence. Brigid's lovely features seemed to twist and gnarl, until she took on the countenance of a wizened old crone.

"In this life you shall have neither the sword nor the woman," she said. "But in another you shall have both, and you shall have to choose between them. How will you choose, Macsen? The sword of the gods, which will make you invincible, or the love of a mortal possessing neither power nor sight?"

"I will have Brigid!" he shouted.

The Hag Goddess laughed. "That is to be seen." Her voice seemed to grow until her laughter filled the clearing, booming as the thunder in the sky. "You may wait . . . but she shall serve me."

Suddenly all sound stilled, plunging the glen into dead silence. Brigid's eyes cleared. Her hands shook slightly. No one moved.

She brought the sword down. At the point where the tip of the steel blade met the sacred stone, a blinding spark rose out of the rock, leaving the spectators blinking. When they could see again, the sky had cleared, the rain had stopped, the thunder had subsided, the lightning had vanished.

And the sword rose out of the rock like a flower growing out of the earth.

Brigid heard the music then, the song of the Cailleach who had taken the gift offered. You may wait, the music said, but in this life she serves me.

In time Brigid would become a goddess herself, she of the clear sight, goddess of women and childbirth, curer of blindness. She would be remembered.

And the sword became famous, too, so famous that even when the Tor no longer held any inhabitants, when the name of the Cailleach was no longer spoken, and the magic of the place was long vanished, the legend of the Sword of Macsen remained, along with the promise of its creator.

He had waited, as he had promised. Through one lifetime after another, his soul had searched for hers, until he found her again, and made her his.

"Arthur," Guenevere said, waking to see his face before hers.

The fog of Morgause's drug was beginning to wear off. Guenevere drifted in and out of consciousness, the images of her dream still prominent in her mind. "I saw the ancient goddess Brigid," she said thickly, trying to sit up. "I *was* Brigid, Arthur! And you—"

At that moment she realized where she was, in the midst of enemy raiders who had taken her from her home and nearly killed her, and that Arthur, her soul's true love, had come to save her.

"You're here," she said, holding on to him fiercely, kissing his eyes, unable to keep from crying any longer. "You've come back for me. . . ." She tried to pull herself into wakefulness, but the dim fog in her mind was spiraling her back into sleep. She saw the sword again, growing out of the rock. And she saw Arthur's face— no, not Arthur, that wasn't his name then, though it was the same soul, saying he would wait for her through that life and others. ". . . just as you promised . . ." Her fingers touched his lips as she sank back into unconsciousness.

They burned against the young man's mouth. Gently he took her small hand in his. "My lady," Launcelot du Lac said.

She was delirious, he knew. In her confusion, the princess Guenevere had obviously mistaken him for the high king. It was Arthur whose eyes she had kissed, whose lips she had touched with such tenderness.

Yet Launcelot could barely contain the feelings that rose within him as he knelt before her, this perfect woman who was destined to be the king's wife.

Softly he touched her bruised face, smoothed the loose strands of her hair. "Yes, I am here," he whispered. "I will always be here for you, my queen." Launcelot rose to leave. "Always."

CHAPTER THIRTY-ONE

LAUNCELOT

Melwas surrendered almost instantly.

Certain as they had been of being able to reach their homeland before the king's troops, the Orkneyans had not prepared for an attack on the road. Arthur's advance guard may have only numbered twelve knights, but they were well armed and backed up by more than four hundred well-armed troops, already visible in the distance.

Even the dullest of Melwas's countrymen understood which way a fight between themselves and the high king's soldiers would go, particularly since the princess Guenevere was either already dead or close to it. Without Leodegranz's daughter, their entire plan had lost its legs. The only question now was whether or not Arthur would put the entire Orkneyan contingent to death for their misadventure.

They steeled themselves for battle, each man and woman prepared to fight to the death.

"Do you see what you've done?" Melwas shrieked in a panic to

Morgause who, alone among the Orkneyans, did not seem overly concerned about their imminent slaughter. "If you hadn't poisoned the princess, none of this would have happened. We'd be back home."

"What's the good of being there?" Morgause answered scornfully. "This is your chance to best the high king of Britain, Melwas. Perhaps your only chance."

Melwas gestured toward Arthur's troops cresting a distant hill, their swords held high against the sky. "Look at them!" he shouted, enraged, spittle flying from his mouth. "We're not going to best anybody!"

"It won't come to fighting," Morgause said. "Arthur won't want to show himself as a tyrant, no matter what you've done. The other kings are watching his every move. Killing you will be a signal to the others that Arthur will use his power to destroy them, and they'll all come after him."

Had it been an adviser, or even an ordinary adult, who had reassured Melwas of his safety, he would have realized that this analysis was sound. But because the words had been spoken by an eleven-year-old girl, he only sneered. "Maybe you ought to tell him that," he said.

"I won't have to. He's not an idiot." She cast a blank but telling look at her brother.

As it happened, Morgause's thoughts were exactly what had been going through Arthur's mind ever since the renegade Orkneyans were first spotted.

The outcome of this confrontation, he decided, would depend on Guenevere's condition. If they had killed her, he would parade Melwas through every one of the ten kingdoms, asking each of the petty kings for a verdict and sentence. Each chief, he knew, would want a part of Orkney. In the end, Octa would have to give up all his lands, his subjects would be dispersed throughout the nine remaining kingdoms, Prince Melwas, sentenced by the entire island of Britain, would serve as a sacrificial goat, and the other nine chiefs would be not only united in a common cause, but richer for it.

And when it was over, Arthur, if Guenevere was dead, would

walk away from the throne. Because without her, what would it matter if he was high king?

Under a flag of truce, he arranged for an envoy to check on the well-being of the kidnapped princess. He longed to go himself, but as king, his place was with his troops, facing down Melwas, preparing either to lay out the terms of a bloodless surrender, or to engage in battle.

The envoy who had been sent was a young knight from Gaul named Launcelot du Lac.

The tale of the sword in the stone had spread quickly even to places well beyond the British Isles. Despite his young age—Launcelot was even younger than Arthur, barely sixteen years old—he had come to try his hand at the magical sword and the exalted reward it carried. He never got a chance to make the attempt, however. His journey from Gaul had been long, and by the time he arrived, Arthur had already taken the great sword.

Seeing the lad's clear disappointment, Leodegranz offered him his hospitality. After all, Leodegranz reasoned, he was already keeping Prince Melwas and half the population of Orkney. One more mouth to feed wouldn't make much difference.

And the young Launcelot was exceptionally talented with a sword. Leodegranz had heard that the Gauls were great swordsmen, but he had never expected to see such skill in one so young. Within days, he asked Launcelot to train his troops in his method of sword fighting. A few weeks later, nearly every petty king within a hundred miles had seen the young man's remarkable skill.

Every king but Arthur. He had been too busy trying to convince the others not to take up arms against him. But when Ector had presented Launcelot in his gleaming armor as part of the advance guard to ride with Arthur toward the Orkneyans, the new high king had accepted him with a handshake.

If Guenevere could be recovered in good health, Arthur knew that the way he handled the incident with the Orkneyans would go far toward uniting the petty kings under the Pendragon shield. They would see that, though young, their new high king could not only mount an attack, but was intelligent enough to find a diplomatic solution that would render one unnecessary.

"Prince Melwas, I will spare the lives of your countrymen," he began, and watched as the tension drained instantly from the entire Orkney contingent. "In fact, I give my promise to you as high king that no reprisals for this misunderstanding"—he allowed the word to hang meaningfully in the silence—"will be taken against you, your father King Octa, or the Kingdom of Orkney, provided that the princess Guenevere is alive and well."

The tension returned. Some of the weirding women made the sign of the evil eye. Several of the Orkneyans, warriors and women alike, muttered ancient prayers under their breath.

Arthur began to feel uneasy. "Where is she?" he asked.

"She . . . That is, the princess . . . she's resting," Melwas said, wiping the corners of his mouth nervously.

"Is she not well?" Arthur's eyes hardened.

"The envoy should be returning shortly, sire," Ector said. Then he called out into the silence that had descended over the assembly, "Launcelot! Say there! Give the condition of the princess Guenevere!"

Guenevere had been placed under the rudest of shelters, a torn old cloak balanced atop some low-hanging branches in the wood beside the rutted dirt road where the princess had fallen unconscious.

When Launcelot first saw her, he cried out in alarm, certain that she was dead. But before he could shout the dreadful news to Ector, indeed, before he could even tear his gaze away from that beautiful face, her eyes opened. Then she called him by Arthur's name, pulled him toward her in a torrent of indecipherable words, and kissed his eyes.

She would never know how much that kiss would mean to young Launcelot, who understood even then that he would have to leave the king's employ immediately, leave Britain itself, if he were to maintain his honor as a knight. And even then, he knew that with every sight they took in, his eyes would remember Guenevere's kiss upon them.

Launcelot stood up in the tent, knocking over the cloak that was suspended above them. Guenevere blinked into the sunlight. "*Excusez-moi, Princesse*," he said, trying to replace the cloak.

"Who . . . who are you?" Guenevere asked.

"I am Launcelot du Lac," he said, feeling very much like the sixteen-year-old boy he was. "I have been sent by the king to see if you are well."

Guenevere smiled. The boy had a sweet accent. "Arthur? Is he here, then?"

"Yes, my lady. Please wait here. He will come to you, I am certain." He backed out of the shelter, tangling the cloak around his head once again.

As he appeared, stumbling against the posts that now fell helter-skelter to the ground, some of the soldiers laughed. The Orkney women were watching him with sly eyes, though they never left their places of obeisance in front of Arthur, who seemed to be the only one who was not staring at him. The silence around him was terrifying.

"Well?" Ector shouted.

Launcelot felt his heart hammering. "*Pardon?*" He bunched the annoying cloak into a ball and threw it into a bush.

"Damn it, man, is she alive or not?" Ector demanded.

Launcelot hesitated for a moment, his breath suspended. Then it poured out of his body in a sigh so light that it was almost a laugh. "Oh, the princess, *oui*. That is, yes. Yes!" He looked around, smiling, his tousled hair shining in the early sunlight. "She is well."

A low murmur rose from the throats of the Orkneyans. The witch-women, whose fingers had been moving rapidly in all manner of spells, nearly fainted with relief. Melwas himself choked on all the saliva which had pooled inside his mouth as he anticipated his death. After he stopped coughing, he whispered, "A miracle," and others closed their eyes and nodded in agreement.

Arthur was puzzled by the demeanor of these strange people. "I beg your pardon?" he asked.

"I said it was—" Melwas sucked in a huge gulp of air as he felt the tip of Morgause's sewing needle pierce the skin of his back. He caught himself. *No, of course,* he thought. *Mustn't tell the fellow we nearly killed his fiancé.* But he was not quick enough to come up with anything better.

"My brother wishes to convey his deepest and most humble appreciation to you for sparing his people, Highness," Morgause said courteously. "Your compassion toward us is most surely a miracle. We will forever be your most loyal allies, and will hold ourselves forth as an example of your compassion and decency to all the other kingdoms."

Arthur smiled. Such politic words sounded odd coming from a child. *This girl was surely the most intelligent individual the Orkneyans ever produced,* Arthur thought. "Well, try not to make a habit of stealing your host's daughter the next time you go visiting," he said lightly. All was apparently forgiven.

Melwas, noticing the young king's approval of Morgause, was not to be outdone by an eleven-year-old girl. "Actually, no one ever intended to do the lady Guenevere any harm," he said casually, producing his most unctuous smile. "We merely, um, wished for her to visit Orkney. Yes. The beautiful forests of Orkney . . ."

As he realized that his words were not having their desired effect on the high king, Melwas's voice trailed away like pebbles falling out of the fixed crescent that was his mouth. The Orkneyan soldiers shifted uncomfortably on their feet. The women narrowed their wise eyes at their bumbling leader.

Arthur's face reddened, insulted by such a blatant lie. "Are you—" he began, visibly restraining his irritation. "Are you meaning to tell me—"

"I beg your pardon, sire," Morgause interrupted softly. "But I must explain for the prince, my brother, who is too overcome with gratitude to express himself clearly on this matter. Melwas took the princess because he loved her. He was heartbroken when his betrothal to Lady Guenevere was broken, and had consented to let her go only because he knew that was what she wanted. But in a moment of imprudence, he sought to take her to his homeland, even though he knew—or at least believed—that you would come to kill him. He did this so that he might spend what short time remained of his life illuminated by the light of her beauty. He but loved her too well." Morgause lowered her lovely head.

"Good heavens, Melwas, I didn't take you for such an ardent suitor," Arthur said. Melwas opened his mouth to protest, but nothing came out except another gasp as Morgause's needle sank into the fat around the back of his midsection once again. "I'm almost sorry I took her from you so peremptorily. I can see why you were distressed, under the circumstances."

"My kinsman has learned his lesson, as have we all, Your Majesty," Morgause said, using a title so grand it was almost laughable among the plain-spoken Orkneyans. "Prince Melwas wishes to offer you a gift: a chapel made of Orkneyan oak, in honor of the lady Guenevere. Please accept it as a token of our loyalty to you and to the federation of our independent kingdoms."

Melwas only stared at her, frowning and openmouthed. Such a gift would be costly. He could only imagine what his father would do to him for permitting such a thing. "Sir . . ." He gasped again as the needle struck.

"No!" Ector tried to whisper out of the corner of his mouth. "Say no, Arthur!" He knew what would happen: The Orkneyans would come back, this time to take advantage of Arthur's or his own hospitality, under the guise of building the chapel, in greater numbers than before. "We'll never get rid of them!"

"I thank you for your generous offer, and I accept and treasure your gift," Arthur said.

Melwas groaned beneath his frozen smile. Ector rolled his eyes.

Morgause smiled sweetly.

CHAPTER THIRTY-TWO

GUENEVERE'S SECRET

Fifteen years later, the matter of Guenevere's barrenness—an issue which would eventually plunge Britain into civil war and destroy the legacy of its greatest king—would be studied and probed, and eventually the truth of the poisoning on the road to Orkney would come out. Some of the truth. The conclusion of the council which investigated the incident was that Melwas had tried to kill Guenevere in retaliation for her rejection of him, and that the poison administered to her had left Arthur's queen unable to bear children.

Much of their evidence consisted of the testimony of Melwas's younger sister, Morgause, who stood before the council dressed in purest white, her still-beautiful face stained with tears as she told of how her brother had beaten her into silence when she learned of his terrible act.

By then, Melwas was dead, but Morgause's testimony was easy enough to believe, as the prince had developed a reputation as a poisoner during his life. This had made him the object of scorn among all the other petty kings, as poison was well known to be a woman's weapon.

No one, of course, thought to disbelieve Morgause. She had been married to old Cheneus, more than forty years her senior, and cared for him until he died in battle along with his sons. Morgause had grown into a saintly and beautiful woman who afterward had married Lot of Rheged, who openly adored her and would have killed anyone on the council who disputed a single word she spoke.

It was not mentioned at this inquiry that Melwas himself had died with a tongue so thick and black that it could not fit into his mouth, always a sure sign of poisoning.

But that, too, was not the truth. Guenevere had not, in fact, been rendered barren by either the fall from her horse or by Morgause's poison. Her childlessness had much deeper and, for her, more shameful origins.

Launcelot had returned to Joyeux Garde, his family's estate in Gaul, determined to forget the young woman who was affianced to the British high king.

In this, he failed utterly. He could not forget Guenevere, nor a single moment of their brief encounter in the Orkneyans' makeshift tent. Each day his face flushed as he remembered the touch of her hands on his face, her lips on his eyes. And each day he hated himself for succumbing to the memory, for needing it, living for it.

He did not marry—a source of great distress to his aging parents, who had already given over much of the responsibility for Joyeux Garde to him. It was not that their eldest son had no possibilities. Launcelot was an extraordinarily handsome young man as well as the son of one of the richest noblemen on the Continent. There was certainly no lack of lovely women eager to provide Launcelot with heirs. But he would have none of them.

To compensate for his lack of interst in finding a suitable wife, Launcelot worked harder than any peasant at the business of administering his family's extensive lands, riding to every village and farmstead regularly, and looking after his tenants with the concern of a father. He trained so diligently at the fighting arts that he gained a reputation as the greatest swordsman in Gaul. And, to the delight of the Christian priests who had educated him, there was no layman in all Europe who went about his religious duties with the dedication of Launcelot du Lac.

Indeed, the young man devoted so much time to prayer that even his mother expressed alarm over his excessive attachment to the New Religion. At least the pagan gods allowed one time to marry, she complained to the priests, who shook their heads and gave her penance. Perhaps he has a vocation in the Church, they whispered hopefully among themselves. Imagine if Joyeux Garde were to become a monastery!

Launcelot assured his family that he would never take holy orders. He did not add that the reason for his certainty was because he, Launcelot, was as far from a holy man as a human being could get, being constantly filled with thoughts of lust over no less than the Queen of Britain.

Prayer helped, being the only thing that kept thoughts of Guenevere even occasionally at bay, so he would try to pray during every waking hour. He had heard of saints who had learned the secret of praying continuously, so that their every act was pure, and their every thought was of God. The continuous prayer was an effort, but he welcomed it, working and praying until he was exhausted and fell into bed.

But even then his body betrayed him, for his dreams were filled with wild images of Guenevere, naked and moaning with desire like a cat, and he would awaken humiliated.

There was nothing for it, then, except for Launcelot to leave Joyeux Garde in the hands of his younger brother, and set off to see the world and perhaps get lost in it.

His parents were dumbfounded. The priests were desolate. His brother was overwhelmed. The tenant farmers were frightened.

But Launcelot was finally, inexplicably, happy. He truly had no idea why his heart had so suddenly lightened. Perhaps it was the prospect of riding through the sunlit hills of Iberia, or living among the country folk in the charming villages outside the ruin of what had once been Rome, on the Etruscan peninsula. And when the sky grew grayer rather than bluer, and the wind grew colder rather than warmer, he did not question why he was not heading toward any of the places he had planned to go. He had no idea where he would end up, he told himself.

Even when he saw Britain's chalk shore across the channel, he was quite surprised at the direction the fates had brought him.

As for Guenevere, she had hardly given a moment's thought to the sweet boy who had announced that Arthur had come to save her from the barbaric Orkneyans in the adventure that had transformed her, in the eyes of her peers, from a silly, spoiled princess to an interesting and strong woman whom the high king had led an army to rescue.

As soon as the couple returned, wedding preparations took up most of Guenevere's time, while Arthur met cordially with each of Britain's tribal chieftains, who by now had judged him worthy of their loyalty. They all agreed to attend the king's wedding, which was to be the most important event of the year.

It did not disappoint. The traditional ceremony of handfasting was performed by the Merlin himself, one of the last great druids on the island, and according to accounts, the most powerful. Immediately following, a priest of the New Religion spoke words over the couple as well, using the Roman tongue which none of the commoners understood. A well-meaning aristocrat explained that the priest was extracting promises from the king and his bride that they would remain sexually pure except for purposes of procreation.

Guenevere's nanny nearly objected aloud when she was told about the vow, but was restrained by her fellow servants. It would not do, she was told, for aristocrats to take their pleasure whenever it suited them, because it would not be dignified.

"Well, so long as she's not too dignified to open her legs for a babe to come out between them," she conceded as the music started up raucously and the dancers took their places.

Guenevere was delighted. There was never a question that Arthur was the man to share her life. They were so comfortable together, so certain of the other's thoughts and feelings, that it was as if when they had come upon one another in the ancient graveyard of Camelot where the magical sword grew out of the stone, their meeting had been merely a continuation of a much longer and earlier relationship.

"We must have known one another in the Summer Country," Guenevere whispered one night after they had made love beneath a blanket of sewn rabbit skins.

"And we will again," Arthur answered. "Because I will never stop loving you."

And he had not. They both loved one another until the moment of their deaths and beyond.

Unfortunately, love was not enough to keep them together.

It had begun, probably, during that minor but decisive act of statesmanship when Arthur pardoned the wrongdoers from Orkney after defeating them in battle. After that, the other petty chiefs gravitated toward Arthur as their high king. He had shown himself to be both courageous and merciful, and intelligent enough to put the good of the unity of Britain before his own pride. They came hesitantly at first, but then in greater numbers and with solid conviction, until less than six months later they had all come under Arthur's aegis, even the self-serving Lot of Rheged.

Through these delicate times, Arthur was advised by the Merlin, who had a genius for diplomacy, and in later years functioned much more as a statesman than as a magician or priest. He was, rather, a brilliant secretary of state who happened to have been trained in the esoteric holy order of the druids. And in matters of warfare, Arthur was trained throroughly and patiently by Ector, who could lead an army to the bottom of the sea and out again, if that was what was ordered by his king.

Between his two mentors and the monumental responsibilities of his office, Arthur's private life suffered. He saw less and less of his wife as the years went on; and when her inability to bear children became apparent, they saw each other so rarely that they came to treat one another as cordial acquaintances rather than as intimates or even political allies.

For Arthur, the loss of a close relationship with his wife was a sacrifice.

For Guenevere, it was a betrayal.

It was well known that Launcelot had once brought a dead man back to life with his Christian prayers. So intense was the man's faith, so potent his entreaties to the young, dead God at the center of the New Religion, so pure was Launcelot's own soul, that the knight slain upon the tournament field was given back the breath which had fled his body and his soul journeyed back from the Summer Country to return to the joust.

So was it said. It was, of course, entirely probable that the knight in question had simply been knocked unconscious by his fall, in full armor, from his horse and consequently revived independently of Launcelot's pious exhortations, but few were interested in this explanation. At the moment, everyone at the tournament who witnessed this extraordinary event was convinced that they had witnessed a miracle.

Guenevere was among them. She, too, had seen the deceased knight return to sweating, cursing life. But she was paying no attention to him. Her eyes, her mind—every vibrant fiber of her ripe and lonely body—was concentrating on the Gaulish knight who had recently come to the Round Table.

His name, delicious as she rolled her tongue over its sound, was Launcelot du Lac. And when, at the tournament, he rose from his kneeling position beside the fallen knight whom he had brought back to life with his prayers, when his eyes met Guenevere's and his nostrils flared as if he could smell her and the scent inflamed him, the queen forgot entirely all she had ever known of God.

She did not love him, not in the way that she loved Arthur. There was not the psychic bond between them, nor the knowledge that they had lived and loved before.

Perhaps that was why Guenevere was able to believe, however briefly, that her life would not be unduly affected by the hot, wet urgings that rose within her. And so long as she did not act upon those urgings, she told herself, why, no harm would come of anything.

Launcelot begged her, quite formally, to be her champion in combat, and she accepted. He was, by then, known as a very skilled fighter. And an excellent horseman. The queen often chose knights close to her husband to accompany her on her morning rides through the countryside. It was not amiss to include Launcelot among this group. And if the others were somehow indisposed, it was not unusual for the queen to ride alone with a single knight, particularly one who could protect her under any circumstances.

Launcelot also was not completely aware that the raw, needful lust he was feeling would destroy his life. Had he been asked about it, Launcelot would have stated, with absolute conviction, that he simply adored his queen, who represented the king to whom he had pledged his loyalty.

And if he would have been asked why he had come back to the court of Arthur, where he had once been so sorely tempted by the beauty of the high king's wife, he would have said that he had ended up at Camelot by sheer accident, that he had been wandering the world, and one thing had led to another, and before long he found himself in a part of Britain that seemed familiar to him. Ah, yes, he would remember suddenly, it was the place where King Leodegranz had sent his troops—and Launcelot along with them—to rescue his daughter, who had been stolen away by a band of rustics from the north. And after that, he would recall quite innocently, he had encountered a man in armor, and had enjoyed some friendly combat with him until he'd learned that the man was the high king of Britain himself. It would become another story that the whole world would remember.

On that day, Arthur had not recognized Launcelot, nor indeed remembered anything about the handsome young man, but had offered the knight a place at his table in exchange for his service to Britain.

Launcelot would have said, had he been asked, that the king's mission to unite all Britain against the invading Saxon hordes was noble enough even for him. He had left Joyeux Garde in order to seek adventure, and he had found it in abundance on this wild and fractious island ruled by the most fair, just, and honorable of men.

That is what he would have said, and what he would have truly believed. Unless he allowed himself to get drunk or to think during the minutes before he fell asleep at night, or to let his mind wander during his travels. Because during those times, he knew that all his good reasons and pure-hearted logic were nothing but lies, and that the reason he had left his homeland and his family's estate—left, in fact, everything he knew and loved in his life, all his responsibilities, his entire future—to come back to Britain, was because he could not erase the image of the woman he had found in the woods from his mind.

The memory of her set his limbs on fire. He wanted her so badly that, in the depths of his loneliness, he would sometimes weep uncontrollably and wish for death to take away his misery.

And so, whether anyone wished it or not, whether anyone believed it could happen or not, everything changed on that day at the tournament.

The dead knight had been brought back to life. The miracle was acknowledged. Then, in front of all the petty kings and their wives, the queen bowed before the handsome knight from Gaul and asked him to convert her to the New Religion.

From that moment on, there was nothing to be done for either Launcelot or Guenevere—or Arthur, for that matter—but to see the tragedy through to the end.

The matter of the queen's conversion had raised quite a fuss among the court ladies, who all made haste to display their own devotion to Christianity, wearing large gold crosses over their bosoms and assuming attitudes of rectitude—eyes heavenward, hands templed—whenever there were enough people watching and the light was right.

Only her nurse, who knew that Guenevere had been raised as a Christian and therefore could not have been instantly converted, as she appeared to have been, was not impressed.

"Oh, you're just an old pagan," Guenevere said dismissively when the nurse brought up that fact.

The nurse had made noises of contempt. "I thought you loved the goddess Brigid," she said. "You found the magic sword on Imbolc. You saw the face of your true love then." She set her jaw. "Your husband, that is."

"Those are just silly superstitions," Guenevere said blithely. "Anyway, I was young then. It amused me to think of lots and lots of goddesses, all doing different things."

"Brigid is the goddess of clear-seeing. You'd do well to stay with her, young miss." The nurse's mouth was set in a defiant line.

"I see perfectly clearly," Guenevere answered airily. "I've come to see that the New Religion holds the answers. I've found the right path at last."

The nurse snorted.

"You're altogether disgusting," Guenevere said. "But then, I suppose you can't help yourself." She was about to leave the room, then turned back with a toss of her head. "I forgive you."

The nurse spat into the fire.

Each night that Arthur was occupied with Ector or the Merlin, or with the petty kings discussing their problems with each other, or away doing battle with the Saxons, or training the army, or negotiating trade with Gaul or Ireland . . . during all those empty, silent, lonely nights, Guenevere sat huddled in her bed, her arms around her knees, her head bowed and weeping, and thought not about her new God and the kingdom that waited for her after death, but about the young man whose glance made her feel wanton and desired.

Sometimes she secretly watched Launcelot training with the other knights. Almost every evening when the troops were home, she saw him in the great dining hall at supper. His gaze would seek hers slyly, and hers would seek his, and eventually they would meet, both blushing and filled with shame, both suddenly unable to eat anything more, both their bodies buzzing with longing.

"I say, who are you looking at?" the knight named Dry Lips asked with a poke at Launcelot's ribs.

"No one," Launcelot said stodgily, his face crimson.

Dry Lips scanned the U-shaped dinner table. "Let's see. There's Lot's wife, Morgause. She's quite a beauty." He added, "Rather a handful, though, I should think."

Launcelot made an irritated gesture. "Don't be ridiculous," he said stonily. "Lot's wife." He tore off a piece of bread with his teeth.

"Well, she's the only one at that table worth looking at," Dry Lips said. "Except for the queen, of course."

Launcelot stared at his trencher and tried to swallow his food.

The followers of the Old Religion did not believe in coincidence. Events, especially important events, did not just happen. They were part of a greater story, a movement of some universal force or other. Practitioners of the old ways, at least those women who understood the nature of the gods from what little had been handed down through the ages since the last of the great priestesses, knew that when one walks into the ocean, one had better be prepared either to ride the wave that comes, or to be engulfed by it.

Had Guenevere and Launcelot been pagans, the lust that had grown between them might have been consummated quickly and pleasurably, and then abandoned. But the New Religion forbade such union. They knew how wrong they were every step of the way, from their forbidden feelings, to their rationalizations, to their lies, to their acceptance of their own evil weakness. By the time they gave in to their desire, they each already knew that they were damned.

It happened in the morning, while the two of them were out riding. The fog had not yet lifted, and the air was so still that each step of their horses' hooves made a distinct sound. Neither had intended to do anything other than pass the time in pleasant conversation, but their horses—yes, they would decide later, it had been the fault of the horses—had come too close to one another, until the two humans' legs were actually touching. . . .

There had been nothing to do for it after that. Their words, so friendly, so formal, dried up in their mouths, and their hands moved toward one another almost as if of their own will, and Guenevere touched his cheek so lovingly that she moaned, deep in her throat, without knowing it, and Launcelot felt himself go hard and ready with such swiftness that it was almost painful.

And then their hands were all over one another, and Guenevere opened her lips (so soft, he thought, so dark and red) and Launcelot moved his mouth upon hers, and felt her quiver beneath his hands.

Quickly he dismounted his horse and came around to wait for her. She slid into his arms, and wordlessly they walked a little way into the fog-soft meadow, where Launcelot pressed the beautiful wife of the high king into the cool grass beneath an overhanging boulder, and undressed her until she lay naked and welcoming.

"My queen," he whispered raggedly, shaking his head in confusion and shame.

"Shh." Guenevere touched her finger to his mouth. "Let us have this moment. For whatever dread may come of it, I need to be here now." There were tears in her eyes.

And in his, as well. "God forgive me," he whispered, running his lips along the swell of her breast.

They had intended never to see one another again. They had both resolved to pray and fast and thereby free themselves from their base desires. They both refrained from touching themselves while reliving the memory of that languid afternoon when they had filled the air with the sounds of their passion, and filled their souls with the sights and tastes of their hungry bodies. They had both vowed not even to permit themselves to dwell upon the memory of the moment for which they had sacrificed everything. They did all this to expiate what they knew to be their sin.

But it was already too late for that. Within six weeks of their encounter, Guenevere knew that the worst had occurred: She was pregnant.

CHAPTER THIRTY-THREE

THE POISONER AT THE WELL

Not for a single moment did Titus Wolfe consider the possibility that a man had been brought back to health instantly after a gunshot wound because of a boy messiah. And yet he had seen it himself: Hal Woczniak had not been wearing a Kevlar vest or a theatrical bag of pig's blood. Titus was more than adequately familiar with signs of death, and they were abundantly in evidence on the former FBI agent. He had gone down with a lethal injury. And then, inexplicably, he had gotten up without a scratch.

The only possible explanation was the water. But the explanation was not that the water was miraculous. Oh, no. Wolfe had been involved with governments too long to be so naive. The "miracle" of the water was due, without doubt, to some compound—probably experimental, possibly deadly over the long term—which the CIA or some other clandestine organ of the United States military apparatus had placed into it.

What was it? A vaccine against a virus intended for warfare? The virus itself, which perhaps healed before it killed? Some substance engineered to enhance genetic mutation? The building blocks of a super race? Or might it be a killing drug in disguise, something that made people feel better while actually speeding up the death process in the infirm and elderly?

It could be anything. Anything, that is, except what it appeared to be, which was a beneficial and benign source of healing that was free for the taking. That was not possible.

While the crowd was still thick, demanding more miracles of the boy whom he had come to think of as the Christ Child, Titus returned to the room at the Tally Ho Motel that he had rented for himself and Pinto. He took a small sealed plastic tube from his shaving kit. The tube contained a half ounce of pure strychnine, enough to kill a cow. Some employer or other—not the Libyans; they wouldn't waste the money on an easy death for their mercenaries—had given it to him in case he got captured and wanted to kill himself.

For some reason, he had been given two such packets. Of course, Titus would not have used either, because he did not regard capture as doom. He had escaped imprisonment many times, in many ways, and none of them had involved a thought of suicide. But he had kept the poison nonetheless, for just such a circumstance as he found himself in now.

Pinto had not come back to the room. He was probably hiding, Titus reasoned, amused at his own ability to inspire fear in others. Pinto had not failed, exactly—he had shot the ex-FBI man cleanly enough. But the fact was that nothing had worked out the way Titus had planned. He had come thousands of miles with a psychopath, his life in jeopardy the whole time, just to kill one man who now appeared to be immune to bullets. In another few hours the television crews which transmitted to the world the whole episode of Hal Woczniak's miraculous return from the dead would be back in force.

Titus had to move fast.

But first he had to test the water at Miller's Creek. Because whatever was in it was important enough for the United States government to stage the most elaborate ruse he had ever seen in order to conceal it. Once he found the secret of the water, he could sell it to any government in the world, and make enough from the sale to live in safety and wealth for the rest of his life.

And perhaps strike a blow for the Coffeehouse Gang while he was at it.

The strychnine in Titus's possession was double-sealed, first in a thin, degradable material, and then in a tube of sturdy plastic. The outer vial was curved, designed to fit easily along the base of one's teeth. Once cracked, the interior packet would melt virutally instantly in saliva.

Titus kept the vial in his pocket as he waited in the line at Miller's Creek. Following the events of the morning, the police had dispersed the crowd that had gathered there, and few had returned so quickly. The police themselves were nowhere in evidence: They were patrolling the house where Arthur and his escort were staying, or searching the vicinity for the gunman who had fired a shot into a crowd. The only people at the creek were two busloads of pilgrims who had left their homes too early to hear about the shooting, and too late to cancel their excursions.

It was a good time for his experiment. Innocuously fitting in with the milling visitors to the creek, Titus pierced the plastic tubing with a pin in his pocket and then held it under the cold water. Within three seconds, the strychnine was released into the creek and flowing freely. He replaced the spent tubing in his pocket, along with a small vial of the creek's water.

Then he sat back and waited to see what it did to the faithful.

Several dozen people obliged him at once. It was a hot day, and even those who had no particular need of healing appreciated the water. They drank it, splashed in it, annointed their eyes and mouths with it. They dunked their babies into the water. They dipped their heads into it.

Nothing happened to any of them, except that one man exclaimed that his toothache was gone, and a woman announced, weeping, that the arthritis that had been crippling her hands for decades suddenly vanished.

No one died, or even reported feeling ill.

Not enough strychnine, Titus decided. Or else it had lost its

poisonous properties somehow. Or it had never been real strychnine in the first place. Perhaps it had been the Libyans who had
given it to him, after all.

He sent part of the water sample, sealed in an airtight container,
by express mail to a lab in New York City, and took what remained
to Beecham Laboratory in Dawning Falls. Beecham's equipment
was at least as sophisticated as that in the lab in Manhattan, since
the Miller's Creek water was of such great interest to scientists of
all stripes. Between the two labs, someone would be able to detect
the presence of strychnine in the water samples if there was any.

He was given the results within fifteen minutes. "You took this
from the water at Miller's Creek, didn't you," a woman wearing a
white lab coat over a low-cut ruffled blouse accused. She was smiling and good natured, as if this sort of thing happened all the
time. "You wouldn't believe how many people want to find out
what's in the water. They think that if they had the recipe, they
could make it themselves."

Titus stared at her, stony-faced, saying nothing.

"Here's the chemical breakdown," she said, producing a printout.
"It's just plain water, similar to the water in every other small town
from Corning to the Finger Lakes. You can keep this, since you're
paying for it." She offered him the paper.

He didn't move. There was something about the woman that
he recognized. Stewardess? he wondered. FBI plant?

"Did you test for strychnine?" he asked, careful to conceal his
British accent.

She reexamined the test results. "Oh, you did ask for that spe-
cifically, didn't you? Here it is. No. There was no strychnine. No
cyanide or arsenic, either. Just good clean water." She smiled.
"Anything else?"

Astonishing, he thought. He would have to wait for the results
from the other lab, of course, but . . . Could it be that the water
had actually neutralized the poison?

That would explain why no one who drank the water after Titus
tampered with it had gotten sick.

It might be miracle water, after all, and if it was, then whatever the government had put into it would be worth a tidy sum.

"Gosh, you look familiar," the woman said.

"Oh, really?" Titus was edging away, getting nervous. "Well, I really must—"

"Bob," she said, snapping her fingers. "I knew I'd come up with it." She giggled. "You went to college in England or something." She looked down, embarrassed. "Maybe you don't remember. It was years and years ago."

He felt faint. The artist. He had slept with her. A wave of nausea rose up in his throat. Of the entire population of Dawning Falls, New York, he would have to encounter the one person who might recognize him despite his efforts at disguise. "Ginger," he said.

"Hey, you do remember! It's Bob, right?"

Bob? Bob? A sensation of profound relief washed over him. Bob! He had used another name! All those years ago, when his future had been so uncertain, he had still had the foresight to use a false name with her!

"Bob Reynolds." She laughed. "Am I right?"

Titus swallowed. Was this a test? Or did the woman just have the memory of an elephant? Either way, running from her was no longer an option.

He only hoped he would not have to kill her. She smelled marvelous.

The fragrance stirred his own memory. Ginger, yes. She always did wear exotic and seductive fragrances. Yes, he was beginning to remember now. A lovely girl who never looked as if she belonged in this silly little American town.

Although she had belonged here, he remembered. In the end, her stunning looks could not make up for a mind that might charitably be described as banal. She had exhibited one interesting quality, though, a titillating aberration of character that had produced some of the best sex he had ever experienced. Titus remembered a long, wine-soaked evening in which Ginger, all those years ago, had told him about her penchant for choosing lovers who beat her. He remembered because at the time he had nearly ruined things by laughing at her odd confession.

"Why don't you leave them, then?" he had asked innocently. "Or strike them back?"

But that would have not been possible for Ginger, and that was why he had found himself so attracted to her. Because, of course, in time he had begun to inflict pain on her himself. Not like the others. He could only guess the sorts of mindless brutes that took her fancy, men who became angry at trifles and released their frustrations with their fists.

But with them, it had been different. There had been pain, but it had been exquisite. Exciting to inflict, and exciting for her to receive. They were bound in pain for those weeks they spent together. And he had felt so much pleasure that he had nearly given up his work to stay with her. One might have said that for a time, insofar as Titus Wolfe was capable, he had loved her.

"How've you been?"

"What?" He remembered where he was. The woman wasn't half bad for her age, he thought. She was still smiling a little too much, too eager to please. There was a bruise on her forehead, artfully covered with a wave of her thick hair.

"Well, if you don't need anything else, I suppose I'd better get back to work," Ginger said lamely. "It was nice to—"

"Could you meet me tonight?" he asked impulsively. He regretted the words almost as soon as they were out of his mouth. It was the bruise, of course, that had prompted him. It had been so long since he had been with a woman.

Ginger looked flustered. "Sure, I guess so," she said. "That would be fun. Talking about old times and all."

He nodded. "Er . . ." He would have to ask a favor. It was not how he liked to begin these things. "Would you mind not mentioning me to the people you work with? Not yet, anyway."

She blushed. "I get it. Married, right?"

"No."

"Oh."

"I would just like to be . . . private with you." He moved a step closer, looked into her eyes, allowed her to see his need. "Do you understand, Ginger?"

She inhaled sharply. "Yes," she said. "Oh, yes, I surely do remember you," she whispered.

CHAPTER THIRTY-FOUR

DADDY

Although Titus knew that he was taking a risk by going out with Ginger, it seemed small enough to chance. The fact that she did not know his real name further reduced any danger inherent in the situation. Of course, she may have been a plant, a woman who only vaguely resembled the nubile girl he'd enjoyed twenty years before. But really, he thought, that would take a lot more effort than the FBI was usually willing to expend on something as ephemeral as a police sketch. He was probably safe with her.

And, too, Titus was not made of stone. He had gone without sex for nearly three months. Working under the strict scrutiny of the Libyans during the preparations for the Warren Air Force Base project, he had not dared to jeopardize himself by buying a woman's favors.

Besides, Ginger Ranier had something not even the most experienced prostitute could offer: that sweet willingness to let him hurt her.

He guessed that the sheets on her bed had barely cooled since

the exit of their last occupant. Clothing left behind by a number
of men still hung in the closet. Titus smiled as he looked through
them. A cheap polyester blazer, two Hawaiian print shirts still
smelling of sweat. Ginger would never change. And she was still,
despite the eighteen years that had passed since they last saw one
another, the best thing he'd ever had in bed.

"I'm ready," she said, emerging from the bathroom wearing a
chiffon leopard-print peignoir.

Titus tried to suppress a laugh. "How often do you get to wear
that in this town?" he asked, stretching languorously on the bed.
He had removed the dental appliance. He would be changing his
appearance again after he left her, anyway.

"You'd be surprised," she said throatily, moving toward him.

"Take it off," he said. She obliged him, and Titus was surprised
that the sight of her was still stunning. Up close, the skin might
be a little looser, he speculated, but she'd kept everything that
mattered. He took her by her hair. A small comb fell out. "Does
that hurt?"

"Yes," she moaned, her fingernails scratching upward on his arm.
"Why are you wearing a bandage on your neck?" she asked softly.

"I cut myself shaving," Titus said.

She smiled. "Must have been a while ago." She pulled it off.

"What are you—" He shoved her away from him.

Ginger's face registered shock and hurt. "But it was just flapping
loose," she explained. "There's not even a mark under it."

Titus raised his hand to the place where the wound from the
spear had been. "Good God," he said. He moved to the mirror. "It
must have been the water."

"Oh, at the creek?" She laughed, anxious to get things back on
a lighter note. "Did you go there?"

Titus did not answer her, but continued to stare into the mirror.

"I guess the water really does work," she went on. "That is,
sometimes. It doesn't work for me, wouldn't you know."

Slowly his gaze traveled in the mirror from the site of his healed
wound to Ginger's face. "It doesn't?" he asked midly. "Why is that?"

She shrugged. "Bad luck, I guess."

He was smiling.

"What's so funny?" she asked flatly.

"The fact that the water didn't heal you. Your bruises, I presume, the places where your lovers kick you and punch you."

"Don't say that, honey. Besides, there really aren't that many—"

"Of course there are, Ginger. You're a masochist. You like being hurt. Naturally you wouldn't heal."

Tears came to Ginger's eyes.

"The question is, how did the water know?" he mused. He looked at her levelly, as if he believed she could give him an answer. "How?"

"Well, it could be just about anything, I guess—"

He never heard her. "Psychologically, I suppose, some people simply don't respond to any sort of help. I wonder if the water would heal you if you had a grievous wound, like a—" He bit his lip. He had almost actually said the word *gunshot* in front of her.

He had been under too much stress. The six months in Libya, followed by the aborted attempt to reach Cheyenne, the bizarre encounter with those thugs, then seeing the sketch of his face on the TV news and the two failures to kill the ex-FBI agent . . . He must not allow himself to unravel just because he smelled a woman.

"Do you think that's a bad thing or something?" Ginger was asking.

He closed his eyes and sighed in relief. At least she was stupid, he thought. Thank God for small things.

"I think you could be very bad," he murmured, drawing her toward him. "Why don't you show me?"

The phone had been ringing constantly since the television cameras had lingered lovingly on the image of Gwen and Arthur reaching out to one another in the middle of the highway.

According to the high school crowd, the boy was indisputably King Arthur, and the miracle of his existence was accepted without question. By being linked with him, Gwen's status among her peers rose dramatically, although none of them could figure out why Arthur Blessing, who could have chosen any girl in school— in fact, any girl in any school—had chosen Gwen Ranier.

She talked with the first couple of callers—girls who wouldn't bother to say hello to her in the hall under other circumstances, suddenly friendly and chatty and inviting her to a day at the mall or a trip to the lake. Gwen had listened in silence, muttered a few terse words of rejection, and then hung up. After the third call, she took the phone off the hook. Even the loud and incessant noise the phone made was preferable to the voices of those girls.

Or the sound of her mother having sex. God, she couldn't wait to get out of this house. Out of Dawning Falls. Out, out, out.

She wrapped her arms around her knees. Her dreams had been more frequent lately, and she remembered more of them. They were all about the strange, handsome boy whose portrait she had drawn before ever having seen him. In the dreams he loved her. And she had hurt him. She awoke feeling disoriented, as if she were not quite sure she wanted to finish out the day, and inexplicably sad.

It was probably all the things that were going on, she decided. That man getting shot, and Ms. B's face growing suddenly beautiful . . . It was just hard to take it all in. She was not experienced in social situations. She had virtually no friends at school. She had never had a boyfriend, much to her mother's dismay. Some of the goth boys had tried, in their apathetic way, to get close to her, but she had felt no interest in them.

Most of her antipathy was due, she supposed, to watching her mother throw her own life away on a steady stream of worthless men. But there was something else, too, a sense of waiting for someone. . . .

She kicked a book across the room. Waiting for someone. How stupid, she thought. She might as well be waiting for Godot, waiting for Armageddon, waiting for Prince Charming.

Or King Arthur.

Titus found the empty tube of what may or may not have been strychnine in his trouser pocket. He dipped it into a fishbowl atop Ginger's television set.

The goldfish in it died instantly.

"What are you doing?" came an incredulous voice. A teenage

girl wearing goth makeup stood in a low doorway. The whole house was low and small and dark, Titus noticed. It was like a rabbit warren, filled with cheap and sentimental souvenirs. He felt suddenly constricted, as if he needed to breathe.

"Who are you?" he drawled.

"You killed our fish," the girl announced.

"Coffee's almost ready," Ginger called from the kitchen.

Titus took out his wallet and threw the girl a twenty-dollar bill.

"Keep your stupid money!" Gwen shouted. "And since you're done screwing my mother, why don't you get out?"

"Now, now, what's this all about?" Ginger came bustling into the room. She was wearing a red kimono over her nightie and carried a plastic tray decorated with watermelons.

Gwen rolled her eyes to keep from crying. "Oh, great. Look at you."

"What is wrong with what I'm wearing?" Ginger demanded. "I'll have you know this is silk."

Gwen turned away. "Fine," she said. "By the way, the stud of the day here just poured poison into the fishtank."

Her mother gasped as she noticed the floating goldfish. "Finny," she said. "He's our pet."

"Was," Gwen corrected.

Titus burst out laughing. "I say, the two of you are better than a West End musicale."

"Are we?" Gwen sneered. "Hey, you know what I say?"

"Gwen, now stop it. Stop it this minute," Ginger interrupted. "As it happens, Bob and I are old friends. We knew each other years ago, isn't that right?" She looked to Titus for affirmation.

He folded his arms over his chest as he looked over the girl with an amused but critical eye. "Who is your father?" he asked.

Ginger brought the tray over her chest like a shield. Her mouth opened and closed, but she said nothing.

Gwen's eyes narrowed. "What do you care?"

It was extraordinary. The resemblance was remarkable. "Come here," he said.

"Get lost."

"Now, honey—"

"Why don't you go back to what you were doing in the kitchen, Mom?" Gwen snapped.

"Just hold still," Titus said, walking over to Gwen. He moved her chin.

She slapped his hand away.

Yes. Yes, the resemblance was unmistakable. The same eyebrows, the same mouth.

Gwen's portraitist's eye saw it, too. "Oh, shit," she said. "How many years ago did you two know each other?" she asked warily.

"Well, honey—"

"Don't tell me." She turned a ferocious glare on her mother. "Well, is he? Is this pet-killing bozo my . . . Shit."

"Your father?" Titus asked, looking at Ginger. "Is that true?"

Ginger stared at the floor. "Finny was just a fish," she waffled. "I mean, 'pet killer' isn't exactly . . ."

Gwen stormed out of the house, slamming the front door so hard that one of the diamond-shaped panes of glass shattered.

After she left, Titus stared at Ginger in silence. "She's right, isn't she?" he asked with mild surprise.

"Didn't know how to reach you to tell you about it," she said coyly. "Besides, I didn't know if you'd want to even know you were going to be a daddy." She put her arms around him. "Hey, I'll bring in the coffee."

Titus extricated himself from her grasp, feeling exceedingly uncomfortable. "Er . . . Don't bother, love. I've got to be on my way."

"Oh." She tried not to sound disappointed. "All-righty. You going back to Miller's Creek?"

"I hadn't thought about it, no. Do people visit the place all during the night?"

Ginger shrugged. "I guess they could if they wanted to, but it'd be dark. There's no lights or anything."

"But the creek is still running?" Titus asked. "That is, nothing controls the flow of water into the creek, does it?"

She found this amusing. "No. I mean, It's not as if the creek water got turned off and on. You've been living in cities too long."

"I suppose I have," he admitted. "Is there a well at the site, perhaps?"

"I think so," Ginger said. "The creek flows right underneath the house. The guy that bought the place put in a new floor to cover it. There's some that think he put something in the water then. It never used to do this magic stuff."

It seemed to Titus that several minutes went by before he remembered to breathe again. The floor! How simple could it be? Something, the something that created miracles out of ordinary water, was under the floorboards of that shack near the creek . . . And the whole town knew about it! He could not believe his luck! He was, without a doubt, the first intelligent being ever to set foot in Dawning Falls. And he was going to leave with its treasure.

"I see," he said with desperate nonchalance, and cleared his throat. "Well, I really do have to go along now. I'm very tired."

"Me, too," she said. "Ooh." She flapped her hands, suddenly animated. "Just a sec, okay? I want to do something before you go." She ducked back into the kitchen.

"Ginger . . ." He sighed. She was already becoming tiresome.

The next moment, she bounded around the corner in a brilliant flash of light. When Titus blinked the spots away from his eyes, he saw her standing in front of him with a disposable camera in her hands. "Now I'll have something to remember you by," she said.

Titus reached her in two steps and batted the camera away. It hit the wall and flew apart on impact.

Ginger was stunned. "Why did you do that?" she asked. "I only wanted—"

"No pictures," he said, his heart still racing. Actually, he hadn't meant to respond so strongly, but a man in his line of work did not want to leave photographs of himself behind.

"Please understand."

"Oh. Oh, sure," she said. She picked up the pieces of the camera. It had cost eight dollars. "You always did kind of fly off the handle easy." She did not look at his face as she spoke.

He was panicking. If he killed her, he would have to kill the girl, too. "I'm sorry, Ginger. I really am." He searched his mind for an excuse that would help her to dismiss the incident. "It's just that I hadn't expected your daughter to be here."

"Our daughter," Ginger amended.

"Yes. Well, I'll buy you another camera."

Ginger tried to smile. "Thanks," she said. "Listen, are you in trouble with the police or something?"

He froze. "Of course not," he said mechanically.

"It's just that . . . well, what you said in the lab about not wanting me to tell anybody about you, and I asked if you were married and you said no, so it's not that. . . ."

She was babbling. She was stupid and talkative, Titus realized. A dangerous combination. He walked over to the place where he had thrown the camera, picked up the pieces, and unrolled the film before putting it into his pocket. "You've seen my face on the telly, haven't you?" he asked quietly.

"Oh, no," she said, obviously lying.

"And you've noticed that I don't look the same as I did when I came into the lab."

"Well . . ." A thin line of sweat was beginning to form on Ginger's upper lip. It excited him. "I did kind of wonder why you'd want to look different. . . ."

"Yes." He moved nearer to her.

"But the thing of it is, I only wanted to know because I, like, don't want any trouble, okay? I mean I have a kid, you know, I don't want any trouble for her. But as to my saying anything, I can tell you that's not going to happen. I'm not a blabbermouth, Bob. Just ask any of my friends—"

"And you know my name isn't Bob, don't you?"

"Shoot, I don't know anything anymore," she said, laughing nervously. She backed away slowly, her cheeks trembling. They were fleshy cheeks, he noticed, jowly. When her back touched the wall, she gasped. Then she cried.

"Take off your pretty silk robe, Ginger," Titus said.

She could barely work her fingers, but she finally managed to undo the knot at her waist. She opened the robe, then let it fall. "It's still good with us, isn't it?" she asked, speaking softly so that the shake in her voice would be less noticeable. "I mean, I didn't call the cops or anything, did I? I'm just me and you're just you. . . ."

He kissed her. Her skin was taut and bumpy with gooseflesh, her nipples were hard. She was scared. The fear exuded from her pores, her breath.

"Do you want me to hurt you, Ginger?" Titus asked softly.

Her breath caught.

He pressed her against the wall as she fumbled with his belt and trousers. "Yes," he moaned. "Yes, my lovely."

She wrapped one of her legs around him. The high heel dangled from her toes.

"Have the authorities offered a reward?" he asked, stroking her long neck.

"Wh-What?"

"Is that why you wanted my picture?"

"No, honest," she protested. "Now come on, baby, it's nice now."

"Yes," he said, slowly closing his hands around her throat. "Very nice."

Ginger began to choke as he took her. Her eyes bulged; her tongue protruded. And all the while the back of her head beat a steady rhythm against the wall as Titus worked himself into ecstatic frenzy, feeling the beat of her heart in his hands, watching her panic and weaken and fight for her life.

"Oh, my, yes," he said as her leg dropped off his back and fell limply. Ginger sagged in his arms, held up only by his hands that caressed her neck as if it were a sexual organ.

Her eyes already possessed the glazed, incurious look of the dead.

Titus laid the body carefully over the kitchen table while he made himself presentable. She was actually going to show a picture of him to the police, he thought self-righteously. The cow. Of course, this was going to make things difficult with the girl, but it wasn't worth going after her. The Feds knew about him already. He would just have to get out of the country as soon as possible.

This entire enterprise had been a fiasco, but it was still not irredeemable. Titus would need nothing less than major plastic surgery to change his appearance enough for him to keep working, plus at least a year underground. For that, he would need both money and friends.

In other words, he would need whatever was at the bottom of Miller's Creek.

If Titus could leave Dawning Falls with the secret of the healing water, there would be no reprisals either from the Libyans for the aborted Wyoming mission or from the Coffeehouse Gang for the loss of his cover.

He flipped back the checked curtain over the window. Outside, the sky was leaden and the wind was high.

Rain, he thought. It was an incredible stroke of good luck, more than he could have hoped for. Enough rain would keep away visitors to the creek. And no lights. Ginger had assured him of that.

"Thank you, darling," he said aloud as he lifted her corpse and carried it out to the car.

When he got back to his motel, Pinto was in bed snoring and there was a message from the lab in Manhattan. Its analysis concurred with the other lab's. The water sample he had sent contained a configuration of the H_2O molecule in a form no one recognized. There was no trace of strychnine.

That night he dreamed of poison. And, oddly, of himself as a woman. In his dream he was lovely and lethal, a mistress of the dark herbs, a wise child who had poisoned a princess. . . .

CHAPTER THIRTY-FIVE

THE SLEEPING BEAUTY

Morgause was still a teenager when she poisoned the wife of old King Cheneus and married him, becoming queen of Dumnonia.

Cheneus was even then not in the best of health, and could no longer travel. This greatly dismayed Morgause, who had married the old man mainly to get out of Orkney. She had anticipated a life of gaiety in the court formed around King Arthur's famous Round Table, with knights from every chiefdom in the kingdom, but things were not turning out the way she had planned. Each day Morgause's eyes shifted toward her grizzled husband, while her thoughts ran toward species of lethal herbs.

Fortunately, the ever ambitious Lot of Rheged invaded Dumnonia, killing all of Cheneus's sons and, once Cheneus himself was mysteriously poisoned, taking Morgause as his own wife.

This turn of events was not looked upon kindly by the other nine chieftains, who had all made efforts to comply with the high king's plans for a united Britain. Since Arthur's assumption of the throne, the petty skirmishes between the chiefdoms had ceased.

Valuable men and arms were no longer wasted in pointless civil
wars. All of Britain's power was now focused on repelling the invading Saxons, and the tide was turning. In Camelot, each day
was a celebration of peace, prosperity, and unity.

Lot had placed all of these advancements in jeopardy, but Arthur had to think diplomatically. It would not do to wage war on
Lot; that would make the other chieftains nervous about the high
king's power.

Arthur decided to punish Lot by putting into effect the plan he
had once conceived for Orkney: He divided the conquered and
leaderless Dumnonia nine ways, giving all the kingdoms a share as
great as Lot's. This way, if Lot objected, every other clan in Britain
would rally against him.

It was a brilliant plan. The chiefdoms remained solidly allied,
Lot was penalized for his aggression without bringing about an
armed confrontation, and Morgause, because of her new husband's
resentment of King Arthur, remained far away from court.

Again she languished in the remote reaches of a provincial fortress. In order not to lose touch completely with the world outside
of Rheged, Morgause sent a woman she knew—a wisewoman's
daughter, like herself, from Orkney, whom she had trained in the
ways of the civilized gentry—as her representative in the court at
Camelot.

It was small comfort to her. At twenty-six, having given birth
to four children, Morgause felt like little more than a brood mare.
She might as well have been a hundred, for all the fun to be had
in Rheged. It had been fifteen years since she had last seen Guenevere or Arthur.

And it was useless to try to reason with Lot. He absolutely refused to show obeisance to the high king, who Lot felt had robbed
him of lands won in fair battle. Indeed, if the Orkneyan woman
she had sent to court in her place had not come to her with great
and strange news, Morgause might well have dispatched Lot in
much the same manner that she had gotten rid of so many other
inconvenient people, and made her own way to Camelot.

But the lady from Orkney did come, and with the most delicious
tidbit of information. The queen was with child!

That wasn't what was delicious about it, of course. In fifteen years of marriage, everyone expected Guenevere to have birthed a castle full of children to perpetuate Arthur's dynasty. What made this particular piece of gossip so tantalizing was that the queen had not told the king about it. And not only had she not told him, but it was also clear that she was afraid to tell him.

"Afraid?" Morgause savored the idea, her lovely red lips stretching until she looked like a satisfied cat.

"Yes, ma'am," her creature answered. "I was in the bedchamber myself when the queen's old nurse—she's dotty with age, and never bides her tongue—when she says, 'I declare, you've got a belly, Guenevere!' " The woman giggled. "Just like that. And the queen got all red, and acted like she never heard her, but the nurse kept on. 'Have you told the king your husband, girl?' she says so loud you could have heard it beyond the pale, and all of us are trying to keep from laughing, because naturally we all noticed it, though no one would say nuffink—"

"Nothing," Morgause corrected.

"Yes, ma'am, nothing, sorry. But it's the talk of the court, all the same. It seems everybody knows except the king. So now we're all saying why isn't she telling him? Well, I say there's only one reason a woman wouldn't tell her husband she's big with his child, and that's if . . . well, you know, don't you, ma'am."

"If it isn't his child," Morgause finished.

The woman smiled slyly. "That's what the word is, Lady. The king's been dreadful busy, always gone someplace or other, or training with the knights what love him something fierce. . . ."

"Who love him," Morgause said absently, drumming her fingers on the table.

"Yes, ma'am. The knights who love him." She laughed aloud. "They love him a damn sight more than the queen, I'll wager!"

Morgause laughed with her. "But then," she said, growing thoughtful, "who would be the one?"

"The one what's putting a smile on the queen's face, you mean? But then, there's just the one. The Christian."

"Launcelot," Morgause said, recalling the handsome face of the young Gaul.

"That's him. The two of them's always praying and such, and making a point of never being in the same room with each other. Why, they might as well be wearing dunce caps on their heads, they're that noticeable."

"Except to the high king."

"Well, not for long. She's starting to stand with her legs apart."

"Does she show to anyone except her nurse?"

"If you look at her the right way and in the light," the woman said.

Morgause thought for a moment. "Less than three months, though?"

"Right about there, I'd say."

Morgause got up and took a book from a wooden chest. Written in her own hand, with painstakingly exact illustrations, it was her herbary, and her most precious possession. She turned the pages carefully, frowning as she read. The Orkneyan woman sat quietly in the presence of such magic.

Finally Morgause spoke. "I'm going to pay the queen a visit," she said.

"Oh, King Lot may not like that much," the woman ventured cautiously.

"Really?" Morgause smiled as she closed the herbary. "I think he'll be delighted."

She arrived at court bearing gifts of great ingenuity—a bird that flew at the end of a golden string, a blanket of wolf noses for the king's bed, and twenty wooden benches made from the finest cedar in Orkney, lest anyone forget that, before her marriages, she had ruled her brother Melwas's kingdom in all but name.

Within a week of her arrival, Morgause's charismatic personality had convinced most of the court that she had also been the power behind Cheneus's throne, and that Lot owed her a great deal more than the keys to his castle, as well. There was a ball in her honor, a meeting with the king which resulted in the establishment of the Royal Shipyard in Rheged and, finally, a private audience with the queen.

Guenevere seemed very distracted, hardly seeming to notice the beautiful young woman paying her court.

"Do you not remember me, Highness?" Morgause asked sweetly. "I am the girl-child who accompanied you on your ill-fated journey to Orkney."

Guenevere moved her gaze toward Morgause. "Melwas's sister," she said softly. "Of course. You were the only one who showed me kindness during that ordeal."

"I thank you for not holding the actions of my brother against me," Morgause said. "A word from you, and the high king could destroy all of Orkney."

Guenevere smiled without mirth. "I think not," she said before adding quickly, "The king's purpose is to unite Britain's chiefdoms, not to destroy them."

She's saying Arthur doesn't care about her, Morgause thought. She felt an impulse to hurt the queen, with her irritating pouting and resentment. What did she expect from the high king of Britain? A shoulder to cry on? Didn't she have a nurse for that?

Morgause touched her hand. "I saw how greatly you suffered, Lady."

At that the queen's eyes grew shiny with unshed tears.

Self-pitying idiot, Morgause thought. "I've brought you a gift," she said, handing Guenevere a bundle wrapped in fine white wool from the western hills of Orkney. Inside was a tapestry, a weaving so detailed and splendid that it almost seemed made of magic. It had, in fact, been woven by the Orkney witches, who excelled at this craft.

"Your name was invoked with each knot," Morgause said, for once speaking the truth. The tapestry, meant for Guenevere alone, was worked through every stitch with magic. "I myself produced the central figure."

Slowly Guenevere unfolded the large piece. It showed a knight in silver armor, kneeling beside a woman who lay asleep on a bed of flowers.

"The Sleeping Beauty," she said, remembering an old story her nurse had told her as a child. The tapestry was truly a work of such magnificence that Guenevere could not immediately find words to express her appreciation. She ran her hand over the stiff fabric. "It's wonderful," she said. "I almost . . ."

Her hand stopped near the knight's face. Launcelot's face. The likeness was uncanny. And the face on the sleeping princess was her own. Guenevere's expression was so stunned, it was almost comical.

"We tried to tell the story of your rescue from my brother's wickedness, Highness."

"But the king . . . It was the king who rescued me," Guenevere said, flustered.

She lies so pitifully, Morgause thought. "Please forgive me, my lady. I remembered, perhaps wrongly, that you were awakened from your slumber by the great Gaulish knight who is your champion, Lady."

"Launcelot," the queen said, so tenderly that the name came out as a sigh.

"Yes, madam," Morgause said. "It may amuse you to know that there are those among my people who believe he brought you back from the dead."

The queen blinked. "I beg your pardon?"

"Oh, I've grown to understand that you were probably only suffering from heatstroke during that long and dreadful ride, Highness, but to the country folk of Orkney, you seemed to have been struck down by some evil spell." She laughed lightly.

"That's not so outlandish as it sounds," Guenevere said, coming to grips with her emotions. "I too thought that for a time. For quite a long time, actually."

You still think it, you weak-minded little fool, Morgause thought, *because it was true. You just won't believe it.* "Well, then you may be able to understand the depth of their worry. Orkneyans may be simple folk, but they worship you, Highness. The thought that you may have died because of the hardships of that journey . . . That was something that could not have been borne by any of us. And so when Sir Launcelot woke you, it was as if he had brought you back to life."

Guenevere breathed in sharply. "Back to life . . ."

"And then, when we heard a rumor that he had brought someone else back to life from the dead . . ."

"The knight at the tournament. Yes, that was true."

"Oh, my," Morgause said slowly. "It would be easy to fall in love with such a man."

Guenevere's eyes snapped warily, but Morgause was only gazing at the tapestry. "He has very distinctive features, don't you think, my lady?"

She felt the queen trembling beside her.

"A son by such a man could not be mistaken for another's, no matter what the circumstances."

Their eyes met. Guenevere's face was dead-white with fear. "What can I do?" she whispered.

From a pocket sewn into the shift she wore beneath her gown, Morgause produced a vial of dark liquid. "Blue cohosh," she murmured.

"Will this kill me?" Guenevere asked.

"Not you, Highness."

The queen knew her meaning. She closed her eyes in anguish.

"Your life is protected by the magic in the knots of the tapestry," Morgause said. Then she rose to leave.

Guenevere did not move.

The queen's physicians were called three days later. They informed Arthur that his wife had miscarried a son, but that she would live.

Two weeks later, when she was well enough to walk, Guenevere took the tapestry into the cook's building and threw it into the fire.

She never conceived another child, thus ending the dynasty of Britain's greatest king.

CHAPTER THIRTY-SIX

THE WHEAT KING

There was darkness in the Summer Country.

"Are you hiding?" the Innocent's voice spoke into the void.

Taliesin started. "I beg your pardon," he said dispiritedly. "I thought I was alone."

"Would you like to be?"

"No, no, madam. You're quite welcome, as ever." With an effort, Taliesin popped into view amidst a bank of fluffy white clouds. "There," he said. "I've made myself visible."

"Not on my account, I hope," the Innocent said dryly. "I'm blind, remember?"

He looked about, distracted. "Oh, quite. That is . . ."

"My, my, little bard. You are upset."

He turned away. "Well, why wouldn't I be? Things are ruddy awful."

"Yes," she agreed with a sigh. "That they are." There was a long silence in which Taliesin waited for his teacher to offer some helpful advice. She did not.

"Well, it's damned disconcerting, not being able to at least see the expression on your face."

"Very well." The old woman's head materialized on Taliesin's lap. "Is my expression satisfactory?" she asked, grinning.

With a shriek he leaped up, the disembodied head springing off his garment like a ball on a trampoline and sailing off into the clouds. "How could you!" Taliesin seethed.

Her laughter echoed riotously around him.

"That wasn't funny."

"I thought it was," she said, giggling. "Now hold out your arms. Here I come."

A baby appeared, apparently affixed to the old man's chest. He grabbed it awkwardly. "Oh, for Mithras's sake," he grumbled. "Can't you just be a . . . a person?"

"I am a person," the Innocent said. "I'm a nine-month-old infant of the Waura tribe. Normally I dwell in the southeastern region of the Brazilian rain forest."

He looked down at the baby with disdain, although he could not help but notice that she was rather appealing, with her black hair sticking straight out from her scalp like porcupine quills and her bright little eyes which examined his face intently.

"You can see!" he said.

"The better to help you discern my facial expressions," the baby said sardonically, her words sounding slightly distorted since her mouth contained only four small teeth. "That was what you wanted, wasn't it?"

"Yes. Er . . . Is it very different for you—having sight, I mean?"

"Oh, no," she answered. "It's a wonderful treat, actually." She gurgled as she waved her chubby hands in front of her face. "If I were ever to be human again, this is who I would want to be."

"Then why do you—forgive me, Innocent—why do you choose to remain blind, even in the Summer Country?"

She stared ahead blankly for a moment before answering. "It is an atonement," she said quietly.

"What? You? But what could you possibly have done that would require your sight as penance?"

"It isn't penance," she said simply. "Just a choice." The baby patted the old man's face. "You really ought to do something about the hairs in your nose," she lisped. "Some are so long, you could weave them into sweaters."

"Thank you," Taliesin said blandly.

"Now, what were we talking about?" The Innocent settled herself comfortably in the old man's lap. "Oh, yes. Your failure with the Second Magic."

"It wasn't a failure! the old man snapped. "I brought them all back. I gave the king back his life. I . . ."

Inexplicably, his eyes filled with tears, and he found it impossible to go on speaking.

"You didn't know that Arthur Blessing would come to mean something to you," the Innocent said gently. "To all of you."

"I didn't know a lot of things," Taliesin said. "He's like a clock that knows when his own mechanism will break."

"Yes," the Innocent agreed. "This Arthur is extraordinary, but finite. He isn't immortal, but he's not quite human, either. You had too much of a hand in his making."

"But how are humans—real humans—different?"

She blinked her shiny black eyes thoughtfully. "Fate is not a paved road meant to be walked upon, Merlin," she said. "We build the road as we go. Things change all the time, and nothing is 'meant to be.' There is only what is. That becomes what was, and leads, vaguely, to what will be. But there is no right way or right thing. There are no mistakes, even for wizards. Only what was, what is, and what lessons we learn. . . ."

"Until we know everything?"

She smiled, shrugged. "I suppose."

"And so to change one's stars . . ."

"One must let go of one's expectations," the Innocent said. "Forget all the rules, Merlin. Everything I taught you. Stop being a craftsman, and become an artist. And then let your creations run away."

"Let him go?" The old man stood up abruptly. "Are you telling me to let Arthur go forever?"

"Yes."

"But—"

"The way I've let you go."

"Oh," he said.

"Too difficult?"

"Well, it's just that . . . it ought to be more than that, I should think. It doesn't seem that letting go of what I want would accomplish much of anything."

"Perhaps that is because you don't want to let go," she said.

"No, I was only saying—"

A glass globe appeared in the baby's hands. She held it up to him. "Take us back to Camelot, Merlin. You may find what you need there, after all."

"Oh, all right." The Innocent was pulling his chain again, talking in circles. Letting go. That wasn't the problem at all.

"Focus," she said.

Taliesin allowed the place in the globe to exist. From the depths of his soul he brought forth the sounds of wind and birdsong and the smell of rye grass. The castle stood new, its stone still sharp enough to cut flesh. And inside, beyond the great hall, in the chamber of the king, stood a man struggling to keep his shoulders back and his head erect.

"Who's that?" Taliesin asked. "And what's he saying?"

"Go there," the Innocent whispered.

"You are the land, and the land is you," Ector said somberly.

He was an old man by then, and meant well, but his nearsighted, almost mythical loyalty to the king he had known as a boy could be unnerving.

"Thank you," Arthur said, looking up from his work with a weak smile.

"When you recover, the land will once again bring forth an abundant harvest."

"I hope you're right, Ector." He nodded in dismissal. Ector bowed, wobbling precariously on his arthritic knees, before walking backward out of the chamber.

Arthur sighed, putting down the quill in his hand. Ector, unfortunately, was not the only one in Britain who blamed the poor harvests of the past three years on their king. The legend of the

Wheat King, the Earth-Goddess's consort whose sacrifice ensures the success of the next season's crop, was still firmly embedded in the consciousness of the people.

Despite the inroads made by the Christian church, farmers and their wives still copulated in the middle of their fields, making sure to spill the man's seed onto the ground as a sacrifice to the Goddess. She, the Primal Mother, Earth, was still a living force to these people. And to the Goddess, men—even kings—were temporal things to be replaced when their time was done in order to keep the earth alive.

In truth, Arthur's malaise was not unrelated to the failed crops. In addition to the monumental tasks of keeping the clans united so that the Saxons would not be tempted to invade again, now the king also had to find a way to keep his people from outright starvation.

The past three years had been identical: a spring so rainy that roots had rotted in the sodden ground, followed by a dry, hot summer with scorched fields in which nothing grew. By September's meager harvest, new parents looked with fear upon their sleeping infants, wondering how they would survive the coming winter, and the old people shivered even before the first frost came.

The cycle had occurred three times. Now the people were looking at their king, asking silently if he had lost favor with the Goddess. If it was time for the Wheat King's sacrifice.

"It's a natural assumption," Merlin said, pouring a glass of wine.

Arthur took it, but did not drink. He had no appetite for food or drink, and had grown thin and gray within the span of little more than a year.

"The common folk love you, Arthur. They believe you to be some sort of messiah."

The king buried his head in his hands. "What an obscene joke that is," he muttered.

"Well, you did rout the Saxons. Before you took the crown, no man could go to bed with any certainty that his family wouldn't be slaughtered and his home burned before daybreak."

"I could have brought peace fifteen years ago, if the petty chiefs had listened to me," Arthur said bitterly.

"Yes, yes." Merlin was becoming bored with the king's harping on the intransigence of the tribal chieftains. It had been Arthur's idea to accommodate the Saxons rather than obliterate them. The fighting, which had been going on ever since the Romans left Britain and the Saxons looked to the divided land as a place to settle, was accomplishing nothing.

Arthur had pleaded with the chiefs to think differently about the situation. He suggested that each of the petty kings give over a small portion of their lands to new Saxon settlers. The chieftains would be permitted to charge rent and receive a portion of the tenants' crops. This plan worked until the first accusation from one of the chiefs that the Saxon farmers were plotting an insurrection.

It was Lot of Rheged who had complained, of course. Lot, who had resisted the idea of having any Saxons on British soil from the beginning, mentioned that a number of Saxons were living in the forests of Britain.

This was true. After each sea raid, a few Saxon warriors found themselves on enemy territory without weapons, homes, or means to return to their homeland. After several decades, their number had grown to the point where the Saxons were a real, albeit powerless, presence. It was these people, many of whom could no longer even remember their native land, whom Arthur had in mind when he suggested a peaceful Saxon settlement.

Some had already taken British wives and started families. Their number would only grow, and Britain, whose own population was kept low as a result of unrelenting tribal warfare, needed the extra hands to wrest the land back from the abyss into which it had plunged after the departure of the Romans and their advanced civilization.

But Lot—and, if the truth be told, a number of the other petty kings—could never adjust to the idea of Saxons living on more or less equal footing with native Britons. As soon as Lot voiced his complaint about the so-called "army" of disenfranchised Saxons living in the wilderness, "getting ready to kill us all in our sleep like the savages they are," as he put it, a nervous rumbling echoed throughout every chiefdom. Weapons were forged, warriors trained, food supplies stored.

And then, in a night raid which Lot subsequently explained away with a feeble excuse, the men of Rheged attacked every unarmed Saxon tenant holding in the chiefdom.

The action brought out the Saxons who had been hiding in the forests. They attacked not only Rheged but every British farm and hill fort they could breach, fighting with rusted battle axes, broken swords, stones, slings, and makeshift bows.

Within days Britain was in the throes of a full-scale war, although the outcome was never in doubt. In the end, the Saxons were slaughtered, almost to a man, their families wiped out, their few farms burned. Feasts were held, and songs written about the valor of each chieftain who had successfully defended his land from the vicious Saxons.

Only Lot had commanded the bards to write the songs of victory about Arthur.

Soon the other chiefs followed suit. Yes, Arthur had routed the Saxons from the land, just as St. Patrick had rid Ireland of snakes. Arthur was toasted in every hall and castle. Arthur's name was spread among the peasantry and the fighting men. Arthur the High King had brought peace to Britain at last.

And Lot had laughed to himself as Arthur had been forced to smile in acknowledgement. The king's plan had failed utterly.

"Well, whatever you may think of it, you'll be known as the king who drove the Saxons out of Britain," the Merlin said.

"For how long?" After a short period of peace, Arthur knew, in which the Saxons regrouped to heal their wounds and train a larger fighting force, the invasions would begin all over again. "The Saxons are so populous their borders can't contain them . . . while here in Britain, after the flight of the bloody Romans, and the plagues, and the constant wars we love to wage on each other, we've hardly enough men to defend ourselves.

"The Saxons were willing to adandon their culture, Merlin. The ones who homesteaded here were more than willing to become completely British in their ways in exchange for having a little land to till. But we couldn't have that, no. Foreigners on our soil? Never!"

He slapped the arm of his chair with his fist in imitation of the petty kings. "The chiefs conveniently forget that most of them have more Roman blood in their veins than Celtic."

Arthur himself was of a Romano-British line, as were Merlin and most of the other educated people on the island. "God knows, without any foreign influence, we'd all be like Octa and those thickheaded dolts from Orkney."

"Nevertheless, Highness," Merlin said, reminding Arthur with a raised eyebrow of his obligations to his people, "the chiefs are grateful that you led them to victory."

"They're just pleased to have been able to fight again," Arthur said. "They like it."

"Oh, really—"

"Of course they do. We haven't come far from the days when we painted our faces blue and ran screaming toward wild boar with pointed sticks in our hands."

The old man sighed. "Well, all right. Ours is a warrior race, it's true. In many cases, how well a man fights is the measure of him. That's why the chiefs respect you, Arthur. Because you fight well."

"I hate fighting," Arthur said sullenly.

"Nevertheless, you are the king of this fighting race."

"And so I must die by the sword, is that what you're saying?"

Merlin looked abashed. "No, of course not. It's just that the chiefs . . ."

"The chiefs are like children, Merlin. Foolish, unruly children who have to be kept entertained and distracted every moment, or they'll get into mischief." Arthur coughed. "If they don't have a foreign enemy to fight, they'll fight each other."

Merlin tried to smile at the king's fractiousness, but he was worried. Arthur's cough had become chronic. In recent months, he had complained of pain in his gums, which were red and swollen with infection. His stomach bothered him whenever he ate. As a result, he had grown gaunt and gray-faced, and his once glossy hair which had glinted red in the sun now hung, dull and thinning, around his shoulders.

He was thirty-six years old.

And alone. He had sent Guenevere away, in accordance with the wishes of the petty kings, who insisted that he take another wife in order to beget an heir.

When informed of her rejection and approaching exile, the queen had said nothing. She had not spoken a single word of recrimination or outrage against Arthur or the petty kings.

Arthur felt as if he were tearing out his own heart.

CHAPTER THIRTY-SEVEN

THE THREE GIFTS

She was barren, the Merlin had argued. There was nothing else to be done, despite what the peasants thought.

The problem revolved around her name; or rather, her name-sake, *Gwenhwyfar*, the ancient Welsh goddess of the sea. It was said that no king could rule a nation of islands without her by his side. To the common people, sending a queen—particularly one who bore the name of one of the most powerful goddesses in creation—into exile among the wicked Christians was an act of despicable folly.

Of course the crops would be affected, and the catch of fish, and the very weather! Of course the Wheat King would grow sick and die! Arthur Pendragon was the best of the best, but he was still a mortal. Only the Goddess could help him, She who had given him the cup of immortality and the sword of invinciblity. Without her, even the great gifts of the ancient gods would not help. Did these modern men know nothing?

But no one consulted the peasants. To the petty kings it was all quite clear. For an ordinary man, a wife who could not bear children was a burden; but for a king, such a woman was a danger. Because of Guenevere, Arthur had no successor. That in itself virtually assured the kingdom of large-scale civil war after the high king's death.

It had only made sense, the Merlin reasoned now, watching warily as Arthur spat blood onto a cloth.

There were already a hundred legends about the boy king who had pulled the fabled sword of Macsen from the stone. Arthur had been meant to be king from the moment of his birth. He had conquered the Saxons, and had brought the first peace in a thousand years to a free Britain. With Arthur, the improvements advanced by the Romans could be duplicated, could even be bettered. The great king would wrest Britain from the darkness and bring her, shining as a jewel, into the light.

Such a man needed an heir. A dynasty must be established. Even Guenevere's father, King Leodegranz, understood that. His daughter had been required to do only one thing, to produce a son, and she had been given eighteen years to do so. Eighteen years of marriage, with only one pitiful miscarriage to show for it. No other king would have waited so long, given the woman so many chances.

In the end, the chiefs had insisted that Arthur put her aside.

Leodegranz announced publicly that he would not wage war on the king or on any of the chiefs as a result of this decision, or even reclaim the land given as Guenevere's dowry. Compared with such weighty matters as the succession of the high king, he agreed, a wife was nothing.

All Leodegranz requested as compensation was that the seat of the high king always remain at Camelot. The chiefs acquiesed at once. Of course Leo should remain close to the seat of power, they agreed. After all, he'd no idea that his daughter would prove to be a useless mate for the king.

Besides, they knew, all the rules would change once Arthur chose a new queen.

The chiefs were in a state of high excitement, despite the failed crops. After all, the weather was bound to improve, and when it did, the first great crop would be attributed to the new queen. Already some of the petty kings were putting about talk that Guenevere's barrenness had brought barrenness to the land. The peasants were superstitious; they would believe that, and it would keep them from putting too much pressure on their tribal chiefs.

As long as they can blame the woman, they won't blame Arthur, Merlin thought. The only problem was Arthur himself. He did not seem to grasp that he was walking on thin ice with the chiefs, that he should be grateful to them for their continued loyalty after nearly two decades without a successor to the throne. These were warrior-kings; sooner or later, one of them—and Merlin could guess who among them would be the first—would make a move to seize the high king's crown for himself.

They all had sons. Sons and grandsons and nephews, literal armies of men who would stand shoulder to shoulder with them in battle. All except Arthur. Arthur had only the knights of the Round Table, most of whom were unmarried, and a growing number approaching old age. And the king was even turning his back on them, it seemed.

How could the loss of a barren wife affect him so?

The chiefs had demanded that Arthur wash his hands of Guenevere and take another wife to his bed.

Well, he had complied with the first demand, Arthur thought bitterly. Now Merlin had come mewling again about the second, as if the high king of Britain were some sort of stud horse in high rut.

He had never been unfaithful to Guenevere. It had not been a boast of his, surely; men did not put great stock in fidelity to women. And with the business of Morgause's son, Mordred . . . well, half the kingdom was convinced that the whelp really was his, and it would do no good to go on objecting.

He had refused to recognize the boy as his son. That was all he could do. Even the high king did not have the power to still the wagging tongues of gossips. What had shocked him was that some of the chiefs had even suggested that he should claim Mordred, just so he would have an heir.

Imagine, Morgause's son as his heir! The petty kings would stoop to anything, it seemed.

He was lonely, lonelier than he had ever been in his life. His one consolation was that Guenevere might not find life in the abbey where he had sent her to be too difficult, since she was such a devout follower of Christianity.

But it did not alleviate his loneliness, or his guilt at sending away a wife who had done no harm. Oh, there were the rumors of Guenevere's adultery with Launcelot. Rumors . . . and perhaps not rumors.

He would never admit to the chieftains that he had harbored suspicions of the queen's faithlessness, of course: To their accusations he railed and raged, and strongly suggested that the evil-minded among them would be justly dismissed from the high king's company; but secretly, silently, almost guiltily, he wondered if they were right.

The legends already springing up about him claimed that the Goddess had given him two gifts, the Holy Grail of Christ, hero of the New Religion, and Excalibur, the great sword of Macsen. The one had allowed him to achieve immortality, and the other, invincibility.

But in truth he had also been given a third gift, perhaps the most precious of all. In the Goddess's wisdom, She had bestowed upon him the gift of love. Guenevere was that most wondrous of wives—a woman who was both friend and lover, easy to be with yet exciting, sensible but fascinating. What had passed between them from the first had been not only a passion, although that had been a part of it, but something deeper as well, a current of knowing, a recognition that the two of them had been meant to be together from the beginning, and perhaps before the beginning.

Yet he had spent almost no time with her. Indeed, during the early years, their nights of intimacy had been so few in number that neither of them even thought that the reason for their child-lessness might be physical.

The worst of it was that it had never been his choice to neglect her. He had thought of it as a sacrifice, a sacrifice of his time, so that he might attend to more pressing matters. How ironic, then, that after all these years, the most pressing matter in the kingdom appeared to be the lack of issue from their union.

Had she given herself to Launcelot? Could he blame her if she had?

In the end, he had sacrificed two of his three gifts. The first, the cup, he had relinquished willingly. Arthur had no wish to live forever, because to do so would diminish the precious time he had. The other was the love, which he had not considered precious enough to fight for. In every choice between the throne and the woman, he had chosen the throne.

That was, after all, what kings did. It had been the only choice possible.

And because of his choice, he had never had to give up the third gift. The sword had always been his. The sword, Excalibur the Voracious, and all the death it brought, was all that remained.

"Do you think we live more than once, Merlin?" the king asked suddenly.

The old man looked up with a start. Arthur suspected that the Merlin had dozed off. "I beg your pardon? Live . . . Oh. Oh, yes. At least that's what I was taught among the druids. I don't have any personal recollections of living before now, of course." He made an attempt at a laugh. "Why, Arthur? Are you thinking about coming back?"

Arthur smiled. "I was thinking about Guenevere," he said quietly. "We didn't really . . . Oh, I don't know, *succeed* might be the right word. I never wanted another woman in my life, and yet . . ." He shrugged miserably.

"That's only because she was barren," the Merlin said quickly, then instantly regretted it. "I meant that the queen—"

"It was more than that."

The old man looked abashed. "I'm sure it was."

"If I hadn't been king, things may have been different."

"No doubt," Merlin said. "But you are king."

"Yes," Arthur said abstractedly. He wondered if Guenevere's initial desire for him had ever blossomed into total abandon. She had always been beautiful, to be sure, lovely and accommodating.

But there had also been something else in her manner, a certain pagan wildness that Arthur had perceived and even loved, but had never been able to tap. It was as if Guenevere were as constricted by their royalty as he was.

Had Launcelot known that wildness, touched the inner heart of the girl named for the Welsh goddess to whom the commoners still made secret sacrifice before sowing their fields? Had he tasted the salt of her armpits, felt the smooth, hard longing of her tongue between his legs?

The king's glass fell out of his hands and crashed onto the stone floor.

"Majesty!" the Merlin said, rushing to summon a servant.

Arthur waved him away. "It's nothing," he said irritably. His voice was hoarse.

In the early days of their marriage, Guenevere had hosted elaborate festivals at Beltane and Samhain, the biggest holidays in the Old Religion, at which time the miracles of birth and death were celebrated. For weeks before the feast of Beltane at the beginning of May, the peasant women would gather bunches of herbs and wildflowers and then bury them in the earth with a wish for the beautiful young queen to conceive a child. And at Samhain, when the spirits of the dead were summoned on the coming winter winds, those same women asked their departed ancestors to release the soul of the queen's babe so that it might at last be born.

But Guenevere never bore a child to the king, and in time the festivals stopped. The queen had become a Christian, the villagers heard. She had been converted by the handsome foreign knight named Launcelot.

And from then on, Arthur remembered, she had slowly withdrawn.

It had been nothing notable or obtrusive—just a bit less disappointment when Arthur had to leave, not quite as much effort to converse with him when he returned. She had always been willing to accept his lovemaking, of course, although that, too, changed with time. Along with her Christianity, Guenevere developed a sort of prudishness about her body. And once, when pressed, she had admitted to feeling shame at indulging in physical congress when it was unlikely to produce an heir.

Arthur had been furious with that, so furious that he'd thrown on his clothes and ridden to his hunting lodge, where he remained for the rest of the night. Now he wondered if he had been angry with her for her lack of enthusiasm, or for her words that so echoed the sentiments of the petty kings.

Or perhaps it was because he had known even then, in some inner, hidden way, about Launcelot.

The queen's champion left Camelot shortly after Guenevere's retirement to the abbey. He traveled to a wild place, to the northern lands of the Picts, or so the stories told, where he had lived as a hermit for the remainder of his life. A life which had ended in that most undesirable of Christian states, suicide.

Suicide! Arthur shifted his aching, thinly-fleshed bones in the hard chair. It was as if Launcelot were consciously turning his back on his faith. Or else ejecting himself from it in shame.

The two of them had felt so much shame!

Yes, the queen and her champion must have had each other, Arthur decided. And though it hurt him, he could feel no real bitterness toward Guenevere for it. After all, he had had his chance with her, and thrown it away. If, after a lifetime of disappointment and neglect, she had managed to find some small share of happiness with another man, then he would not begrudge her that.

But neither he nor Launcelot had ever touched the real Guenevere, the goddess from the sea. And she had withered away in the waiting.

The king wiped his eyes. Was he weeping, or only sick? He could no longer discern the difference.

CHAPTER THIRTY-EIGHT

THE BROKEN SWORD

"Do you see, little bard?"

With a pained expression, Taliesin looked around at the bland clouds surrounding him. He had been immersed in the agonies of the king in his castle. On his lap the Amazonian infant spoke animatedly. "How they all suffered and struggled, the high king whose sense of duty had cost him everything, the banished queen, driven by guilt to become a dessicated shell . . ."

"And the evil magician who orchestrated everyone's downfall," Taliesin said flatly. "I say, you're not going to wet on me or anything like that, are you?"

"That depends on how annoyed I become with you." Laughing heartily, the baby grabbed his long beard. "Actually, you don't come off half bad. You were only following your reason."

He felt himself warming to her, despite himself.

"That's the point, you see. You were all three following scripts that you'd written for yourselves. Guenevere could have run off with Launcelot and become his puritanical mistress. Or she could have embraced paganism entirely, and made herself into the wild woman of the wood."

"The queen?" Taliesin asked, incredulous.

"Well, I know that seems odd, but only because she didn't make those choices. All the great queens after her were influenced by her reticence and powerlessness."

"Hmmph," the old man said. "And the king?"

"Good heavens, the king might have done all manner of things. He could have kept Guenevere, and told the chiefs to go hang themselves."

"But he wouldn't have been a good king if he'd done that!"

"What difference would it have made? The Saxons would have invaded again, anyway, and eventually conquered Britain, as they did."

"He was obligated to please the chiefs," Taliesin explained. "That was his unspoken pact with them."

"Which sealed his doom right from the beginning," the baby said. "Actually, the only really good idea he had during those dreadful days was to talk with the Saxons."

"How can you say that?" Taliesin answered, his body twitching defensively. "The Saxons couldn't have been stopped at that stage. Perhaps earlier—"

"I didn't say the idea was effective. I said it was good. It was good because it was outside the king-mold he had forced himself to conform to in every other area of his life. He was creating a new destiny for himself."

"Hell's bells, Innocent, that's what got him killed! Because he couldn't get the petty kings to support him, he ended up on the losing end of a civil war! Don't you see, that was what went wrong! That was what should never have happened!"

"But it did," she said, waving her fat little arms in the air. "It happened because he wanted it to." She squirmed. "How uncomfortable your bony knees are becoming!"

The Innocent vanished from his lap and reappeared a moment later as an elderly blind woman seated demurely beside him. She was dressed in finely woven white silk, with a diadem of clear stones in her wispy white hair.

"Oh," Taliesin said. "You're lovely."

"Thank you," she answered with an ethereal nod of her head. In the next instant she was standing in front of him, dressed in a filthy gown and corset, her hair streaming long and wild behind her. She was wearing an eye patch and scratched her belly with gusto. "Do you see, you motherless blighter?" she roared. "Do you see we can do anything we want?"

"Good gods," the old man said, his nostrils flaring. "You smell abominable."

"Arrgh," she roared.

"Innocent, please . . ."

"But we don't!" she shouted, hitting her chest and belching. "We almost never do what we want, because we're afraid that what happened to Arthur will happen to us, that we'll be thrust out of the great scheme of destiny and go floating about—"

"Innocent, I must protest in the strongest terms—"

"Shut your flap, arsewipe, and show me your ball."

Taliesin's mouth formed an outraged O. "I say, I have never—" The glass globe struck him in the head. Moaning, he staggered backward. "Why, you horrid old beast!"

"Back at ya." She farted. "Take another look, matey, and tell me if I'm not right."

"I need to speak with the Saxon king," Arthur announced.

The Merlin whirled around to face him. "What? Surely you're not going to try for a treaty again. Not after what happened to the forest settlers."

"That's why I have to do it. They're angry, and justified in their anger. Even now the Saxons are massing along their shores, with dozens of good ships at the ready. We'll have another invasion before long."

"Then call the chiefs—"

"For another round of battles," Arthur said flatly.

"By Mithras, yes!" The old man moved toward him with a speed he had not exhibited in months. "Don't you see, this could be your chance to consolidate your power among the petty kings. Unite them once more against a familiar enemy—"

"And meanwhile marry the daughter of the strongest among them—"

"The strongest is Lot, of course, but—"

"To save my reign at the expense of all Britain."

"Actually, Cornwall has a daughter . . . What?" Merlin frowned at the king, puzzled. "What are you talking about?"

"How much longer do you think we can keep the Saxons at bay?"

"Why . . . indefinitely, I should think. They haven't attacked us for nearly ten years."

"That was before the slaughter of the forest Saxons."

The Merlin was silent.

"So. Ten years, then? Is that what we'll get if we trounce them again? And it's a big if, Merlin. You see, while we've been using up men and weapons killing unarmed men hiding in the forests, the warriors of Saxony have been busy training and building ships. They may win this time."

The old man sputtered. "Pfft . . . Saxons defeat Britain! Sometimes you talk like a madman, Arthur."

"Really? I don't find the possibility at all mad. There are more of them, they've got more weapons, and since we haven't been willing to consider any alternative to all-out warfare, we're virtually inviting them to invade us." He shrugged. "If I were the Saxon king under those circumstances, I'd attack, too."

Merlin crossed his arms over his chest. "I suppose you're going to tell that to the chiefs."

"Why not?"

"Because they'll turn against you!" the old man shouted. "You said it yourself, Arthur—the Celts are a fighting people—"

"They've got to stop fighting," Arthur said quietly. "If we are ever to establish ourselves as a nation—as a civilization—we have to look beyond the costly thrill of bloodshed and toward a lasting peace."

"Yes, yes." Merlin tried not to sound exasperated at the king's adolescent idealism. "Those are fine sentiments, and I agree with them. But your problem right now is not to achieve a lasting peace with the Saxons. Your problem is to keep the petty kings in line."

"So that I can go on being king?" Arthur said stridently. "Is that all it's about?"

"Yes, yes, it is!" The Merlin's eyes blazed. "Because you are Britain, Arthur. Don't you understand? If you aren't king, someone else will be. Why, already Mordred is courting the chiefs. And some of them are taking him seriously."

"That's Lot's doing," Arthur said dismissively.

"Of course it is. And the chiefs know it. Lot's power and wealth, behind a legitimate male heir—"

"Mordred is not legitimate!" the King railed. "There is not even a possibility that he can be my son!"

"His mother says otherwise."

"To gain the crown for him!"

Merlin held out his hands in a calming gesture. "A king is what the chiefs need," he said softly. "That is all I am saying. A king who can provide an heir—"

At that, Arthur stood up and walked out of the room.

Arthur called upon the petty kings to meet outdoors, so that they would see him mounted upon a stallion, rather than sitting like an invalid in a too-warm room. But the day was wet and dark, and his voice barely carried in the cold drizzle. He began to shiver with fever even before he finished his speech.

"And so," he said, trying to stifle the cough that threatened to wrack his chest with pain, "you must see that the only way to a lasting peace is through treaties of trade and homesteading—"

"Am I also to let the bastards tup my daughter?" shouted the king of Cornwall.

"And your wife as well," someone else chimed in.

Lot of Rheged stepped forward. The crowd parted deferentially to let him pass. Always a threat to the other chiefs, Lot had been kept in line solely through the laws created and enforced by King Arthur, which ensured equality among them all. But after his invasion of Dumnonia and subsequent marriage to Morgause, who still effectively controlled Orkney, Lot's power slowly swelled. It had all been perfectly legal. Much of it, in fact, was purely psychological: Lot was a strong man who would be a fearsome adversary. But the result was the same. Any balance that may have once existed among the petty kings had been destroyed long ago.

It left the chiefs with a difficult choice: to remain faithful to a weakened, childless king in ill health, or to side with Lot, who would surely wipe them all out, one by one, to rule Britain as a tyrant.

"With respect to my king, Sire," Lot snapped, "and to the oath of loyalty I have taken as one of ten kings, to defend my country against all who would harm her . . ." He paused and looked around, lest anyone miss the intention of his words. "I swear by all that is holy that I shall not suffer a Saxon invasion upon Britain's shores without a fight!"

The petty chiefs hesitated for only the briefest moment, then cheered in support.

"We'll not have the blood of Saxon dogs running through the veins of our families!" someone chimed in.

"The only Saxon blood on my land will be what's spilled in battle!"

"And good riddance to them!" Lot finished.

More cheers.

Arthur put up his hands for silence, but he had already lost his audience. Inadvertently, today's meeting had made the chiefs' choice easier. Arthur had not only grown weak himself, many of them felt, but was actually willing to give the country over to the Saxons. Lot, on the other hand, had begun to make it clear that he would not claim the crown for himself, as the chiefs had once feared, or even give it to one of his own sons. Rather, his petition was for Mordred, a young man whom his own mother—Lot's new wife—proclaimed to be the bastard son of the high king himself.

Mordred was, it seemed, the perfect compromise between the great but failing Arthur and the powerful, ambitious Lot.

He appeared now, as if on cue, riding a magnificent black stallion, and came to a halt a short distance away from the crowd. In the chill October air, the horse stamped impatiently, steam rising from its flared nostrils. Its rider, too, dark and close-faced, was a picture of restrained strength. The contrast between the two men was stunning: The chiefs looked from the battle-ready young man seated high on his virile mount to the sickened, gray-faced king shivering beneath a cloak that looked too heavy for his shoulders to support.

Almost imperceptibly, the group shuffled away from Arthur to assemble loosely around Mordred.

Lot did not make a move to stand beside him. He did not have to.

Far away, it seemed, isolated and alone, the king doubled over in a paroxysm of coughing.

Lot cocked his head, like a vulture observing a lion in its death throes. *Take your time*, his eyes seemed to say. *I can wait. I can wait.*

Even Arthur's own men were embarrassed.

By the time the king dismissed the meeting, almost no one was even listening. Only the knights of the Round Table were still gathered about him.

"It was a failure," he said quietly to Merlin. The shame and despair in his heart felt like an actual, physical weight in his chest.

"Of course it was!" the old man rasped. He wanted to add that the debacle on the moor could not have been more damaging if Lot had planned it himself, but he restrained himself from rubbing salt into Arthur's wound. "The idea of getting the chiefs to consider peaceful negotiation with a longstanding enemy was perhaps too bold," he said diplomatically.

"No." Arthur shook his head. "That's not it. A year ago I could have commanded them. It was I who lost them—myself, my bearing, my health . . . my weakness. They smelled it, and turned away from me as if I were offal."

Merlin looked down at his hands helplessly. As usual, the king had perceived the situation perfectly. The man who had once been the nation's savior, the king who would reign forever, had become, in the eyes of his subordinates, a useless fool.

"Who will make the first move against me?" he asked quietly.

The old man sniffed. "It's too early to think that way. For Mithras's sake, Arthur, you can still turn this around. Marry Cornwall's daughter—"

"It will be Lot," Arthur said flatly, as if Merlin hadn't spoken. "Lot, with Mordred as a figurehead. He'll need Mordred at first, because of the boy's claim to be my heir. But unless Mordred so endears himself to the other chiefs that his position becomes unassailable, Lot will be rid of him before long."

"Then ally with Lot," Merlin urged. "Bring him to our side. Neutralize Mordred."

The king laughed mirthlessly. "All that, just by marrying? My, my, wizard, for a pagan, you apparently set great store by the institution of wedlock."

The old man could no longer contain himself. "No, marriage might not accomplish all that without any additional effort," he said slowly, "but it may mitigate some of the damage you've done by proposing to bring Saxons back to Britain and insisting that the chiefs live cheek by jowl alongside them!"

"I've told you, we have to move beyond those days of constant war. The chiefs must learn that peace—"

"Yes, yes," the Merlin said impatiently. "They must. And they will, under a wise ruler who will first ensure their safety by begetting a son to take his place!" He finished with a roar, then brought himself under control. "Under the circumstances, Arthur, could you not at least consider marriage? It doesn't seem like such an onerous task, in exchange for saving your crown, your dynasty, your future, your country, perhaps your very life—"

"Is my life so important?" the king asked quietly. "For what am I known? For driving the Saxons out of Britain, preparing the stage for a full and permanent invasion by a greater power. In the end, my legacy will have been that of a shortsighted warlord who sacrificed the future of his country for a momentary victory." He shook his head bitterly. "No, wizard. It is better that I leave behind none of my blood."

Merlin's anger was such that he could barely breathe. "If that's how you feel, then you might as well give the throne over to Lot and be done with it—"

At that moment, the young knight named Perceval entered the room. Seeing Merlin's furious countenance, he stepped back a pace.

The old man threw up his arms in exasperation. "What do you want?" he shouted. The young man's cheeks blazed.

"I sent for him," Arthur said. He looked pointedly at the Merlin. "Do you mind? The last time I checked, this was my residence."

The wizard sighed. "Forgive me," he said for the benefit of the knight. Inwardly, he wished he could push the fellow back out the door so that he could hammer some sense into Arthur's head.

"Perceval, come here," the king commanded.

As the young knight approached, Arthur opened a wooden casket inside which was a single, shining object: the sword Excalibur.

He lifted it gently from its silk casing. The light from the candles in the ceiling wheel danced in its silvery depths. The jewels in its hilt shone.

"Macsen's sword," he said with a faint smile.

The old man watched him as he held the sword to the light. Even now, sick and middle-aged, there were times when Arthur still looked like a boy. It was the clarity of his eyes, perhaps, a complely unselfconscious directness that lent his face an air of youthful ingenuousness. Merlin's heart broke, remembering the thoughtful, sensitive boy who had never possessed the ruthlessness of a Celtic tribal chief.

And yet he had been chosen by the ancient gods to rule.

That boy. This self-doubting king, crushed and dying.

But there was still Excalibur. That, which Arthur held, was his badge of office more than any crown. It was the proof of his having been chosen by the Gods themselves. Macsen's sword was what made Arthur the king, the true king, the once and always, Forever King.

He handed the sword to Perceval. "I want you to cast this into the lake," he said.

The young knight's face registered such shock that it seemed he would faint on the spot.

With a low moan, the Merlin sank into a chair, his knuckles white and trembling on its arms.

Perceval looked to him, and then to the king. "My Lord—"

"Do as I say. If I am killed, I will not leave the sword for Lot of Rheged—or any of the attacking Saxons—to take. I owe old Macsen that much."

"And if you are not killed?" the Merlin asked hoarsely.

Arthur ignored him. "Take it," he said gently, pressing Excalibur into Perceval's hands. "Make sure it is sunk in the deepest part of the lake. And tell no one. Swear it."

"I . . . I will tell no one, my Lord. I swear it."

The king nodded once, dismissing him. The knight's gaze, as stricken and helpless as that of an animal caught in a trap, flickered toward the Merlin in search of some other, better counsel.

But for once, the old man had no idea what to do. He closed his eyes and his shoulders moved slightly, as if too weary even to shrug in resignation.

The young man swallowed once, then backed out of the room.

"He's a good young knight," Arthur said conversationally after a moment. "Reminds me of Galahad, even down to the dubious parentage. For all I know, Launcelot may have sired him, as well. Funny, for such a devout Christian, Lance seems to have found his way into all sorts of forbidden beds."

The Merlin looked out the slitted window at the waning moon. Was that why, he wondered, feeling leaden in the pit of his stomach. Was his wife's petty trifling with some hot-lipped soldier the reason why Arthur was throwing away the sword of the gods as if it were garbage? Was this man, this man who was to have been the greatest ruler in history, really so weak as that?

"Galahad was a fine knight, though. As good a fighter as his father, and loyal beyond question. Why, do you remember—"

"Excuse me," the Merlin said. "I find I am very tired. Perhaps we might continue our discussion at another time."

"Of course," Arthur answered.

The old man hadn't moved from his seat. His knotty fingers still clutched the chair arms like the talons of a vulture. For what may have been the first time in all his long life, he finally looked his age, and more. His eyes were rheumy, his lips cracked and dry, his skin ashen.

Arthur was silent as the wizard slowly rose and then moved with difficulty toward the door.

"Merlin . . ." he said hesitantly, as if he were about to share a secret.

The old man held up a waxy hand. Whatever the king wanted to say now, it was too late.

Too late for everything.

"Good night, Majesty," the Merlin said.

He walked out of the chamber and out of the castle. For a long time he ambled aimlessly in the darkness, numb to the cold and wind of the night. At last he found a cave, one of many carved into the side of the hills at the base of the great Tor, and entered it.

Inside, the smell of moss and bat droppings was strong, and the chill dampness oppressive. On the druids' island where he had been trained, such a cave would have been used as a test of his firestarting abilities. In his first year there, he had been able to create a blaze from nothing but two stones and some leaves.

But he made no fire now. Feeling his way through the blackness, he found a wall of rock, sat down on the cold earth with his back against it, and wept.

CHAPTER THIRTY-NINE

THUNDER

Arthur Blessing sat in the room that had been assigned to him, staring out the window at the darkening night. Emily lived in a small house down the same street. He could see its red door illuminated by the streetlamp outside. She had called—nearly everyone in the world, it seemed, had called—but he hadn't wanted to talk just yet.

The knights understood. They allowed him the privacy of his room, knowing, perhaps, that privacy would be a rare luxury for him in the future.

He looked at his hands. What had they done, he asked himself. How had they acquired the power to take the scars from Emily's face and heal Hal's wound?

No, no, another part of him answered. *It wasn't me. It was the cup.* What he had felt was the cup, its vibrance coming up through his hands, power surging through his hands . . .

He ran his fingers through his hair. Had it been the cup? Had the accident on the road been only that, an accident filled with coincidence? Or was he becoming something he had never guessed at, something different, not quite human, perhaps, something . . . other . . .

And, too, there was the girl in the crowd, the one he had recognized not only from his memories of Guenevere, but also from the inexplicable visions of an ancient priestess named Brigid. She had said her name was Gwen, and she had known him, just as he had known her.

The moon shone dimly through thickening clouds. He felt sick. This burden of unwelcome gifts felt nauseatingly, dangerously familiar. The memory of it danced around the outskirts of his consciousness. He knew that this gift, like that other, would destroy him. But first, which was so much worse, it would destroy his dreams. It had before.

The king had thought that discarding Excalibur would save him from his destiny. He had no wish to be known as a warrior who led his people into battle against an unbeatable foe, the Celtic king who had brought about the extinction of the Celts.

He did everything he could to get the tribal chiefs to listen to reason, but they were as voracious as Excalibur. They hungered for blood, even if it was their own, spilled in battle.

When they learned of what Arthur had done with the sword, they despised him. This was not the same king who had led them bravely into battle against the Saxons, they said among their clans, but a weakling who would go begging to his enemies with nothing in his scabbard but talk.

Before long, even the speculation about a royal marriage ceased. It was no longer important that this coward king bear a son.

Mordred began to travel. He visited each of the petty kings, making promises, sealing alliances, assuring them that he would not permit Lot's power to grow unbounded should he, Mordred, come to rule.

The Saxons, meanwhile, aware and amused at Britain's self-destructive unraveling, sat back and waited. The inevitable civil war among the Celts would decimate their number so much that in a year or two, the army of Saxony would be able to take the entire island without losing a thousand men.

Merlin went into seclusion. He was no longer needed.

And then the final stone dropped into the glass, causing it to overflow: Lot of Rheged died, suddenly and with a black tongue.

Mordred, his heir, now ruler of Rheged, Orkney, and part of Dumnonia, was solidly in power. Urged by his mother, he called the petty kings to arms and challenged the king's forces to face them in combat on the field behind a village known as Camlan.

It was the thirty-eighth year of Arthur's life. On the night before the battle, he received a message from the abbey where she had taken the veil.

It read:

> *Please come tonight.*
>
> *Guenevere*

Nuns were not required to confess the contents of their dreams. Nevertheless, Guenevere was so bothered by hers that at times she believed she would burst.

Some of them, understandably, were of Launcelot, naked beside her on the grass while Arthur looked on brokenhearted. These had occurred from the beginning of her stay in the abbey, and had brought on such guilt and shame that she had felt compelled to flog herself for the remainder of the night afterward.

Each nun kept as one of her few possessions a small flail used to flagellate herself as discipline against thoughts of the flesh. Guenevere still had the Launcelot dreams, but no longer minded them. She viewed them, rather, as an opportunity for penance. Whenever Guenevere used the flail as an antidote for her memories of lust, she felt, in her pain and humiliation, that her great sin was being in some measure expiated.

But it was another dream that worried her now, a dream that had come to her now and again since childhood, but which had increased markedly in frequency over the past few years. It occurred with such frequency now, in fact, that she feared sleeping, and kept herself awake long after compline, reciting prayers until her legs grew numb from kneeling upon the cold stone floor and her hands shook with fatigue. But then in time she would invariably collapse into sleep—usually on the floor—and she would be caught up in it again, feeling the old woman's voice rasping out of her own throat:

"Will you choose the sword or the woman?"

It was not even a particularly terrifying dream, except for the fact that she knew the answer: Arthur had chosen the sword. One look around at her surroundings verified that.

No, Arthur, she moaned as she drifted, bodiless, beside him. She was not Guenevere, but someone else, a priestess who had loved Arthur when he was not yet Arthur Pendragon, but another version of Arthur, as she was a version of herself. They were both dream-people, dreams of visions of imaginings, unreal beings whom Guenevere remembered only while she slept, and with such deep sorrow.

Throw away the sword! Guenevere's ghost-self called to him. Throw it away and find your life again. . . .

But the only sound made by her warnings was the soughing of the wind scented with the stench of spilled blood.

Throw away the sword. . . .

In the dream, that had become impossible. The sword Arthur carried would follow him through death and into another existence. It was the Goddess's ironic gift to him, a sword that would bring him victory through lifetime after lifetime. Victory and loneliness, forever. In the end, the sword would be all Arthur possessed. And it would never leave him.

No one knew this better than Guenevere. Her isolation in the Christian abbey had sharpened her senses and opened her soul. Had she been younger when she had entered this place, she might have eschewed the pagan fancies of her youth as mistaken forays down a path of error.

But she did not come to this place as a young woman. She came as a disgraced queen, barren, ashamed, but fully cognizant that the events of her life, however tragic, had not occurred as a result of having followed the wrong gods.

She had, in fact, been a full-fledged, practicing Christian at the time of her fall. No one had talked her into anything; no serpent had lured her into Launcelot's arms.

She regretted the loss of the child, of course. For that she would either burn in the Christian hell or return, in the pagan manner, in a way that would make amends to the unborn child. She might herself become an unborn child, she thought. She seemed to recall a dream in which she met two other women, both of whom were herself. The one had been a priestess of the ancient Hag Goddess. The other had been a young girl wearing leg coverings, like a man's. Both had been dead, as Guenevere herself was dead. A prophetic dream, perhaps.

Ah, of course, she thought without surprise. The young girl had died before she had the chance to bear children. That would be Guenevere's penance in that other, future, life.

So she would lose Arthur again, she thought. The pattern was set; it was not likely to end. Excalibur, the voracious one, the gift of the Goddess, exacted a high price.

The sword was what made Arthur a king. It was as a king that Arthur had chosen the sword over Guenevere. He had not wanted to put her aside; she knew that. Despite her failings, her faithlessness, her barrenness, her ruination as a woman and as a human being, he had loved her. Perhaps, in his way, he loved her still.

But he had given her up. And not for the crown. Arthur Pendragon was not a man who lived for power, or even desired it. But power came to him, always, because he had been chosen by the Goddess to carry out Her will.

He had been a hero and a king. What would he be in the future, Guenevere wondered. A prophet? A worker of miracles? He had found greatness, but at the cost of his human happiness. He had never found any of that. Happiness was not in the fabric of Arthur's destiny. He had been meant to live not a mortal life, but an immortal one, to be a legend rather than a man.

"Goddess, haven't you had enough?" Guenevere whispered into her silent cell. To have lost the love of her life once was a tragedy; but to lose him three times, knowing that for all eternity he would be lost and lost again . . . this was more than the former queen could bear.

She wished with all her heart that Perceval had not come to her with the sword that night. He had promised Arthur that the thing would be tossed into the lake.

Arthur had known exactly what he was doing. By ridding himself of the sword, he was turning his back on the old gods and their plan for him once and for all. He would sacrifice no more lives to them.

But those gods, the ancient ones, the storm gods and the nameless elementals too old for men to understand, and the Great Hag known only as the Cailleach, the Goddess, had made him king, and they were not so easily fooled. The sword had come to Guenevere for safekeeping, while the king slept easily, deluding himself into thinking he had bested the immortals.

"Please, my lady, tell me I have done right in coming here!" young Perceval begged. And he had been so hopeful in his innocence that she had not had the heart to scold him. "You have," she had said, and closed her eyes to the silent sound of the Goddess's laughter.

Oh, yes, the Hag was exacting her revenge. On Launcelot, for giving in to his weakness, on Guenevere, to be sure, for killing the child that had come as a gift to all Britain, and on Arthur, for accepting the great hungry sword as his master.

A sadness of such force overtook her that for a moment she could barely breathe. Launcelot was dead along with his son Galahad, his perfection lost forever to mankind. Arthur was a sickly monarch beseiged by ambitious men determined to take away his crown and his life.

And she herself, Guenevere . . . *Well, look at me,* she thought, not without a certain bitter humor. A forgotten woman, stripped of all her queenly finery, locked in a nun's cell like some drab orphan without possibility of marriage. I suppose it was my particular penance to end up here, among the joyless Christians. The Goddess had given me her favor, and I threw it away.

Just like Arthur.

She reached beneath her narrow bed of fragrant straw and

pulled out the sword Excalibur. "Well, here you are again," she said, her voice heavy with irony. "Come to take him for good, I suppose."

For she could not keep it from him, she knew. The Goddess was using Guenevere as Her tool, it was true, but if she refused, the Hag would find another way.

Arthur would possess the sword until he himself chose to make the sacrifice that would remove it forever from the world of men. And with it, himself.

When he arrived, she held it out to him wordlessly.

He stared at the sword for a moment, then smiled slightly, the corners of his mouth barely lifting. "I thought that was long gone," he said.

"It's been here." She smiled in return. Her eyes were rueful and compassionate.

"Why are you giving it to me now?"

She shrugged. The gesture struck Arthur as almost unbearably pretty. "I thought it might be useful to you."

He grunted. "I doubt if even Excalibur can bring me victory against that one. He's got a bigger army. Not to mention a younger one." He allowed her to place the blade reverently into his hands. "Since Lot died, a lot of the fence-sitters have gone over to Mordred. He's offering some of Lot's lands as spoils of war. Not to mention Morgause."

Even the name was repugnant to Guenevere. "What can she do?"

Arthur smiled. "Oh, quite a lot. She'll marry anyone who's advantageous."

"What about you? Marry her and make Mordred your heir. It will avert a civil war."

"And I'll be poisoned on my wedding day."

"Two can play at that," Guenevere said. "Clap her in irons immedately after the ceremony."

Arthur shrugged. "Then Mordred will finish the job. Don't you see?" He spoke softly. "It's time." They both knew what he meant.

After a long silence, she nodded. "In that case, you should have Excalibur with you," she said.

He smiled. True to her blood, Guenevere understood just what it meant to be a warrior. "I wish I'd spent more of my life with you," he blurted out.

Guenevere bowed her head.

"The young think that there will be time to right every wrong," Arthur mused. "They believe, contrary to everything they know, that they will live forever."

"And so you will," she said. "In your way."

"I love you, Guenevere."

"I love you, Arthur."

And in the glance that passed between them, all the regret and anguish of their wasted lives stood between them like a stone monolith.

At last Arthur put the sword under his arm and turned blindly, his eyes swimming and burning with tears which he refused to shed.

"Godspeed," Guenevere said to his retreating back. "Perhaps we shall meet again."

He hesitated for a moment, the muscles of his back tensing. Ah, yes, the thought passed between them. The Goddess always gives another chance.

Then he stepped through the small stone doorway and was gone.

The air outside was gusting. Arthur Blessing smelled the coming storm. The moon had disappeared, and the first wave of thunder rolled in.

She's going to die, he thought.

He stood up, feeling the dryness in his throat. Who was? Had he been asleep? It was so hard to tell anymore. That was part of his becoming. Or his madness, whichever he believed at the moment. He could no longer discern waking from sleeping, or truth from illusion, or fiction from memory.

A faint thrum of electricity passed through his hands and feet, up his body and into the top of his head. This was going to be a bad storm.

"Gwen," he whispered aloud. That was the girl's name. It sounded close to Guenevere. Was she Guenevere, he wondered. Was she the one he was meant to find in this life?

That was the problem with living two lives at once, he thought. Aside from the drawback of losing your mind, there was also the challenge of discerning whether you were recalling the past or predicting the future. And what was worse, he was beginning to suspect that the two lives were becoming three. The blond priestess named Brigid was visiting him more and more often, as was Guenevere. And the girl on the road. Gwen.

A young girl wearing leg coverings, like a man . . .

Guenevere had seen Gwen in a dream. How was that for convoluted, he mused. His dreams were having dreams of real people.

Dead . . . Dead before she could bear children . . .

Gwen?

He closed his eyes. No oh no oh no oh no oh no. He wished he could just shut his mind off for once, rest, throw away this horrid thing, this ability that clung to his back like a beast.

Her name was Gwen, and she was going to die, and he did not know if he could stop it.

Wearily, wanting to scream with the horror of his isolation, Arthur walked out the door.

The first fast drops of rain, smelling of dust and still warm from the heated summer air, slapped against his face. The thunder called again.

CHAPTER FORTY

THE CUP

The half-block walk to Emily Blessing's house seemed to Hal like the proverbial journey of a thousand miles. He had turned back again and again, certain that Emily would have nothing to say to him. Her recent message commanding his appearance in Dawning Falls had been terse at best, and he had not known what to make of its verbal adjunct, the strange announcement that she had been horribly disfigured years before.

He had not seen her disfigurement, though. When he awoke after the gunshot, her scars, if that was what they had been, had been healed along with his own. He shook his head. It would be like Emily Blessing to accept a face that had been altered by fire as a triviality, worth mentioning only because of its possible effect on whoever had to look at it.

Emily was a strange woman, immune from most feminine vanities. It was conceivable that she did not consider facial scars to be of adequate importance to make use of the powers of the Holy Grail until it was convenient for her to do so.

She was tough.

By the time he finally reached her door, the rain had begun to fall in ribbons. Hal hesitated before knocking. There was still time, he thought in a panic, to run back to the rented house.

But he did not have the opportunity. Emily opened the door while his hand, balled into a loose fist, still hovered tentatively in midair.

She seemed pleased to see him. "Emily, I hope . . ." His voice died away. she was wearing the yellow dress.

It was the same yellow dress she had worn on their last day together. All those years before, when life still made sense, he had kissed a woman in a yellow dress, and for one moment, the whole of his miserable life seemed to make sense.

"I hope I'm not bothering you," he finished hoarsely.

"I'm glad you've come," she said.

Then he walked into her house, and eight years vanished in an instant.

They lay in a tangle of arms and legs, each almost surprised to be with the other, neither quite believing that what they were experiencing was really happening. Emily's hair streamed across her face, her lips inches from Hal's. "You're beautiful," he said.

She ran her hand over his chest, the unbroken expanse of skin and hair that had been a bloody mortal wound less than twelve hours before. She closed her eyes. She did not want to think about miracles now. The bizarre had become the matrix of their lives; in the face of the reality-bending events of the past few days, it was nearly impossible for anyone in Dawning Falls to attend to what had once been the ordinary things of life—working, going to school, being with family, making friends, falling in love. . . .

But that was what life was, Emily thought, all of those ordinary things. All of the things she had scorned as trivial and useless for most of her life.

She knew better now. For her, lying in this bed with this man at this moment was more important than the fact that he had been brought back from a state near death or that her face had grown suddenly, inexplicably beautiful. It was more important than the death of a supernova, or the birth of a messiah. This was her life, now, in this moment, and she would have it.

"I love you," she said.

Hal stroked her hair. "I love you, too," he said.

Her eyes welled with tears. "I thought I'd lost you today."

He thought of himself tumbling through the void, headed for the Summer Country. "And miss out on this? No way."

"Did the police find whoever shot you?"

Hal shook his head. "No, but I've got an idea. I was shot a few days ago by a crazy biker in South Dakota," he said. "In the scuffle, a car came by, and the biker got in it."

"Wouldn't that have been a carjacking?"

"That's what the cops believed. But I found something near where the car had stopped. A detonator. Handmade, seamless, custom."

"For a bomb, you mean?"

"For a big bomb."

"Would this have something to do with the scare at that military base in Wyoming?" she asked.

"Maybe," Hal said.

"The news is saying that the person responsible is an Arab terrorist."

"Except the guy in the car wasn't an Arab."

"He may just have been a bystander," Emily reasoned. "If the car were hijacked . . ."

"The car was stolen," Hal said. "The Feds found that out fairly soon after I gave them what I could remember of the license plate."

"And so they're thinking that these guys—the biker and the other one—are somehow connected with Hassam Bayat because of this detonator you found on the ground?" She sounded dubious. "It could have been lying there for months."

"Okay, I know it's not the best argument," Hal said, putting on his trousers. "But there's one other thing. The FBI checked out all of Warren A.F.B.'s regular vendors. Turns out a guy from Minneapolis selling metal dies had an appointment in one of the central supply offices for the day following my run-in with the biker."

"So?"

"So he was found murdered and stuffed down an air shaft in a hotel. The work was very professional, and the victim bore a fair resemblance to the guy I saw in the car."

"How do you know? I thought you didn't work for the FBI anymore."

"I called my old boss," he said.

"What's he think of your theory?"

"Well . . . frankly, not much," Hal said. "But I've asked the local cops to keep an eye out. They've got a pretty good sketch of the guy in the car. I think he and the biker might both be here."

"And they might not," she said. "In other words, Arthur may have been the target all along."

Hal sighed. Emily always took the shortest route, and she could see through the thickest smokescreen. That was what had made her such a good researcher, he thought. "It's a possibility," he said. "He's getting so overexposed that that kind of thing is going to become a problem unless we can find a way out of all this. And I don't know that we can." He ran his hands through his hair. "I'm sorry, Emily. He should have stayed with you. That was what was supposed to happen, you know. He was going to come back to you as soon as the danger passed, only—"

"It's all right," she said, putting her arms around him.

Hal realized he was babbling. "I'm sorry. It's just that I've been thinking about this so much, trying to find a way . . ."

"There is a way," Emily said. "We'll stay here, you and I and Arthur, until the media storm blows over. Or we'll go somewhere else. People forget, Hal."

"Not as long as Arthur keeps doing the things he's doing."

"Then we'll make him stop," Emily said. "It'll be for his own good—"

"How can he stop?" Hal shouted. "He doesn't even know he's doing it!" He took a deep breath. How could she know how much thought he had given to Arthur's strange and unwelcome gift? "The water didn't heal the gunshot wound in my chest, Emily," he said softly. "It was Arthur's hands."

She put her hands over her mouth.

"He said it was the water. So the crowd wouldn't know."

Emily was silent for a moment. "He healed my face, too," she said at last. "The water doesn't work for me, but my scars went away as soon as he touched me."

"Jesus," Hal said.

"What's happening to him?" she squeaked.

He was about to say "nothing," but couldn't bring himself to tell the same old lie again. "I don't know," he answered. "It's as if he's growing into some kind of god in front of me." He paced the room. "And I'm scared shitless over it."

"Why?"

"Because there's always a payback. You don't get hands that heal the sick and bring manna from heaven and not pay a steep price somewhere down the road."

A long moment passed between them "I just wish there were someplace safe where we could take him. . . ." He didn't want to say too much.

"But there isn't any such place," she finished.

Hal sat down. "That's right. There isn't. Not in this world."

Outside, a bolt of lightning illuminated the street. The crash of thunder was so loud that the very floor seemed to shake.

Titus and Pinto began digging that night. Titus had hoped to have another day to think through his plan more carefully, but when the thunderstorm blew up and promised to last through the night, he knew he had to act.

He began by making five small bombs. It would have been easier for him to make Molotov cocktails, but he knew that if he bought ingredients like saltpeter and hydrochloric acid anywhere in a town the size of Dawning Falls, people would remember him.

So carefully, almost regretfully, he took minuscule amounts of the powerful explosive filler from the one-of-a-kind bomb that had been intended for a nuclear silo in Wyoming, and encased it in several plastic eggs from a vending maching in the entrance to a K-Mart. One of the thumb-sized eggs was enough for Titus's purpose—they would not have to dig very far, and the explosives he used were very powerful—but keeping a few extra was always a good idea.

He sent Pinto into the store for the other items he would need: a roll of duct tape, some hair dye, and a box of garbage bags. There was a dicey moment in the parking lot, when Pinto opened the car's trunk to see Ginger's livid head protruding from the blanket in which Titus had wrapped her.

"Holy shit!" he shouted, his cigarette flying out of his mouth. "You should have warned me there was a—" He slammed the trunk of the car.

A young couple huddled beneath a yellow umbrella stopped, startled.

"What are you looking at?" Pinto snarled. They moved on.

Pinto got in the car, drenched from the rain, his eyes slitted. Titus had vacated the driver's seat. "Friend of yours?" Pinto asked, more than a little put out.

"No one you know."

"Well, that's a damn good thing, since I like my women on the warm side. Were you just going to leave her in there till she drew flies, or what?"

"Have no fears, my good man," Titus said expansively. "I've arranged for an excellent funeral. Shall we?"

Pinto shook his head. He had never seen a more natural born killer than this faggy Englishman. "By all means, old chap," he said, revving the engine.

On the way to Miller's Creek, Titus assembled the weapon which had been packed in the same custom-made case as the bomb designated for Warren Air Force Base: a leggy spider of a handgun with a laser site accurate to within five millimeters at a thousand feet.

"What the hell is that?" Pinto demanded. It was the strangest weapon he had ever seen.

Titus held it up admiringly. "One of a kind. Lovely, isn't she?" Then he folded it up into a neat rectangle the size of a cell phone.

"Just what is it you do for a living, your lordship?" Pinto's eyes narrowed, then widened. "Whoa, man. Your neck."

"The wound? It's better."

"But you took a spear, or some damn thing. How'd it get better so fast?" Apparently Pinto had spent no time talking to the denizens of Dawning Falls about the miraculous water in Miller's Creek.

"I'll show you," Titus said.

They pulled into the private driveway beside the rickety house, ludicrously named the Sanctuary, beside a Jeep Cherokee belonging to the security guard.

"I don't think it's such a good idea to park here, man," Pinto said.

"It'll just be for a minute." Titus winked at him. "Help me with the lady, please."

The rain was pelting as the two of them unwrapped the stiffened body of Ginger Ranier and carried it to the house.

Titus knocked, loudly and urgently. When the ancient security guard opened the door and saw Ginger Ranier in Pinto's arms, he let them in at once.

"We found her by the side of the road," Titus said as Pinto set Ginger on the floor.

"There's a couch—" the guard began, but by then Titus already had his gun out. With a tap, it unfolded into its working configuration.

The guard reached for his phone—perhaps the least effective mode of self-preservation under the circumstances, Titus thought as he shot the old man through the head.

"Now you can move the car," he told Pinto.

While Pinto was hiding the car, Titus planted one of the plastic-egg bombs behind the house. They met in the woods some distance away with a detonator fashioned from the remote control for the television in their motel room. Nature obliged with a huge, booming thunderclap less than five minutes later. If it were not for the flash and a spray of mud, even they could not have heard the tiny bomb exploding.

"Coulda used some of these in prison," Pinto said, idly tossing and catching one of the egg-shaped explosives like a beanbag. "Can't hardly hear 'em."

Titus caught it for him in midair. "They can still kill us, though."

They went back to the house to examine the damage made by the bomb. It turned out to have been a perfectly-sized explosive, removing and loosening dirt without really blowing anything apart. The two of them had excavated down to the well within an hour.

It was a primitive affair, little more than a cistern encased in cement. "Astonishing," Titus said, thinking that the corner tavern had better security than a well filled with water that neutralized strychnine. "The wankers don't seem to know what they have."

"What do they have?" Pinto asked, blowing rain off his lips.

Titus ignored him, setting the second explosive against the cement.

"You going to blow it up?" Pinto asked with some surprise.

Titus felt the slightest pang of indecision. It was his contention that the water, which was ordinary water until it reached the well of the Sanctuary, was not the healing agent. There was, he believed, something inside the well which gave the water its properties. He was looking for a device.

It was probably not a very large device, because the land around the Sanctuary had not been dug up. The well had been dug directly beneath the house, through the floorboards. The setup was rather like the old farm spring houses, in which vegetables and other perishables were kept cool by being set into a running stream at the bottom of a trap door in a building.

So the device would be small, Titus reasoned. Small enough to fit into a cement enclosure. Small enough to take away without notice.

There were problems, of course. The thing might be destroyed by the explosion. It might be radioactive. It might be wired to an alarm system, or contain a failsafe by which anyone who tried to tamper with it would be electrocuted or subjected to poison fumes or blown to kingdom come. There was no way to know.

Titus set the bomb, then enclosed the exposed cement with a thick blanket before retreating into the woods again.

"If anything untoward happens, run for the car," he said.

Pinto shifted his eyes to one side.

" 'Untoward,' " Titus explained, "means unexpected. Like if an alarm goes off, or if the place bursts into flames."

"Okay," Pinto said, somewhat resentfully. "You could have said that in the first place." They hunkered down, waiting for the thunder.

When it came, Titus detonated the second explosive. Water sprayed up in a fountain. The men waited for ten seconds before Titus spoke. "Now," he said.

The cement casing, now lying in rubble, had been built around another cement box. This, too, had been affected by the explosion. One corner had been blown off, and a large crack ran up from it across an adjacent side.

"This might be what we're looking for." Titus thrust his fingers through the mud to grab hold of the cement cube. It came up from the mud with a sucking sound.

"Bastard of a storm," Pinto said, blowing the rain from his lips.

Titus was cheerful. "I promise you, this will be well worth the discomfort, my friend." He adjusted some components of the weird weapon he had used to kill the guard, then aimed it at a corner of the concrete box and fired. The box shattered into popcorn-sized pieces.

"Jesus, that's some kind of gun," Pinto said. Unable to restrain himself any longer, he reached tentatively for the weapon. Titus looked at him from beneath his wet brows. Pinto withdrew his hand.

Inside the rubble of the box was the last thing Titus expected to see. Not a high-tech device, but a simple small bowl made of some greenish metal he had never seen before. There was nothing impressive about it. It was dented and out of round, too small to be useful as a container, too ugly to be decorative. It was the sort of thing one might find at a garage sale, along with a dirty embroidery of daisies or a set of plastic coasters, something that might once have been a lid to something else, or part of a floral arrangement, or a weight for balloons decorating some festive table.

Titus picked it up and examined it slowly, thinking all these things about it, not noticing for some time that, while his mind was racing to understand the meaning of the homely cup that someone had taken the trouble to encase in cement and hide in the bottom of a well, he was, meanwhile, experiencing a sensation of profound well being.

His arms and shoulders, sore from digging, felt suddenly rested. A headache that had grown with each explosion and boom of thunder and had finally blossomed into full-blown agony with the murder of the guard instantly subsided.

Slowly he reached up to touch the place on his neck where he had once been wounded, where the water from the stream had healed it without a trace.

Pinto was looking at him. At the place where the wound had been, then at the cup.

Before he could speak, Titus picked the gun up off the ground and fired it into Pinto's thigh.

Pinto sucked in air. As the sound formed in his throat to scream, Titus ripped open the pant leg and thrust the cup onto the wound.

The blood, which had shot up in an arc from the bullet hole in Pinto's flesh and cascaded down his leg, stopped flowing. Pinto closed his eyes as warmth from the cup throbbed throughout his body like a second heartbeat. He gasped as the cells of his bone and muscle began to regenerate with such speed that he could actually feel himself mending.

The two men watched with fascination as the wound healed before their eyes from the inside out. First the opening knit together, extruding white cells. Then the top scabbed over, lightened, and then faded away, leaving skin that was at first pink, and then, a moment later, indistinguishable from the rest of the leg. Hairs grew out of it. The healing was complete in less than thirty seconds.

Pinto looked over to Titus with a look of childlike gratitude. "That cup . . ."

"It can keep you alive forever," Titus said. Then he stood up, wiped the rain and some splashed blood from the barrel of the gun, and shot Pinto in the heart.

Pinto tried to raise his hand, as if to grasp the cup again, but

Titus shook his head. "This is where we part ways, friend," he said.

He left Pinto in the mud as he went inside to distribute the rest of the plastic eggs. There were seven of them. After they were detonated, it would not matter a whit where any of the bodies had been placed. Nothing would be left of them, anyway.

CHAPTER FORTY-ONE

STORMWALKER

Gwen was becoming worried about her mother.

Ginger had probably left with "Bob," or whatever this latest stud's name was, but it wasn't like her to stay out so late on a weekday. Of course, she had been particularly enamored of this one, apparently—she'd even tried to make everyone believe that he was Gwen's father! Leave it to old mom to find a new twist on classic old shotgun wedding. The marry-me-'cause-I-was-pregnant-seventeen-years-ago ploy.

Naturally, Ginger hadn't bothered to remove the rapidly decaying Finny from the fishbowl before going on her joy ride. She'd left that for Gwen, the same way she'd left the vacuuming and the laundry and the dirty dishes from last night.

Damn her, Gwen thought, tossing on her pillow. She wasn't going to waste another minute worrying. So what if her face was too black and blue for her to go to work in the morning? It was time little Ginger grew up, maybe stopped going to bed with men five minutes after meeting them.

Oh, that's right, this one was different. She'd known old Bob for years, isn't that what she said? It was probably more like the time it took to drink a bottle of beer. The nerve of her, saying that he was Gwen's father!

Gwen punched her pillow. That went beyond shallow. Didn't it ever occur to her that her daughter might not like being known as the town bastard, that maybe a father was a special thing that was worth more than a line on a date?

The worst thing was that the guy sort of did look like her. For a moment, Gwen had actually believed it might be the truth. She had been angry about it at first, just the sheer surprise of it all, but it had been exciting, too. He had seemed pretty bright, even though he'd killed their fish. He might have been an okay father.

But then, after she'd had a chance to think about it and clear her head, Gwen realized that it was just another stupid thing her mother was saying. Another date, another pain-in-the-butt man who'd send her back to the battered women's shelter sooner or later.

"Damn you!" Gwen shouted, and realized that she was crying.

She made herself calm down and checked the clock. Nearly two in the morning. Outside, flashes of lightning illuminated the heavy rain. Thunder boomed so loudly that it seemed to rock the whole house.

The battered women's shelter was a long walk from their house: through the park, and then across Miller's Creek and the Germantown Pike, and then over the big meadow and into Dawning Falls. An hour at least.

"The hell with her," Gwen muttered, squeezing her eyes shut. Besides, Ginger might not even have gone to the shelter. Her car was still in the driveway, so she wasn't driving.

She might have gone to the hospital.

Gwen would call. That was it. She would call around, find out where her mother was. At some motel, probably. Hi, honey, Ginger would say sleepily. Oh, didn't I leave a note? I'm sorry you had to worry, I'm having a fine old time.

Gwen got up, looked up the number of the shelter, then picked up the phone.

It was dead. "Oh, hell," she said.

Annoying, but no big surprise. The cul-de-sac where they lived was always losing power of one kind or another. The neighbors would not have phone service, either, not that she would have invited any of those nosy cretins to listen in on her conversation with the shelter.

As she stood in the kitchen, the lights went out. Great, she thought. This makes it perfect. She felt her way for the junk drawer where the flashlight was. That is, where it would be if her mother had not used it and left it lying somewhere else.

She was in luck. The flashlight was in the drawer, and the batteries hadn't died. The first thing the light shone on was Finny's empty tank. And beside it, Ginger's handbag.

Gwen felt the first stirrings of panic. No woman ever left her house without her bag. Quickly she went into her mother's room and scanned the closet with the flashlight. Ginger had been wearing a red silk robe. It wasn't hanging among her clothes. It wasn't in the hamper, either, or in her dresser. She checked the bathroom. No red robe on the hook.

She wouldn't leave wearing a bathrobe, Gwen thought. Not unless she was running for her life.

Four huge bolts of lightning glowed like spider legs through the window. Then a sudden gust of wind blew through a crack near the bottom, making Gwen's scalp shiver, and she knew.

"Oh, Mom." She sighed. She had to go.

She pulled on a pair of jeans, a Rage Against the Machine T-shirt, and a black oilcloth rain jacket. Then she walked out into the rain.

Oddly, she felt immediately better. Gwen had never feared thunderstorms. It felt good, the coolness of the rain and the icy electricity of the lightning.

She wondered if that was a sign that she was crazy. You were supposed to be afraid of weather—rain, snow, heat, wind. Whatever it was doing outside, most people didn't seem to like it.

Gwen did. She had always felt more at home outdoors in the elements than inside buildings. Even if she were uncomfortable, there was a wildness about the natural world that she loved. She could feel the pull of the moon, she could smell rain coming, taste the metallic tang of lightning storms.

Not that she felt no fear: The unpredictability of storms was part of its appeal. It always felt as if she were in the presence of something far larger than herself and the paltry little dramas that made up her life. In the midst of a storm, she was certain that there was a God.

The first time she had walked the length of the park during a storm, with the black sky lit up by white veins of lightning that looked to her like cackling, shrieking banshees flying overhead, she had been terrified. Gwen had almost decided to swallow her pride and go back home when she saw a group of kids she knew from high school dashing toward the exit with their jackets pulled up over their heads. They were part of the clique, the rich, popular, attractive kids who, of course, only hung out with one another.

As soon as Gwen spotted them, she straightened up, fixed her face into a mask of proud disdain, lifted her chin, and sauntered past, making it clear that she was entering the park as they were running out of it. And after, when she was a short distance away, the popular kids laughed loud enough for her to hear them, but not very convincingly. They knew they were cowards. Gwen felt like the queen of the world.

By the next day, the rumors were already circulating around the school. Gwen did something by herself in the park in the middle of thunderstorms. She was a witch, a goth, a weirdo. She was burying babies as part of some kind of blood cult. She was a vampire. She was crazy.

That had always struck her as funny that she was called crazy for wanting to be a part of nature. It was at odds with her appearance, she supposed, but that was a different matter entirely. She didn't want to look like them, like the kids in her school, like everyone who lived in Dawning Falls. She didn't want them to know her.

And they didn't. That was why they called her crazy, she supposed.

During the first half of her sophomore year, she had been scheduled to see the school psychologist for an hour every Monday. It was part of a county program. The psychologist traveled around to all the schools in the county talking to crazy kids—kids who'd been busted for drugs, kids from alcoholic families, kids in foster homes, that sort of thing. Gwen knew as soon as she found out about the traveling head shrinker that she would be on the list. Kid of the town roundheels, yeah, she'd qualify. And, true to form, the shrink had asked all the predictable questions. Why do you wear all that makeup? Do you mutilate yourself? Which rock groups do you listen to?

A waste of time. Gwen just lied to her, anyway. After a while, the shrink had not even pretended to be interested.

She thrust her hands into the pocket of the oilcloth coat she was wearing. Her hair was plastered against her head, channeling rain into her eyes. She blew it away and kept closer to the trees, where there was at least a little shelter.

Few people ever came to the park, even during the day. Gwen supposed it was because it had no activities—no seesaws for little kids, no pool, no baseball diamond, not even a lake. The park used to be part of the Miller farm, but it had been sold to the township for taxes sometime in the eighties, and had never been developed.

Certainly no one else was around now, she thought as a horizontal bolt of lightning shot across the sky. With some surprise, Gwen noticed that there were no longer any trees above her, which meant that she had walked out of the park and onto the grounds of Miller's Creek. The rain was falling much harder here. Lightning zigzagged around her, making the hair on her arms stand on end, the incipient electricity crawling over her skin in a slow, exploratory burn.

And so it was that she felt, rather than saw or even heard, the explosion that came from the creek. It was a vibration, like an earthquake, that shivered across the bottoms of her feet.

At first she had panicked. The sensation had been vaguely electric, like what she imagined the first intimations of a lightning strike must feel like. Gwen held her breath, certain that she would die. The only question would be how much pain she would feel. Was death by lightning swift and merciful? She'd never read about anyone who had been executed by electrocution screaming their heads off, so she assumed it would be a fairly painless way to go.

But by the time she had the presence of mind even to think these thoughts, the vibration had passed. And in the distance, through the darkness and the rain, she thought she detected movement.

All of the grass within a hundred yards of the creek had been worn away long ago by the crowds of tourists. Now it was nothing but slick mud. Gwen's shoes were so heavily caked that she felt as if she were standing in blocks of cement. She left gigantic footprints behind her.

Cupping her hand over her eyes like a visor, she squinted into the night. And then, perhaps because of the rain, or a sudden shift in the wind, she heard a *pop* which was like nothing else she had ever heard.

She walked toward the noise until she saw that there indeed had been movement. Near the house that the papers were calling the Sanctuary, two figures appeared to be kneeling in a pile of mud and rubble. As she was walking toward them, she heard another *pop* that made her jump.

One of the figures fell over. The other rose and walked swiftly into the house.

There had been some kind of accident, she thought. Beside the house she could see the outline of the Jeep belonging to Mr. Santori, the security guard. Whoever had been outside must have gone in to ask Mr. Santori to help.

She hoped he would be able to do something for them, although she was doubtful. All the volunteers at Miller's Creek liked the old security guard, but it was common knowledge that his mind was slipping. Mr. Santori might not be the best bet in an emergency.

She ran, sweating through the tremendous effort of moving through what was becoming nearly ankle-deep mud, to where a man lay on his back in the midst of a pile of rocks and broken cement. Something had happened to the house—lightning, maybe—and this poor guy had been in the middle of it.

There was blood all over him. It looked black in the dim illumination of her flashlight. Tentatively she reached out her hand to him, thinking she would check for a pulse, but it was obvious that the man was dead. She shivered. She did not want to touch him.

She moved on to the house. Mr. Santori was probably looking after the second man, who had at least managed to walk inside. She looked through the window beside the door. "Mr. Santori," she called, wiping the glass. "Mr.—"

Gwen had raised her hand to knock, but it remained suspended in midair. On the floor were two bodies. One was Mr. Santori. The other was her mother.

Gwen froze in the spot where she stood. *No,* she thought as a low, wavering moan escaped from her lips as if the sound were not connected to her. *No, no, not my mother, not here, this is just something I'm seeing because I'm crazy, because it's dark, because . . .*

Then Titus's face appeared at the window, looking first surprised, and then inexpressibly sad.

The next moments seemed to occur in slow motion: First, his eyes, looking around and behind her, questing, and then, as she backed away (so slowly, so painfully slowly), the window shattering, glass spewing pieces of light into the dark night. A towel wound around Titus's hand loosened and fell to the ground; and something beneath it now, some sort of gun that looked as if it had been made from an erector set, swinging up, then aiming directly at her, steady, holding steady . . .

"Oh, God," Gwen whispered. She turned to run, but even then she knew that she could not make it back into the woods in time. There was a third pop, this time behind her, and simultaneously a pressure thudding into the left side of her back, as if someone had pushed her so hard that she was propelled to the ground.

The pain was not instantaneous; it came a moment after the thud, the surprise, the sudden spray of blood, like an aerosol, from her burst lung through her mouth and out from between her lips. After all that, the pain shot through her like a burning pinprick of flame, causing even her feet to kick out wildly.

The door of the house creaked open. Then he was there beside her in what seemed to be no time at all. The horrible pain shooting through her chest one second, and then Titus's face above her the next. But then, she thought, more time must have elapsed. She was on her back, which meant he had turned her over, and he was kneeling beside her.

He was wearing a plastic parka. The hood was pulled over his head, but rain still ran down his face in rivulets. His expression was very concerned.

"Daddy?" she asked.

He looked down at something in his hand. Gwen by this time was seeing only dimly, but it appeared to be a little cup, or a bowl. She did not wonder at all why Titus would be holding such an object. She was at the stage of trauma where all realities were acceptable. An angel walking out of the park would have been every bit as possible to her as the appearance of an ambulance.

Unfortunately, she got neither. Only Titus contemplating his cup and occasionally looking at her face as if trying to memorize it.

"I'm . . . I'm cold," she managed to say. The blood in her mouth tasted metallic, too strong.

For a moment it seemed that Titus held the cup tentatively out to her. Again, this action seemed perfectly normal, as would any other. But he withdrew it again. "I'm sorry," he said. "I haven't anything to put over you."

Her teeth chattered.

"It won't be long," the man whom she now knew only as her father said. He put the cup in his pocket.

"You're going to the Tor," she said.

Titus was getting up off his knees. "What did you say?" he asked softly. He leaned over her, his hand cupped over his ear. Rain dripped from his fingers onto Gwen's face.

"The Tor," she whispered. "You'll go to the Tor to make things right." Her speech was so soft that someone whose whole body was touching her would not be able to hear it.

But Titus did. Through the rain, through the deep rumble of thunder, he heard the dying girl's incoherent words so clearly that he thought they had originated in his own mind. "To make things right," she repeated.

"Yes, of course," he said, sorry that it had had to come to this.

With her face washed clean, he saw that the girl was clearly his daughter. He saw it in all her features. She was the only child he had ever produced, as far as he knew, and she was quite lovely. "I'm sure you would have had a nice life," he said. Then he shot her again, through the head, to put her out of her pain.

CHAPTER FORTY-TWO

GUENEVERE'S JOURNEY

Aah, she thought. Dying was easier than she had ever thought it could be. Almost pleasant, actually, once the fear was gone. And Guenevere had lost her fear long, long ago.

She was Sister Guenevere now, in the convent where Arthur had chosen to put her away nearly twenty years before, although she almost never thought of herself as a nun.

There were different categories of nuns at the abbey. The contemplative nuns, who took on biblical names, were quite devout, living only meditate on Christ through prayer. Even though most of them had come from very good families, they lived lives of penitential simplicity, dwelling in wretched little boxes of rooms with only a straw mat for a bed and no other furniture except for a tallow candle, and ate communally.

Then there were the working nuns, from the laboring classes. These sturdy women performed the menial chores of the convent, from plowing the fields to cooking. Unlike the contemplatives, they brought little to the abbey in terms of material possessions, but without them the place would surely fall to ruin.

And then there were the women like Guenevere—well, naturally, none were quite like Guenevere, since she had been high queen of Britain—but nevertheless women of great stature and wealth, who had found their way to the abbey after their political roles had been fulfilled. There were only a few of them, mostly widows of petty kings who had fled for their lives after their husbands' dynasties were overthrown.

By this time civil war was raging through Britain as a result of Arthur's dying without leaving an heir. Mordred, Arthur's principal adversary, had been killed in the same battle that had taken Arthur's life.

After that, a number of people including, strangely, Morgause, had briefly ruled Britain. But in the end, the Saxons took over the country, and proved to be competent if harsh administrators who finally bent the disparate clans to their will by killing all the petty kings.

It was during those harsh times that Guenevere lay dying in the Abbey of Glastonbury, where many great ladies from the era of Camelot found themselves grateful for the sanctuary of the New Religion.

The abbey was not very rule-bound then, at least not for highborn women. Guenevere ate in her room, and had two servants, including her former nanny, to look after her, although in fact it was Guenevere who looked after Nanny rather than the other way round until the old woman died. Guenevere herself lived only two years more.

Her last years were spent in virtual solitude, remembering the two men who had made up her life: Arthur, who had been the fabric of her being, as much a part of her as her skin or her breath, and Launcelot, who had blazed for one white-hot moment in her loins and her heart.

That moment had exacted a terrible price. Arthur had died, betrayed and brokenhearted, the last great native king of Britain. Guenevere had given up the rest of her life to languish in this single stone room. And Launcelot had wandered away, some said to the wild northern lands of the Picts, a broken man gone mad with shame.

And then, of course, there was Britain itself, which would never be the same. The Saxons would change the very look of the population. They would bring their own gods, and name the days of the week for them. As for the Old Religion of the Britons, its magic and power would become lost in the storms of war. There would only be a few druids left by then, anyway. After Britain became a Saxon holding, no one would pay any attention to the ancient ways. Only the old women in the countryside would remember the Sabbats and Esbats, or chant the spells for love and fertility and protection, or mix the potions from the earth and the sea that cured sickness and eased pain. Only the old women would keep what was left of Britain alive.

All because I did not give birth to the child within me, Guenevere thought. Because ultimately, her country had not been lost because Arthur was a bad king. On the contrary, he had been the greatest king their island had ever known. He had been doomed only because he had begotten no heir.

The terrible irony of it all was that Arthur had been raised in the old ways. Had Guenevere simply told him of her indiscretion, he might not have been ruined by it, as he was by the circumstances as they happened. He might have accepted the child she bore as his heir, even if he knew it was made from Launcelot's seed. Practitioners of the Old Religion were not so sticky about whose child was whose. They believed all life belonged to the Goddess, anyway, the Great Mother, and that human beings were merely custodians, not owners, of one another. One child was as good as another under the old rules.

Not a bad way for people to be, she thought, knowing how blasphemous the thought was, but no longer really caring. She was fifty-five years old, the oldest woman in the abbey. Considering that the average life span was under twenty-five, even Arthur had been thought of as an old man at the time of his death at the age of thirty-eight. Cheneus, universally acknowledged as ancient, had been perhaps sixty when he succumbed to his wife's lethal potion.

Only the Merlin had lived longer, but he could hardly be counted as human.

Guenevere had no doubt that she would not remain long on earth. Her lungs were filled with the congestion that came of damp and cold. The Merlin had known of a hundred ways to cure it, but he was long gone. He had become a hermit shortly after Arthur's death, Guenevere was told. He had died inside a cave, with a wolf watching over his body, so that no one could claim it for burial.

The sisters at the abbey, meanwhile, knew of no cures besides prayer. And so Guenevere prayed, when she remembered the words, although she knew she would die of this foul thing in her lungs. This, this coughing, the black phlegm, the honking pain in her chest, was was just penance for her sin with Launcelot.

And yet she never could quite bring herself to truly regret that morning in the field when she lay naked with Launcelot, their limbs entwined, feeling his breath on her, his lips, his sweet tongue; the electrifying moment when she opened her legs to him and gave over to him her passion while she took his, took his love, the deepest love of his heart, into herself.

Was that so horrible? Her eyes welled with tears. If it was, it was only because Arthur, too, had held her love in his heart. They had loved one another, it seemed, since the beginning of time. Yes, she thought as she grew drowsy, she had known him lifetimes before, and loved him then, too.

The sin lay in the knowledge that she had not chosen between them. She had taken what was offered by both Arthur and Launcelot, and and treasured it all. That, she supposed, was what made it all a horror.

"But can love ever be a horror?" she said aloud, although the sound was little more than a croak.

She was glad she was here, in the nunnery, rather than back at the castle with a hundred attendants to record her last breath. People were meant to die alone. It was more intimate. When God—or the Goddess, in case her old nanny had been right, after all—came to take her, she did not wish to walk away reluctantly, as if she were leaving the party.

But then, perhaps no one would come for her at all. After what she had done, perhaps her sinful little soul would just dry up and turn to dust. And in the morning, when her body was taken away, one of the sturdy working nuns would sweep up the ashes of her soul in a dustpan and throw it out among the chickens.

She smiled. The picture the thought generated was amusing. Suffering had brought Guenevere the gift of humor, even though it was of the black sort.

Yes, it would be fitting to be tossed out among the chickens, she thought. *All of us, with our mighty plans and clever ways. In the end, it seems, fate always has its way.* All of the compromises Arthur made to appease the petty kings were for nothing. He had forsaken his wife, whom he had loved, for them. He had abandoned his plans for a peaceful assimilation of the Saxons, thereby making them enemies, in order to feed the chiefs' lust for battle. And although he had geared his whole life toward achieving peace, Arthur had died by the sword.

As for herself . . . Well, here she was, an old sinner dying alone, filled with phlegm and regret. She coughed, and her thin body doubled over in pain. Blood trickled from between her lips.

Are you coming? she asked silently. *Goddess, have you come to take me?*

She did, in fact, see someone. It was the beautiful fair-haired woman she had seen so many years before, in a demented vision as she hovered near death beneath a makeshift tent along the road to Orkney. The woman, a priestess, was holding an obsidian dagger, just as she had in that long-ago vision.

"Brigid," Guenevere said, delighted. "Have you come for me?"

"I *am* you," the priestess said.

"Ah, I understand." She looked down, and there she was, standing, dressed again like a queen, in a gown of fine red wool. "I am Guenevere. I am you."

"And me, too." The two of them turned to see a third female, this one a young girl with eyes rimmed in black, wearing blue jeans and a wet jacket.

"My, that's an odd one," Guenevere said.

"Gwen." Brigid held out her arms. "She is from the future," she explained to Guenevere. "Have you ever dreamed of her?"

The queen thought. "Hmm. I do believe I have."

"And I know you both," Gwen said. "I've drawn you."

"An artist," Guenevere said. "I always wanted to draw."

"And I would have liked to be a queen," Brigid said.

"And I would have liked to call down the Goddess," Gwen said.

Brigid cocked her head. "But you did, child," she said. "At the end, when you were suffering so. You told your killer to come to the Tor."

"The Tor?" Gwen asked.

Brigid smiled. "It's where I lived."

"And where I found the sword in the stone," Guenevere said.

"And where you will . . ." Brigid covered her mouth. "Well, things will be made right, as you said."

"Did I say that?" Gwen asked.

"In a way. It was the Goddess who spoke. But her words came from your mouth."

"I didn't know that could happen."

"Oh, yes," Brigid said. "It is the way of our kind."

"Our? But I'm not—"

"You are everything I am." She gestured toward Guenevere. "Everything the queen is. Whenever you need us, you will find us all within yourself."

"Unfortunately," Guenevere said dryly, "I'm afraid you won't be needing much of anything. Nor will any of us."

Gwen looked around. "Am I dead, then?"

The two other women smiled gently.

"Oh, but I can't be," she said, looking about her. "I have to go back."

"Oh, dear," said the queen, who had lived such a long time that the prospect of returning to her sickness-wracked body did not seem tremendously appealing. "But how do you propose to do that, child?"

"I don't know," Gwen said. "Maybe Arthur . . ."

"Arthur," Guenevere said.

"Arthur," Brigid echoed.

"I beg your pardon, ma'am?" It was her servant. Guenevere had forgotten all about her. She was new. Both her former nanny and her handmaid were dead. This girl—oh, what was her name again? It didn't matter. The girl had been sleeping. She could tell by the way the little simpleton was blinking.

"You could at least stay awake for my death," Guenevere said archly.

"Yes, ma'am."

Well, there were some good things about death, she supposed. She wouldn't have to be waited on by fools. "Go away," she said.

What had she been thinking? Oh, yes, Brigid. The priestess whom she had been in another life. Fascinating. And the other, the strange girl with the covered legs. Very odd, that one. But she, too, had been Guenevere. How many other lives have there been, she wondered. Hundreds, perhaps thousands.

Oh, my, she thought suddenly. That's blasphemous. Or something. She blinked slowly, sleepily. Or nothing. "Just the wanderings of my confused mind," she rasped. "I'm sick. I'm dying. These imaginings . . ."

They are not imaginings, came a voice. It was very close, right inside her ear.

"Brigid?"

"Yes, my child."

"Child, indeed! I'm twice your age."

"And I was born sixteen hundred years before you."

"Oh, dear. I see. Where's the other? The maiden who wraps her legs?"

"She wants to wait. For Arthur."

"Arthur, yes," the queen said faintly. "Will he come?"

"I think so."

"I'm glad," Guenevere said. "We were always meant to be together, but we couldn't . . . that is, I didn't . . ."

"I understand," Brigid said softly. "It was the same with me. That is why we're being given another chance."

"Through the maiden."

"Yes. We'll try again. Sooner or later, we're bound to connect."

"So much always seems to get in the way, though."

"That is why we're given other chances."

"Ah," Guenevere said. "Fate does have a habit of getting its way, doesn't it?"

"Indeed." The women laughed.

"But about these imaginings of mine . . ." Guenevere began.

"They are not imaginings," Brigid repeated. "They are the journey home."

Guenevere blinked. "Oh," she said softly. "Are you God, then?"

Brigid thought. "Why, I suppose I am. And you, too."

"What?" The old woman laughed out loud. "Hardly."

"Well, why not? Who else is going to look after us?"

"But that's . . . that's . . ." Her eyes met Brigid's. "That's marvelous," she finished.

Then, putting her arm around the ancient priestess, they walked together into the great white light that grew around them like a halo. And in that radiant, loving light, Queen Guenevere laughed about what she now knew, too late to tell anyone, of gods and humans.

CHAPTER FORTY-THREE

A NEW DAY DAWNS

"I think someone's at the door," Hal said.

It was hard to tell. The rain was pouring seemingly straight down, and thunder boomed so loud that it was difficult to hear anything.

Emily pulled aside the curtain to look outside. "Who in the world . . . It's Arthur!" she said, running to let him in.

He was soaked and shivering, his red hair plastered to his face, and his eyes looking lost, with the vague, wide aspect of someone in shock. "Emily, is Hal here? I . . . I need . . ."

"What is it?" Hal demanded, knowing that Arthur would not hunt him down idly on a night like this.

"It's a girl," Arthur said, embarrassed. "Her name is Gwen."

"Who?"

"Gwen Ranier?" Emily asked.

"Yes. I have to find her, but I don't know where she lives."

Hal made an effort not to laugh out loud. "Are you telling me you've been out in this rain looking for a girl?"

"I called all the Raniers in the phone book, but I couldn't reach her." Arthur wiped his face with his bare hands. "I think she's in trouble, Hal."

"How do you . . ." Hal was going to say "know," but the one thing he had learned from his experience with Arthur was that it made no difference how the boy knew the things he did. He simply knew them.

"I think she's going to die."

Emily gasped.

Hal took a last, long look at the storm outside. Then he grabbed his coat. "All right," he said. "If you want to look for her, I'll help."

"Haven't you heard the radio?" Emily shouted. "There are tornado warnings . . . Wait," she said, rummaging in her pocketbook. "At least take my car." She tossed him the keys, then scribbled Gwen's address along with some quick directions.

"Thanks," Hal said. He was halfway out the door when he turned back to face her. The wind was gusting so hard that she had to squint against it. Rain sloshed in a puddle inside the doorway. Dressed in her bathrobe, she embraced him. "Please come back," she pleaded.

He kissed her mouth. "Get inside," he said. "You'll catch cold."

The rain hit the pavement of the street so hard that there seemed to be a fog three feet high snaking over the neighborhood. Into this river of vapor walked the two men Emily loved.

It was the last time she saw either of them.

Even with the windshield wipers on full, it was nearly impossible to see. All the streetlamps were out. The only thing going for them was that there were no other cars on the roads.

"I think we're in over our heads," Hal said.

Arthur knew he wasn't talking about the rain. "You mean I am." He shrugged. "I can't help it. What's happening, I mean. I can't."

"I know," Hal said. "Is the girl . . ." He didn't know how to phrase it. ". . . part of the story?"

"I think so."

Hal's jaw clenched. "It's the old man," he said. "He's trying to bring back Camelot, the bastard. Lock, stock, and barrel."

"He's not just trying, Hal. It's working. We're all here." He held
out his arms, as if displaying himself. "All ready to serve good old
King Arthur himself. The only problem is, I'm not a king this time
around. I'm a nut, as far as the world goes. But the truth is worse
than that."

"Arthur—"

"I'm an artificial man, Hal. Only instead of being made of steel
and electricity like Frankenstein, I'm made of ghosts. And everyone around me, except for you, is a ghost."

They rode in silence for a time, aware only of the wall of water
against the car's windshield and the blinding intermittent flashes
of lightning.

"Are you going to marry Emily?" Arthur asked finally.

Hal looked startled. "Where did that come from?"

"It would be good for you if you did."

"Why?"

"She's not a part of this," Arthur said. "You could have a life.
A real life, instead of being a character in a fairy tale."

Hal waffled. "I don't know if you're right about all this, Arthur."

"No? Do you remember Lakeshire Tor, Hal? Where there used
to be a legend that the ghosts of King Arthur's knights would ride
through the streets every year on the night of the summer solstice?
Well, I've been reading about it. That doesn't happen anymore at
Lakeshire Tor. Do you want to know why? Because those ghosts
have been brought back to life. They're in Dawning Falls, New
York, right now, along with Merlin and Guenevere, and just a short
distance away are the young king himself and his champion, Sir
Galahad."

He stared at Hal. "It's like some weird dream, except that it
doesn't end. We're all caught up in that story all over again, only
there's nothing for us to do except to keep on running. Forever."

Hal drove in silence for a time. "Besides, there's this new stuff
that's happening," Arthur said quietly. "The healings, the trances.
Something's happening to me. Something bad."

Hal tried to control his alarm. "How does it feel?"

"Like . . . like I'm dying," Arthur said. "Every time it happens, it's harder for me to come back." He looked out the window at the patterns of rain on the glass. "Maybe that's for the best."

"Listen, Arthur—"

"I'm telling the truth. I don't have much longer, and I don't think things are going to get better before the end."

Hal's knuckles shone white on the steering wheel. The rain pounded on the car's metal roof. "What about the knights?"

"They'll go with me. Wherever that is."

"You're talking about dying."

"They can't die, Hal. They're already dead."

"I mean you."

"Nobody can stop that. The point is, it's time for you to get out," Arthur looked meaningfully at Hal. "You still have a chance for some kind of life. Take it."

Hal smiled. "Suggestion noted," he said.

"Meaning what?"

"Meaning I can handle it, okay?"

"No." Arthur was getting belligerent. "Don't you get it, Hal? It isn't going to end. Look where we are. In the same place as the Grail. We can't get rid of it. The story just keeps on playing itself out. . . ."

At that, they both looked at one another.

"The creek," Arthur said. "That's where she is. By the cup."

Hal turned the car around and stepped on the gas.

"Will you think about it, at least?" Arthur asked. "About marrying Emily?"

"Yeah, all right," Hal said.

But both of them knew he wouldn't. Hal would never leave Arthur. He would sacrifice his entire life to stay with the boy who was brought back to be king of a world that no longer existed.

Titus set the egg-shaped bombs in the house and scattered papers around the floor. He could not be sure about the efficacy of the bombs. The first two that he had set off had been fairly controlled, but they were the weakest of the bunch. The last three might blow the place sky-high, but they could just as easily fizzle. If that happened, Titus would have to rely on fire to achieve the effect he wanted.

He had been careful to shoot Pinto directly in the heart. No bones broken, no telltale bulletholes in the skull. When all the evidence was in, the place would look as if Pinto—wearing mud-wet leather gloves to preserve his fingerprints—had killed the guard and the girl (*your daughter, Titus*, the unwanted voice in his head taunted) before being trapped in an accidental explosion from a homemade bomb. It would come out that the cup, now removed from the building's foundation, had been destroyed in the blast.

For good measure, he would leave something of his own inside, in a place where part of it might be retrieved. Something that would identify the innocent bystander kidnapped in South Dakota by the homicidal biker named Pinto. Something that would make the FBI stop looking for a second man.

You'll go to the Tor . . .

What had she meant by that? Titus squeezed his eyes shut and forced the memory away.

The arrival of the girl had been an unfortunate coincidence. It had thrown off his pace. He was not a man who enjoyed inventing life as he went along. For Titus, occasions were better when they were planned, when they were expected . . .

. . . to make things right

Wasn't that what she had said? He took a knife from his pocket. *Go to the Tor to make things right.*

He set his left hand on a table strewn with papers. Then, clench-ing his teeth, he cut off his index finger at the second joint.

Panting with the exertion, he groped in his jacket for the cup. "Come on, come on," he said, as he fumbled the thing into his hand and placed it over the stump of his knuckle.

He waited for the throb of vitality from the cup, its warmth, the sense of well being he had felt before.

But nothing happened. His blood poured onto the table. Sweat mixed with rain dropped from his sodden hair into his eyes. A feeling of panic welled up inside him.

Go to the Tor, the Tor, to make things right. . . .

Titus slapped himself to make himself think clearly. The pain from the wound was clouding his mind. He needed air.

He staggered out of the house. What had gone wrong? Why hadn't the goddamn cup worked? He looked dolefully at the two bodies outside. He had meant to bring them into the house, but what did it matter, really? They would not need to be consumed. In fact, it would be better if they were found murdered. It was just a question of getting away before . . .

Oh Titus, you killed her.

. . . before the police came around. But they wouldn't see the bodies anyway, most likely, not in this rain.

Your daughter. You killed your daughter.

He checked the detonator. His finger was losing a lot of blood, but he would be all right, he told himself. He just had to get to the woods, explode the five bombs inside the house, and then take off for Atlantic City.

Sea Legs would be waiting for him.

He scrambled toward the woods like a crab, his hands held over his body to protect the detonator and the cup, his face red with his own blood. Just as he reached the treeline, he stopped to vomit.

Why hadn't the bloody cup worked? he wanted to scream.

Because you killed her, you killed your daughter, Hassam Bayat, and now you're going to

"There's something over here, Hal!"

Titus inhaled sharply. It was the boy, he thought, amazed. The Christ Child, of all people, out here in this tornado. Titus stared at his finger, where white gristle showed through his raw red flesh. He toyed with the idea of shooting the boy, but such an act would probably only add insult to injury. If the baby messiah were operating true to form, he would have a mobile news crew behind him to film Titus's arrest. The Coffeehouse Gang would play the film clip for the next fifty years. He wondered as he fashioned a bandage out of strips of cloth from his undershirt if anything else could possibly go wrong.

The boy knelt over Gwen's body as another figure ran up the hill past the house.

Titus almost laughed when he recognized him. Of course it

would be him, he thought. The ex-FBI agent, the one who had supplied Titus's description to the authorities. After two very nearly successful attempts on his life, the lucky bastard was going to see Hassam Bayat in all his blue-eyed British splendor get carted away by the constabulary of Dawning Falls.

Even though he knew it would probably be a fruitless move, Titus was about to make a run for his car on the other side of the woods. It all just seemed so common, he thought, to be caught running, red-handed, as it were. . . .

And then the girl sat up.

Titus vomited again.

She was dead, I knew she was dead. He swallowed hard. A voice, very deep, very far away inside his mind, laughed.

The FBI man backed away, then walked slowly toward the house, his head swiveling from side to side, watching for danger. "Jesus Christ," Titus heard him say as he peered in the doorway.

There were no other vehicles on the road, Titus noticed. No TV vans, no police escorts.

Hal walked inside.

"Oh, yes," Titus said aloud as he pressed the detonator.

It had been clear from the moment Arthur saw her that the girl was dead. She had felt like meat from the butcher's, cold, flat, slow in the process of decay, but already beginning. The hair at her temple was matted with blood, congealed around the charred-edge hole of the bullet's entry.

"I'm sorry," Hal said. "She's gone. This one, too." He wiped Pinto's hair out of his face. "Oh, good God."

"What is it?"

"This is the biker who shot me in Sturgis." Hal looked through the man's pockets for ID. There was none. He looked back at Arthur. "You sure you're all right?"

"I'm okay," Arthur said flatly.

"Look, you are what you are, and you do what you can. And sometimes you can't do anything. You may not like it, but that's the way it is."

"I know," Arthur said.

"Then I'm going to check things out. You stay put."

The boy nodded.

They had arrived too late. Arthur heard his breath pour raggedly out of his mouth. It would have been better not to know, he thought. The gift for healing that he possessed meant nothing in the face of death. Even the cup could do nothing now. All the miracles in the world stopped short of death.

Keeping his natural revulsion in check, he reached over to close the dead girl's eyes. *You are what you are and you do what you can,* he thought. Now, all he could do for the girl who had struck the deepest chord in him that he had ever felt was to close her eyes in death.

"Good-bye, Gwen," he said.

At the moment he touched her, the first image appeared, blinding, inside his eyes. It was the image of Guenevere speaking the word "Excalibur" at the same moment that Arthur himself learned the name of the great sword. That image flashed inside his brain with such intensity that Arthur was rendered physically immobile. And then came the other images, of Guenevere hurtling through the air as her horse bolted; of Guenevere, veiled and bedecked with white flowers, accepting his ring on the day of their marriage; of Guenevere sad-eyed, childless, meeting his eyes as he told her that he would have to put her away in a Christian nunnery in order to please the petty kings.

She had never objected. Her acquiescence was what broke his heart the most.

"I'm sorry," Arthur the king, who had forgotten how to be a man, said to the woman he loved.

Guenevere was silent for a moment. Then she said, "This is how it must be. For my sins."

"For mine," he corrected.

Guenevere's brow creased. "Arthur," she said wonderingly, "Do you believe that we will return to live an earthly life again?"

He was taken aback by the question. Guenevere had been a Christian for many years, and had forsaken such pagan beliefs. "I don't know," he said.

"Who shall you become?" she asked. Unconsciously her hands had risen, almost into an attitude of prayer. The look in her eyes was pitifully earnest.

"No one can know that," Arthur said gently. "Even the Merlin of Britain cannot see that far."

"Sometimes I see . . . that is, I dream, or perhaps it's something I see before I dream, I don't know . . . I see myself as someone else, a woman with long golden hair and a dagger made of black glass in my hands . . ." She took in a swift inrush of air and blushed. "I know it sounds outrageous—"

"No." Arthur spoke quickly, then held out his hand to touch her own. "No, I've . . . What you've said . . ." Their eyes locked together in mutual torment. "My sword was there."

"Excalibur," Guenevere whispered.

Their hands, clasped tightly together, broke apart. The two were silent.

"Everything is possible," the king said to relieve the silence.

"Then perhaps we'll see each other again," Guenevere said, smiling to conceal the pathetic hope in her eyes.

"Of course. I'll come by the convent to visit." He did not look at her when he spoke. He knew how shallow his words sounded, how inadequate. It was not what she meant at all, he knew. But he could not bear to think that he would not see her again until they were both beyond death.

And it was his fault. She had not asked to be put away like an unwanted toy. He was wronging her, wronging her so greatly that he dared not even ask for her forgiveness.

He rose, wanting to run away from his shame.

Guenevere cast her gaze down. Of course he had not understood. Perhaps it was not even his desire to encounter her again in another life. Why should he? She had betrayed him with his best friend.

"Well, good-bye, then," Guenevere said, smiling gently.

Arthur looked at her once more, seeing the girl whom he had known was to be his soulmate the instant their eyes met, and then walked away from her for what he believed would be forever.

———

"Guenevere," Arthur said now, kneeling near the body of the young girl.

"Here. Over here." The voice called him through time, through death and life and death again. "I'm Gwen this time, remember?"

Through a white mist he saw her, spiky black hair, tight jeans. "I've stayed behind for you," she said. "It's hard to do. The others have left."

"What others?"

"Brigid. And Guenevere. There's just me. I've waited."

He looked at her for a long moment through the mist. Then he smiled. "I'm glad you did," he said.

She looked down shyly. "You hardly know me."

"That's why I'm glad you waited."

"Guenevere was sad because she had sex with Launcelot."

Arthur laughed. "I guess everyone knows that."

"Yes, well, she wanted to be punished for that, so she suffered for a long time."

Arthur thought of Launcelot. That was why Lance had gone away, too. To punish himself. "For what," Arthur said. "For loving someone."

"We mess up our lives by thinking too much," Gwen said.

"I know."

"What will happen when you take me back into the world, Arthur?"

He hesitated. "You'll have a wonderful time," he said.

"With you?"

Arthur turned away. "I don't think so."

"But I've waited my whole life for you! We all have, Guenevere and Brigid, too. Over and over—"

"I don't have much time left," Arthur said.

Gwen looked puzzled. "To live?"

He nodded. "I don't really have a life of my own this time around. Actually, I'm just somebody's magic trick, living out someone else's last days."

"But it's someone you used to be."

"It's not who I am now."

"Who is that?"

Arthur smiled. "That's the problem." He held out his hand. "Come on."

Arthur's eyes rolled back in his head. His back arched. His hands and feet shook uncontrollably, even as he held fast to the dead girl's body.

"You have to come back with me now," Arthur said, in the netherworld they occupied. "We can't wait."

"But your body! What is it doing?"

"It's allowing me to bring you back, Gwen."

"But it looks as if it's dying."

"It is. In stages. Humans aren't supposed to be able to do this. Bring you out of this place."

"Are you not human, then?"

"Yes, but it's a different sort of human. It's like having a life in the second octave. Most of the time, we come back with no memories at all of who we used to be. We start over from zero. But I know what it's like to be alive and to die. So there are new things for me to learn."

"Like bringing people back from the dead."

"Yes," Arthur said.

"But it's killing you."

"That's because the earth plane isn't where I should be learning this. It's not compatible with being human." He laughed. "So now you can ask me again if I'm not human. The riddle just goes on and on, like a merry-go-round."

"Couldn't you just be Arthur? That is, you, who you want to be, and forget all this other stuff?"

Arthur looked at her levelly. "Then I wouldn't be able to bring you back, would I?"

Arthur felt the rain hitting his face like needles, then running into his mouth, tasting of his own sweat. He felt exhausted. How long had he been here, he wondered, clutching the dead girl as if he could bring her back to life? "Gwen," he said softly. "Gwen, can you answer me?"

His hands throbbed, hot, giving off heat in waves. Beside him,

Gwen stirred. The vibrance of her life seemed to hum around her. Her cheeks flushed red. Her eyes opened.

She stared vacantly ahead, unable to speak.

"Just rest," he said, putting his arm around her. Though the rain was chilling and the mud uncomfortable, Gwen was in too fragile a state to move, and Arthur was too tired.

They had both almost fallen asleep when the earth exploded and seemed to turn inside out.

Above everything was the mud, a tidal wave of mud flying around them, slapping them with rocks and splinters of wood, mud so thick that Arthur was certain they would be suffocated by it. It took them both down in the first second. By the time the sound of the explosion subsided, they were buried in mud two feet deep.

Behind them, the house had collapsed. Only one wall remained standing. A stairway was attached to it. A chimney still stood, as did several radiators and a few random pieces of furniture that seemed to float in a sea of splinters. A dozen or more fires smoldered through the mess, occasionally breaking into flame, then subsiding in the rain.

"Hal!" Arthur cried, scrambling to his feet. Gwen only blinked, the fingers of her hands splayed out in front of her, her mouth open and filling with mud.

Arthur looked back at the smoking, burning wreckage, and then at the girl. "You have to stay here," he said gently, pulling her out of the mud and onto a part of the wooden platform that had not been destroyed. He put her hand on one of the fallen guardrails.

She looked up at him. "You're bleeding," she said. She reached up and touched his head. Her hand came away bloody.

"Wait for me here," he said.

He slogged through the slime and debris, blinking away the blood and rain that was pouring into his eyes. His mind was still foggy from the seizure, but he forced himself to focus, running into the nightmare landscape, tripping over the piles of boards and nails and scraps of paper and metal and wood that lay everywhere and still fell out of the sky like confetti.

"Mom?" Gwen called behind him. To Arthur's dismay, she was

lurching into the wreckage, her legs scraped raw, blood streaming from her nose. "I saw my mother . . ."

"Gwen, don't," Arthur said. He held her by both shoulders. "Go to the road and wait for the fire trucks. Someone's got to have reported this. It's not safe here."

"But you—"

"Just go!" he shouted, pushing her toward the road. She staggered away, sobbing.

It would be better for her not to see what lay among the fires.

The body of Mr. Santori, the security guard, was recognizable only by the nametag which was pinned to his uniform. One dismembered arm lay near his feet. His face was gone.

"Hal," Arthur whispered, choking as he beat out a fire that was threatening to billow. He felt sick. What was happening was not within the realm of possibility. All of the strange, impossible things that had gone before—the healing water, the trances, the power of his hands, even the uncanny occurrence when he brought Gwen back from the state beyond death—all these were acceptable to his mind. But losing Hal was not.

"Hal!" he shouted, throwing boards aside, burrowing into the piles of matchstick-sized wood. He had to keep looking, keep digging, because he could not bear the thought of being able to do nothing.

Beneath a radiator he spotted something. It was a finger. Near it was a metal watchband. Arthur dug wildly through the rubble, his hands bleeding and filled with splinters. Beneath a ceiling beam he found a body, and his breath caught. Could he heal Hal? Arthur wondered. If there were enough left of him . . .

He turned the body over. The face was a woman's. Its naked body contained no internal organs.

His eyes stung from the smoke, though so little of the house was left that it was clearing rapidly. He heard himself whimpering as he searched the same places again and again. There was not a single object within sight that was larger than a bicycle wheel. "Oh, Hal," he moaned. "Please come back. Please, Hal . . ."

He isn't here, Arthur thought, suddenly brightening. Swallowing quickly, he bustled through the wreckage once more, telling himself that Hal had not been in the house when it exploded, willing the idea to be true. Yes, that was it, he knew it. He could feel it. Hal's going to come walking through the door any minute. He must have been outside when the bomb went off.

He dug through the wreckage faster. His hands were running with blood. Yes, Hal had probably been outside. Checking out the security guard's car in the driveway. He'd gone out another door, on the other side of the house. Or he might have gotten stuck behind something when it happened, and been blown into the yard somewhere. There were always stories in the newspapers about cows being picked up by tornadoes and deposited in the next county, still chewing their cud. Or maybe he's in the basement, stuck underneath a beam, and in another minute I'm going to hear him cursing and yelling at me to get him out.

He dug deeper.

At the bottom of the pile, where the trap door had once been, Arthur found a single motorcycle boot.

He stared at it for a while—a minute, perhaps, or an hour—before holding it to his chest. His hands trembled.

In the distance, the wail of police and fire sirens cut through the silence. The rain had stopped. The first rays of sunlight shot through the cloud cover.

Hal was gone. It was the only thing that Arthur was certain of.

The day was dawning, and a messiah was about to be crucified.

CHAPTER FORTY-FOUR

MESSIAH

The first spectators began arriving just after the police and the fire trucks, in the soft light of dawn. From the first scream, the scene was one of chaos and horror.

The television cameras were there almost from the beginning, and the press poured in until, by six A.M., there were more news-people than onlookers. And that is what the ordinary people had become—onlookers. There were no more faithful, no more devotees, only witnesses who stared in horror as the paramedics sorted through the debris for bodies and the firemen waited behind them for the bodies to be moved so that they could hose down the already rain-soaked ground.

A group—no one seemed to know where they came from—began to chant, "Arthur Antichrist." People who had traveled long distances to experience the healing water found the well smashed and the water ineffectual.

And through it all the cameras rolled.

The police questioned him again and again. In another part of the grounds, Gwen was subjected to the same scrutiny.

"No, he didn't kill anyone!" she shrieked hysterically. It was clear that she was on the verge of shock, wild-eyed, trembling, her speech rapid, her thoughts disconnected. "He healed me. Someone shot me. . . . It's my blood, only I don't have the wound anymore. . . . The guy was one of my mother's boyfriends, only it was my real father. My mother's dead, too. I think he killed her. His name was Bob, at least that's what he said. Then he killed me. I knew I was dead because I saw my past lives. . . ."

The paramedics were taking the bodies of Pinto and the guard into the waiting ambulance as a television camera followed them.

"Messiah or murderer?" a news reporter asked into the camera. The next shot was a telephoto image of Arthur's face, seen only briefly between the heads of two policemen. "The famous healing waters of Miller's Creek, New York is the unlikely scene of a bizarre murder involving a young man who had been touting himself as a latter-day Jesus Christ and his girlfriend, who claims that she was resurrected from death by her lover."

Here the network news showed the photograph of Gwen and Arthur touching hands on the day of his arrival in Dawning Falls. It was followed by Gwen Ranier's unsmiling senior class photo, showing her in full goth makeup, with kohl-rimmed eyes, black lipstick, and six earrings.

"Police discovered the couple covered with blood at the site of a devastating explosion that destroyed what thousands have called the 'Healing Sanctuary' because of what many considered to have been miraculous properties in the water here.

"Apparently the explosion has destroyed the well which fed the healing waters of Miller's Creek. Pilgrims, some of whom have traveled hundreds and even thousands of miles, are being turned away disappointed."

The network now showed an old woman in a walker standing beside the muddy banks of the overflowing creek, shaking her head and wiping a tear from her cheek.

"Meanwhile, there is no official explanation for the two brutal murders which, according to police sources, may only be the tip of the iceberg." Here the reporter consulted a notebook.

"Police have found a finger that may belong to yet a third victim, and an arm from what might possibly be yet a fourth victim," she read. "Also, since the devastation here has been so extensive, it is possible that even more people were present at the time of the explosion, but have not been recovered because there are simply insufficient remains."

The reporter spoke directly into the camera now. "At this time, there is no way of determining the death toll from the deadly explosion at this site known as the Healing Sanctuary that has saved the lives of so many. But the overriding question is, why?"

The group accusing Arthur of being the Antichrist took up their chant again as Arthur was led by a police escort toward the waiting patrol cars on the road. "Killer!" they screamed.

The media people and the other spectators rushed to surround him. All Arthur saw was a sea of faces, a mob of screaming, wailing mouths.

"Messiah!"

"Satan!"

"Antichrist!"

"Why didn't you heal the others?"

"What have you done to the well?"

"Why did you let them die?"

Arthur looked around at the wall of faces, all of them shouting. The words they spoke no longer made sense to him. "Hal," he said quietly. "Oh, Hal, did you have to go?"

But of course he did. Arthur knew that.

The reason nothing was left of Hal was because he had thrown himself on a bomb. It was something Hal would do without question.

You are what you are, and you do what you can, he had said. Hal had lived by those words, Arthur thought as the police led him through the mob. In the end, Hal had died, just as Galahad had died, in service to him.

Oh, Hal.

Maybe you were right to leave, Arthur thought. After the events that had happened, he was not at all sure that dying was not at least partially a conscious decision. This life had not brought Hal much of what he had wanted. Perhaps he had simply made up his mind to leave, and events had accommodated him.

Well, Arthur thought, *I can leave, too.*

That was something he had known ever since the incident of the loaves and fishes at the crossroads. When he had closed his eyes, it was not to bring rain, as it had, but to leave his body. His body, and eventually the planet. He had been preparing to die.

It hadn't worked. Something had happened: a slight shift in consciousness, a small fear of death, perhaps. Whatever it was, instead of oblivion, the rain had come, and Arthur had returned to the screaming, shouting, adoring voices around him without remembering what he had intended to do.

But there were no adoring crowds today. The adulation had turned overnight to hatred, the blind faith to suspicion. As it had with every messiah in history.

These people were not prepared for what he was. He still did not understand his gift, this strange outgrowth of the Merlin's magic gone wrong; but he did know that whatever power he had been given was wasted on human beings.

The taste of life in his mouth was bitter. He had had enough.

He closed his eyes, hearing a deep thrum inside his mind, the silent sound that would engulf him and lead him to the Summer Country. The noise around him grew muffled. All the shouting and commands directed at him, the jarring sounds of traffic and claxoning horns and machinery, the purposeful, probing questions of reporters, the chatter of idle passersby, the occasional burst of laughter or wail of an infant . . . All of the auditory detritus of life around him dimmed, as if a giant bell jar had covered everything.

He could no longer feel the humidity in the air or the sun on his face. He was traveling far, through that plane of memory and illusion, into something clearer, stiller, into the eye of the storm.

"Arthur . . ." It was Gwen's voice, entering his silence.

"Are you all right?" he asked with his mind.

"I'm afraid I'm going quite mad down there," she answered wryly. A moment later she appeared beside him, just the two of them in a limitless expanse of white.

"How did you get here?" he asked. "I didn't know . . . Oh." He realized that the woman he was talking to was Guenevere. "I thought you were Gwen."

"I am," she said patiently.

"I think I was supposed to get to know her, but . . ."

"But you're going to kill yourself instead?"

"It's only a matter of time, anyway, Guenevere." He paced. "And not much left of it at that, from all indications."

"Then hadn't you better do what you came to do?"

"I beg your pardon?" he asked archly. "I've hardly had the opportunity to do anything, in case you hadn't noticed. Thanks to the Merlin, the life I was supposed to have lived as Arthur Blessing was blithely exchanged for another that I'd already lived!"

"Now, now," Guenevere said. "You did enjoy being king, didn't you?"

He blinked, touched his face. He had a beard. He shook his head, astonished. "Why, that's who I am now, isn't it!"

The queen made a noncommittal gesture. "You are who you are," she said.

Arthur sat down beside her, on a bench that materialized as soon as he thought of it. "What, er . . . what exactly was it I was supposed to do, Guenevere?"

She raised her eyebrows. "Don't you remember?"

"Well," he waffled. "I . . . I suppose . . ."

"You came for me," she said, quietly but firmly. "You said you would wait for me. But instead, I've waited for you, again and again. For three lifetimes I've waited. But something always seems to get in the way."

"Oh. But naturally, there were matters that had to be taken care of. Your vow as a priestess in one life, my duties as king in another. And in this one, of course, they're all making me out to be some kind of tinpot god created for their entertainment. . . ."

"It has nothing to do with them," she said irritably. "It's about knowing who you are, and what you are, and what it is you want, and what things you have to leave behind. . . . As Hal said, it's about doing what you can." She arranged her skirts around her. "He was giving you a message, you know."

"Hal?"

"No one ever loved you more," Guenevere said. "Except for me. That is why I am here."

"You are what you are, and you do what you can," Arthur repeated.

"Go back," she said. "Finish out the story." She took his hands in hers. "And remember who you are."

He came to abruptly as a rock struck him, the pain in his head throbbing.

"Antichrist!" someone shouted from the crowd.

"Look, he's bleeding!"

"Heal yourself, miracle boy!"

"It was a fraud. And the girl's in on it."

"Those punks on motorcycles, too."

"Heal me!"

Again the cameras swiveled toward him. Gwen, too, was being led away. Two police squad cars were waiting on Germantown Pike. One for each of them. He caught her eye. She was terrified.

Don't be afraid, he tried to tell her, but he knew she would not understand him in this way. She was fully human; while she was conscious, she had no inkling of being anything except Gwen Ranier, a friendless girl who the police believed had killed her own mother.

If she only knew her worth, Arthur thought. And then he looked out on the crowd around them. *If they all did.* He stopped cold. The idea made his breath stop. All these people, the invalids, the accusers, the complainers, the vicious ones, all of them were here because they did not believe that their lives were good enough to do the things they wanted to do.

Just as he himself had not believed.

Oh, my God, he thought. That was why the Grail didn't work all the time.

"It can't give you what you don't already have," he said.

"What'd he say?" a reporter shouted. A dozen microphones were thrust through the protective circle of the police. The officers shoved them away.

"Hurry up, goddammit." A television camera was bearing down on them, and its operator, a sweating, smelly man with greasy hair and an expanse of belly showing beneath his shirt, motioned for the reporter to come forward.

"I think he's trying to give a statement," the reporter said in her most outraged tone to the police. "Will you . . . Officer . . ." The reporter took a deep breath, then looked directly into the camera with eyes of steel. "Police are strangely unwilling to permit the young man at the center of this tragedy to speak," she said.

"Oh, for God's sake," the chief of police said. He motioned for Arthur's escort to stop. "Okay, kid, you want to say something? Go ahead."

Suddenly Arthur found himself in the middle of a silent circle, with microphones arrayed like spears around him. He almost wanted to laugh. It was all so simple, really. The people there— the ones who had come to the healing waters, who had looked for a messiah, who had eventually needed only to kill the one they had once worshipped—suddenly they seemed harmless to him, childlike, understandable, worthy, forgivable.

"They're just afraid of dying," he said into the microphones. He looked out over the crowd. "But that's the easy part."

"Arthur!" a woman's voice called. It was Emily, running up from the road. Someone shouted her down. The protesters began chanting again. The reporter who had gotten the police to grant the interview with Arthur slipped in the mud and fell hard against one of the officers. Misinterpreting the event, another policeman drew his club. Instinctively, the other officers formed a circle around their prisoner, pushing the microphones out, causing the media people to complain loudly and shout questions at Arthur. The din grew even louder as the news helicopter once again appeared overhead. In the distance, the ambulance taking away the bodies receded. The fire truck pulled away.

Into this cacophony of voices and mechanical sounds came the motorcycles.

With a roar that rent the air, the knights lunged into the police circle like a herd of bison. They came, single-minded, powerful, and fearless, the horsemen of the apocalypse come for their own.

As they barrelled through the crowd at breakneck speed, Launcelot extended his arm and plucked Arthur out of the police circle like a daisy. On a parallel course, Dry Lips grabbed Gwen around the waist and slapped her neatly in front of him. The rest never even slowed down.

"Where are we going?" Curoi MacDaire mouthed as they barrelled down the highway.

"Somewhere that's not here," Launcelot shouted in response.

The pursuit began at once, with the police making up only a segment of the group of vehicles following them. A van from a television news team kept trying to weave through the traffic, despite loud warnings from police bullhorns. Observing the success of the van, the other motorists were not about to fall away. It was a strange procession, a parade to nowhere.

About a half mile down the road, someone dressed in rags of such an extreme condition that he looked like a beggar from the Middle Ages stood directly in front of them, gesticulating wildly. Arthur recognized him at once. It was Taliesin, theatrical as ever, directing them into the woods.

As the motorcycles veered off the road, the cars behind them pulled over immediately. A siren wailed, coming closer.

The knights rocketed their bikes along a deer trail as far as they could go, until the path ended at a sheer wall of rock. On one side of the cliff was a thicket of thorns. On the other was a small stream overflowing with muddy water from the previous night's downpour.

Agravaine flipped off his helmet with the hook at the end of his arm. "A fine road you sent us on, Merlin," he said, scowling.

"Quiet," Taliesin said. "There's no time to waste. Are we all assembled?" He looked around, counting. "Good." He grabbed Arthur by the arm and propelled him forward, toward the wall of rock.

"Walk," he commanded. He looked deep into the boy's eyes. "You know what I mean, don't you?"

"Walk . . . walk through the rock?" Arthur asked.

The old man nodded. "I'll be doing it for you. All you have to do is trust. Can you trust me, Arthur?" His eyes pleaded, as if what he were really asking was, Can you ever trust me again?

The boy looked at him for a long moment. Worlds passed between them. "I can," he said, "and I do."

Taliesin's eyes shone. "Thank you," he said.

Arthur walked over to Gwen, who was riding in front of Dry Lips. "Will you come with me?" he asked.

A look of overwhelming anxiety passed over her face as she dismounted. "I don't think I have much of a choice," she said.

"You always have a choice," Taliesin said softly. "That's right, isn't it, Arthur?"

The boy smiled. "Yes," he said. "Yes, I think we do." He held out his hand to Gwen. "Are you coming?"

Her fingers wound around his as they faced the wall of rock. "I'm with you," she said.

"You always were, my lady," Taliesin said, stilling himself for the spell he was about to perform. "Walk," he commanded.

With that, Arthur and Gwen entered the wall and disappeared into it.

Behind them came the knights, who apparently did not find this act to be in the least bit unusual. They all tumbled through the stone wall as if it were a holographic illusion.

Not far behind came the pursuers from Miller's Creek, on foot and led, not by uniformed police officers, but by the camera crews of broadcast news agencies. They were catching up quickly. Someone was shouting. A flashbulb popped.

Taliesin waited for them. Just as the TV cameraman burst through the crowd of running spectators, he bowed theatrically, then backed into the rock as if it were made of water, disappearing an inch at a time.

"Bye, bye," the old man said as his lips—the last visible part of him—vanished from view.

CHAPTER FORTY-FIVE

SEA LEGS

ATLANTIC CITY, NEW JERSEY

Sea Legs was in its appointed spot, crowded in among other pleasure boats. She looked particularly tawdry, the painting of exaggeratedly large human hindquarters chipped and fading, the cheerful lettering looking old-fashioned.

Titus Wolfe came aboard feigning good cheer. It was difficult, particularly since the stump of his finger had become infected and throbbed painfully with every step he took. "Ho, Cap'n!" he called, holding aloft a bottle of whiskey. "Care for a short run around the harbor?"

That was the password. Edgington appeared in short order, his face drawn and gray.

"I say, would you care for a short—"

"Get belowdecks," Edgington growled, not looking Titus in the eye as he pushed past him.

Titus found his way to a cabin. It was filthy, but there was a blanket inside. Edgington's drug use was getting the best of him, he decided. He'd seen the rapid deterioration of junkies before. Among the Coffeehouse Gang, a number of optimistic young men had turned to drugs once the euphoria of schoolboy idealism wore off and reality came galloping in. Faced with the choice between being double agents and going to jail, more than one had opted out of either scenario. A few, brave or foolish, killed themselves quickly, by hanging or with a bullet in the brain. The others died slowly.

Edgington was clearly one of these. From the looks of him, his habit—it was probably heroin—was nothing new. Always thin, he was wasting now, and his eyes had that incurious, unfocused look.

But he could still pilot a boat, Titus imagined. The Coffeehouse Gang would eliminate him in a day if he couldn't.

The two men didn't meet again until dinner. There was beef stew from a can. Edgington didn't eat much of his. His beverage was straight whiskey in a tumbler, around which he kept his fingers tightly clasped.

They spoke desultorily for a time—mostly Titus spoke, with Edgington looking glassily elsewhere—until the captain drained his glass and set his gaze squarely upon his passenger.

Titus felt immediately uncomfortable. They were old friends, after all. Titus knew the difference between heroin and trouble. All was not well.

"What is it?" he asked quietly, though they were the only ones in the galley.

"The Coffeehouse Gang knows what you've been up to," Edgington said. Even after all the years of hiding among the proletariat, his voice still maintained the crisp upper class accent that had been the hallmark of the "old money" aristos at Cambridge. "There's a photo of you."

Titus felt his entrails constrict. How was there a picture of him? He had broken Ginger's camera to avoid being photographed.

"Off a security camera, I think. Said it was black and white. Could be worse."

A security camera? Where? He had always been careful to keep his back to those. In the drugstore, where he had bought the hair dye? No, he had spotted that camera before he even went in.

"It was in connection with some woman who worked in a laboratory or some such. She'd been killed, apparently by her daughter and a boyfriend. Blah, blah, the usual. I don't know how you're involved, but there you have it."

The water analysis lab. There must have been a camera in the ceiling. Titus had been too shocked by Ginger's recognition of him to pay attention.

That, he knew, was how careers were lost. "I see," he said. "Who's got it? Besides the Gang?"

Edgington gave a lazy snort of mirth through his stony, waxen face. "Everyone, apparently. FBI, CIA, all of them, every local bobby along the east coast. Surprised you made it this far."

So they had his face. "For murder?" he asked quietly.

"Not really. The girl claims you tried to kill her. She also claims you're her father, although she only knows you by the sobriquet 'Bob.' But since she's the prime suspect in the murder of her mother, the authorities aren't taking her completely seriously." His mouth twisted into a wry smile. "Anyway, she's bolted, so nothing's on paper. You're quite safe from the Feds."

But not from the Coffeehouse Gang. Darling and the others would only see the huge, publicized mess Titus had left in his wake. Very, very poor PR for a firm that specialized in extreme privacy.

He exhaled noisily. The other bad news had been about the girl. He had been hoping that that particular part of that nightmare night had been his imagination.

He knew he had killed the girl.

How could she have sat up for the Christ Child? What in hell had the boy done?

"What happened to your finger?" Edgington asked, smacking his lips slowly. He was high, Titus thought. Shot up just before dinner, when the going was apt to be smooth.

"Accident," Titus said tersely. "Am I wanted for anything else?"

The captain shrugged, indifferent.

"There wouldn't be anything else," Titus affirmed, feeling sweat bead on his forehead.

Edgington blinked slowly. "Right-o."

"So the Coffeehouse Gang wouldn't have anything to worry about, would they?"

The captain grunted.

"Christ," Titus said, deciding to concentrate on his meal. Edgington was no help at all. After a few minutes, the captain stood up and shambled out of the galley, taking the bottle of whiskey with him.

Fat lot of good he is to the Coffeehouse boys, Titus thought. Edgington was so far gone, he'd probably give the lot away for a fix if he needed it badly enough.

He put down his fork. The food in his mouth seemed to turn to cardboard.

That was it, of course. Edgington was a liability, and the Coffeehouse Gang never kept those.

So why was he still alive to make this run? Why had the Gang agreed to have anyone meet Titus at all, since he, too, was a liability, now that his face was known?

Suddenly he knew. He inhaled deeply with the shock, as if someone had just stabbed him with a knife. Edgington had been ordered to kill him. That was why he'd been so talkative about Titus's photo; he'd felt guilty. The man had never been any good at wetwork.

Afterward, of course, after Titus was dead, Edgington himself would be put out of his misery.

Titus sat back and allowed himself a short, bitter laugh. They'd never had a chance, either one of them. They'd been performing dogs from the beginning, driven to work at the peak of their ability under threat of death. And then, after one mistake on Titus's part and a slow and inevitable decline on Edgington's, the threat was made real.

That was how all the bright young boys in the coffeehouse ended, their dreams exposed for the rhetoric they were, their little lives unnoticed beyond their criminality, plucked like weeds in the garden of treason.

Titus found Edgington on the bridge, steering the helm while he scratched idly at one arm. The tracks on it were black, long threads of needle marks from years of abuse. His face, waxy and impassive, resembled a skull. Titus doubted if the man even saw him come in. He moved squarely into Edgington's line of vision and leaned against a wall.

The captain's body stiffened with dread. His obvious revulsion at having to kill Titus was evident, and touching. If Edgington weren't an addict, Titus thought, he might even have refused the assignment. Of course, if he weren't an addict, he would know that such an assignment was a prelude to his own death.

Edgington, in his early years at least, was the sort who might have killed himself rather than stoop to such degrading work. He most probably would have killed himself if he had known he was going to die as soon as he carried out the murder.

Not any more, though. Addicts never believed they were going to die. That was part of their denial; the future didn't exist for them.

It certainly didn't exist for Edgington, Titus thought. That was a fact.

"I've brought you a gift," he said softly, smiling.

The captain squinted at him with the exaggerated suspicion of someone not quite in his senses. He looked like a cartoon caricature of a spy.

He's expecting me to take out a gun, Titus understood. Instead, he brought from his pocket a glassine envelope into which he had placed the contents of the remaining strychnine capsule from his suitcase. "I had to kill someone, a junkie. He had this on him. Heroin, I think." He shrugged and laid the envelope on a wooden shelf. "Consider it a tip."

Edgington didn't move.

"Or you can throw it away. It makes no difference to me, surely, although I admit to hoping you might swap me a glass of whiskey for it." He nodded toward the half-empty bottle Edgington kept beside the helm.

The captain stared at him for another moment, his eyes rheumy and red-rimmed. The envelope filled with white powder quivered on the ledge. Finally, in a quick, sweeping motion, Edgington snatched it and stuck it in his pocket.

Titus had known he wouldn't be able to resist. Even suspecting poison, the captain would think of his habit first. If he thought at all anymore.

He folded his arms. "Where are you planning to do it?" Titus asked casually.

Edgington started; but after a moment of hesitation, he stared stonily ahead.

"Well?"

A tear trickled down the captain's cheek. *He's crying,* Titus thought. Crying, over having to kill someone. Edgington really had gone over the hill.

"I'm sorry, Titus," he said.

Wolfe shrugged.

"I guess it was the photo thing."

"Probably."

"I'm supposed to put you overboard before we reach Panama. That would be just after dawn."

"Put me overboard?" Titus could not help smiling. "How do you propose to do that?"

"Oh, Christ, I don't know. Buggers, all of them. I'm not going to, of course. That's why I'm telling you."

Titus wondered what Edgington was more grateful for—the drugs he'd given him, or Titus's knowledge of the situation. The relief in the man's eyes was evident. If Titus knew, then Titus would know what to do. That was how it had always been.

"We'll be passing the Bahamas late tonight," the captain said. "You could take a dinghy then." His eyes were scanning the ceiling, trying to think as he spoke. "But then you'd have to get lost. Lay low for a time."

"A long time," Titus said mildly. "I suppose I'd have to change my identity and hide for the rest of my life."

Edgington scratched his arms through his sleeves. "Could be," he said noncommittally. "You could keep the authorities at bay, that won't be a problem. There's just the boys. . . ." He made an involuntary gesture, something like a spasm of his head.

"Will they kill you if I go missing?"

"Oh, no, never." Edgington dismissed the thought with a too-large wave of his hand. "I've been with them too long. Besides, I'm just the ferryboat driver." He grinned. His teeth had rotted, Titus noticed. "I'll say you went overboard during the night. You can leave the dinghy at sea, if you would. They'll think you drowned."

Titus laughed. The Coffeehouse Gang would think no such thing. "Whatever you say, Captain."

"Good, then." He grabbed the whiskey bottle and handed it to Titus. "Here you go. No glasses, I'm afraid, but help yourself."

Titus raised the bottle in salute. "*L' chaim,*" he said, meeting Edgington's gaze warmly. "To life."

When Titus returned to the bridge, Edgington was dead, his fingers curved and splayed with the effects of the strychnine.

Couldn't even wait to get back to his room, Titus thought with disgust. Edgington had used all the strychnine—shot it, probably—without even sniffing to see if it was poisonous. He hauled the body to the deck and pushed it overboard.

Quickly he fitted himself out in a life jacket and a pair of Edgington's boots. From the captain's cabin he took five hundred dollars—apparently all Edgington had to his name—and sixty packets of heroin in a watertight container. Drugs were always useful. Look what they had done for Edgington, Titus thought as he lowered himself in the dinghy off the coast of Grand Bahama Island.

CHAPTER FORTY-SIX

CAMELOT

"Where are we?" Gwen asked. Her voice, echoing and tinny, sounded as if she had spoken in a cavern. She could see nothing. White haze swirled around them all, thick as cotton candy. "Is this a cloud?" She swallowed hard. "Are we . . . dead?"

"Probably," Launcelot answered. "We were the last time. The wizard may well have killed us again. 'Tis well within his dark power."

"What?"

"Oh, stop." Taliesin's voice boomed, seeming to come from all directions at once, clear as a bell and loud enough to make Gwen jump. "You're not dead, girl. We're merely existing on a plane—a zone, if you will—where you're not accustomed to being."

"And this is where you brought us?" Arthur asked, annoyed. "All we needed to do was to get away from the police. You could have taken us to Tahiti."

"Instead of this nothing," Launcelot finished gloomily.

"What ingrates!" Taliesin sputtered. "Oh, well, I suppose it doesn't have to look quite so lackluster," he said with a sigh, as if he were giving in to a bunch of spoiled children. "I can make it into whatever—well, here's an idea."

Suddenly the entire group found themselves in the middle of the Great Hall at Camelot, seated at a long table piled with meats and roasted fowl and steaming loaves of fresh bread.

"Now this is more like it," Dry Lips said, helping himself to a turkey leg.

MacDaire rubbed his hands together. "How long has it been, boys?" he asked. "Eh?"

Lugh Loinnbheimionach began to blubber.

"Ah, it's all right, lad," MacDaire said, putting his arm over Lugh's shoulder.

"I miss it," the big man said.

"Aye, we all do," Kay said softly. A hush fell over the room. Even Dry Lips set down his food.

" 'Tis but a dream, anyway," Launcelot said bitterly. "Something the wizard's cooked up to trick us into thinking we're home."

"But it is home," the Merlin said, walking jauntily down the stairwell. He was dressed in his magician's robes, slightly frayed but still stiff with magnificent medieval embroidery. "This plane exists, every bit as much as the one we just left. We may say 'the past,' as if time were something real that comes and goes, but actually, there is no past. No future. We are here now, as we were then, as we will be."

There was a long silence. The knights stared at Taliesin uncomprehendingly. Finally Gawain, a man of few words, expressed his sentiments by farting.

"Aye, and we all feel the same," Kay shouted, trying to keep his voice from cracking. "You took us from our home to defend the king, but the king's nowt but a poor lad that's had not an hour of happiness for all the trouble you've brought upon him."

"What—why, the nerve—"

"Kay's right," Curoi MacDaire piped up. "Change me as you may into a mute and ugly beastie, Merlin, I owe this much of the saying to the lad I've come to think of as me own son," he said, quaffing a tankard of stout, "as well as as the king I honored to my dying day.

For it's glad I am he has a young girleen to warm his nights, since all the world around him has gone mad with fear, and will kill him sure for his trouble." He slammed the tankard on the table, to the shouts and thumping of the others.

"That's not true—" Taliesin began to protest. "It was just—"

"And where were you and the other great druids while the peasants struck Arthur upon the head with stones?" Agravaine shouted. "Where?"

"You saw those men with their clubs and noisemakers, the ones called 'cops'!" Fairhands said, his mouth turning down at the corners with disdain.

"I'd like to have seen a one of them try to use one of their cursed sticks on us," Dry Lips said, clunking down his tankard and wiping his mouth with the back of his hand.

"That's enough," Arthur said softly. Absolute silence fell. He moved to the head of the table. "I know you miss this place, this life. I know it's hard for you." He looked down at his hands. "But you know that you're only acting this way because Hal isn't here."

Some of the knights spoke up to protest, but Arthur silenced them with a gesture. He walked over to Launcelot. "I'm sorry," he said, putting his arm on the knight's shoulder. "I know he was your son, and I know you loved him. I loved him, too."

Kay bit his lip. They all knew that Hal was the only father Arthur had ever known.

"Aye, we all did," Launcelot said.

Arthur swallowed the lump in his throat so that he could go on. "He always knew what to do," he said. "And though I'll never be Hal, or even close to the man Hal was, I know what he'd say now. I know because it was one of the last things he said while he was alive. He said, 'We are what we are, and we do what we can.'"

He looked around. The men were all subdued. Launcelot put his face in his hands. "You're all soldiers," Arthur said. "I, too, was once a soldier. I didn't like everything about soldiering, but I know that what Hal said was true: When your back's against the wall, you do what you have to do. We can still make it right."

Slowly Lugh nodded. "Truth," he said.

"Can we go on?"

Launcelot came over to stand with him. "Aye," he said, his voice hoarse with emotion. "We can. Lead us, my King, and we shall follow you back into hell, if that is where you command."

In the silence that followed, footfalls echoed through the hall. A soldier, from the sound of the walk, steady and strong, perhaps a knight. The men listened, waiting, until he appeared under the arch, in the place where, in days of old, visiting chieftains would stand to receive accolades.

The man was indeed a knight, dressed in a tunic of fine blue wool, covered with a vest of silver mail. "Hello, Arthur," Hal said.

"Hal," Arthur gasped. He reached for him, but his hand went through empty air.

"You . . . you're not there," he said.

"Neither are you," Hal answered. "Not in the way you think."

"But I see you."

"Yes. I'm still with you, Arthur. I always will be."

Arthur felt his eyes welling. "Why did you die, Hal? Why'd you have to die?"

"Well, I didn't plan it, if that makes you feel any better," he said. "You know, you don't really know any more after you're dead than you do while you're living."

"No?"

Hal shook his head. "But my guess about why I died is that I was supposed to. I died the last time around when you needed me, too, remember? I found the Holy Grail, but I was killed before I could get it to you. I guess that was to show you that you didn't need it."

"But I did. I died without it," Arthur said.

Hal smiled at him. "You know that doesn't mean anything."

Arthur grinned back. "I know," he said. "Will you stay?"

Hal shook his head. "Can't. I don't belong here."

"Does the Summer Country look like this?" Arthur asked.

"It looks like whatever you want. That's why people call it heaven."

"What does it look like to you?"

Hal looked embarrassed. "It looks like a duplex on the south side of Chicago."

Arthur was taken aback. "That's where I grew up," he said. "Well, sort of. Until all this." He gestured vaguely at the castle and its trappings.

"I know. In heaven, I'm there with you. And Emily. We eat pizza and go to Cubs games. My crazy old father lives with us. We've got a three-year-old Chevy and a cat."

"And you're a cop," Arthur said.

"Yep, I'm a cop."

Arthur's eyes welled. "It doesn't seem like a lot to wish for."

Hal shrugged. "Maybe in the next life," he said.

Arthur tried to touch him again, and failed. "Will you wait for me?" he asked. "In the Summer Country? I won't be long."

"Sure, kid," Hal said. "I've got all the time in the world." He raised his sword, saluting the company. "Be valiant, knights, and true," he called.

Launcelot rose. He balled his right hand into a fist and placed it over his heart. "Godspeed, my son," he said as Hal slowly faded from view.

Taliesin walked the Tor until he found the big yellow stone stone where Excalibur had been placed by the gods. The sword was there, waiting for Arthur to take it once again.

The wolf sat on her haunches beside it. The old man settled onto a tree trunk.

"You did well, walking them through the rock."

"They put me to shame," he said softly.

"Who?" the wolf asked archly. "Those humans, with their worthless, common lives?"

"The boy is going to die," he said.

"Yes."

"Instead of being a king, he became a kind of god."

"That was all he could be," the Innocent said.

"But he cannot be both a god and a human. And he has chosen to be human."

The wolf looked over the breathtaking landscape. "Did you expect anything less of a man who gave up the Holy Grail and its gift of immortality?" The animal seemed to smile. "That one has never needed to be more than he is."

"He could have had a wonderful life, if I hadn't interfered. Arthur Blessing would have been a fine man."

"Yes," she said. "I believe he would have been."

The old man wiped his eyes. "Please teach me the Third Magic, Innocent. I cannot watch Arthur go to his death with such acceptance. It was my fault that his life has become such a horror. It was my arrogance, my unconcern for the consequences of my actions, my foolish audacity . . ."

"Your love," she said. "You loved Arthur the King so much that you could not accept that his time was over."

"But it was not," Taliesin said. "I know that now. Only his life was over. One life . . . It's as nothing." He faced her. "Please help me, Innocent. I will do anything, sacrifice anything."

The wolf stared ahead for a long time, her blank eyes unblinking. Finally she turned her head toward him. "Anything?"

"Everything," Taliesin said.

She raised her head and looked at him through narrowed eyes. "Well, well," she said. "That's something new."

"Please teach me. I beg you."

The wolf got up and sniffed around the grass. "The first great lesson of magic, little bard, is that it is possible." She ate a flower. "The magic wasn't in walking through the rock. It was in knowing that you *can* walk through the rock. Do you understand the difference?"

"Yes," he said.

"Good. Because all magic stems from that one principle. If one does not believe that spirits exist, one will never see them. If one does not acknowledge one's talent, it will never blossom. To make magic—even the most outlandish and sophisticated forms of magic—one must first accept, with certainty, that the magic is possible. Then the intent must be summoned, enough intent to ride the winds of change. But by then one knows one can do it, doesn't one?"

"So that is the second lesson?"

"After one knows that one can do it, one must know that one is doing it, yes. That is how we Bring the World into Being."

"And so the third lesson . . ."

"You tell me."

"I think that it must be to know what one has done," he said quietly. "because by understanding all that can happen, the magician can correct his errors."

"At what price?"

He faltered. "I . . . I don't know that," he said. "But I will pay any price."

"Will you? Can you give up your dreams?"

"My—"

"Your convictions. Everything you hold sacred. Everything you fear losing, you must lose. To perform the Third Magic will mean the destruction of the whole world for you, the death of your gods, the end of your existence." She was silent for a moment. "Can you do that?"

He looked at the sky, as if he were seeing it for the last time. "Yes," he said. "I will let go. I will let it all go."

The wolf looked up at him with her wise, blank eyes. "Then perhaps you are ready." The glass globe appeared in Taliesin's hands. "One last story," the wolf said.

In the globe, the Tor appeared once again.

CHAPTER FORTY-SEVEN

THE CAILLEACH

3500 B.C.E.

She had once been human, although her tribe had never named her. Born small and silent during the cold times, the girl had not been expected to live through infancy. And though she had lived—had, in fact, thrived—she had remained silent, and so was not given a name.

Later, when the weather became too harsh to live, and her tribe made plans to migrate southward, the girl's family decided to leave her behind as a sacrifice to the spirits who ruled the cold mountaintop, the Tor, where the people had lived for as long as anyone could remember.

She was an appropriate sacrifice. She was special. Although she had never spoken a word of human language, the girl had known how to summon the snakes and bring about rain. As a baby, a hare had lain across her chest without fear. Her mother once found her on the outskirts of the wood, petting a grown stag between its antlers.

As she grew older, more of her strange gifts became manifest. She could stare at something until the object moved. She could make herself so still that she became invisible. She could Walk Through the Rock, and so appear to materialize in a place remote from where she had been. And once, just once, when an older boy taunted her for her difference from all the others, she pointed her finger at him and caused him to die.

Or that was what the elders said. Perhaps she had not caused his death at all. Some argued that the boy had choked on a bird bone he was chewing. He may have laughed at the girl's outrage, or taken a deep breath in preparation for an onslaught of words he was planning to use against her; or he may simply have choked at that particular time.

But most of the tribe did not see it that way. The girl was "other," not like the rest of them. The girl drew the attention of the spirits. She was not a safe person to have on such a dangerous journey.

On the day of the exodus, all of the members of the tribe held their hands flat against a wall of the cave where, years before, they had been forced to live by the cold conditions of the Tor. While they held their hands to the damp stone, an artist named Tuwa pressed charcoal powder around each hand, producing a signature for every member of the departing clan.

While this process was going on, the old women wept. They feared change. They feared the coming journey. They believed they would encounter the end of the world, and none of them thought they would live beyond that encounter. Still, they collected their possessions and made ready to leave with the others, because anything was better than staying behind.

They looked at the nameless girl, and then away, their tears drying on their wrinkled faces. No, they would not be left behind.

The children laughed excitedly, looking forward to fighting strange new beasts in exotic lands fit only for gods and demons. They, too, looked over at the girl who did not speak. She stood apart from the others, watching, her face blank. That was what happened to you when you did not listen to your parents, they had been told.

One young toddler ran over to her mother and attached herself to the woman's legs. The mother narrowed her eyes at the nameless girl. Why couldn't she leave now? Having her here during the preparations made everyone uncomfortable. She made a motion with her chin toward the girl, conveying the message that she wanted her to move farther away from her and her young daughter.

At the end, when all the others had left their palm prints on the wall and were joking about their black hands, Tuwa the artist led the nameless girl to another wall where the imprint of her hand was made. One hand, alone, left behind. It told the story to anyone who cared to know.

The last act before they left was to take the nameless girl to a deep cleft in the Tor. Only a few accompanied her into the ravine. The rest, including her mother, remained on the rim. They stood silently with their possessions and their infants on their backs, their figures black against the rising sun behind them.

The girl was frightened. One of the elders put his hand over her eyes and told her to keep them closed. He pushed her gently toward the ground, where she waited in a crouching position with her head touching the earth.

Then the elder picked up a rock and threw it to hit her squarely on the back of the head. She fell forward with a cry. The next rock silenced her. Then a third, and a fourth. Blood poured out of her nose and mouth.

Above, on the rim, her mother turned away, her shoulders shaking violently. The sacrifice had been made.

The elders climbed out of the ravine. As they passed the cave where they had once lived, they saw the newly made images of their own hands, looking as if they were waving good-bye.

The other, the one left behind, was not visible to them as they walked southward, toward the warm lands, into the future.

———

In the ravine, a wolf who had smelled the intoxicating scent of blood licked the girl's face. Then it raised its head, its ears twitching, rotating, its nostrils quivering. Others were coming.

Eight other wolves gathered around the girl, nine in all. Each licked her bloodied face, then moved back into the protective circle around her. They ate no other food. When night fell, they adjusted their bodies into a tense reclining position, straight on their forelegs, backs slightly arched, supported by their haunches. They rested, but did not sleep.

Two days later, the girl moved a finger.

A day after that, she was able to stumble to a stream for water. She drank, slept, sat up, and then screamed. Screamed with all the outrage and terror that her young body had absorbed during those terrible moments when death had hovered nearby, touching her, kissing her with its hot, bloody lips.

She pointed skyward, and a bird fell at her feet, dead. She sank her teeth into its warm neck and drank its nourishing blood.

Then she turned toward the woods above the ravine. A deer, a young buck, burst out from between two trees and hurtled, screeching, to the floor of the chasm.

The wolves followed that with their eyes, but did not leave until the girl clapped her hands and pointed, giving them permission to eat.

While the animals feasted on the meal their goddess had brought them, the girl climbed slowly, on all fours, out of the ravine. She did not go back to the cave, but lived cold in the open air until she had the strength to fashion a rude dwelling for herself out of twigs and leaves.

Later, she would build a house of stone, where wild wolves would come to share her fire. For they already knew what the girl herself would not for many years to come: that her blood was sacred, and gave her the power to create magic.

The Cailleach had been born.

Taliesin pulled away from the events inside the globe. He was once again sitting on a tree trunk beside the yellow stone where the miraculous sword waited for its owner. The blind wolf had not moved.

"She had neither speech nor a name to call herself," he said of the girl who died to the world and was reborn into the full power of the ancient magic. "Is this how gods are born, then?" he asked. "Not in fantastic circumstances, as the myths suggest, but in blood and pain, like ordinary humans?"

"Why do you need to know?" the Innocent asked. "Are they no less gods for having been human?"

She lived her entire life in the shadow of the great rock, the Tor.

The woman still had no name. She had no need of one, since she never saw any other of her kind. Indeed, she had almost forgotten the tribe of people who had made sounds with their mouths, the Speakers, who had been so different from her that they had taken her into the ravine and beaten her until they thought she was dead, then left her behind to be devoured by wolves.

Almost, but not quite. She remembered the pain of the beating, and of their leaving. She had thought, when the wolves who had protected her while she healed came to share the warmth of her fire, that her own kind were worse predators by far than these creatures. For generations now, the wolves had brought their young to her, to cluster around her, sleeping in circles, when the nights were cold; but never since the day of her beating had she encountered another human being.

She had been alone for so long that she had begun to think that perhaps she was the only one of her kind in the world. The others had probably been killed, she reasoned. That thought filled her with a terrible longing. Even the pain she had felt when her mother had turned away from her so decisively was better than thinking of her as carrion for the raptors, the eyes that once looked upon her with love now crawling with maggots.

No, she could not bear that. One day they would all return, she told herself. They would come back to the Tor, chastened by their adventures in the wild places, and they would welcome her into their open arms.

And she would teach them what she had learned. For in her

years of solitude, the woman had learned to amuse herself by mov-ing things with her mind: food for her friends the wolves; wood for fire.

She had begun by watching a wren bring blades of dried grass to its nest in a mulberry bush growing out of the side of the Tor. It seemed to be so much effort for the little bird that the woman willed a feathery shoot up off the ground, where a gust of wind picked it up and brought it closer to the nest. Then she willed it again, holding her breath, keeping the bit of grass suspended in the air, moving slowly toward the nest, down and in.

The wren had cast a glance back at her, and she had laughed. But she never thought that what she was doing would be called magic.

The extraordinary things she did were not even difficult. In time, as her powers of concentration grew, she was able to move heavier items—small rocks, fallen branches, rotted wood. Soon she had built a wall around the shelter she had made, a wall made entirely of things that had come to her when she asked.

And too, during her days and years of solitude, she learned to Walk Through the Rock, which was much the same thing. Both feats involved seeing objects as they really were—as illusions, re-flections, visions. To walk through the rock, she found, she had to disbelieve its seeming solidity.

Her greatest triumph, her initiation, was the yellow boulder. She had seen it in a field, all of a piece, like some great doorway into the earth. She had looked at it for months, touching it, feeling its life, its slow beating heart. All objects had such hearts, she had learned. Living creatures, of course, from the big thumping organ in her own chest to the flutter of hummingbirds, had very distinc-tive heartbeats. But insects had them too, fast, jumpy rhythms, and so did slugs and tadpoles. The rhythm of trees and plants was quite different, much softer. Not all trees felt the same: Oaks felt square and sticky, willows soft, and rowans exuded little sparks of excitement, and she could feel them all.

The trees breathed, too. When she sat very still, she could see the faint wisps of life exude from their bark and wind around their trunks like smoke.

And then there were the rocks, with their slow life, their rhythm so deep that she had to slow her own body down just to perceive it. It was an ageless rhythm, eternal, lacking all desire.

When the woman could feel the beating heart of the great yellow stone, she knew that she was welcome inside it and she entered it, weightless, soft as a lover, feeling what it was like to be ancient and unmoving, to need neither water nor air, to be complete.

She walked outside of the stone and knelt down in reverence.

And then the stone moved.

At first it only lifted slightly off its earthen bed, revealing hosts of small blind creatures scuttling around in panic. Then, as the woman began to grasp the extent of her power, it moved upward. Grass and dirt fell off it in great clods.

She pointed her finger toward her dwelling at the top of the Tor, and the great stone flew there like a feather on a gust of wind. The sun shone upon its smooth yellow surface as it sailed toward the flat top of the hill and settled there. It gleamed like gold. The woman ran up the hill, panting and cackling with laughter.

On the rock she carved a sunburst, sign of a new day. And next to it, the soot-blackened outline of her hand.

She lived there in her bower for several more years. The woman was quite old by then, and had all but forgotten the tribe that had walked away from her those many years before, when one day she heard voices.

Voices. The sound made by others of her kind. Her heart began to pound. A vision came into her mind, not of the beating or her abandonment by the tribe, but of their laughter, their excitement as they prepared for the long journey into the world, the shy smiles of lovers and the songs of the women as they prepared food.

She missed them, missed them so much that her tongue ran over her lips in anticipation. Then, slowly, she emerged from her fortress of rock and wood and smelled the clean air upon which lay the scent of humans. She stopped short, her nose twitching. They were meat eaters. Closing her eyes, she could think of only one thing: Mother.

The tribe had come back for her! What else could it be? The

old woman broke into a crooked lope, waving toward the approaching humans with both hands high in the air. Her face grew tired from the unfamiliar grin creasing it. There was a lightness in her heart that was almost unbearable.

The faces of the newcomers were not familiar to her. But naturally, she thought, how could they be? It had been so long.

How long? she thought in a sudden panic. How old was she? She had no idea. Her steps faltered. She touched the matted snarl of her hair hanging over her shoulders, and felt suddenly shy.

But what did it matter, she thought. These were the grandchildren of the ones who left her. Grandchildren and great grandchildren! And yet she craned her neck to see if she could catch a glimpse of a woman whose features she strained to remember.

One of the boys, very handsome, picked something up off the ground and then came running at her so fast that she was startled at first. He was smiling broadly. There was a radiance about him that she could actually see, a bright vibrance. It frightened her.

Too late she realized that the aura she saw was one of malice. The boy pulled his arm back and let fly the stone he had picked up. It hit her on the arm, so hard that the sudden pain brought tears to her eyes.

Behind him was another, coming over the crest of the hill. The first boy shouted, and the other came running also, hurling a stick. The old woman deflected it with her forearm, but caught another stone on her breast. She turned away, and a stone struck her on her back, knocking her to the ground. The boys laughed and shouted loudly at her in a language she did not understand.

Behind the boys were other voices, older voices chiding them, but they paid no heed. A third boy crested the hill, and a fourth, and they all thought it great fun to throw things at the funny old woman who now faced the ground on her hands and knees. As she tried to rise, a stone hit her elbow. It was already swollen with arthritis, and the pain felt as if her arm were exploding. As she cried out, another hit her on the head, and she fell to the ground, dazed.

For a moment she thought that she had gone back to the awful moment when the elders of the tribe had bludgeoned her with rocks in an attempt to kill her.

But these were not her tribe. They were cruel children, like the ones who looked down from the Tor, smiling, as the elders smashed the stones into her head.

Oh, she should never have come out! She had been so seduced by the sound of humans that she had forgotten how cruel humans really were.

The rocks that struck her were bigger now. The boys drew closer, sniggering. One spat on her. She looked up. The first boy was showing her an exaggeratedly innocent face while he took his penis out of the cloth that was wrapped around him and wiggled it at her.

The others fell into paroxysms of laughter at this rudeness. One of them looked over his shoulder to see the approaching men of his tribe, their faces stern and angry. He said something to the boy who had exposed himself, but this one was not to be deterred. Calmly, with half-closed eyes, he began to urinate on the old woman.

She scrambled out of the way, outraged. And then, before the boy could even stop urinating, she cast her eyes toward a flat, sharp stone. It flew at incredible speed, slicing off the boy's arm.

The faces of the other boys grew ashen as they watched. When the boy began to scream, they ran.

The first to run had his head smashed in by a rock. The second's back was broken.

It took the adults a few moments to grasp exactly what was going on, and even then they could not believe it. One, the leader, carried a sling, and some others had spears, but their weapons did them no good. One by one they were struck with uncanny accuracy by flying objects from the makeshift fortress. Stones, branches, logs, rivers of pebbles . . . they all seemed to pour toward the newcomers as if thrown by invisible hands.

Invisible, they said in their language. Demons.

The woman laughed. She stood up amid the flying debris and placed her bruised hands on her hips, and opened her toothless mouth wide in laughter while the mass of logs and stones parted around her like water.

"Witch," one shouted, pointing his finger.

"Goddess," said another.

It did not matter what they called her. They all died.

All but one.

The man carrying the sling was so horrified that he did not even seek shelter from the Cailleach's wrath. He dropped his weapon on the ground. He did not kneel before her, nor beg for his life. He simply watched.

And as he watched, the Cailleach fell to her knees before the first child she had killed, the boy who had been bled white without his arm. She raised her arms to the sky. She screamed. She wept until she had no tears left.

And when she had used her eyes for the last time, she plucked them out with her own hands and laid them upon the great yellow stone.

Then, weeping tears of blood, she began to walk, widdershins, in a circle of undoing, while her bodiless eyes followed her from their place on the great rock.

The watching man did not count how many times she circled the Tor. But she walked until the day turned to night, and then to day again. When the first rays of sunlight broke upon the flat summit of the mountain, they reflected a trail that circled it like a halo.

Her eyes were withered and eaten by ants. Never again would she look upon the sunburst she had carved into the side of the yellow stone, that assurance that another day would come.

In the distance, the Cailleach heard voices approaching. A man wearing a coat of badger skin would be among them, she knew. He would be carrying a sling, but would not use it. She would find him.

The spell was complete.

"Ho, there! Stay with the group!" the leader called to the boys who ran ahead.

They were local boys, a little too high-spirited to serve as guides, perhaps, but the only ones willing to make the trek up the Tor.

There were eleven men in all, come from the balmy climate of the Southern Sea to this cold and desolate place in atonement for a wrong committed long before by their ancestors toward one of their own.

She was known as the Cailleach, the Watcher. A magic woman. Their grandfathers had killed a magic woman once, long ago, before the people arrived in the new land. No one had spoken of it for many years, and they had been good years, with sunlight and green fields.

But then the storms came, and grew more evil each year, until the once-lush fields had broken off and fallen into the sea, and all the people's possessions and animals with them.

And so the first whisperings began of the magic woman who had been left behind so many years before. The Watcher, whose magic had reached out like long fingers to find her people and punish them for their wickedness.

The people were certain they were doomed. What had they done, the shamans who knew the magic sounds but were still only men? Had they sought to kill one who possessed the true magic, one who could not be killed? If so, Her punishment on them would be terrible. And unending. The storms were only the beginning. The babies would die, the sea would drown them all.

As soon as the misfortunes began, the family of the magic woman had been sacrificed under the shaman's knife, but that had not been enough. Now, decades later, eleven young men came on foot to right the wrong done to the one who had once blessed her people with her magic. They would bow at her feet. They would offer themselves in sacrifice. They would do anything they must to turn the Cailleach's power away.

At the tail end of the group walked the shaman himself, a medicine man named Alder who wore a coat of badger skins brought from the Tor during the time of the exodus. The pelts were old. They stank and disintegrated in the rain that fell. Alder's armpits and belly itched from the badger hair that covered them. He had been warned about the cold of the Tor, but not of the rain, rain so different from the warm monsoons of his native land. This rain was vicious, spiky as pine needles, icy, blown by frigid wind.

He had been a small child when the tribe had left this place. At least he thought this was the place. There had been a flat-topped mountain, with a lake on top. A lake and a canyon, where the elders had stoned the silent one, the watcher, before they left.

She had never spoken. All the old ones who remembered the journey away from the Tor agreed on that. And the fact that the nameless girl had possessed powers from the beginning. She had killed a boy, Alder's mother had told him. "Killed without ever opening her hand."

"You should have kept her," the boy had answered, which had earned him a hot slap at the time.

But he had been right, and after the disasters began, the others in the tribe knew also that killing the magic woman had been a mistake. Within one moon of the first big storm that had wiped out their homes, a mysterious fever had spread among the people and sucked the life from the old and weak. A year later, nearly half of the men who were left were killed by a roving band passing through the hunting fields. The women and children had stayed hidden for nearly a year. And then the second storm came. And the third. And then their very land had disappeared beneath the sea.

It was during this time that the last shaman died. Alder had trained to take his place, but the training had not been complete. And so he was now called shaman, but all the tribe knew he was not truly a medicine man.

The magic woman—and yes, her magic would be stronger than his, he was sure—would be fearsome, would kill him. She who took her strength from this cold air, these cold rocks, would see him for what he was, a soft creature of sun and sand and bright flowers, and laugh at his softness.

He looked around at the barren landscape. How he wished he could learn magic from her! In his imagination he pictured her creating these lakes with her gigantic footsteps, forming these mountains with rocks that she carried in her apron. She was the

Cailleach, rock-woman, hag, witch, sorceress, goddess, source. Womb where warriors are born, a tunnel of fire between her legs. Woman in her most fearsome aspect, all the parts that mortal women hide from men because they know that to reveal their strength would be so frightening that their seed could not be lured out of them.

How he would have liked to learn the magic from her!

But he knew that would not be. Already he knew that he would die, that they would all die, that the Cailleach would not be appeased. And so he stared for a moment into the cold northern sun, pale and small and hard, and filled his lungs with stinging air, and walked forward, up the rocky spiral path leading to the top of the Tor.

The young boys with them had come from a village at the base of the mountain. They had told the travelers excitedly about the hag who lived alone at the top of the Tor.

"In a fortress," one of them volunteered.

"She's old and ugly," another said, making a face. "Sometimes we go up there and throw rocks at her animals."

"You'd be too cowardly to hit her, though," a third boy taunted.

"I could hit her if I wanted to!"

"She lives with deer and wild rabbits," the first boy said. "And wolves."

This last had convinced the members of Alder's expedition that they had come to the right place. Of course, Alder thought with admiration, the wild wolves would come to her.

And so the eleven men of the tribe began the long climb to the Tor. The village boys, who had accompanied them unbidden, danced around their legs like bees, chattering and boasting, thrilled to meet strangers from so far away, ecstatic at the prospect of seeing the witch herself, and perhaps besting her in battle.

It was one of the boys, then, who was the first to reach the flat summit of the Tor, the first to encounter the Cailleach who waited for them, the first to throw a rock at the hag.

She caught it.

The boy was stupified. The old woman had her back to him.

And yet, at the moment he let fly the pebble that he hoped would strike her hard enough so that she would cry out and prove his triumph to the other boys, she reached up with one hand and caught it, *thuk,* as if it were a slow-moving fly.

The other boys, who were just cresting the hill, saw it as well. They all stopped in their tracks.

She smiled.

They bowed down to her, to a man. All but Alder, who was too surprised to move, but could only watch.

The Cailleach walked toward him. *She knows,* Alder thought as she approached. *She knows this is not what I see in my vision. I see her killing me, killing us all, taking our heads and carrying them by our hair to the yellow stone. I see her walking in a long circle. . . .*

And then he could see her face clearly. The woman had no eyes.

"I am Alder," he whispered when she drew close to him. "Thank you."

"Alder," she rasped, as if she recognized him. It was the first word she had ever spoken.

With that sound, the Cailleach had called him to her and initiated him into the Mystery. What the shaman felt, from that moment to the present, in which, after countless lifetimes, he still found himself learning from her, was something like love.

The globe dropped to the ground. "It was you," he said in quiet astonishment. "That's why you're blind. It was the spell. The End of the World."

"Rather a grandiose term," the Innocent said. She assumed her guise as an old woman. "You were Alder, you know."

He was stunned. "I? I've lived before?"

She smiled. "Even magicians come and go," she said.

He hesitated. "Our lives . . ." He looked pained. "They just go on and on, don't they."

"Are you disappointed?"

He looked about, confused. "I thought the gods, at least, would be immortal."

"We are all immortal," she said softly.

"Are there gods beyond the gods, then?" he asked. "Unknown gods to whom the gods we know pray?"

"Oh, yes."

"And are they, too, destroyed before they are worshipped?"

"Perhaps."

"Where does it end?"

A small smile played at the corners of her mouth. "At the beginning," the Innocent said.

Morning broke.

"Go, little bard." She patted his knee. "Be who you are and do what you can."

CHAPTER FORTY-EIGHT

COMING HOME

Titus made it safely to Panama, where he immediately found work on a freighter headed for Dover. Why he would want to go to England, of all places, was something he asked himself again and again during the sea voyage. The Coffeehouse Gang was centered in London, for one thing. So was MI-6, which still employed a number of people who might recognize Titus as a former field agent who was supposed to have died many years before.

That the FBI meanwhile had a perfectly accurate photo of Titus Wolfe was a source of some anxiety to him, although the FBI was not Titus's main concern. The significance of the photo was not lost on the Coffeehouse boys. It was only a matter of time before they found Edgington's body and figured out the truth.

But they wouldn't think to look in England, Titus told himself. Right under their noses. He could get lost in London, easily. He would make himself bald, tan, with contact lenses and a stone in his shoe to make him limp, put on a hundred pounds, get a job in a small college somewhere, or shoot billiards for a living. . . .

He knew he was lying. For in truth, he had no good reason for coming to England except that when he learned that the freighter was headed there, he knew with uncanny urgency that he must be on it. His call to return to his native land was as strong as the need to mate.

The peculiar thing was that he did not know why he wanted to go there.

On the journey, he puzzled over his desire. It would be almost certain death to dangle himself in front of the Coffeehouse Gang. They would have found him even in Panama; surely the wide network of information the Boys had created would find Titus Wolfe in England. And yet he stayed on the freighter.

By day he worked at whatever job was given him—cleaning lavatories, washing dishes. That didn't matter. Those hours flew by without a thought. He spoke to no one, absorbed in his own obsession to reach England. Sometimes he felt as if he were single-handedly guiding the ship toward its destination by the power of his will alone.

At night, though, he felt the threads of his reason unraveling. He began to draw, for one thing, obsessively and badly. One of the motifs of his dubious artistry, drawn with lead pencil on lined notebook paper, was a flat, ziggurat-shaped mountain. He caught himself doodling again and again, and each time he tore out the page and threw it away in embarrassment. It was like something he'd seen in a movie once. Yes, that must have been where the idea came from. A stupid American movie.

He was compelled to draw other things, too: figures as crude as the drawings on cave walls, of hunters or something. Or rather, one hunter, a single man with certain characteristics which always appeared in the doodles, even if they were drawn in a state of stuporous drunkenness, which had become the norm during the long, frightening nights.

His stick figures always had tongues, for one thing. Big, bulging black tongues. They were creepy images, real meat for any psychiatrist worth his salt, Titus thought, although he himself did not understand any of it.

Then there were smaller figures, children from the looks of them, throwing stones. One of them was missing an arm. It was lying on the ground at his feet, while blood spurted out of the torso in paisley-shaped droplets. Another was a girl with spiky black hair and a bullethole on the side of her head.

Daddy, she said.

Sometimes the figure would come to life in his mind. She would stand up, the bullet wound still fresh and dripping at her temple, and walk off the page, trailing bubbles of blood that exuded from her wound. The bubbles would turn into faces, grimacing, disembodied, disturbing as the floating heads in Picasso's "Guernica."

The faces filled Titus with so much dread that he took pains to burn these drawings as soon as he realized he'd made them. And then, feeling utterly embarrassed, he drank more of the whiskey he'd taken from Edgington's boat.

Unfortunately, the whiskey was gone by the second night. On the third day, after viewing his creation of the resurrected child who, this time, was speaking to him through a cartoon bubble containing the words, "You'll go to the Tor to make things right," his hands shook as he held the empty bottle to his lips, hoping for a drop to fall into his mouth.

He became so distraught that at one point he rummaged through his duffel bag and held the misshapen little cup in his hands, hoping that somehow, in some magical way, it might take away his sorrows and his fears and the memory of his daughter's eyes as she lay dying. But of course, the worthless thing did nothing.

It had all been for nothing. What was left of the finger he had cut off was festering. His fever, rising steadily, caused all the stick figures he drew to jiggle and move now, the one-armed boy, the black-tongued warriors, as if they were trying to come to life. The girl with the bullet in her brain, of course, hardly ever kept still anymore.

Weeping, his tears running hot down his fevered face, he opened Edgington's stash of heroin.

After Edgington's death, Titus had taken the stash from the captain's cabin, earmarking it for use as bribes. Indeed, he had been recommended for the job on the freighter as a result of just such a bribe.

Titus had followed Edgington's addiction from the beginning. During their years at Cambridge, a number of the idealistic young men in Professor Darling's inner circle experimented quite openly with the more popular recreational substances. They were actually encouraged to do so by their teacher, who was then able to determine who among them might be prone to addictions. These were washed out of the program on some pretext or other, or—more likely—sent on assignments of extreme danger.

Edgington had been one of these. In retrospect luck, rather than skill, had probably been the deciding factor, but the fact that he had survived the first assignment, and the second, which had been equally dangerous, had bought Edgington immunity for a long time.

Eventually, of course, his time had run out. Titus knew that if he himself had not killed his former classmate, someone else would have, probably within days. As it was, that killer was now looking for Titus Wolfe.

He was well aware of this fact as he heated the heroin in a spoon in one of the ship's heads.

Edgington had never thought of himself as a heroin addict. The term conjured an image of proletarian squalor which the aristocrat found laughable. Instead, he—and the other users, too, Titus recalled—would talk about the drug as a kind of ultimate solution.

There was no other substance, Edgington would argue passionately, with quite the same blanket effect at making one's problems disappear. He had said more than once that when a man's troubles became unbearable, heroin was the best way out.

That had certainly held true for Edgington, Titus thought, although there had hardly been any philosophical thought behind the man's demise.

It had been easy to talk about easy death when death itself was so remote as to be nearly imaginary, he thought as he shot the liquid into his arm. When death lay under your bed, when it came up out of the bathroom sink every morning or snaked into your window like a vine, it no longer seemed so pleasant.

The heroin worked. For an hour that felt like eternity, he experienced nothing but blessed, perfect oblivion. He had found the elixir of life. Heroin, he decided, put everything into perspective. If someone was waiting to kill him in England, it didn't matter a whit. Life was today, now, this liquid, soft moment when he was wrapped in arms more secure than any mother's.

He got sick afterward, puking into the head in the middle of the night. Several people heard him. He used the incident to go off duty the following day to get high again. The experience had left him with a gray feeling, which was dispelled the instant the magic liquid entered his arm. Then the perfection returned, the blissful state of pure being unburdened by thought, emotion, or conscience. He slept.

In his dream, an unwanted and disconnected image of Edgington spoke to him from the plane of death:

You'll have to go back to make it right, old bean.

No, Edgington hadn't said that, Titus recalled. The girl had. The girl he'd killed because she had seen the bodies at Miller's Creek.

His daughter. Ah, yes, he remembered now. He had killed his own daughter.

As she lay dying, she was the one who had spoken those odd words to him: *You'll have to go back to make it right.*

He remembered that he had wanted to hold the cup out to her, the magic cup that would save the girl from death. She reached out for it, gratitude in her eyes. But Titus had snatched the cup away again and left her to die.

You'll have to go back. . . .

He shot up again, and felt immediately better. Everything was going to be fine, Titus told himself. He was clever and resourceful, probably the best mercenary in the world, Lucius Darling's protégé. Nothing bad was going to happen to him.

He screamed himself awake.

"Shut up!" someone called, tossing a shoe at Titus.

But he did not stop. He couldn't. It seemed the scream crawled out of him like a snake, long and agonizing.

"Asshole." An ashtray filled with cigarette butts hit him on the head.

But still he could not stop. He made other noises, frightened, panting sounds, and he vomited again, this time all over himself in his bunk, but he came back to the scream again and again. His hands shook. He held them in front of his face as if staring at something alien and terrifying, and continued to scream.

"Gone buggy," someone said.

"Get frigging security."

In the end, still screaming, Titus was dragged out of the room and thrown into the brig, where he remained until the ship docked at Dover. There he was unceremoniously dumped, blinking into the unaccustomed sunlight. His duffel was thrown on top of him.

It was not raining in Dover that night, but there was no moon to see and no stars. Titus struggled to his feet, clutching feebly at the strings of the duffel bag. It was too much for him. He felt as if worms were crawling beneath his skin. He dragged the bag for a few feet, then let it go.

He looked up blearily. The only thing visible in the night sky was a highway billboard illuminated by powerful floodlights. It showed a silhouetted skyline of Lakeshire, with a castle that was supposed to be Camelot superimposed upon it. Beneath the castle were words advertising a travel agency. They read: "Come to the Days of Adventure."

Titus did not notice the castle. All he saw was the silhouette of the Tor, the flattopped mountain, looming in the distance. It called to him. He began to babble. He walked away from the docks with empty hands.

Some distance away, a man in a telephone booth put a pair of infrared binoculars into the pocket of his jacket. He inserted some coins into the phone box and dialed a number.

"I've found him," the man said. "This isn't going to be difficult."

From the opening of the forgotten duffel bag, the unprepossessing little cup rolled out and traveled along the dock for a few feet before plopping into the water and disappearing from view.

Titus never noticed it. Long before now, he had forgotten all about it.

CHAPTER FORTY-NINE

THE TOR

The police lines at Miller's Creek had been taken down that morning; it had been two weeks since the explosion. In another hour a bulldozer would come to knock down the single tenuous wall that still stood in the rubble that had once been called the Sanctuary.

In the days immediately following the murders, people had continued to come for the healing waters, going past the police lines into the woods, but there was nothing special about the water anymore. The local newspaper quoted a spokesperson for Beecham Laboratories, who claimed that according to extensive tests performed at Beecham and other labs, the water at Miller's Creek appeared to have lost all of its unusual properties.

Since one of Beecham's employees, Ginger Ranier, had been among the murder victims, everyone at the lab had done whatever they could to help the police with their investigation. But neither the photograph taken by the security camera at the lab nor the dismembered missing finger discovered in the wreckage had served to identify the man she knew as Bob Reynolds.

Whoever he was, it was generally conceded that he had died in the explosion along with a known felon named John Stapp, aka Pinto, who was wanted for the murders of four physicians in Sturgis, South Dakota, a biker named Banger in Pittsburgh, Pennsylvania, and Enrico Santori, the security guard at Miller's Creek.

Hal Woczniak's body was never found, and so there were no remains to be shipped. And since he had no relatives, there was no funeral in the part of Manhattan where he had been raised.

The only service for him was going on now, observed by a mourning party of one.

Emily Blessing placed a flower on the broken boards of the wreckage.

Far away, in a plane between life and death, Gwen walked along the shore of a lake. Three thousand years before, six men chasing a wild boar had fallen to their deaths on the spot where she now walked. She could almost see them tumbling through the honeycombed earth, screaming as they struck the rocks at the bottom of the chasm.

"Goddess," she said aloud, about to pray.

She remembered. She had been the fair-haired woman with the obsidian dagger, the priestess.

The incident near the lake had brought her to the Goddess in that distant life. In gratitude for sparing her father, Brigid had left behind the man she loved.

And he in turn had sacrificed the great sword, Excalibur, to win her back.

I will wait forever, if I must.

And they had. They had both waited. And the waiting would go on.

She could picture him, Macsen, trembling as he held it out to her as an offering. Created from his mind and his will and his sweat, Excalibur had been as close to a child of his own flesh as he would ever know. All of his dreams lay within its gleaming blade.

How will you choose? the Cailleach had demanded. The sword of the gods, or the love of a woman?

Suddenly her nostrils flared. She felt the burdensome gift of prophecy stir within her now. She could smell someone coming, one with poison in his blood.

"Goddess," she said again, but this time it was a hiss, a snarl. There would be more death. The air was thick with it.

He was coming to the Tor. Yes, that was it. Coming . . . to make things right.

She herself had first said those words. She, Gwen, the maiden.

But for the one who was coming, she would need the others. The Mother. The Crone. The Goddess.

She ran toward the meadow where the altar stone lay. Magic was afoot. Strong magic.

The end of the world.

By the time Taliesin returned to the castle, the Great Hall was deserted except for a single servant, an enormously fat woman whose job it was to clear away the dishes and goblets from the previous night's feasting. Taliesin remembered her. "Danna," he said with unexpected delight.

Her expression of calm jollity was replaced instantly by a look of studied blandness. She curtsied to him, her eyes downcast. "Yes, sir," she said reverently.

Taliesin's spirits sank. He had forgotten that this was how servants—and most other people—had always treated him during the Middle Ages, as if he were some otherworldly creature capable of turning her at will into a gnat or a toad.

He put his hands on his hips. "Where's the boy?" he asked querulously.

"In the king's chamber, sir," she said, licking her dry, fear-quivering lips.

"Superstitious peasants," Taliesin muttered as he strode down the hall. The servant woman breathed a sigh of relief.

"Are you in here, lad?" he called before entering the room.

"Yes," Arthur answered. He was seated at the king's enormous carved desk. For a moment the old man was taken aback. The boy looked so natural there. It was as if they had both gone back in time, to when young Pendragon had just taken the sword from the stone and was setting about the business of unifying Britain.

Those had been wonderful years, back in the beginning, when the world was so young. . . .

And then he saw the boy, saw him perhaps for the first time, and realized that, for Arthur, the world *was* still young, still new and brimming with possibility. It was himself who had grown old. The past that Taliesin had clung to so desperately had been his own.

"They've missed this place," Arthur said.

"What?"

The boy pointed toward a high slitted window in the wall. Sounds of horses and men's laughter came from the practice field on the other side of the wall.

"That . . . Oh, yes." For a time the only sounds in the room were the happy shouts from the practice field. Bedwyr was Master of Horse again, in charge of the gleaming beasts they rode as if they were extensions of their bodies. Kay and Dry Lips and Gawain, veterans all, formed a knot of bawdy laughter as they swapped old stories about former campaigns. Fairhands and Agravaine and Tristan and Geraint Lightfoot, still too young and thin to be pitted against the older men in terms of sheer muscle, but clever and fast in battle. Curoi MacDaire and Lugh Loinnbheimionach, inseparable, the one always looking for trouble, the other always finding it. And Launcelot, solitary, apart, still unable to forgive himself for his humanness.

"I've missed it too," Taliesin said in a small voice.

He was so caught up in his memories that when Arthur spoke again, it took the old man a moment to remember where he was.

"I'm going to need the sword," Arthur said.

Taliesin's breath caught. "Will you use it?" he asked.

"Yes."

Taliesin's mouth felt dry with excitement. Could it be that the Magic would be unnecessary, that the boy was ready, at last, to accept his role as king? "Then you . . . you'd like to stay here?" he asked.

Arthur smiled. "You know we can't do that. The knights are mine for life. My life. Once I'm gone, they can go back to the Summer Country."

"But that would be just like this place!" the Merlin said brightly.

"Not exactly," he said softly. "I wouldn't be there. Your king would."

The old man hung his head. Had the boy known that all along? It had taken himself sixteen hundred years to figure it out.

Arthur Pendragon, High King of Britain, only existed in the Summer Country. This boy might share the king's soul, but his life had always been his own. The life which the Merlin had taken from him, and which was now coming to an end.

Trembling, the old man bent slowly until he knelt on the cold stone in front of the boy. "Please forgive me," he whispered.

The boy touched his shoulder, and Taliesin felt a radiance wash over him, as if the sun itself resided in the tips of Arthur's fingers. "There is no question of forgiveness, old friend," he said.

"I will do anything you ask of me," Taliesin said.

"Good." He helped Taliesin back to his feet. "We need to go back. To my time."

"But why?" the old man said, agonized. "There is nothing that awaits you on that plane."

"Just the one thing." Arthur smiled crookedly.

He meant his death. It was coming swiftly. They could both sense it.

"Would it take a lot of magic to send the knights home before I . . . before it happens?" He took a last look out the window at the men who had cared for him so loyally and lovingly since he was a child, in a world as alien to them as the moon. They should not have to see their child murdered.

Because that was how it was going to happen. He saw that very clearly now.

"I'd like to send them off with dignity and a certain amount of ceremony."

"I understand," Taliesin said, his gaze downcast. "I can arrange it."

Arthur turned back around, calmly, serenely, as if he knew that his life would last for another fifty years.

"I'll tell the men to get ready," Arthur said.

Arthur called the knights off the practice field and lined them up. "We're going back," he said. The pleasant breeze stilled, and the air felt suddenly thick. "Tomorrow morning, you will return to the Summer Country, and your proper king."

"But that is you, Highness," Fairhands said.

"No." He smiled. "Although it has been my privilege to know each of you, I am not your leader. Camelot is not my home." He stood tall. "My name is Arthur Blessing. That is who I am. It is who I have always been."

There was a long silence. At last Bedwyr called out, "Then I shall follow you, Arthur Blessing, unto the ends of the earth!"

Fairhands bent onto one knee. "I, too, my lord."

"Aye," Lugh agreed.

In a body, each of the knights bowed before him. Then Launcelot rose to stand before the boy. "Do not put me from you," he said huskily. "For I would rather remain in hell with you than find my way to Paradise."

Taliesin watched from the window of the king's chamber. How bravely does he accept his mantle, the old man thought. What a good choice the gods made.

That night, while the knights and wizards and ghosts slept, Arthur kept vigil by the yellow rock of the Tor.

Here there were no lights except for the stars overhead, no noise except for the forest creatures who moved by night. It was into this dark and silent world that Arthur Pendragon had come, he mused. For the first time in many years, he did not think of that distant being as the Other. The high king had once been a living being like himself, neither man nor boy, but poised between the two, and burdened with a responsibility that he had not pursued.

He sat up. It was true: The great king of the Celts had never sought the crown. He had never jockeyed for power. He had not pursued his own ambitions. He had not even insisted on keeping his woman.

But he had done what he could. Every day until the moment of his death, which he knew with certainty was coming on the day of the battle at Camlan, he had done his best in service to that crown which had been thrust upon his head.

Could he have stopped the Saxon invasion if he had stood up to the petty kings?

Would he have been a happier man if he had kept Guenevere as his queen?

Might it all have been different without the sword in the stone?

A figure appeared in the clearing, her face lit by the light of the full moon.

"Gwen," he said softly.

"Someone is coming," she said urgently. "A man. I think he's going to try to kill you."

He took in this information without emotion. "So that's how it will be," he said.

"We have to get out of here."

"And go where?" he asked calmly.

"I don't know. Back home."

He nodded. "What will you do?"

She hesitated for a moment. "I need to bury my mother," she said.

"Could you check on Emily for me?" he asked.

"Sure, but won't you . . ." She frowned. "Arthur, aren't you coming?"

"I won't be able to stay long," he said softly.

"Oh." Her face fell. "I'd hoped . . ."

Another lifetime, thought the part of her that was Brigid. And for that moment, Gwen knew just how long she had loved this boy.

Slowly he took her in his arms and brought her to him. Their lips touched. A thousand images flashed behind their eyes as they struggled out of their clothes to come together as they had for thousands of years, the two of them, by whatever names they had taken, Brigid, Macsen, Guenevere, Arthur, the boy, the man, the king, maiden, mother, crone. None of it mattered. Nothing mattered now except that they were, however fleetingly, together once again. That at last, they both belonged.

She touched his face. "Don't go," she said.

His eyes welled. "It's not my choice."

She made an almost imperceptible gesture of acceptance. "I understand."

"Do you?"

Her eyes were sad, old, wise. The eyes of the dying queen. "Yes," she said. "I do.

"I love you, Gwen," he said.

"I love you, too."

He held her fiercely to him. "I said I would wait for you forever," he said, "and I will. However long it takes, wherever you are, I will find you. I promise you that."

A tear fell from her face onto his cheek. "I'll remember," she said. She kissed him again. "But all we have in this lifetime is tonight."

"Yes."

"It will be enough."

"It will," he said.

The moon shone upon them, naked in a field of wildflowers.

It was all either of them had known of happiness in their lives, and it was enough.

In the blue predawn hours, Arthur, Merlin, and the knights gathered on the Tor.

"Not too close to the stone," the wizard said, preparing the magic that would take them back. "The thicket's grown considerably in sixteen centuries. Wouldn't want to be stuck inside it." He chortled. "Now, then." He shook back the sleeves of his robe.

Then there was one white flash and a moment in which they felt as if they were floating in fog. When it cleared, they were standing just where they had been, except that a huge expanse of impenetrable brambles now surrounded the great yellow stone for a mile in each direction.

Launcelot drew his sword.

"Not that way," Taliesin said gently. He raised his bare hands, and the brambles and thorns shimmered before him, then melted away into air, closing again behind them as the men moved forward.

Behind the wizard walked Arthur and Gwen, side by side. Although nothing had been said, the others stayed apart from them, allowing space for the invisible nimbus that surrounded the young couple like a shroud. The knights pulled up the rear, with Launcelot in the middle of the front line.

Death lay thick on the air, heavy as ropes. Launcelot did not know why Arthur was going to die, or how. He only knew that it would come to pass, just as it had before. How many more times would he be forced to walk behind Arthur on his way to death? For even in his hell nothing, nothing could be worse than this: to feel the same sorrow in life after life, the same regret, to watch the great king fall time and time again because of the venal desires of cruel and petty beings, like a lion brought down by jackals.

And who were the jackals this time, Launcelot mused. Who had taken the place of the petty kings in this life? The ones with the sirens and guns, or the ones who made the pictures on the television?

Or was it just all the lost ones clinging to Arthur, wanting him to bring them the happiness they could not find for themselves? Were all kings expected to provide what only each man himself could find, and therefore always fail?

He looked up from his ruminations to find, to his astonishment, a large white wolf, very old and quite blind, loping beside him.

"Don't be alarmed, Lance."

The knight's face reddened. It was the damned pagan magician again, he thought, his fist clenching around the hilt of his sword. "What the devil are you doing now?" he growled.

"I absolve you," the wolf said. "When this is done, you can go to your god."

Launcelot coughed. "Blasphemy!" he sputtered. "How dare you, you heathen trickster—"

"Because you understand. It was for you that he came back."

The knight was taken aback. "What? For me? What are you talking about?"

"To show you that he forgave you. And Guenevere. And the Merlin, too. That he'd forgiven all of you from the beginning." The wolf panted. "It was the love he had for you that mattered, not your betrayals."

Launcelot stood stock still.

"You'll go home this time, knight. To heaven."

At first he did not respond. His gaze darted from the wolf to the Merlin, and then back again. Then his jaw began to tremble. His lips worked, trying to bring himself under control before he allowed himself to speak. "I'm a soldier," he said hoarsely. "A soft afterlife will be no reward for me." He kept his eyes facing forward, unwavering. "With Galahad gone, I'll stay with the boy, if it's all the same to you."

The wolf cocked her head, understanding. "There are many ways to look at heaven."

In the next moment the animal was gone. Launcelot looked to the others, who had passed him and continued walking toward the rock.

Finally they came upon it. The altar stone stood in the center of the clearing Merlin had made, massive and yellow and worn smooth with time. In the middle of it jutted the ancient sword Excalibur, just as it had sixteen centuries before, when Guenevere first came upon it, just as it had been left sixteen centuries before that, when the priestess Brigid had thrust it into the altar of the Cailleach.

CHAPTER FIFTY

VORACIOUS

The Tor first appeared to Titus Wolfe through the window of a taxicab. Parched and shivering with fever, he had taken the cab from Dover, giving the driver all the money in his possession—a wad amounting to some four thousand pounds—for the trip.

There was something forbidding about the sawed-off mountain. To Titus, it looked like some ancient ziggurat standing as a challenge to him. As the cab approached the village of Lakeshire and the Tor at its outskirts, he felt his heartbeat quickening, thudding louder with each passing moment.

"What's that you said?" the driver asked genially. It was his last fare of the day, and the luck was with him. It hadn't been the first time a drunken sailor had given him a month's pay for a ride. Usually that ride ended up at a whorehouse, but he didn't mind making the extra effort to drive the fellow to Lakeshire. There was still plenty of time to get home, play some darts, buy the lads a pint. . . .

Titus grunted fuzzily.

"Is this where you wants off, gov?" the cabbie said, louder. "Not that it matters. I can drive you wherever you says, long as it's—"

"Here." Titus tried to rouse himself to action. His lips felt stuck together. It hurt to pull them apart. He blinked twice and propped his hands on the arms of the doors. They shook. He could smell himself, stale, unwashed, redolent of whiskey and vomit. "I'll get out here."

He rummaged in his pockets, turning them inside out. "I'm sorry."

"Already paid in full, sir," the cabbie said with a grin. The grin wobbled uncertainly as his passenger lurched out onto the open road. The poor sot had given him every cent he'd had, and didn't even remember doing so.

Feeling guilty, the driver reached into his pocket for a bill. The least he could do for the man was to leave him enough money for a meal and a phone call after he sobered up. "'Ere you go," he said, holding out a tenner, but Titus had already spilled out of the cab and was shambling across the road toward the Tor.

The driver got out, put the bill away, and then closed the back door which Titus had left wide open. "Christ," he said, shaking his head as he got back behind the wheel.

As he drove back the way he'd come, he passed a car parked alongside the road. The driver of this vehicle, a tweedy sort in his late sixties, was getting out as the cab passed. He gave the cabbie a cordial nod and stretched grandiloquently.

The cabbie might not have noticed the man at all, had it not been for one thing: The tweedy man had been taking something out of the car as the cab crested the hill, something he had hastily placed on the front seat as the cab passed.

The cabbie had only seen the object for a moment, but he had been fairly certain of what it was, if only for its incongruity in the hands of the professorial looking gent who had been carrying it:

It was an automatic rifle with a telescopic lens.

Odd sort of place for a hunt, the cabbie thought.

Lucius Darling looked after the receding taxicab for some time, holding his breath and cursing silently. He was getting old. He should have heard the cab's engine as it crested the hill. He should not have taken out the rifle so carelessly.

Chances were that the driver had neither noticed nor cared. And Darling would be changing cars within the next ten minutes. Lakeshire's parking lots would be filled with cars so easy to steal they might as well have their keys in the ignition. He would choose a Honda, if he could find one quickly. The favorite of car thieves everywhere, a missing Honda would cause no more concern to the police than a domestic argument.

As for his being identified by the cabbie, he'd take his chances. Darling had no police record whatever. If anyone cared to trace him through the rented car to his home, he would simply bring out a large barometer approximately the length and shape of a rifle, complete with canvas shoulder bag, and explain that he had been indulging in a hobby of weather tracking.

But it would not come to that. It never did.

He had killed sixteen of his former protégés. Titus was one of the last of them, the Coffeehouse Gang's bright young things. They had been recruited and developed to be the muscle of the organization, the eyes and hands of the KGB in Britain. But their time had passed. With Titus went the end of the dream, if it had ever been a dream. The very word seemed like an obscenity now, after all the killing, all the deceit and betrayal.

Darling had not meant to become a monster, no more than had Titus and Edgington, and the rest. Monsters all, slain by their own kind.

He followed the small figure of Titus Wolfe as it staggered up the winding path leading to the top of the Tor. What he was planning to do there was anybody's guess. But then, Titus was not well in any sense of the word. Whatever demons he planned to meet at the crest of the hill were his own concern.

Darling would wait. He would give his beloved student a few more minutes.

He took a deep breath, reflecting on the fragility of life. For the man climbing the Tor, these breaths were his last. Within minutes his heart would explode and his legs would buckle beneath him.

Titus's eyes, once eager with curiosity and aflame with passion, would circle dully and then open wide in surprise before glazing over, his juices inviting the insects to feed upon him.

Titus Wolfe's ascent up the hill was laborious and stumbling. After a time, he did not even know why he was making the arduous climb. Only the image of the Tor in his mind kept him at his task.

Once, when he fell, the spidery weapon he had assembled before the debacle at Miller's Creek fell out of his jacket. He picked it up, barely able to hold it, so great was his shaking. His left hand, with its missing finger, was swollen beyond recognition. The bandage that had kept the area clean had long since fallen away. Now the stump was red and pus-filled, its edges turning black.

The infection had spread. He was burning with fever. He had neither eaten nor drunk anything in days. He was parched. His eyes hurt.

Come back to the Tor, the familiar voice sang to him. *You will come back to make things right.*

He was on all fours now, scrambling over the dry stones, cresting the final ridge. Yes, the Tor, he thought. He was almost home. Blinking from the dust, he crawled toward the clearing he knew he would find. He had seen it in a hundred visions since the night he had left Dawning Falls. There would be a man there, waiting for him.

The man he was supposed to kill.

Titus halted, confused. He could not remember who the man was or why he was supposed to kill him.

To make things right, the voice reminded him.

Oh, yes. It was a king of some sort. An assassination. It had all been planned long ago, even before the Libyans.

Squinting, he thought he could make out shapes in the clearing. Taking out the gun with its high-powered telescopic sight, he snapped it into position. Just to see.

The man would be waiting to die, Titus thought. It would not be a problem.

But he did not see a man at first. In the sight of the gun stood a woman. He frowned, adjusting the scope. What woman would be here?

And then he saw. It was his dead daughter, come back to life like his stick figure drawing. And in the foreground a white blur, moving, blocking his view.

Titus staggered backward. A wolf the color of clouds was coming, running straight for him. He tried to scream, but the wolf leaped into the air and in one astonishing bound was on him, its jaws fastened around his throat. Strangling, grappling desperately with the wolf and fighting with all the strength of a dying man, Titus managed to fire one shot. It struck the wolf.

Then he sank to one knee and aimed the gun at the boy-king.

The Christ Child, he thought. Oh my God, the king I've been hired to kill is Jesus Christ.

He hesitated. But that was all written long ago, he realized. He, too, was a part of the tapestry, come to life like the stick figures of his dreams. You must die, he thought, because I am here. He pulled the trigger.

I have come back, back to the Tor, to make things right.

With all the knights gathered around the yellow rock, Arthur placed his hands upon the hilt of the great sword.

"Thank you for your service to me," he said. "For a time, we created together a community that now is thought of as a perfect world. We know it was not a perfect world. Far from it. It was a time of fear and bloodshed and betrayal, of early death and failed dreams. A time like all times. But we lived it together, and in that we made memories.

"The memories, my friends, are all that are perfect. Because when it is all done, does any of it matter? Any of it, except for the joy of having lived?"

The knights were silent. Launcelot, standing apart from the others, wept. Taliesin swept the field with his gaze. He was very uncomfortable. Something was coming, something dark and unknowable.

Gwen, too, felt as if she were jumping out of her skin.

Slowly, Arthur pulled Excalibur from the rock and held it aloft

with both hands. It was magnificent in the sunlight, its gold un-
tarnished, its blade smooth and sharp as a razor.

"With this, I send you home, back to Camelot, to the perfect
world that we did not live, but remember having lived. With this,
I give you freedom."

The first shot drew their attention. The second came moments
later.

"No!" The Merlin screamed as Titus Wolfe's bullet sped through
the clearing and into Arthur's beating heart.

The knights mobilized at once. Launcelot was the first to spot
the man lying on the grass beyond the clearing, and in one motion
unsheathed his sword and turned to run toward him.

He never made it. With the last bit of life within Arthur's body,
he thrust the sword back into the stone, and the knights began to
fade.

Launcelot felt himself disintegrating. "My King!" he shouted.
"Take me back, I beg you!"

Ahead of him lay the blind white wolf, dying, its fur streaked
with blood from the bullet which had passed through it.

"You were valiant, knight, and true," it said in its way so that
only the knight could hear. Its eyes were bright and unafraid.
"Godspeed, Launcelot!"

Arthur, too, was fading. "Oh, no," Taliesin moaned. He never
thought it would happen so quickly. "Arthur, please, by all the
gods . . ."

Arthur's eyes, soft with forgiveness, met his. "Friend," he whispered.

He reached out for Gwen. He could no longer speak. She kissed
his lips. *I will find you,* she said to him silently. She spoke with
Brigid's voice, with Guenevere's, with her own. *Wherever it is, however long it takes, I will be with you again.*

She held him in her arms until he vanished from sight, along
with the sword Excalibur, gone at last to the Summer Country.

In the distance, the crack of a rifle sounded. A shabby looking
man holding a gun of some kind arched his back before falling
forward into the grass.

Gwen sank to the ground. Beside her, on the great yellow stone, the light shone on the Cailleach's ancient carving of the dawning sun with its eternal message.

There would always be another day.

CHAPTER FIFTY-ONE

THE THIRD MAGIC

Taliesin stood silently at the altar stone. They were all gone now, the knights, Hal, even Arthur, for whom he had tried to recreate the whole world. Even the great sword was gone.

Behind him, Titus's body lay crumpled on the grass. No one had come to take it. No other shots had been fired. The weapon that had been used to kill Arthur lay next to the dead man. Such a strange, small thing, the old man thought, yet deadlier than the greatest sword ever made.

Excalibur's time, like Arthur's, had passed.

Nearby lay the dead white wolf. Gwen lifted it off the ground and brought it back to the altar stone.

"Begin," she said, raising her arms in the ancient pose of a priestess.

The Merlin did not question her, or her authority, or her meaning.

He began to walk, widdershins, the wide circle around the Tor, and did not stop until the sun had arced completely across the sky, and the moon rose and faded, and the next day dawned.

When he had completed the spell, the wolf was still lying on the altar stone.

The old man's heart felt like a lump of lead. "Innocent," he whispered. The animal's fur was cold. He stroked it with trembling hands. "I'm sorry," he rasped. "The magic failed." He lay his head on the wolf's still body and sobbed.

"There, there," someone said. A wet tongue licked his face.

He bolted upright. Another wolf panted close to him, its aromatic breath moistening Taliesin's skin. "Earth suit," the wolf said, showing off its pelt. "Easily replaced."

The wolf had blue eyes, and sight to see through them.

Gasping, Taliesin scanned the clearing. "Where is she?" he demanded.

Gwen was gone. So was the man in the meadow, and his spidery gun.

1996
CHICAGO, ILLINOIS

"Gwen!"

The girl looked up from her drawing. It showed a fair-haired woman standing over a flat rock on which lay the body of a wolf. In her hands was an obsidian knife.

Her mother bustled into the room. "I'm going now. Make sure you . . . What kind of scene is that?" She turned the sketch pad. "It looks like some kind of animal sacrifice."

"Oh?" Gwen squinted at it, frowning, for a moment. Then, with a few strokes of the charcoal in her hand, she altered the drawing so that the wolf was one of several, panting eagerly at the feet of the woman.

Ginger Ranier laughed. "I swear, you must be the best artist in the fourth grade," she said. Then, picking up another piece of charcoal, she turned the priestess's knife into a rubber chicken. They both grinned.

"And speaking of artists, your mother the painter is off to school!" She turned around in a circle. "Do I look all right?"

She was wearing a lavender poncho over pants. In her hair was a big pink silk hyacinth.

"You're beautiful, Mom," Gwen said.

"Oh, I'm so nervous! Can you imagine, someone my age getting a scholarship to Cooper Union!"

Gwen kissed her cheek. "You'll do fine. School isn't that hard."

"Well, make sure you don't give Hal and Emily a hard time while I'm gone. Or old Mr. Woczniak, either." The Woczniaks lived in the other half of their duplex. So did Hal's father, Lance, who was senile but still fun.

Ginger collected Gwen's sketch pad and a sweater. "Oh, they said to keep an eye out for Merlin. He's missing again."

"No, he's not." The girl scooped a rangy gray cat into her arms. "He's been with me. He likes to sleep on my feet." Gwen kissed the cat's head. White tufts of fur stuck out over its eyes and beneath its chin, so that he looked like a wise old man with a long beard.

"Well, bring the ugly old thing along," Ginger said, "before Hal has the whole precinct looking for it." She helped Gwen on with her parka before venturing outside.

Next door, old Mr. Woczniak was sitting on a folding chair on the front stoop, even though it was January. He liked to catch some rays every day, he'd explained.

"Catching some rays, Lance?" Gwen asked, as she always did.

"Get inside!" her mother said. "And don't call Mr. Woczniak by his first name. It isn't respectful."

Mr. Woczniak waved dismissively. "See?" Gwen said. "It's okay. And we'll go inside in a minute."

Ginger rolled her eyes. Her daughter was going to be a handful. "Okay, but try not to freeze." She waved good-bye.

"My mom's a pain," Gwen said. "But she's all right."

Lance Woczniak smiled. "You've got the cat," he said, delighted. "Did he try to turn you into a toad?"

"Nope."

"He'll do it if you give him a chance," he said. "Your kitty was a wicked sorcerer once, a long time ago. . . ."

The cat yowled in protest and streaked away.

"I don't think he likes it when you tell that story," Gwen said. She herself had heard the story many times. It had been Mr. Woczniak, in fact, who had given Merlin his name.

"He's a cranky old critter," he said.

MUNICH, GERMANY

As soon as he turned the key to his apartment, Titus Wolfe knew that someone was inside.

He also knew who it was.

"No precautions?" Lucius Darling asked from his position on the living room sofa. "Not even a gun?"

"Would it do any good?" Titus asked.

Darling laughed. "Surely you don't believe the stories about Cronos," he said.

Titus did not answer. He did believe the stories. Nearly everyone in the Coffeehouse Gang was dead, and those who remained alive had no illusions about their safety.

Cronos was coming. It was just a matter of time.

"Why are you here?" Titus asked.

Darling's face was somber, his eyes filled with regret. "I think you know," he said softly, taking out something that looked like a large Swiss army knife—lightweight, leggy, a metal spider that opened into a handgun in less than one second.

Titus said nothing. It would do him no good to plead for his life, he knew. Not with Cronos.

It was just a matter of time, and his time had come.

CHICAGO, ILLINOIS

The alarm at the Riverside National Bank was ringing. Arthur Blessing had seen two men running down the sidewalk a minute earlier, and wondered idly if they were bank robbers.

His hands were cold. It had snowed while he was in school, so he had stopped in the park to enjoy it before people walked all over everything. Usually Gwen came with him on these excursions, but she'd had to get home early so that her mom could leave for art school. Besides, she'd be staying at his house anyway, so big deal.

He checked in his jacket pocket to make sure the bird's nest was still there. It was old, probably left over from last spring. The wind must have knocked it out of the trees.

It was small, maybe a wren's nest, made of fine hairlike filaments, and almost perfectly round on the bottom. It was hard to believe that birds could make something so complicated.

Gwen would like it.

She had kissed him once. He hadn't told anyone.

His sneaker, which was stiff and freezing, banged against the curb. The impact made the bird's nest fly out of his hands into the gutter.

"Damn it!" he shouted. The neighbors would probably tell Hal they heard him swearing, but he didn't care. Angry, he stooped to pick it up. Luckily it was cold enough so that the gutter wasn't filled with gunk the way it usually was. He blew at it carefully, in case there was dirt on it.

And then he saw, lying beside where the bird's nest had been, another treasure. It was a cup, he guessed, although it had no handles. In a way, it looked like the little cups in the Japanese tea set that Emily kept in the dining room and never used.

He picked it up. No, the Japanese cups were a lot prettier than this. It was made of some greenish metal, and was so banged and dented, it looked like it was a hundred years old. Still, it was interesting, in a way.

He held the cup and the bird's nest side by side, comparing them. Maybe Gwen would rather have the metal thing. It would be more useful.

And it was warm. That was the strange thing. It was so warm in his hands that it nearly vibrated.

Actually, now that he thought about it, it felt wonderful. As if everything in life were going his way, and everyone in the world were on his side. He felt . . . well, like a king. This cup—

"I beg your pardon, sir." A distinguished old man tipped his hat to him. It was one of those brimmed felt things that people in old movies wore when they went mountain climbing. It had a little feather on the side.

"Me?" Arthur said.

"I seem to have lost something around here," the old man said. "A cup. Actually, it's more like a bowl . . . I say, I believe that's it!" He pointed to the cup in Arthur's hand. "Er . . . that is, would you mind?"

Arthur kicked at a stone. He had liked the cup.

Sulking, he handed it over.

"Oh, jolly good!" the old man said. "Here, I'll make you a trade." He reached in his pocket and pulled out a handkerchief. Inside it was a small resin replica of a wolf.

"A white dog," Arthur said, examining it from all angles. "What are its eyes made of?"

"Moonstones," the old man said.

"They make him look blind," the boy noticed.

"Her. She's a female. Is it a fair trade?"

Arthur held the bird's nest in one hand and lay the white wolf inside it. Gwen would love it, he knew. She liked animals. And the blank eyes were very cool.

"It's a deal," Arthur said, holding out his hand. The old man shook it.

"Very good," he said. Then he touched two fingers to the brim of his funny-looking hat, and walked briskly down the street. In another minute he was gone.

Arthur examined the dog statue again before putting it back in his pocket. All in all, he decided, this was turning out to be one of the best days of his life.

CRISTOBAL, BRAZIL

In the southeastern quadrant of the Amazon rain forest, in a ravine fed by a tributary of the Tapajos river, lay an infant. She was nine months old, and left in the ravine to starve. Her tribe, an offshoot of the Waura, had been decimated by leprosy, and the young mother had fled to the city, where she would not be faced with living her life alone in the jungle.

Later, the baby would come to question why her mother had left her. She would long for her and wait for her return. And after that, years in the future, she herself would leave the rain forest and venture to a place she would not even hear of until she was more than twenty years old: America.

Through a series of coincidences she would arrive in New York City, where she would learn European magic from a kindly old white-haired man named Alder Taliesin. In return, she would teach him all she knew about the healing herbs of the rain forest.

But for now, she only wriggled among the leaves and the black earth of the jungle floor. Around her, in a circle, stood monkeys and capabaras and tapirs. In the trees was a panther, ferocious and watchful; and in the river, a cayman. These were her guardians. These were the family who would protect her, who knew instinctively that a special being had come among them.

In the baby's hands was a cup. It was a small, misshapen metal thing that had traveled from the coast of England in the belly of one fish and then another, and on board a boat filled with dead tuna, and in a bucket as chum for shark, and flying high in the beak of a crow. And then for a time the cup had been dragged in a net behind a freighter on the vast Amazon River, and then carried as a drinking vessel on a banana boat traveling up and down the *igarapes* of Brazil's deep interior regions. From there it had been eaten by a cayman which died on dry land.

After the cayman's body decomposed, a howler monkey carried it to its goddess: a tiny girl with black hair that poked out in all directions and shiny, beadlike eyes that saw everything.

Cailleach! the monkey shrieked. But of course the baby girl could not understand what it was saying.

She had no name, and her life was just beginning.